Enola Gray Mysteries

Volume 2

A. S. French

Neonoir Books

Enola

Ginger

Bruce

Kronos

Becky
Becky

Parker

A. S. FRENCH

The Blurred Girl

An Enola Gray Mystery

Chapter 1

Shifting Perspective

I was staring at a life-size doll of Darth Vader when the first applicant strode out of his interview and threw up in the corner, spewing over a stack of tattered magazines. The manager of Games & Comics stared at the guy before grabbing a can of lemon air freshener and spraying it everywhere. I coughed into my hand as the boss switched his attention to the next poor sod in line, a young woman with hair like an exploding green jelly and a tattoo of Wolverine on her arm. She scampered into the room as the vomit festered near a box of *Star Trek* books. It was my third job interview in two days, and I guessed it might not go well.

The man wiped spew from his chin and smiled at me. 'It must have been a dodgy burger from the place next door.'

That was Bagels & Burgers, where I'd had my first interview of the week. I didn't get the job. *Overqualified*, they said.

The bloke slithered out of the room as I scanned my surroundings. It was cramped and cluttered, filled with several discarded items that seemed to have no purpose.

Piles of old comics and magazines were stacked haphazardly on each other next to a broken desk with a rusted lamp. The walls were coated with peeling paint and grime. I shifted in my seat, feeling the rough texture of the threadbare couch beneath my fingers. I rubbed my palms together, the grit and dust coating my skin, but still not enough to hide my scars.

The girl near me spoke. 'I don't mean to be nosey, but what happened to your hands?'

I held them up so she could view the marks better. 'I fell into a pit of poisonous spiders.' I flexed my fingers. 'The rest of my body is worse. Would you like to see?'

She grimaced and slithered back from me. 'Eh, no thanks.'

People always stared at my scars, but few asked about them. I alternated between fiction and lies when they did, never speaking the truth about the fire and my parents' murders.

A buzzing fly caught my attention as it circled the steaming vomit. It was a perfect metaphor for me, rushing around a bunch of shitty job interviews to get off my friends' sofa and find my own flat: the bagel place, then the mobile phone shop, and now the comic store - jobs that needed no qualifications or experience and were minimum wage. However, beggars couldn't be choosers, and the holes in my shirt and shoes put me firmly in the spot of the soon-to-be impoverished.

The persistent hum of an old fan in the corner of the room was a stark contrast to the occasional creaking of the wooden floorboards beneath my feet. My throat croaked, and I reached for the half-empty water bottle on the floor beside me, taking a sip of the tepid liquid. The taste of plastic lingered in my mouth as the stink of the spew wormed its way up my nose. I wriggled my toes until the big one pushed through the hole in my shoe and revealed my dirty sock to the world.

'I can help you with that,' the girl said as she gazed at my foot.

'Are you a cobbler?' I replied.

A veil of confusion settled over her face. 'What?'

'Shoemakers are called cobblers.'

'Oh. My mum told me cobblers means rubbish. She always said my dad spoke a load of old cobblers.'

'Your mother was right. I don't know about your dad, but cobblers is slang for nonsense derived from the Cockney rhyming slang for balls, testicles, of "cobbler's awls".'

She shook her head. 'I've got no chance now, have I?'

'What do you mean?'

'With you being so clever, you'll get the job with no problem.'

I removed my phone from my pocket and showed her the screen. 'I have a lot of spare time, and when I'm not walking my friend's dog or looking after the neighbour's ten-year-old kid, I waste it browsing useless websites.'

She nodded. 'That's amazing.'

'Yeah,' I said. 'What did you mean about my shoe?'

'Oh, I know where you can get replicas of authentic designs of clothes, shoes and, well, everything. CDs, DVDs, electrical goods, even food.'

'Knock-offs?'

She whispered. 'Yes, but don't say it out loud. The people who run Counterfeit Alley don't want the coppers finding out where they've relocated to.'

'Counterfeit Alley?'

'That's what everybody calls it. It started in an abandoned factory next to the by-pass, then it moved to the old shopping mall before they got a tip-off the police would raid it. So now, it's in that row of abandoned shops on the other side of the river. Do you know where that is?'

'Yeah, near the run-down funfair.'

She sighed. 'I used to love going there as a kid. It's a shame there's nothing for kids anymore.' She beamed at me. 'That's why we need places like Counterfeit Alley.' She touched my arm. 'It's the only place where people like us can afford to buy life's essentials.'

'How do you know about it?'

She lowered her voice. 'My boyfriend sells dodgy mobile phones there.'

'Stolen mobiles?'

'Oh, no; fakes. They're all from China, I think.'

'And they sell cheap shoes and clothes there?'

She patted my arm. 'They have everything. If they don't, ask a seller, and they'll have it for you in a few days.'

I peered at my toe, peeking out of my shoe, and pictured myself buying myself a new set of clothes. My friends Bruce and Ginger had offered to give me money, but I didn't want to take it from them, especially as they were kind enough to let me sleep on their sofa for the last few months.

The door opened, and the jelly-haired woman stumbled out. She looked unhappy but didn't throw up.

'Whose next?' the manager said.

I got up, stepped over the spew, and entered the room, thinking I might be able to get that Kitty Stardust T-shirt I'd been after for so long.

Then the bloke breathed on my neck, and I knew the interview wouldn't go well.

Chapter 2

From Trash

We sat opposite each other. He was a portly man with a receding hairline and a disturbing grin, resembling one of the comic book characters whose images covered the walls. There was a half-eaten burger on his desk and an open bottle of Coke. I tried to inhale the food's aroma as a distraction from the smell of rotten cabbage coming from his mouth.

He looked me up and down like an angler ready to bait a hook. 'You don't look like the typical comic book fan.'

I rolled my eyes. 'I didn't know there was a dress code.'

'Clothes are important in a professional work environment.' He glanced at the paper in his hand, and I assumed it was my CV. 'We can't have any scruffs working here.'

My nose twitched from what crawled out of his mouth, staring at the Bruce Lee t-shirt that was way too small for his frame and the impressive mustard stains on the front.

'I'll smarten myself up.'

He didn't seem convinced. 'So, why do you want to work here?'

I took a deep breath and launched into my prepared speech. 'Well, I've been a fan of comic books since I was a kid. They've always been a source of comfort and inspiration for me. I love how they transport you to different worlds and show that anything is possible if you believe in yourself.'

Comics and music were the things that got me through living in children's homes after my parents died, and I assumed my specialist knowledge would help in the interview.

He wasn't impressed. 'That's all nice and inspirational, but what can you do for me?'

I bit my tongue, resisting the urge to grab the Wonder Woman figurine on the shelf and stick it into his eye. Instead, I described my skills and background, emphasising my familiarity with comic book lore and customer service expertise.

'I'm great dealing with customers,' I lied.

He flicked through my CV. 'You worked for our disgraced former MP, Kate Frost.'

I spent three days helping our local member of Parliament in my previous employment. 'It didn't last long.'

He had the permanent gaze of a man who ate his own toenail clippings. 'Were you involved in that money she embezzled?'

Frost didn't embezzle the cash, but I took it to the bank for her, a hundred grand in US dollars. Of course, I couldn't tell him that.

'No, that was before my time.'

He glanced at the CV. 'Before that, you were the IT manager at a computer shop?'

'Yes, for two years.'

'Why did you leave there?'

'Somebody set the building on fire.'

He gazed at my hands. 'Is that how you got those scars?'

'No, they're from another blaze.'

He opened his legs as wide as possible, and an unpleasant smell drifted off his crotch, resembling swamp gas. I grimaced and wished I were in the other room with the fresh vomit.

'You have a hole in your shoe,' he said.

'You hum the tune, and I'll sing it.'

His eyes shrunk to the size of pinholes. 'What?'

'It's a song. Don't you know it?'

His gaze darted left and right like a caged bird searching for an escape, but finding none. 'I hate music. It's a waste of everybody's time.'

I sat back in surprise, remembering my childhood and the long car rides with my parents, singing along to the radio, recalling the mixtapes my best friend had made, filled with songs that spoke to my soul. And I thought of the times when it had saved me from despair, providing a glimmer of hope in the darkest periods.

'Music is far more than entertainment or a method to pass the time. It's a lifeline, a constant companion that has seen me through some of the most challenging moments of my life. Whenever I feel lost or alone, I turn to my favourite songs and artists, finding comfort in their lyrics and melodies. Music is a language that transcends words, a way to connect with others on a deeper level. And it's a means of connecting to people, which is an important skill to have when working in a place like this.'

He peered at me as if my jacket should have been tied up at the back. 'Did you learn all that woke bollocks from the dodgy MP?'

'Woke?'

'Yeah, you know, progressives who seek to take away our history through cancel culture and virtue signalling, all those left-wingers.' He opened his mouth wide enough to fit Thor's hammer. 'That's why I'm a lifelong Conservative voter.' He reached over and put his hand on my knee. 'If you want to work here, you must think as I do.' His fingers were like a slug crawling over my brain. 'The country needs the right leaders in government, so they won't waste money on woke ideas; folks who don't steal from ordinary hard-working people like me to give it to lazy good for nothings and foreigners. I hope you agree with me.' He squeezed my leg, and I controlled my breathing.

'First, woke means someone is informed, educated and conscious of social injustice and racial inequality. Therefore, it's a compliment, not an insult. That's unless you're a petty-minded, gammon-faced, ignorant moron. Second, do you know those parents who go to the shop, spend a fortune on cigarettes, and then tell their kids they can't afford to buy them some sweets? Yeah, that's the fucking Tories.'

I grabbed his hand and pushed his fingers back. The bones didn't crack, but they made a pleasant snapping sound. He wailed like a baby and dropped to his knees.

'Stop, please stop!'

I didn't, rubbing against his grubby, wrinkled skin. 'Are you like this with all women? Did you also try to intimidate the woman you interviewed before me?' I pictured the bloke throwing up outside. 'Did you harass that man? Is that why he threw up?'

Fuck! What to do with the scumbag? I had Detective Inspector Jack Parker's mobile number on my phone, but it would only be my word against the bloke's unless the others spoke out. And he might want to press charges against me.

I stared into his pained eyes and let go. 'Thanks for the

job offer, but I'll pass.' Tears swam down his cheeks as he rubbed his fingers. 'However, I'll watch you, so you better behave yourself. Do you understand?'

He nodded, and I left.

And I was still unemployed.

Chapter 3

The Blurred Girl

The interview left a bad taste in my mouth, but I had to get rid of it as I was picking up Becky from school. Julia, Becky's mum, was working another of her long shifts as a carer, and I didn't mind helping with the kid. She was like the younger sister I'd never had.

Walking through the town, I examined the boarded-up shops and empty buildings. It was a stark reminder of how the government had abandoned the community. The streets were quiet, with only a few people out. A gaggle of kids rode past on their bikes, shouting and laughing. I smiled and pushed the image of the comic-book man from my mind.

As I turned the corner, I saw the school ahead. It was a small building surrounded by a fence and a group of adults waiting for their children. I recognised some of them to nod and smile at, but we didn't talk. At my age, a few weeks from twenty-one, I guessed they probably looked at me as just another child. Most of them were at least ten years older than me, though one woman might have been in her mid-twenties. And most of them were women, with only a couple of blokes outside the gates.

While I waited, the memories of my school days returned. Considering I'd only left there five years ago, it wasn't hard for the images to resurrect themselves of all those schools I drifted between after the murder of my parents: the playground fights, the disgruntled teachers, and all the other kids who hated me.

A bell rang, and excited children burst out of the building a few seconds later, running and shouting. Becky was one of the last to leave, looking down at her feet. My heart sank as I realised something was wrong.

She glanced up and shuffled towards me, her voice barely above a whisper. 'They were calling me names again.'

Anger and sadness surged through me. 'Who are *they*?'

She shrugged, staring at the ground. 'Just some girls from my class.'

I scrutinised the other kids, watching them laugh and smile with their parents, families, and guardians. 'Who were they? What did they say?'

Becky's voice shook. 'They said my clothes were ugly, and I was stupid.'

I stared at her, noticing the hole at the elbow of her coat, how frayed her skirt was and her scuffed and dirty shoes.

I squeezed her hand. 'You're not stupid, Becky. You're smart, kind, and brave. And your clothes are fine.' My blood boiled at the thought of those kids bullying her. I knew I had to do something about it, but first, I needed to calm her down. 'It's going to be okay,' I said, putting a comforting arm around her shoulder. 'Let's grab a snack and talk about it.'

She wiped her cheeks and smiled at me. The café was two minutes away, and by the time the server had put burger and chips in front of her, she seemed to have forgotten her troubles. The aroma of freshly brewed coffee hit my nose as I lifted the cup to my mouth, the sweetness sending a jolt through my veins.

'Can I have a coffee?' she said with tomato sauce dripping from her lips.

I laughed. 'You're lucky I bought you that Coke.'

'Would you let my mum know?'

'About the Coke? Of course not.'

'No, will you tell her about the bullies?'

'I should. Have you told your teachers?'

Becky shook her head. 'I'm afraid to. I don't want to make it worse.'

It was hard to see her like that. A few months back, she'd stood up to more difficult challenges than school bullies: a lunatic with a gun, drug users, and local gangsters. She'd taken all those things in her stride and was calmness personified when her supposedly dead father returned from the grave.

I took a deep breath, trying to keep my emotions in check. 'You don't have to be afraid, Becky. You deserve to be given respect and kindness. Speaking up is important if someone is not doing that. I'm here for you, and we'll figure out how to handle this together.'

She smiled and devoured her burger. Then she finished the Coke and burped loud enough to disturb the elderly woman sitting opposite us.

'Can I have a cake, Enola?'

'Do you want a blueberry muffin?'

Becky nodded. 'Please.'

I went to the counter, already planning how to deal with her bullies. I'd dealt with my tormenters by responding in kind, discovering my propensity for violence early in the children's home. The three girls who enjoyed hitting me every night soon stopped when I used the poker from the living room to bruise their knees and legs. A boy who got his teenage kicks from pulling my hair gave up when I set his on fire. And the twin sisters at my school quit bothering me when I stuffed worms in their mouths. For Becky, I needed something more subtle and less violent.

As I considered that, a woman spoke behind me. 'I'm sorry to interrupt, but I couldn't help but overhear you talking to your daughter.'

I turned, recognising her: tall, long dark hair down to her shoulders, ocean blue eyes and wearing clothes that would have paid my rent for a month if I paid any.

'You're a parent from the school?' I asked.

She held her hand out. 'Claire King. My Fiona is in the same age group as your daughter.'

I shook her hand. 'Becky's not my kid. I'm Enola Gray, a friend of her mother, Julia.'

'Well, it's nice to meet you, Enola.' We moved forward in the queue. 'Regarding your conversation with Becky, I spoke to the school last year about kids bullying Fiona, and it seems they've done little about it.' She reached into her bag and gave me a card. 'My number's on there if you want to talk about it sometime.'

Then she left the café and dragged a young girl with her. I ordered the cakes and returned to Becky, who was busy drawing in her schoolbook. I looked at the text on the card.

Claire King: King's Clothing Emporium.

King's Clothing. There was a shop on the high street and a large factory on the town's largest industrial estate. I slipped it into my pocket and wondered if fate had given me a solution to my unemployment problem.

Chapter 4

The One Who Walks Through You

I dropped Becky off with her mother and returned to the flat. Kronos greeted me as I stepped inside, jumping up to drool on my face. Bruce grabbed the dog and slipped a lead on it.

'I'm taking him to the woods if you fancy a walk, Enola.'

'I've hardly got through the door, and you want to drag me out again?'

I went to feed my pet tarantula, Dirty Harry.

Bruce whispered in my ear. 'I'm doing you a favour. Ginger's friend, Nora, is here. She's a bit strange.'

He shuffled out of the flat with Kronos, and I threw my jacket over a chair. Ginger came out of the kitchen with her mate.

'Enola, this is Nora. You've heard me talking about her, right?'

I nodded. Nora's appearance was striking: jet black hair and porcelain face, and her eyes possessed a certain intensity that drew me in. She wore a flowing flowery dress with several scarves and bangles, looking like the missing hippy cousin from the Addams Family. She rushed over, threw her arms around me, and hugged me like it was going out of fashion. She eventually let go, and I took a deep breath.

Then she touched my arm. 'I sense you have some difficulties in your life.'

I pulled back, startled by her sudden touch. 'Uh, yeah, don't we all?' I tried to brush her off, but she was persistent.

'No, I mean serious challenges. Financial problems, perhaps even something dangerous.' Her eyes bored into mine, and my arms and legs stiffened.

Ginger jumped in. 'Nora, maybe we should change the subject.'

However, she wasn't deterred. 'I want to help you, Enola. I sense you have a powerful aura and a fighting spirit. You can overcome whatever obstacles are in your way, but you need guidance.'

She reached into her bag and pulled out a deck of tarot cards. Ginger was a tarot card reader – we'd met at a psychic evening in a room above the local pub, though she was there as a "professional", and I'd gone because I was bored – but I'd always resisted her prompting me for a reading.

But after the crappy job interview and Becky's problems, I needed a distraction.

'Okay, sure. Why not?'

We sat at the table, and Nora shuffled the deck and laid out several cards. As she read them, it surprised me how accurate they appeared. She talked about my recent struggles with unemployment and my money worries, amazed by how much she seemed to know about my life. I glanced at Ginger, thinking she must have got all the information from her.

Then I realised what it was: most people in the town were experiencing the same difficulties, unable to find work and facing hardships in buying food and paying the bills. I stared into her eyes and assumed she thought I was one of the many struggling with life.

'You think this is all fake, don't you?'

I shrugged, more concerned about not hurting Ginger, who believed in such nonsense, than upsetting Nora. 'Who am I to say what is or isn't real?'

She moved her hands over the cards. 'The Fool indicates you'll have a fresh start if you're brave enough to take a leap of faith. The Chariot is telling you no obstacle can stop you now. Death is the card of endings and beginnings if you're willing to let go and change.'

I pointed at the Devil. 'And what does this mean?'

Nora grabbed it. 'You're not a puppet. Nobody possesses the power to control you unless you let them.'

I glanced from it to the other cards. Ever since the fire in the computer shop and losing my flat, I'd felt like a ship caught in a storm, twisting back and forth with uncertainty, unsure which direction to take. It was as if I'd lost my compass, adrift in an endless sea of confusion, desperately searching for a return to solid ground. I thought things would change with the job working for the local MP, but that quickly turned into a shit sandwich.

Ginger jumped up. 'Well, that was great, Nora. Now, who wants a drink?' She whispered to me. 'She normally charges £50 for a reading, but you got that for free.' She smiled at Nora. 'I'll put the kettle on.'

She went to the kitchen. 'Yeah, thanks, Nora,' I said.

Nora collected the cards and replaced them in the pack. 'I still don't think you believe me, Enola, but that's okay.'

I changed the subject. 'How did you get involved in the psychic world?'

She removed a scarf and placed it on the table. 'My

mother and grandmother were both psychics, so it runs in the blood.' She reached over and touched my arm. 'Ginger told me what happened to your parents. I'm so sorry.'

'It was a long time ago.'

'It's affected your aura; I can see that. You've had a lot of negative things in your life, but if you're prepared to grasp your opportunities, I think that will all change soon.'

'Opportunities?'

'Yes, there are unexpected openings on the horizon. That's what I saw in your cards.'

Ginger returned with tea and biscuits. 'Did you hear what happened to our ex-MP?'

'Kate Frost?' I said, picturing my former employer.

She poured drinks for us all. 'Yep. Apparently, nothing was illegal in what she did with that donation from America.' That was a good thing for me. 'But with her reputation ruined, she's quit politics.'

I bit into a custard cream and wondered if I was a jinx: my parents were murdered in front of me, the computer shop where I worked was torched, killing three people – my colleagues – in the building, and then my last employer was caught in a political scandal. Disaster appeared to follow me wherever I roamed.

Ginger and Nora continued talking about Frost as I went to the bathroom. I peered into the mirror, struggling to recognise the person staring at me. I reached into my pocket and removed my cash, seeing I had £60 left from my universal credit to last a month. Then I glanced down and saw the hole in my shoe.

It was time to buy new clothes.

Chapter 5

Sidewalking

I took a deep breath before entering Counterfeit Alley. It looked like any other retail shopping district, with people drifting in and out of the shops and stalls. The air smelled of cigarettes, cheap cologne, and the noxious odour of imitation leather and plastic.

I scanned the crowded street, seeing everything from fake designer bags to knock-off electronics. Several faces turned to me, suspicious eyes judging me from a distance. Then two teenagers approached me, a boy and a girl.

'What do you want?' the lad demanded. There was a scar under his left eye and a permanent twitch under the other. She chewed gum and created a huge pink bubble before it burst, sticking to her lips and chin.

'I need children's clothes,' I said. My new shoes could wait. I had to get something for Becky first. 'They're for a ten-year-old girl.'

The teenage girl wagged a finger at me, and I noticed the scars on her wrist. 'You don't look old enough to have a ten-year-old.' She turned to her mate. 'I bet she's a nark.'

He sneered at me. 'We need to check you for a wire.'

I shook my head. 'I don't work for the police.' However, I had Detective Inspector Jack Parker's number on my mobile.

The lad touched my shoulder. 'We can take you to one of the units and frisk you.'

I smiled. 'You won't be able to do anything with broken fingers.'

He snatched his hand away and spat at my feet. Then the girl dragged him to the side and got her phone out. She made a call as I walked down the road, glancing up as if I were in a film, searching for the snipers on the rooftops. When I was younger, before several children's homes, this street was one of the most prosperous in the town, full of busy shops, cafés and pubs. Then, economic pressures forced them all to close. I hadn't realised what had happened to it until now, but I wondered what the land-lords of the buildings thought about it all. Or perhaps they were the ones running Counterfeit Alley. It wouldn't be the first time organised crime had funnelled their illicit gains into property acquisition. The individuals peddling coun-terfeit goods were also likely involved in other unlawful activities. The unemployment rate was high, and many had turned to illegal deeds to put food on the table.

I couldn't take the moral high ground. After all, I'd broken the law several times and had no right to question the behaviour of others. And I needed those clothes for Becky. So I strode past converted shops selling jewellery, mobile phones, CDs and DVDs, and bags until I reached stalls full of clothes and shoes for all ages. Some designer items were impressive in their fakery and nearly impossible to tell between the real things, with the vastly reduced prices being the giveaway.

However, they weren't what I needed. It took a few

minutes to find the cheap, non-designer stuff, grab two tops, a skirt in the correct uniform colours for Becky's school, and a coat that would do for all purposes. Her birthday was three months away, but I could present them to Julia as early presents so as not to make her feel guilty about me helping them out. But it left me down to my last ten quid. Still, I didn't have to pay for the plastic bag.

As I exited the shop, the teenagers returned to stalk me, shadowing me from the opposite side of the street. The girl continued to chew her gum while the boy fluctuated between sneering and winking at me. I was half expecting a bullet from the roof when there was a commotion ahead: raised voices and the occasional obscenity. I intended to ignore it and leave Counterfeit Alley until I saw a man harassing someone I recognised: Nora.

I increased my pace to get there as he harangued her, his thick face resembling a distressed puffer frog.

'You claimed this cream would heal my eczema.' He rolled up his sleeve to reveal a scarred arm. 'It's made every-thing worse.'

He went to hurl the container at her as she cowered behind the stall, so I grabbed him. 'Calm down, mate.'

His fingers shook as he dropped the cream, and it bounced along the ground, rolling away and resting on the other side of the street near my new teenage admirers.

He glared at me. 'Who the fuck are you?'

I stepped back. 'Don't panic.'

Nora thrust a twenty-pound note at him. 'Here, take your money.'

He pushed his arm at her. 'How is that going to make this better?'

I grabbed his shoulder and threw him into the street. He stumbled around like an irritated wasp, hands flailing towards any unfortunate bystanders before he tripped over and hit the ground. My teenage fan club laughed, and the girl exploded strawberry bubblegum over the bloke. He groaned as he stood, ready for a fight, until the boy said something, and the angry man stopped. He glared at me before scuttling off and tossing threats at Nora.

The girl popped more gum in her mouth. I expected trouble, but she grinned at me. 'Do you want a job here?'

'What?'

'We're always looking for extra security. We could do with someone who would blend in with the punters instead of all the brick shithouses we currently employ.' She nodded to the side, and the two rejects from the SAS staring at me. 'So, what do you say? We pay well.'

'We?'

'Yeah, my brother and me.' The teenage boy waved at me.

'You don't run this place,' I said.

Her giggle made her seem younger than she was. 'Who says so?'

I brushed the dirt from my jacket. 'Me.'

The girl shrugged. 'It's all about the optics, love. How do you feel about my offer?'

There was no point in offending whoever was running Counterfeit Alley. 'I'll think about it.'

She grinned. 'Great. You know where we are.' Then she marched over to her brother before they left and took the two goons with them.

I should have done the same.

Instead, I spoke to Nora.

Chapter 6

Someone Else's Clothes

Approaching her, I noticed the beads of sweat on her forehead and how tense she seemed. 'Nora, are you okay?'

She looked up and relaxed when she saw me. 'Oh, Enola. Yes, I'm fine. Just a bit overwhelmed with everything.'

I saw the stress on her face, so I changed the subject. 'What are you selling?'

She grabbed a small, brightly coloured gem and handed it to me. 'This is a rose quartz crystal. It promotes love and healing.'

I examined it, turning it over in my hand, trying to think where I'd seen one recently. Then it came to me. 'Ginger has one of these in her bedroom.'

Nora beamed. 'Yes, she got it from me. That's why I tell her she has me to thank for her latest romantic success.'

I peered at my reflection in the crystal. 'Ginger's dating? She kept that quiet.' Yet, to be fair, I'd spent little time with her since losing my job with the MP. With no work to go to, my mind and body had hit a sudden lethargy, and I rarely had breakfast anymore. It meant by the time I got up, Ginger and Bruce were out. Even though they both worked from home, they continued to help at the food bank, as I occasionally did.

Was there such a thing as an early twenties life crisis? I seemed to be having one.

She came around the table. 'I think she's worried about your reaction.'

'My reaction?'

'Yeah, considering who she's dating.'

I tried to picture the worst person I could imagine Ginger in a relationship with. 'The guy from the post office with the Metallica tattoos?'

Nora laughed. 'No, the police officer.'

A copper? Then it hit me. 'Jack Parker?'

She nodded. 'Yes, the detective inspector. He's quite a catch. I told her I'd be in there unless she moved fast.'

I struggled to believe it, though I didn't know why. Ginger had met Parker several times over the last few months, but I'd noticed no attraction between them, and definitely not on her part. And I assumed he was wed to his job.

'How did that happen?' I said.

'He attended one of our spiritual healing sessions at the community centre. That's where they hit it off.'

My brow furrowed. 'I thought she had better taste in men.'

Nora laughed. 'Oh, she always went out with the wrong types at university.' She pushed a bar of absinthe soap towards me, as if trying to tell me something. 'But this was different with Jack. Ginger told me all about it.' Nora's eyes took on a distant, dreamy quality, and she wove the story. 'It was during a stormy evening, Enola. Rain hammered on the windows like a thousand tiny drumbeats. The scent of damp earth and the soothing aroma of lavender oil burning in a corner filled the place. The air felt charged, like electricity before a summer thunderstorm.'

I peered at the tin of bath salts with Jesus on the label, the Messiah appearing to wink at me. 'It sounds very romantic.'

Nora's tone softened, as if she were revealing a secret. 'Their eyes met across the room, as if time had stopped. The air crackled with tension, like the moment just before a lightning strike. Ginger's heart must have been pounding so loud she could almost taste it in her mouth.' Her voice dropped to a whisper. 'They didn't speak for the longest time. It was as if words had lost their meaning, and all that existed was their connection. The room seemed to hold its breath, the silence so profound you could nearly touch it.'

My guts rumbled, and I thought I might throw up all over her stall. 'When was this?'

She waved a hand before me, resembling a magician ready to pull a rabbit out of a hat. 'Oh, about three weeks ago. I'm surprised you didn't know since you're living with Bruce and Ginger in that little flat of theirs.'

I shook my head and tried not to picture them together while I was sleeping on the sofa. I glanced at Nora's items on the table to distract me, lifting a tube of cream to see what it was. A large stamp on the bottom said NOT TO BE SOLD IN THE UK.

'Where do you obtain your merchandise, Nora?'

'Online, mainly from China and Asia. There's a lot of demand for organic healing products you can't get here.'

She glanced at the scars on my hands. 'I might have something for your skin.'

I ignored her offer. 'What happened to the guy who was shouting at you earlier?'

She lowered her eyelids. 'Oh, he must have had an allergic reaction. I warned him about the possibility when he bought it.'

I replaced the cream with the other products. 'How did you end up here?'

'In Counterfeit Alley? A friend told me about it. Initially, I came here looking for a new phone and heard about the opportunity to open my own stall. That was last month, and I've done great business since. It's a godsend, really. The tarot readings have dried up, and I don't know what I'd have done without this. It's a struggle to pay the bills nowadays.'

I looked up and down the street. 'Do you know who runs this?'

She shook her head. 'No. Those two kids you spoke to before are the ones I pay rent to. They provide security as well. They would have dealt with that man if you hadn't arrived, but thank you anyway.'

'Does Ginger know you have a stall here?'

'No. She'd only worry if she did. And now she's dating the police officer, and it's probably a good idea to keep it from her.'

She didn't instruct me to hide it from Ginger, but it was a clear enough hint.

'That teenage girl offered me a job here.'

Nora beamed. 'Great. We'd have more time to get to know each other.'

Indeed. And I'd be earning some money at long last.

But at what price? By breaking the law. That would be the cost.

'I told her I'd think about it.'

'You're concerned about the legality of it?'

'A bit.'

'Well, it doesn't hurt anyone, Enola.' Of course, I didn't mention the guy her medicinal cream had harmed. 'All the counterfeit products are only duplicating the big brands run by billionaires. The only people who lose out are too rich to notice.'

She'd simplified a large moral quandary to the basics, but I wasn't in the mood to argue with her. And with a bag of fake goods in my hand, who was I to disagree with her?

'Are you here every day?' I said.

'Most days. My few bookings for tarot readings are usually done at night now, so I can combine both. I used to get several weekly online requests, but they've dried up in the current economic climate.' She sighed. 'And many fake psychics have popped up on the internet to undercut genuine people like me.'

I resisted the urge to mention the irony of her saying fake psychics.

'Enola Gray?'

I turned to see a woman approaching me, wrestling with my memory to remember where I knew her from. Then it came to me: in the café yesterday.

'Claire King?'

Her smile revealed perfect teeth. 'Fancy meeting you here. Can I buy you a drink?'

'Drink?'

'Yeah, there's a lovely little place near here. They do an excellent chocolate muffin, and my sweet tooth is tingling.'

Nora patted my arm. 'You go, Enola. I've got work to do. And think about that offer they made you.'

'Offer?' King asked.

'I'll tell you about it over a coffee,' I said.

We left Counterfeit Alley as I wondered how far I was prepared to stumble over the criminal line just to survive.

Chapter 7

This Jungle

I sat opposite King as we drank our coffees. The café smelt of freshly baked cakes and had a heady coffee aroma. Every table was full, and it looked like most people had bought something from Counterfeit Alley.

'It surprised me to see you there.'

She grinned. 'You mean with the dodgy bags and fake watches?'

'Yeah,' I said. 'You own a clothing factory and a high street boutique, so why lower yourself to walk amidst the underclass?'

'The underclass? Is that how you see yourself, Enola?'

I sipped my coffee. 'I don't place labels on myself. Plenty of other people do that. Still, it shocked me to observe a successful businesswoman striding between the fake goods. Or were you checking to see if any of your clothes were there?'

King bit into the muffin, and bits of chocolate stuck to her lips. 'Something like that. Or maybe I was revisiting my youth.'

'Your youth?'

'My family was poor and owned nothing, even renting the TV and fridge by the month. I spent a lot of time with my mother scouring places like Counterfeit Alley for cheap goods. My father ensured I dedicated myself to my studies, so I was always at the top of my class. This led me to study business and economics at university. It was there I discovered my passion for entrepreneurship.'

'It sounds fun.'

She shook her head. 'After graduating, I worked at a clothing factory, rising through the ranks to become the manager. However, I wanted to build something of my own.'

'My ambition is to have ambition,' I said.

'In my mid-twenties, I started a business with a loan from the bank and rented a space in a nearby industrial park. The early days were tough, with long hours and struggling to make ends meet. Then I had Fiona, and things got harder, but I never gave up.'

I was already feeling sorry for her. 'No help from the father?'

'No. Over time, the factory grew. I took on more clients and hired extra staff. As the business expanded, I invested in new technologies and modernised the operations. Eventually, I opened the boutique shop on the high street, selling my clothing brand. But even with all that, I've never forgotten where I came from.'

It was a nice speech, but I wasn't sure I bought it. 'You're a shining example of the capitalistic work ethic.'

She stuffed the muffin into her mouth, eating as she spoke.

'I operate within the limitations of an impractical system, which will only deteriorate at the current rate. It's a shame your former employer lost her job. This town might have had a chance if she was still here sticking up for it.'

'Kate Frost? She had noble aims for the community, but I can't see how anyone not within a political party can achieve anything.'

'I'm twice your age, Enola, so I don't wish to come across as a lecturing mother figure, but you're wrong. Specific individuals have changed this country's course for the worse in the last few years. The UK is no longer a cohesive unit but a giant neighbourhood fast falling into a rack-and-ruin slum ghetto. Its residents look on, jaws dropping, as the bloody war of terror conducted by warring gangs of politicians tears apart the open streets. It's surpassed the point of being interesting and is now devoid of power or policies, purely about retribution, gang-on-gang, and disregard for the population. The acquisition of money drives everything. The rich want to be richer and fuck anybody who tries to stop them.'

The coffee warmed my throat. 'Hasn't that always been the way?'

King nodded. 'To an extent, yes, but now greed has infested every part of society, from top to bottom. Money is money, whether clean, dirty, or dripping with blood. Regardless of whether it belongs to a Mexican drug cartel, the mafia, big American pharma, corporate tax evasion, Russian oligarchs, Middle East tyrants, or British politicians driven by ideology, all are welcome at a money laundering facility near you. It's the only thing keeping so-called Western democracies going, and the villains know it.'

Passion blazed behind her eyes. I could see how she'd dragged herself up from a difficult background to where she was now.

'You don't think this country is democratic?'

King laughed. 'There is no democracy, not in a meaningful way. Private grifters profiting from the deep pockets of multinational corporations: this and poor education, lack of investment and a dreadful voting system keep us indolent, past caring, comforted by the teat of capitalism, the plague of social media disinformation. I fear what this country is becoming and what it will be like for Fiona and Becky, as well as kids like them. And the environment is going to hell in a handbasket. And none of the fuckers who could do something about it takes a blind bit of notice apart from spouting useless conditions they know they'll never stick to.' She took a long breath. 'Apologies, I haven't talked with an adult outside of work in a while.'

'No need to apologise,' I said. 'It's good to see somebody passionate about improving the world. I agree we don't get that from our so-called leaders.'

She finished her coffee. 'Anyway, enough of my rambling. What were you doing in Counterfeit Alley? Was it anything to do with that hole in your shoe?'

'No.' I showed her the bag of clothes. 'I wanted to find Becky a present for school.'

'That's kind of you. So you think it will stop the bullies from picking on her?'

'Probably not, but I have to try something apart from storming into the playground and terrorising a bunch of kids.'

'You could speak to their parents.'

I nodded. 'I might have to.'

I pictured it in my head when I heard the sirens approaching. A few people clutching bags of fake goods sprang from their chairs and bolted from the café as the police cars sped towards Counterfeit Alley.

Then I thought of Nora.

Chapter 8

Crash and Burn

I clutched the bag as I ran towards Counterfeit Alley. My legs throbbed as sirens rattled through my head. Everybody else was going in the opposite direction, and King hadn't joined me. She probably had the right idea, but I needed to find Nora. I hardly knew the woman, but she was a good friend of Ginger's, so I had to try to help her.

The police cars took the long way around, so I cut across the field to get there before them. The ground stretched before me, a vast expanse of sun-drenched grass swaying in the warm breeze. As I sprinted over the uneven surface, my feet felt springy, the sensation of soft soil and thick weeds pressing against my shoes. The aroma of the grassland was intoxicating, a heady blend of earth, wildflowers, and the faint hint of rain that had fallen earlier in the day.

Beads of sweat formed on my forehead, and the taste of salt coated my lips as I ran, clutching the bag of Becky's new clothes in my trembling hands. As I neared my destination, the distant sirens of the police cars echoed through the air, their wailing cries growing louder with each passing second.

Invisible fingers clawed at the pit of my stomach, a palpable sensation that tightened my muscles and quickened my breath. The urgency of the moment was like a drumbeat in my chest, matching the rhythm of my heart.

People were packing up their wares and running away. When the coppers approached, spotters whistled the alarm while others shot fireworks into the sky. Sellers slammed the metal shutters shut and disappeared into the shadows. I ran to where I'd seen Nora, seeing the table with all her goods. They were there, but she wasn't.

I glanced around as the police shouted instructions to each other. Maybe she'd scarpered at the first sound of the sirens, and I'd run back for nothing. And I still had the bag of dodgy clothes with me. What would the coppers do if they caught me with that?

A vein in my head throbbed as I turned towards the sirens and saw a line of police cars approaching, blue lights flashing. They swarmed the alley, jumping out and fanning in all directions. I spotted Jack Parker, his tall frame towering over the other officers. It was going to be awkward.

Then somebody pulled me into the building behind Nora's stall.

They released me, and I stumbled over a box into the wall, cracking my shoulder.

'Fuck!' I gritted my teeth and rubbed my arm. 'Nora, is that you?'

It wasn't. The teenage girl stepped out of the shadows, still chewing gum. 'We can hide here until the pigs leave.'

I went to the door and peered through the gap, seeing officers rounding up people and putting them in vans. 'Where's your brother?'

'Safe, I hope,' she replied.

'Do you know where Nora is?'

'Is that the woman who was selling the spiritual junk?'

'Yeah, that's her.'

'I never saw her. My name's Claudia. You?'

I watched Jack moving down the street. 'Enola. The police are checking each building.'

She peered through the broken window. 'Damn! We'll have to hide upstairs.'

Or I could go outside and admit everything to Parker. Then Becky wouldn't get her new clothes, which was more important than anything else. I had to do something to brighten the kid's life, even if it meant breaking the law and hiding from the coppers.

'Is there a way out the back?' I said.

Claudia shook her head. 'It's swampland out there, leading into the river, unless you want to swim across it to the woods.'

It was tempting. 'Let's get the lie of the land from upstairs first.'

She led me through the dirt and damp, with peeling wallpaper and cracked plaster on the walls. 'This place is supposed to be haunted.'

I peered at the faded wallpaper, waiting for ghostly arms to burst out, even though I was a non-believer in anything supernatural.

'Are you scared?'

She shrugged. 'Only of the living.'

As we crept upstairs, I heard steps approaching. We froze, and I held my breath at the sound of the police radios crackling with static. I pressed myself against the wall, trying to disappear into the shadows. The footsteps stopped outside the front door as two people spoke.

'Make sure we search every building. I want to know who's behind this whole operation.' It was Parker's voice.

Claudia grabbed my hand, her skin cold against mine, and dragged me upstairs. As we went, I touched the cobwebs on the wall, getting to the top as the police entered. That was when I realised I'd left the bag of clothes downstairs.

Fuck!

My legs shook as she hauled me across the dirty carpet and into the bedroom at the end. There, she let go of me and ran to the window. I stood by the door, hearing the coppers moving below. Maybe they'd get bored and not bother going upstairs.

'We'll climb out the window and enter the garden,' Claudia said. 'We'll lose them through the swamp.'

I went to her and studied the outside, seeing the wetland on the other side of the fence. 'You want to go through the river?'

'Not really,' she said. 'I can't swim.'

'You should head downstairs and give yourself up, then.'

The shadows swallowed her up. 'My life wouldn't be worth living if I did that. I'm better off risking the river.'

'Bad things happen in those woods.'

She narrowed her eyes. 'What?'

I didn't mention the dead man I'd discovered there not so long ago. 'Nothing. Kids sometimes mess about in the trees, pretending to be witches and playing with Ouija boards.'

Claudia grinned. 'Drink, drugs, and sex – that's what teenagers get up to there.' Her smile disappeared as soon as it appeared. 'I heard about a woman who drowned in the river before I was born.'

My shoulder trembled as I pressed my head to the door, listening for the coppers. 'She didn't die – she vanished.'

'Isn't that the same thing?'

I didn't answer, focusing on those trampling through the rooms below.

'Who runs Counterfeit Alley, Claudia?'

'Are you a nark?' she said. 'Did you bring the pigs here today?'

Before I could reply, I heard footsteps coming upstairs.

I rushed to the window. 'It's now or never.'

There were sounds in the corridor as I climbed through the broken window and got onto the roof, holding the ledge. The wind swept across my face as I saw the river in the distance. The voices were loud on the other side of the house, and I suddenly wondered what I was doing. What was the worst Parker and the others could do to me? I assumed they weren't after buyers like me, but those who ran Counterfeit Alley. People like Claudia, even though she was only a front for the criminals that organised the operation.

But what could I do? I had too much experience dodging the police to turn around and walk towards them, open-armed. I edged my way to the end of the roof and dropped six feet to the ground, tucking into the grass without a sound. Then Claudia followed behind me, grabbing my arm before I ran across the garden.

'You'll look after me in the river, won't you?'

'Sure,' I said. 'Now come on.'

We dashed to the fence, scrambled over it, and landed on the wet earth below. The water slithered over my shoes, entering the hole at my big toe and soaking my feet. I expected to hear shouting behind us, but it didn't arrive as we trudged through the sludge, the wind whipping over my face. The reeds were between the river and us, only a few feet away. Once we got across, we could lose ourselves in the woods.

That's when I saw the body float to the top of the water.

'Fuck!' Claudia said.

I moved forward and stared into Nora's vacant eyes.

Chapter 9

This City

As Detective Inspector Parker spoke to Claudia, I sat on the cold pavement and dried my feet. Uniformed police officers littered the street like discarded pizza boxes, putting glum-looking people into the back of vans and confiscating fraudulent goods. Nobody bothered me as I picked dirt from my toes, my mind full of the image of Nora in the river.

'Do you need medical help?'

I let go of my aching foot to look at Parker and his open notebook.

'It's nothing a hot drink won't fix. Can I leave now?'

'Tell me what happened with the body.'

'Nora. Her name was Nora.' I'd seen more than enough dead bodies in my short life, but you never got used to it. 'I spoke to her earlier and was looking for her when your lot raided the street.'

'And she was just floating in the water?'

I couldn't get rid of the image of her wide-open eyes staring at me.

'Yeah. That's when I called you.'

He glanced at Claudia, who was chewing gum while ignoring a uniformed officer talking to her. 'And that girl was with you?'

'She must have panicked when you arrived. I don't know who she is.'

Parker read from his book. 'Claudia Kane is a fifteen-year-old runaway with her twin brother, Adam. She claims she was here to buy a mobile phone.'

'Runaway from what?'

'Their foster home, which they disappeared from three months ago.'

'I hope you're going to investigate why two kids felt they needed to live on the streets instead of with their foster parents.'

'That's up to social services,' he said. 'Do you know Nora's surname?'

'No. I only met her last night. I thought you'd know her.'

He narrowed his eyes. 'Why would I?'

'Because she's Ginger's friend. That's where I bumped into her, at the flat.'

Parker rubbed at his forehead. 'Christ! Somebody needs to tell Ginger.'

'Do you want me to do it?' I didn't think it was a good time to mention their relationship.

'That would be great if you could. The body had no ID, so we don't know where she lives or if she has family. Ginger might know that.'

'No problem, but I'm not doing it over the phone. One of your lot can take me to the flat.'

'I'll do it,' he said. 'But there's something else I need to ask you.'

'What?'

He dropped the bag of Becky's new clothes next to me. 'We recovered that from the house. Is it yours?'

The sensible thing would have been to deny it, but I needed those things for the kid.

'Do you know Julia Cross and her daughter Becky?'

Parker nodded. 'I've met them before.'

'Well, Becky's getting bullied at school because of her clothes, so I bought her some new ones to help. So that's what's in the bag.'

'There are plenty of shops selling school uniforms in town, Enola.'

'Not all of us have a copper's salary, Jack.'

'Is that your excuse?'

Police cars drove away with their sad-faced occupants as we spoke.

'Isn't it heavy-handed, sending so many officers here for a few fake goods? Don't you have better things to do?'

He sat next to me, and I noticed how old he looked, with dark shadows under his eyes and two days of stubble covering his face.

'Is that what you think we're here for, bits of knock-off designer gear?'

I shrugged. 'Isn't it?'

'No.' He pointed to the now-empty shops and stalls. 'This is a part of the town where organised crime groups operate with or against each other, whose leaders manipulate defenceless people to carry out their illicit activities, including coerced labour and the abduction of vulnerable child asylum seekers from government-sanctioned hotels.'

I glanced at the bag as guilt swept through me. 'Yeah, I saw that on the news. So how do the gangs get away with it?'

Parker sighed. 'Organised criminal organisations target

easily exploitable individuals nationwide, including the hotel network that accommodates asylum seekers. Hundreds of kids have gone missing that way. We need to catch those running Counterfeit Alley and stop the people trafficking. That's why we're here today.'

'Any luck?'

He shook his head. 'It doesn't look like it. Those we took away are only customers, or so they claimed. What about you? Do you know anything?'

It was my chance to deny everything, but I looked at the bag of clothes and wondered who had been forced to make those things.

'Do the police still use informants?'

'The official name is a Covert Human Intelligence Source or CHIS. Why?'

'Because the girl, Claudia, offered me a job working as security here.'

His face darkened further. 'Why?'

I told him about the irate bloke outside Nora's stall. 'Claudia might have been joking.'

'This angry customer. Could he have returned to hurt Nora?'

'You think somebody murdered her?'

'We won't know until after the post-mortem. My initial impression was drowning, but we can't rule anything out.'

I pictured the man I'd dragged from Nora. 'It would have been me he'd want.'

'So you might be in danger. Did Nora mention a name?'

I shook my head. 'No, and I doubt she kept records.' Claudia had finished talking to the copper and was on her phone. 'What's going to happen to her?'

'We'll return her to the foster home,' Parker said. 'But she'll only run away again.'

'I guess whoever ran Counterfeit Alley will set up somewhere else soon?'

He nodded. 'They always do.'

'So I could get close to Claudia and maybe find out who's behind it all.'

'You want to work for the police?'

Considering how several officers had hurt my family and me over the years, I wanted nothing to do with them. Yet, I was there talking to a copper, and I needed to stop the gangs from exploiting people. And perhaps I could earn some money from it.

'How much does it pay?'

He stood. 'No, it's too dangerous. We should speak to Ginger before Nora's death is all over the internet.'

I got up as forensic officers took Ginger's body into an ambulance. Then I followed Parker to his car.

But not before grabbing the bag of Becky's new clothes.

Chapter 10

Stepping Softly

Ginger was at her laptop when we entered the flat, my heart aching at the thought she might have learnt about Nora's death online. She looked up and saw Parker with me, her cheeks turning flaming red.

'Are you in trouble, Enola?'

I went to her. 'Come over here and sit down.'

She didn't argue as I led her to the sofa. 'What's this about?'

I sat near her while Parker sat opposite. 'I'm sorry, Ginger, it's Nora. She's dead.'

Ginger's eyes widened, and her lips trembled. 'What?'

I explained the situation as best I could, leaving out the more gruesome details. She listened intently, her expression a mix of sadness and concern.

'I can't believe it,' she said when I finished. 'Nora was such a kind, gentle soul. I can't imagine anybody wanting to hurt her.'

Parker spoke. 'We don't know the cause of death yet, but did she ever mention anyone who might have wanted to harm her?'

Ginger frowned, and I could see she was holding back the tears. 'No, not really. Nora wasn't the type to make enemies. She was always so focused on healing and spreading positivity. But one person caused her a lot of pain: her ex-husband.'

'Her ex-husband?' I repeated, surprised. 'What happened?'

'They had a messy divorce,' Ginger explained. 'He was abusive towards her, both physically and emotionally. It was a tough time for her, but she eventually found the strength to leave him.'

'Do you know where he is?' Parker asked.

She shook her head. 'I haven't heard from him in years. But I know Nora feared him. Maybe she never fully felt safe, even after leaving him.'

He got his pen and notebook. 'What was Nora's surname?'

'Miller,' Ginger replied. 'Nora Miller.'

The way she said the name, I could tell she was desperately trying to cling to her friend, to deny what had happened.

'Did she have any family apart from the ex-husband?'

Ginger's sadness turned to anger as her eyes flared. 'He wasn't family.'

He reached over and touched her arm. 'Yes, I'm sorry, Ginger. Do you have an address and contact details for her?'

She nodded. 'I'll get them for you.' She stood and went to her bedroom.

'I'll leave you two alone,' I said.

'Why?' Parker asked.

I got up. 'I know about you two. Nora told me.'

He sank into the sofa, his face flustered. 'We wanted to tell you, Enola, but, well....'

'You know how I feel about coppers.'

Ginger returned before he could reply and handed him a piece of paper. 'It's all on there.'

I went to her, and we hugged, her tears settling on my shoulder. We stood like that for several minutes before parting.

'Will you be okay?'

She rubbed at her face. 'I guess so. Are you going out?'

I grabbed the bag of clothes. 'I've got early birthday presents to deliver to Becky.' I glanced at Parker. 'You'll be fine with Jack.'

I left them and stepped out of the flat just as Bruce returned with Kronos.

'Did you hear about the commotion on the old Micklewood housing estate?'

The mutt jumped at me, and I snatched the dog's lead from Bruce.

'Take me to the pub, and I'll tell you all about it.'

'But you don't drink,' he said.

My stomach grumbled to wake the dead. 'Yeah, but I haven't eaten all day, and you can treat me.' He'd have to since I had little money after my clothes-buying spree.

It was a three-minute walk there. Once inside, I sat near the jukebox while he ordered the food and drinks. Kronos lay at my feet, chewing on a pink plastic dinosaur. Watching him roll it between his teeth reminded me of Claudia and her fruit-flavoured gum. Had I been serious about offering my services as a police snitch? The money would come in handy, and I could do some good in helping people forced to work for whichever criminal gang or gang was running the fake goods operation. In addition, I might even be able to help Claudia and her brother. Yet, I had her name, but no way to contact her. Then again, Parker would have the address of Claudia's foster home so I could visit them there.

I texted him while I waited for Bruce to return.

How is Ginger?

He replied immediately. *She's okay, reminiscing about how she met Nora at university. How are you?*

Fine. Do you have Cladia Kane's address?

Why?

I'm worried about the kid.

You know I can't give you her personal information.

Do you trust social services to check that foster home thoroughly?

No.

Exactly, so who better to look at it than someone who spent ten years in children's homes?

It was a delayed reply. *Okay, but behave yourself.*

Then he sent it to me.

'Your grilled chicken and salad is on its way,' Bruce said as he sat and gave me an orange juice. 'Now, will you tell me what happened?'

I did as somebody put Joy Division on the jukebox. 'How well did you know Nora?'

He rubbed at his neck. 'Only a little, really. She took the spiritual healing paraphernalia much more seriously than Ginger, but it wasn't that which got on my nerves.'

'So what was it?'

He shrugged. 'The usual stuff with me.'

'Politics?'

'Yeah, she was a fervent Tory, and we always argued about it.' He laughed. 'She called me an extremist Marxist yesterday. And just because I said I don't understand how we have such an enormous number of genuinely stupid people running the country, world-beating moronic levels of misunderstanding and malice. If that's what an expensive education buys, their parents should ask for their money back.'

My food arrived, and my guts groaned. I stuffed the chicken into my mouth and stared at him. If somebody had murdered Nora, would the police add him to their suspect list?

I tried not to think of death as I ate, instead showing him what I'd bought for Becky.

He grinned. 'She'll like those.'

I sat back, listened to love tearing poor Ian Curtis apart, and looked forward to making at least one person happy.

Chapter 11

Distant Smile

It was a cold evening, and the air inside the small flat was heavy and stagnant. Julia sat in the kitchen, her long brown hair tied back in a messy bun as she sipped on a glass of water.

'Do you want a drink, Enola?'

My neck ached, and I thought of Claudia Kane in that foster home. 'I'm okay, thanks.'

Dirty dishes and cutlery filled the table with a lingering smell of fried onions.

'Mum cooked spaghetti,' Becky said.

Julia used a stained towel to wipe her head. 'It's easy to make and cheap.' A weary smile crept across her face. 'How's the job hunting going?'

'It's a struggle,' I replied. 'The jobs are too few hours and minimum wage, or the prospect of working for douchebags. Sometimes it's a combination of both.'

'What's a douchebag?' the kid asked.

Julia glanced at me for an answer. Instead, I offered Becky the clothes.

'I got you some early birthday presents.'

Her eyes lit up, and she snatched the bag from me, pouring the contents onto the floor.

'Clothes?' she moaned. 'Where are the toys?'

'Becky!' Julia shouted. 'Show appreciation to Enola.'

The kid scowled. 'Thank you, Enola.'

'That's better,' Julia said. 'Now go to your bedroom and try them on.'

She lowered her head and collected the clothes, lugging them to her room like somebody from the Middle Ages carrying plague bodies to the pit.

'How was work?' I asked Julia.

She cleared the table and made coffee, the aroma invading my senses and adding much-needed adrenalin into my veins. I could still see Nora's body floating in that water.

'It's hard, you know, but rewarding helping others.' She sighed. 'It's terrible sometimes, seeing people struggling with their health and having nobody to spend time with them apart from me and the other girls. It makes you appreciate how lonely it must get for some folks.' She glanced at Becky's bedroom. 'But I'd do anything for her.'

I reached over and touched her arm. 'She knows that, Julia.'

She sipped her coffee and sighed. 'What you did, Enola, getting those clothes is a big help. I want to get her new stuff, nothing fancy, just what she needs for school, so the other kids don't laugh at her, but it's a struggle to buy food and pay the bills even when I'm working sixty hours a week.'

'Any time you need a break, you know I'll look after her for you.'

She nodded. 'I'm so grateful, Enola, and Becky looks up

to you like a big sister, but don't Ginger and Bruce get annoyed when you take her to the flat?'

I laughed. 'Bruce only gets pissed off by politics, and Ginger loves Becky. Plus, she's got other things to focus on now.'

'Oh, do tell. You know I like a bit of goss.'

I didn't mention Nora's death. Instead, I gave her the juicy gossip. 'Ginger and Detective Inspector Jack Parker are, as the kids might say, stepping out together.'

Julia's laugh lifted the weight from her face, which was good to see.

'Wow, the copper. He is a catch. I always thought you and he could have a thing.'

I nearly spat coffee all over the floor. 'He's about ten years older than me.'

She shrugged. 'So? You're twenty-one soon. It's not like you're a kid, is it?'

Becky burst out of her bedroom before I could reply, her smile lighting up the room.

'These are so lovely, Enola.' She ran her fingers over the top and skirt. 'They feel so much better than the crummy stuff I have.'

Julia waved a finger at her daughter. 'You'll need to keep the older ones as well.'

The kid frowned at her mother. 'Why? They're horrible, and these are nice and new.'

Her grumpiness made me laugh. 'Yeah, but you can't wear them every day, Becky.'

She put her hands on her hips. 'Why not?'

Julia shook her head. 'Because they'll get dirty. Especially with you always climbing trees and rolling in the dirt.'

I'd never thought she'd need more than one outfit.

Damn! So, I had to earn money to buy her more clothes. And if there wasn't the prospect of a legal job on the horizon, I'd have to take an alternate route. That meant talking to Claudia Kane and hoping her offer was still open, as long as the counterfeit operation opened again elsewhere.

So, I could kill two birds with one stone: make cash to help Becky and her mum and maybe get information about who was running the fake goods business.

Becky pirouetted like a ballerina, and witnessing something so simple bring her so much happiness was a delight. Only it wasn't simple for her and Julia; having a clean school uniform was essential to their well-being.

I had to get more money.

I went to the window, pressing my nose against the open glass. The view was of concrete and brick, the buildings towering above us in a monotonous display of beige and grey. But there was life down there, laughter and chatter echoing through the narrow streets. I inhaled the sweet scent of flowers blooming in the planters lining the pavement, hearing children playing in the park down the road and the distant hum of traffic.

'Don't you want to play with your friends, Becky?' I said.

It was the wrong thing to say, the words knocking the joy out of her.

'No, I like to stay home with Mum when she's here.'

Julia smiled at me. 'Too many night shifts mean I don't see her as much as I want. But you know that since you look after her for me.'

'Anytime, Julia.'

'And I really appreciate it, Enola, but you have your own life to lead.'

'Yeah, and speaking of which, I better get back and leave you alone.'

I hugged them both and left, with a mixture of weariness and joy sweeping through me as I stepped into the night.

That's when two giants crawled out of the shadows.

Chapter 12

The Man Who Dies Every Day

The stale scent of warm beer and cigarettes drifted my way.

'Somebody wants to meet you,' the tall bloke said.

'Do they need a signed autograph?' I asked. 'The links are all on my website, but you have to be able to read to understand them.'

The little goon stepped forward, resembling Napoleon in a striped suit. 'He wishes to see you now in the Red Raven. We have to take you there.'

'And if you don't?'

The big thug grinned, showing vampire-like teeth. 'Then the twins will suffer.'

'The twins?'

The small thug nodded. 'You've met them, Adam and Claudia.'

'I fucking hate those kids,' the tall bloke said. 'All I need is an excuse from you to hurt them.'

The fury in his eyes told me he wasn't bluffing. 'Okay, but one of you is buying me a Coke.'

It was a twenty-minute walk to the pub, striding ahead of them. I pushed the door open, hit by a waft of sweet cider, testosterone and desperation. The few patrons inside shot me hostile looks as the goons escorted me to the corner. They left with an old man sitting across from me. He was tall and thin, with long grey hair and a thick beard that almost touched the table. And he smelt of fish and chips, with the look of the last surviving minor member of some sixties supergroup who made millions by playing the bass and not dying.

He nudged an unopened can of Coke towards me. 'They texted ahead with what you wanted.'

I grabbed the drink, ready to pull the top off, until I realised it wasn't a genuine Coke, seeing the slight changes in the design. The small print at the bottom said, "Made in North Korea."

I pushed it away from me. 'Who are you?'

'It doesn't matter who I am. What's more important is what I represent.'

'And what's that?'

He placed his hands on the table, highlighting the scars. 'The future, Ms Gray. I represent the future. You must ask yourself, do you want to be part of that future?'

I nodded at the fake Coke. 'Is that your future?'

'Can I call you Enola?'

I shrugged. 'Whatever.'

His smile unsettled me. 'The schools might fall down with pupils in them while you wait five hours for an ambulance if you break your leg. It takes weeks to see your GP, and you'll likely die before you get treated. The police ignore burglaries and other crimes, while most coppers escape punishment for serious offences, including sexual assault and the harassment of women and children. And all the while, our towns, cities and countryside become tatty, neglected and full of problems.

'We can't rely on trains, roads or air travel to transport you and your luggage to where you need to be or on time, or for rivers and beaches to be clean or to get excellent service pretty well anywhere because companies cut costs to pay executives and shareholders more.'

I laughed. 'So that's it – you're here to put the world to rights.'

He shook his head and dislodged a long grey hair that settled over his eye. 'We've all been scammed and now exist within a global corporatocracy. The disparity between the wealthy and the rest has increased massively, and the cornerstones of a well-functioning society have been eroded. We're told the market drives wages, and the rates offered have steadily declined. Globalisation is part of the problem, driven by large corporations farming out operations to the cheapest market and effectively getting into bed with regimes that do not reflect civilised values. These decisions feel so embedded that we have to tread carefully when making choices that might upset the status quo, and we are entirely at the behest of the supply chains and flow of money this has created.

'Banks have financed this change to the point they control every single part of our lives, from government borrowing to the micro-finances of individuals where it's now commonplace to finance purchases on credit for everyday items such as clothes and food. Most folks rely on credit to ensure life continues in the current economic model. So why not have a system where somebody other than the usual financial suspects offers people a credit facility that accurately measures their lifestyle needs and their ability to repay their debts?'

I put one hand on my heart to control the laughter. 'You're a loan shark, is that it?'

'That's an outdated term, Ms Gray. I and others like me prefer to be called credit counsellors.'

I shook my head. 'How much do you charge for interest – four hundred per cent?'

'Charges fluctuate, but that's not the point.'

'So what is?'

He grabbed the fake Coke and opened it. It hissed as dark liquid fizzled from the top and slid down the side, creating a sticky pool on the table.

'Have you considered our offer?'

'What offer?'

He sipped at the can, revealing nicotine-stained teeth. 'To come and work for us.'

'You're the person running Counterfeit Alley?'

The old man shrugged. 'I am one of several controlling interests in that endeavour. Not everybody is eager to give you a position with us, but enough are. And I know you are seeking employment.'

'Claudia and her brother are on your payroll?'

'They are.'

'And how many other kids have you forced into your organisation?'

'Would you rather they were deported to a foreign country against their will?'

'You're such a philanthropist.'

'So, what's your answer?'

I gazed deep into his yellowing eyes. 'I'll think about it.'

He slurped on the fake Coke. 'No, you won't.'

'Why me?'

He wiped the dark liquid from his wrinkled chin. 'We

saw how you handled that hooligan today. You would be useful in a forthcoming operation we have.'

'What operation?'

'I need an answer first, Ms Gray.'

I could only give one if I didn't want others hurt. 'Sure. When do I start?'

His smile irritated me as he removed a mobile from his pocket and pushed it towards me. 'We'll contact you when we require you.'

I glanced at the phone. 'You won't tell me what the work is? Or your name?'

'Do you like the title of this pub?' he said.

'The Red Raven? It reminds me of my favourite Stranglers album.'

He laughed. 'The Stranglers? I saw them in the early days when they played the back rooms of pubs a lot worse than this one. I remember the seething tension in the crowd and how violence could erupt any second for the most trivial reasons.' His eyes lit up. 'The world was much better then. When we become more acquainted, perhaps I'll tell you stories of those days, but for now, you can call me Raven.'

The table creaked as he stood, pushing past me without another word. His goons followed him out, and I sat there unmoving, staring at the sticky mess near me.

It was a sticky mess, and I didn't know how to get out of it.

Chapter 13

Walk Away

I slammed into the shadows as I left the pub and limped into the deserted park, the chilled breeze brushing against my face. The rustling of leaves and the distant chirping of crickets serenaded me as I walked. The darkness was both comforting and unnerving at the same time. Somewhere in the distance, dogs were barking as I heard Raven's voice in my head and felt the way it infected my heart. It had been pounding relentlessly since leaving the stink of booze behind, a desperate rhythm turning my blood into steaming lava.

I moved further into the park, trying to distract myself from the fear gnawing at me. My eyes scanned the area for any signs of danger. The shadows were deep and shifting, and I couldn't shake the feeling of being watched. I tried to ignore it and focused instead on the details of my surroundings, the damp earth and the faint fragrance of freshly cut grass. I heard the soft trickle from a nearby fountain, where the water reflected the moonlight, creating an ethereal glow.

A group of stray cats scattered at my approach. They'd

been rummaging through a garbage bin, and I felt sad for them, recognising how much we had in common. I sat on a bench and leaned back, gazing at the stars. I breathed hard and experienced a sense of release, a momentary respite from the weight of my situation. My thoughts drifted to my childhood, growing up in children's homes, and how it had led to that point.

Both anger and sadness bubbled up inside me. It wasn't fair that I had to make those decisions and worry about those I cared about. Then I remembered the words of my grandmother, who had always told me that life wasn't fair and it was up to me to create my own destiny. That was as she lay in the hospital dying of cancer. A week later, both my parents were dead, murdered by the type of people I now might have to work for.

Maybe this was the ideal opportunity for me. An old man and two blokes in a pub were unlikely to be the front line of an organised crime gang involved in human trafficking, but the so-called Raven was connected to those who ran Counterfeit Alley. This meant that if Parker was right, Raven was probably also linked to the missing refugee children.

Parker?

I took the phone from my pocket and stared at the detective inspector's number. I could sever my responsibility from the issue with a call to him.

Yet how many people would that put in danger?

I gripped the mobile and knew I couldn't tell him or the police.

So what to do?

I looked at the device Raven gave me. It was empty, with no numbers, internet or apps. And he hadn't given me a charger for it. So, I checked the side and noticed that the connection was identical to my phone, which was no coincidence.

How much did they know about me?

'They've got you for life now.' I smelled the strawberry gum before I saw her. Then she appeared out of the shadows like a ghost. 'There's no going back.'

'Where's your brother, Claudia?'

'Adam? Probably doing something for them.'

She stood and stared at me, blowing the gum, busting it, and then sucking it into her mouth. 'How old are you?' I said.

'About the same age as you.'

'Yeah, right? Did they threaten you and Adam into working for them?'

She swallowed the bubblegum and laughed. Then she sat near me and rolled up her sleeve, revealing several cigarette burns on her arms.

'Does this answer your question?'

Icy fingers gripped my heart as my brain and legs told me to rush back to the pub to strangle that old man. 'They did this to you? Was it the grey-haired bloke who calls himself Raven?'

She answered my query with her own. 'Didn't you live in a children's home?'

'More than one. Why?'

She raised her arm. 'The gang didn't do this to me.'

The veil lifted from my eyes. 'Your foster parents?'

'It's worse for Adam because he's a boy.'

Fuck! She pulled down her sleeve, but the image was burnt into my mind, the heat searing through my veins. 'What happened to your parents?'

'Dad was shot, and Mum's in prison.' She suddenly looked like the teenager she was. 'Do you like my name?'

'Claudia? Sure.'

'Mum named me after a vampire girl in a novel. Adam's named after the guy in the *Bible*, but I got to be a vampire girl, which is much cooler.'

'Do you still go to school?'

She shrugged. 'Sometimes. I'm good at French, and my teachers think I could do languages at college, but that's never going to happen.'

'It could, Claudia. Don't give up.'

She shook her head. 'Nah, like I said. They've got us both for life now. Once you're in, there's no getting out.'

'If you're not at the foster home, where do you and Adam live?'

She grabbed a strangely patterned leaf from a tree and stared at it briefly before thrusting it into her jacket pocket. 'We move around different places. Some are nice.'

We had a five or six-year age difference, but sitting on that bench, it felt like an eternity.

I showed her the phone Raven had given me. 'Did they give you one of these?'

'Yeah, but there are no numbers on it. I don't call them; they always ring me.'

'Where are you staying tonight?' I pictured her in that foster home in pain and knew I couldn't let that happen.

'Not sure.' I should have called Parker there and then, but I didn't. She peered into my eyes. 'What happened to that woman, Nora?'

'The police don't know yet.'

'Was it an accident?'

'Maybe. Do you think differently?'

'I'm clueless. I heard some things about her down Counterfeit Alley. She upset a few people there.'

'Do you know why?'

She stood as her phone rang and she answered it. 'Okay, I'll see you there.'

'Who was that?'

'Adam. I've got to go now.'

'Wait,' I said, but she vanished into the trees before I could stop her.

Claudia. Adam. Nora. Becky. Julia.

Raven.

Was I the link that couldn't be broken?

Chapter 14

Obscene Chemistry

I didn't sleep through Bruce and Ginger's early morning racket.

'How are you, Ginger?' I said, pushing the cover from me and slipping off the sofa. Bruce was frying bacon and eggs in the kitchen while she filled the coffee pot.

Her hair was in disarray, and she was in her dressing gown, which wasn't like her at all. 'Oh, you know, Enola, still trying to come to terms with what happened to Nora. Have you heard from Jack?'

'Parker? No, why?'

'He told me about Counterfeit Alley and that you saw Nora there.'

'Were you aware she was selling illegal goods?'

Ginger shook her head. 'No, not at all. I'd realised she struggled with money, but I didn't think she'd do that.'

Bruce brought the breakfast out. 'Morning, Enola. Are you coming to the meeting?'

I sat before the food and split the egg with a fork. The yolk flowed over the bacon and called out to my stomach. 'What meeting?'

'After yesterday's events,' he replied, 'the council and the police organised an emergency gathering at the community centre at ten this morning to address the issue of the avalanche of fraudulent and illegal goods in the town.'

'What good will that do?' I asked.

He shrugged. 'Probably nothing, but at least they'll be seen to be doing something.'

I dropped two sugars in my coffee and watched Ginger. 'So, how's it going with the detective inspector?'

She stopped halfway through buttering her toast. 'Who told you?'

'Why didn't you?'

Bruce buried his head in his phone.

'It's only been a few weeks, Enola. I'm not sure where the relationship is headed.'

'Does Parker feel the same way?'

The bread lingered close to Enola's lips. 'To be honest, with his work, we don't see much of each other.'

That was probably why I hadn't seen them together at the flat before yesterday, when it was nothing but bad news.

'It's none of my business, Ginger. I just thought one of you might have mentioned it to me.' Silence crept through the room, and even Kronos didn't make a noise. I glanced over the table at the stack of photo albums. 'Were you reminiscing last night?'

A sparkle returned to Ginger's eyes. 'I showed Jack and Bruce my university photos of Nora and me.'

'When did you graduate?'

'Ten years ago,' Ginger replied. 'It's hard to believe where the time has gone.'

'I was in Hong Kong then,' Bruce added.

I sipped my coffee, and the overdose of sugar soothed

my throat. 'You were part of a tech start-up?' He'd told me the story before, but I'd paid little attention.

'Yeah, the Asian version of Twitter. It was great while it lasted, but I cashed in my shares at the right time, which meant I could set up my consultancy business here.'

They reminisced, and I watched them, glad that Ginger looked happy but knowing it would be torture for her on the inside. They were ten to twelve years older than I was, but the age gap hadn't been a problem when I'd moved into the next-door flat, and we'd hit it off. Our shared love of music helped - though they obviously had worse tastes than me, especially Ginger - and it was always easy between us. And when I couldn't pay the rent and the landlord kicked me out, they quickly offered me somewhere to stay.

So, I was as close to them as I'd been to anyone outside of Seraphina and Amy, my mentor and best mate from the last children's home. But Seraphina was dead, and Amy and I had a problematic, estranged relationship. I loved Becky and Julia, but Ginger was my closest female friend, which made her pain mine. I could do nothing about Nora's death, but I wanted to help her grieve. And I needed to know how Nora died. If somebody in Counterfeit Alley was responsible for her death, I'd find them. And they'd pay for what they did.

Bruce stood and started clearing the table. 'Are you coming to the meeting, Enola?'

'Sure,' I said. 'Why not?' It was that or wait in the flat for Raven to call.

And I hated waiting for anything.

As we arrived at the community centre, the place was nearly full, and we had to sit at the back. Claire King was in the second row but didn't see me. Jack Parker was sitting at the front with what I assumed were council members. The air was tense, and everyone seemed on edge. The meeting began with the leader of the council introducing herself.

'You have all probably heard about the police operation at the Micklewood housing estate, commonly known as Counterfeit Alley, yesterday. Detective Inspector Parker will provide details of that in a second, but I would like to say that the council takes the matter of fraudulent goods seriously, and we work closely with the Trading Standards to stamp out every instance we find. And we won't hesitate to issue fines if necessary. This relates to the people selling the counterfeit goods, those who help them, and those who handle the items.'

She stared at the audience for twenty seconds before sitting, seemingly satisfied with the veiled threat she'd issued us all. I thought of the dodgy clothes Becky was probably wearing at school while we sat there and pictured the poor kid behind bars in a juvenile detention centre while her mother blamed me for turning her daughter into a criminal.

Parker stood, introduced himself, and explained what happened yesterday. His tone wasn't as accusing as the councilwoman's, but he clarified why the counterfeit goods trade was terrible for everybody but the criminals.

'If you buy fake and illegal items, your money helps fund organised crime gangs, including some who call themselves paramilitaries. These gangs can be involved in crimes which may happen in your area, including armed robbery, ATM and card-skimming scams, ATM physical attack incidents, child sexual exploitation, counterfeiting, cybercrime and cyber threats to individuals and businesses, drug dealing and trafficking, extortion where companies have to pay protection money, loan sharking, fuel laundering and illegal waste dumping, human trafficking, illegal weapons, paramilitary activity, and prostitution.' He paused for breath and gazed into the audience. 'That might seem a lot, but I would like you to hear the individual human cost of purchasing fraudulent or illegal goods.' He nodded to the middle-aged woman sitting behind him, and she came to the front.

She recounted how she had unknowingly bought a fake product in Counterfeit Alley, which turned out to be dangerous and caused her skin to react severely. She had to spend weeks in the hospital recovering from the side effects. The woman's story was heart-wrenching, and the audience listened in silence.

And I thought of the angry man at Nora's stall and his claims against her, none of which she denied. As the woman spoke, I wondered how many others like Nora had been drawn into that life out of desperation. It was all too easy to see how the gangs behind the counterfeit goods took advantage of vulnerable people's circumstances.

The meeting finished with a question-and-answer session, but I'd had enough, getting up to leave.

'I'm staying to talk to Jack,' Ginger said. 'I want to see what the news on Nora is.'

Bruce came with me. 'Kronos needs his walk. Do you feel like joining us, Enola?'

'Sure,' I replied. 'It might clear my head.'

As we stepped into the street, I noticed how different everything felt. The sun appeared dimmer, the colours less vibrant, and the sound of cars passing by seemed duller. It was as if the meeting had sucked life out of the world.

I waited for Raven to call me.

Chapter 15

Collision Architecture

'What do you think will happen now?' Bruce said as we crossed the road near Becky's school.

'About what?' I replied.

'Whoever was running Counterfeit Alley. They won't just give up because of a police raid, not when so much money is involved.'

Raven's phone was heavy against my heart. 'I guess they'll find somewhere else to peddle their illicit wares. There are plenty of other abandoned or empty spots in the town. There's that run-down industrial estate on the outskirts, but it's difficult to get to without transport.'

'Yeah, I suppose so.' I heard the noise of a frenzied schoolyard ahead. 'What do you think happened to Nora?'

I shrugged. 'Probably only an accident. The police should know soon enough.'

As we approached the school, I noticed the open gate, plus the shouting and hollering, followed by the unmistakable sound of a fight.

'I didn't imagine kids fought at school nowadays,' Bruce said.

I rushed forward and saw a group of children screaming and cheering as two girls pulled each other's hair. There weren't any adults or teachers, and my first instinct was to move on and leave them to it; a few fisticuffs never hurt anybody. They'd taught me a few valuable lessons. It was good for young kids to learn about life's harsh reality early so they could look after themselves as they got older. That's what I always told myself.

Then I saw Becky was one of the girls fighting.

My heart sank as I noticed the bruises on her face, and I felt a surge of anger towards the other girl. Then, instinctively, I dashed toward the fight and pushed my way through the crowd. I grabbed the bully by the shoulders and pulled her off Becky, lying on the ground.

'Stop it!' I yelled at the other kid. 'What the hell are you doing?'

She sneered at me and tried to push me away. 'Mind your own business,' she spat. Then she lunged at Becky, and I got between them.

Bruce appeared beside me, his face grim. 'What's going on here?'

The girl's sneer disappeared as she saw him. 'Nothing, sir.'

'That's not how it appears to me,' he said. 'You should be ashamed of picking on someone smaller than you.'

Then I recognised the girl. 'You're Fiona King.'

The kid put her hands on her hips like the queen of the castle. 'Yeah, so what?'

Becky buried her face in my hip. 'Just wait until I tell your mother about this.'

Fiona laughed at me as if I was the child. 'Mum knows

all about it, you stupid cow. She's the one who told me I have to be strong.' She glared at the other kids, and they all winced. 'Stand up and fight if you have to, that's what Mum says. Don't be small like the others. They're all weak.'

An adult finally came running out of the building, her flaming cheeks resembling wrinkly carrots. 'You're not allowed in the school. Why are you here?'

I glared at her. 'Doing your fucking job!'

Becky pulled away from me. 'Enola!'

Bruce grabbed my arm and spoke to the flustered woman. 'I'm sorry, the gate was open, and we came in to break up a fight.' He pointed at Fiona. 'That kid was hitting Becky.'

'That's a lie!' Fiona shouted. 'She hit me first.'

He dragged me to the side. 'Come on, let's leave them to it.'

I frowned at King before turning to Becky. She seemed okay.

However, I wasn't.

I wriggled free from Bruce's grip and stepped through the gates, marching away from the school and in the opposite direction to the flat.

'Don't wait for me,' I said.

He ran to catch up. 'Where are you going?'

'To Claire King's fucking boutique. If I can't punch the kid, I can hit the mother.'

I strode towards the shop, with Bruce keeping up with me and trying to talk me out of it, but he'd have had more luck winning the lottery.

My hand shook as I shoved the door open and stormed inside. The boutique was bathed in soft, diffused lighting, casting a warm, golden glow upon the merchandise. Rows of elegant dresses lined the walls, each piece displayed on polished mahogany hangers. There were mirrors every-where, reflecting the garments from every angle. As jazz music flowed through hidden speakers, a plush, crimson carpet led the way. I hated jazz, and the rambling noise only fuelled my anger.

The place smelled of lilac and lavender as I pushed through the customers and past the expensive items hanging around me. Claire looked up from the counter, her expression widening in surprise.

'What did you think of the meeting, Enola?' she said.

My lips trembled. 'Cut the shit, Claire. You know exactly why I'm here. Your daughter has been bullying Becky at school.'

She rolled her eyes. 'Oh, please. Kids will be kids. It's not like anyone's getting hurt.' She grinned at me. 'I bet you were as mischievous as them at their age, always causing trouble.'

I snapped. 'Becky's getting hurt! She's been coming home in tears every day because of your daughter.'

Claire scoffed. 'Come on. It's not like I'm the only parent whose kid has picked on someone else. Besides, those girls need to toughen up. The world is tough, and they must learn to assert themselves.'

I was about to go all Krakatoa on her when Bruce strode in. 'Perhaps you should save this for later, Enola.'

I ignored him and glared at her. 'There are no excuses for bullying,' I said through gritted teeth. 'And I won't stand by and let it happen.'

Claire smirked. 'Well, what are you going to do about it? You can't shield your little friend forever. Eventually, she'll have to learn to deal with people like Fiona on her own.'

My temperature increased, and I stepped closer to her, fists clenched at my sides. 'I'll do whatever it takes to protect

Becky, and if that means taking matters into my own hands, then so be it.'

Claire raised an eyebrow, unimpressed. 'Oh, please. Is that a threat? What are you going to do, Enola? Punch me? Call the cops? You're just a silly little girl who doesn't know how the world works.'

Her words seeped into my brain, digging through my blood and heart. Scorched lava swam through me, and I was ready for my head to take off like a rocket.

I grabbed an expensive dress from a hanger and tore it apart in front of her and the shocked customers, throwing the bits all over the shop.

'Since you're so keen on it, Claire, I know how violence works.'

She grinned and pointed at the camera behind her. 'I hope you've got £400 to pay for that?'

Bruce whispered in my ear. 'Come on, Enola, before this gets worse.'

But I didn't move, wiping my nose on the last bit of torn dress in my hand. 'You won't get away with this.'

She laughed. 'Good luck with that, sweetie. You're going to need it.'

I brushed past Bruce and stormed out of the boutique, contemplating all the terrible things I could do to Claire King.

Then my phone rang.

Raven's phone.

Chapter 16

No-One Driving

I was shaking when Bruce caught up to me. 'That was nuts, Enola.'

I stopped and glared at him. 'What should I have done?'

He held up his hands. 'I'm not sure, but probably not destroying a £400 dress on camera and in front of witnesses.'

I could see in his eyes he wanted to ask me how I'd pay for it, but he didn't. A chorus of car horns blared out around me as traffic inched along the road. The acrid smell of exhaust fumes mixed with the mouth-watering aromas drifting from the stalls from the weekly food market. Grilled meats sizzled on open flame grills, releasing a tantalising smokiness that drifted through the air and settled on my tongue. The sharp tang of hot mustard and the rich, savoury aroma of simmering curry permeated the senses, but none of it was enough to calm the fires sweeping through my veins.

Teenagers skateboarded past us, and I thought of Claudia and the mobile in my pocket whose ringing I'd ignored. I dug my nails into my palms and tried to ease my beating heart, which was busy trying to crawl from my chest by breaking through my ribs.

'Yeah, okay, you're right, but I had to do something.'

The phone rang again.

'Do you have a new ringtone?' Bruce asked.

'I'm experimenting with them. Are you going to the flat?'

'You know I am. Kronos needs his walk, and I thought you were coming with us.'

I touched his arm. 'Sorry, I've just remembered something. I'll see you later.' I rushed across the road and didn't look back.

'Do nothing stupid, Enola,' he shouted as I entered the park.

I found the nearest bench, sat down, and answered the phone.

'Where were you?' Raven said.

I smiled at a granny knitting a jumper opposite me. 'Having a shit.'

His sigh was like radioactive poison down the line. 'I have a job for you.'

'Great,' I replied. 'I hope it's something thrilling.'

'There's a warehouse twenty minutes from you. Inside it is Turner's Mechanics. You are to go there and collect a small package the size of a mobile phone. Then you will walk across the wasteland and deliver it to Claudia. Do you understand?'

'Nothing exciting, then?'

'If the task becomes exciting, Ms Gray, you'll likely be in trouble. Please remember what's at stake here. Your friend's relationship with the policeman won't help you.'

He ended the call before I could swear at him.

I sat there for two minutes, staring at the phone and wondering if that was how he knew where I was. Then I got up and marched through the streets, a vision of me with my hands around Claire King's neck helping me ignore all outside distractions.

Turner's Mechanics: I had a vague memory of my father taking the family car there while I was with him. It must have only been once or twice for minor repairs, because he took me onto the nearby field while we waited. I would have been five or six, running to the swings. They were long gone, leaving a wasteland of weeds, rubble, and potholes.

I pictured my dad standing there. The playground was alive with laughter and play, adults and children scattered throughout, each engaged in their adventures. I watched in awe as older kids swung from the monkey bars, and I pleaded with my father to show me how to do it. He was never one to back down from a challenge and seized the opportunity to impress his little girl.

'Watch this, sweetheart,' he said, pumping himself up for the feat. With a burst of energy, he launched himself onto the first bar, swinging smoothly to the next. Other kids and parents gathered around, intrigued by the spectacle. My dad was doing well, showing off his prowess as he navigated the bars like a professional gymnast.

Despite this, his overconfidence got the best of him. On his final swing, he attempted a daring move, reaching for the last bar while twisting his body mid-air. However, the laws of physics were not on his side that day. He missed his mark, and his momentum carried him too far. My dad hung upside down, his legs tangled in the monkey bars. His face turned ruby red as he dangled, his embarrassment growing with each passing second. I burst into giggles, unable to contain my amusement at his predicament.

Adults and children erupted into laughter, and someone even snapped a picture of my dad's acrobatic mishap. It took a team effort to rescue him from his upside-down position, with one man steadying the bars while another helped him regain his footing.

My father saw me grinning and joined in, laughing with everybody else as they christened him the "Upside-Down Dad." It seemed as if nothing could go wrong in my life then.

How misguided I was.

The memory lingered in my mind as I strode into the building. There had been other businesses in the warehouse back then: printers, a card shop, and a mobile phone emporium, but only the mechanics remained now. The place was dimly lit and filled with shadows, the air thick with the smell of stale cigarette smoke and motor oil. The machinery hummed as I approached, the rats skittering across the floor.

Several men were hard at work. One peered over a car engine, fiddling with a spanner, while another was underneath a vehicle, his legs sticking out. I stood by the entrance, waiting for somebody to approach me. A bloke glanced over, his eyes dark and unreadable. He wiped his greasy hands on a rag before walking over.

'What do you want?'

I didn't see any point in messing around. 'Raven sent me.'

He looked me up and down but said nothing. Then he turned and exited the room. I watched him leave and thought Raven must be playing with me, like people told to go for a long stand on their first day at a new job.

Then he returned and offered me a plastic bag. 'This is yours.'

I took it and left, feeling the weight inside and guessing it was a mobile phone. The skies darkened as I headed over the wasteland, hoping it wasn't an omen. I thought no more about the package, nor did I consider opening it to see what it was. My mind was somewhere else, picturing Fiona King hitting Becky in the playground.

What would I tell Julia about the incident? Or maybe the school already had. How could I advise Becky on how to deal with the situation?

Then what would I do about Claire King? It wouldn't be a surprise to get back to the flat to see she'd set the police on me. Perhaps I could convince Raven to take care of her. What was the point of working for an organised crime gang if I couldn't have them settle difficult situations for me?

It was a tempting thought gnawing at my brain as I crossed the barren landscape. The ground was hard and uneven, with broken concrete and shattered glass littering the path. I dodged the disused needles and used condoms, hurrying through the weeds. The clouds cracked apart, and the sky crackled like electricity. The rain arrived in a rush, and a river tipped onto my head, soaking every part of me. There was no point in searching for shelter because it was back in that warehouse. I reached the edge of the wasteland, seeing the motorway ahead and watching the cars and trucks speeding past the town.

However, there was no sign of Claudia.

I looked on either side of me and behind, yet nobody was there. As the weather turned me into a drowned rat, I assumed it was one big joke on me.

Then, a car swerved off the motorway and drove towards me. The wheels kicked up dirt and dust as water bounced off it. I stood and watched it, knowing there was nowhere to go. I was a sitting duck if the driver wanted to hit me.

I gripped the bag, thinking it was an extravagant way to die.

Chapter 17

Dancing Like A Gun

The car screeched to a halt, throwing dirt, mud, and rain over my trousers. I stood there shivering, my feet rooted into the sludge, slipping over my shoes and creeping through the hole at my toe. The car's windscreen wipers pushed liquid from side to side to reveal a shadowy figure behind the wheel. I moved closer, wiping water from my eyes and peering at the driver. Then the passenger door popped open, and a familiar voice spoke.

'Are you going to stand there like a wet tap all day?'

I slipped into the seat and closed the door, shoving damp hair from my face to stare at Claudia. 'Raven sent you?'

She glanced at the soaking plastic bag in my hand. 'Is that it?'

'I assume so.' She put her foot down and headed back to the motorway. 'Where are we going?'

She turned the radio on, and Harry Styles serenaded us. 'Newcastle.'

'Newcastle? Why?'

'I have to show you something.'

I dumped the bag at my feet. 'Do you know what's in that?'

'No. Do you?'

'It feels like a mobile phone.'

'That's what it probably is, then.'

She sped down the motorway, seemingly without a care in the world.

'Where's your brother?' I said.

Claudia shook her head. 'Were not joined at the hip. And anyway, he's scared of getting into a car.'

Water seeped out of every part of me, and I shivered. 'How come?'

The traffic meant she had to ease off. 'Are you trying to get to know my family?'

I shrugged, and rain fell from my shoulders into the back seats. 'Why not? There's a long drive ahead, and it looks like we'll be working together from now on.'

She gazed at me in the rear-view mirror. 'And then you'll tell me something about yourself, right?'

I squeezed the water out of my jacket. 'Absolutely.'

Her knuckles tightened as she gripped the wheel. 'We lived in a rundown dump on the crummiest estate in town. It was the place where everybody resembled zombies from a movie. Crime was everywhere, matched by the lack of jobs. Our house was an old, crumbling relic with paint peeling off in sheets and a roof that sagged like it was about to give up. The windows were cracked, and you had to wrestle with the front door to open it. Some families rallied around each other, providing support and encouragement, but not ours.'

She took a deep breath, struggling to speak. I continued to drip all over the car and thought it might be better for her to concentrate on the road.

'It doesn't matter, Claudia – you don't have to share any of this with me.'

Her laugh was a nervous one. 'Are you getting squeamish on me, Enola? I assumed you were tougher than that.'

'Sure,' I replied. 'Tell me everything.'

She continued. 'Our old man was a terrible human being. He used to lock Adam in the car's boot and leave him there for hours. He wouldn't even let him out to go to the toilet, so he had to piss and shit in there. I'd hear my brother screaming and crying, but I couldn't do anything.' She turned to me. 'Do you know how it feels to see somebody you love suffering and not be able to do something about it?'

'Yes,' I said.

Darkness covered her face. 'You might not have noticed it the other day, but my brother has a condition that brings out large red blotches on his skin. Adam hates himself because of it, and our dad called him a freak and a monster. The kids at school were no better. He'd always get into fights and have to put up with our old man when we got home. So every day is a living hell for him.'

'Did your father hurt you?'

'What do you think?'

I didn't want to ask, but I did. 'Did he lock you in the boot?'

Claudia shook her head. 'No, that was reserved for Adam. The bastard had something special for me.' The music on the radio changed to Young Fathers. 'We lived in a small street house probably built in Victorian times. There was a tiny, cramped cupboard under the stairs where my mother kept the Hoover. My father would remove it and throw me in there, in the dark and the damp. But I wouldn't be alone.' She took a deep breath. 'He'd put mice or rats in there with me. They'd run all over my arms and legs, trying to get on my face, but I always clawed them off.' I saw her chest rise and fall as she steadied her breathing. 'But I wasn't like Adam. I never cried or shouted, keeping perfectly quiet. Sometimes, I had to kill the rodents.'

'Where was your mother?'

She laughed. 'Mum? She was doing drugs or tricks, usually both. Our dad didn't care as long he got some of her money and the smack.' Her fingers trembled as she gripped the wheel. 'You would have thought it would get better when the old man died and Mum was locked up, but social services sent us to that foster family. And that place is just as terrible.' She drove faster and took her eyes off the road, staring straight at me. 'How bad was it for you in the children's home?'

Claudia had been honest with me, so I owed her the same.

'I lived in more than one. The first was a nightmare, nothing but cruelty and violence. But I was lucky that later, when I lived in a different place, I met somebody who helped me, and she kept the bad things away from me.'

'How old were you, then?'

'Fourteen.'

'When did you first drive a car?'

'I was twelve.'

She slammed her hand on the wheel. 'Damn! That's two years younger than I did.'

'I crashed into a wall my first time out.'

She stared at me with admiration. 'Maybe you could teach me a few things.'

'Such as?'

Claudia shrugged. 'I dunno. Anything useful. You'd be a much better teacher than the goons I waste my time with. Adam will like you as well once he gets to know you.'

I tried to suppress thoughts of becoming a tutor for two wayward teenagers. 'Why are you and Adam working for Raven and his gang?'

She shook her head and laughed. 'Why? Because they saved us, Enola, that's why. Raven got us out of that foster home. We owe him.'

I recognised the pain in her eyes. 'But you must know what they do, Claudia. They don't save everybody. They exploit children, some much younger than you and your brother.'

'They're not my responsibility.'

I sat back in the seat, still soaking and unsure how to help the kid or myself. I only knew I had to stop Raven and his thugs from hurting anybody else.

'Where do you think this life will take you, Claudia? Are you going to climb your way up the criminal ladder?'

She grinned at me. 'You're asking me if I know what I'll do with my life? Did you at fifteen? Do you now?'

She was right, and I struggled to make sense of it. 'I can help you and your brother.'

Claudia laughed as she drove. 'You can't even help yourself, Enola.' She shook her head. 'But even if you got Raven and his gang locked up, what would the authorities do with Adam and me?' She denied me the opportunity to reply. 'We'd go back to that foster home and the pain and the humiliation those two put us through.'

My phone pinged with a text. I removed the mobile from my jacket and wiped the dampness from the screen. It was from Ginger.

I spoke to Jack. He says someone murdered Nora but didn't give me any more details. Bruce told me what happened at the school and the boutique. When are you coming back?

Got something I need to do first.

Okay. Take care of yourself.

I put the phone on my leg. 'Somebody killed Nora.'

Claudia didn't bat an eyelid. 'That's a shame.'

'You don't know who might have wanted to hurt her?'

'I only saw her at the stall. I never spoke to her.'

'Could Raven or his thugs have done it?'

'Why? She was making money for him.'

Yet, in my brief meeting with him, he seemed like a man who would hold a grudge.

She turned off the motorway towards a large industrial estate and a sign for Fathom Fabrics. The rain continued to pound the car, and I pictured Nora floating in that river. Perhaps I should leave Jack and the police to deal with that. However, I had other problems concerning me, none more so than the two giant goons standing near the factory as Claudia parked outside.

'What is this?' I said.

She turned off the engine, snapping the last remnants of "Gangsters" by The Specials out of the air.

She smiled at me. 'Don't you like surprises?'

I fucking hated surprises.

Chapter 18

Metal Beat

I glared at Claudia. 'What is this?'

She grinned at me. 'Calm your farm, Enola. You'll find out soon enough.'

Had all that soul-searching in the car only been an act, an elaborate ploy to get me to trust her before she unfurled some devious plan designed by Raven inside this building miles from anywhere?

The thugs parted like a broken Twix bar, and Claudia led me into the factory. It stank of oil and smoke, with no visible windows, making it dark and oppressive. Dust hung everywhere, settling on my tongue with a bitter, metallic tang. It coated my throat, leaving a dry, gritty sensation.

I brushed against cold, corroded machinery, silent and still after years without use. The metal was rusty under my fingers. In the distance, the skittering of tiny feet hinted at the rats lurking in the shadows. The factory creaked and groaned, the ghost of its former industrial past. Emptiness and neglect surrounded me, the structure an ageing, empty shell.

We approached a metal door, and Claudia knocked

three times before a large bearded man opened it, like a negative Father Christmas giving you the worst gifts. She looked at him, and he nodded as he let us in.

As we entered, there were dozens of people working, some using machines while others handled various goods, including bags, shoes, jewellery, and mobile phones. They lowered their heads and focused on their work as several men wandered nearby, observing them. The floor was dirty and covered in debris, making walking difficult. There were no windows, the only light coming from a few overhead flickering bulbs, casting eerie shadows on the walls.

Claudia led me through the maze of machinery and workers, and I tried to see their faces or catch somebody's attention, but they never glanced in our direction. The noise of the machines was deafening, matching the rhythm of my increased heartbeat.

As we neared the back of the factory, I noticed men standing in a circle, speaking in low voices. Claudia motioned for me to follow her, and we approached the group. One of them looked up, and his eyes narrowed when he saw me.

'Who's this?' he said.

'She's with me,' Claudia replied, placing a protective arm around my shoulder.

The man gazed at me suspiciously, but nodded and returned to his conversation. She led me through a door and into an office. Hanging from the walls were old calendars with half-naked women on them while piles of dirty, yellowed files filled the desk.

'What's going on, Claudia?'

She pointed at the desk. 'You can leave the bag there.'

It was in my hand, but I'd forgotten all about it on the tour through the factory. I dumped it in the middle of the papers, scattering dirt and spiders everywhere. She saw them, grimaced while I thought of Dirty Harry in the flat, and hoped somebody had fed him.

I watched the arachnids crawl over the bag, some getting caught in the damp still attached to the plastic. 'I have a pet tarantula.'

Her mouth shrunk, and her eyes widened. 'What? Why would you do that?'

'When I was ten years old, I was hiding in a cupboard from some bad people, and there was a spider nest near me. So I knocked it, and dozens, maybe hundreds, of tiny spiders scuttled out and crawled all over me.' Claudia touched her face, and I thought she might faint. 'But I wasn't scared, and after that, I had such a fascination with them I bought one as a pet when I got my own place to live.'

'What do you feed them?'

I laughed. 'Small children and unruly teenagers.' Her expression told me she didn't appreciate the joke. 'No, I give Dirty Harry a diet of crickets supplemented with other insects, including mealworms, super worms, and roaches, though you can feed large tarantulas, pinkie mice and tiny lizards.'

The colour drained from her face. 'That sounds gross.'

'Spiders have to eat, Claudia. They're not vegetarian.'

'I guess so.' She glanced at the little ones crawling over the plastic bag. 'Why call him Dirty Harry?'

'He's named after the Clint Eastwood character Harry Callahan from the *Dirty Harry* movies. Do you know them?'

She shook her head. 'I don't watch TV.'

I touched her arm. 'Look, Claudia, tell me what this is all about.'

Darkness covered her face. 'Mr Raven told me all about you.'

'What did he say?'

'He said you helped the coppers break up a county lines drug operation a few months ago. Is that true?'

I nodded. 'It is.'

She scowled and pulled away from me. 'So you do work for the police?'

I shook my head. 'No, Claudia, I don't. That gang were hurting people, including friends of mine. That's why I did it.'

Her scowl grew bigger. 'I hate the coppers. My dad was mates with them.' She lowered her voice. 'They knew what was happening to me and Adam, but did nothing.'

'I'm sorry.'

'Well, Mr Raven said it didn't matter, anyway.'

'Why not?'

'Because whenever the police capture somebody or disband an organisation, there's always another one to take its place. He doesn't care that the coppers shut down Counterfeit Alley because he has factories like this all over the country, making goods he'll deliver everywhere, even abroad.'

'Was bringing me here a warning or a promise?'

She shrugged. 'He told me to bring you here and pass on that message. That's all I know.'

'Why is he so bothered about me?'

'I have no idea.'

There was more to it than that; there had to be. I opened the door a crack, peering at the workers and those who watched over them. If Raven wanted to get rid of somebody, the factory would be an excellent place to do it, with those pits outside the building and the machinery to fill them in. I scanned the room, looking for another exit or a window. I approached the shelves and studied the wall behind them. It was solid.

I turned to Claudia. 'Open the bag and see what's in it.'

Fear gripped her face. 'I can't. He'll hurt Adam if I disobey him.'

I went to the table, and the spiders scattered before me like an arachnid queen. I wondered if they could smell Dirty Harry on me as I grabbed the sack and emptied the contents over the grubby papers. A mobile phone fell out, and I picked it up.

'That's mine,' a voice said at the door.

I threw it at him. 'Here you go.' He caught it one-handed. 'There's no need to thank us for bringing it here.'

His grin revealed a gold tooth in the middle of his mouth. 'You can bugger off to your dirty old town now, girls.' Then he turned and left.

I looked at Claudia, shivering in the corner. 'Come on.' I said. 'I want a hot bath and some clean clothes.'

We exited the factory the same way we'd entered, and I wondered what game Raven was playing, knowing something he didn't.

I was an excellent cheat.

Chapter 19

Ghosts on Water

Claudia drove away from the industrial estate, sticking a CD into the player as she did.

'Do you like the Big Moon?' I nodded. 'Excellent. I saw them live in York a few weeks ago. It was a cracking gig in a great venue that used to be a workingmen's club.'

I watched the countryside approach us as she hit a back road. 'What were you doing there?'

'I said, Enola – I went to see the Big Moon.'

'Were you working for Raven at the same time?'

She shrugged. 'Don't you mix business and pleasure sometimes?'

'Was Adam with you?'

'Of course. He loves a good gig.'

We passed a field of bored-looking cows. 'What were you selling?'

Claudia laughed. 'I'm not in the industry of flogging stuff. What do you think I am?'

That was the problem. I still wasn't sure if she was hiding her fear behind the bravado or if she was under instructions to weave some fiction to worm her way into my trust.

I peered at her reflection in the mirror. 'I'm guessing you're a scared kid.'

Her stomach rumbled. 'I'm starving, that's what I am.' She spotted a sign for a fast food drive-thru and headed for it. 'What do you want? It's my treat.'

Before I could reply, she veered into a drive-through. She pulled up to a large speaker with a giant chicken on it and spoke to somebody on the other end.

'Two burger meals with fries and Cokes.'

She paid with cash and then parked in the corner underneath sizzling neon signs declaring how good the grub was.

'How do you know I'm not a vegetarian?' I asked.

Claudia laughed. 'Raven told me all about you, Enola. I know your favourite food, how you like your coffee, and which booze you prefer for a nightcap.'

'I don't drink alcohol.'

She shook her head. 'That's something we don't have in common.'

Yet, I saw a lot of me in her, the fifteen-year-old version of me who shouted the loudest to hide her fears. 'Are you scared of Raven?'

'Of course not. He's just another bloke. Adam and I will move on once we've saved enough money to leave that shitty town.'

'Does he pay you well?'

She narrowed her eyes and looked me up and down like I was a cheap pair of shoes in a charity shop. 'Are you still fishing for information, Enola?'

'Nope. If I'm going to work for Raven, I want to know how much I'll make from it.'

'Don't worry. Someone with all your experience will do okay.'

The way she sounded like a thirty-year-old woman and not a teenage girl was unnerving. 'What has he told you about me?'

'Well, how those people killed your parents and how you lived in all those children's homes. It sounds terrible.'

'It was, but you'll have seen some horrible things working for Raven. I guess it must be frightening being with his gang.'

Our food arrived, and she drove a few yards away to park. She supped on her Coke and considered her answer. My guts groaned again, so I tucked into the chicken burger while she drenched her fries in tomato sauce.

Then she replied. 'Raven and his goons don't worry me. The only things I'm afraid of are nuns and clowns.'

'Nuns? Were you in a convent?'

She spat Coke out of the window. 'Shit, no. It's from watching too many horror movies and reading Stephen King books.'

Fried chicken dribbled over her chin, and the look in her eyes told me she was putting on a brave face. 'Do you have any friends your age apart from Adam?'

She replied as she ate. 'You can't have mates in a dog-eat-dog world, Enola.'

The weariness in her voice made me tired. 'What do you mean?'

Claudia finished the burger and dropped the wrapper near her feet. 'If someone's been talking about you behind your back and saying things that aren't true, or if she's been making threats, then you front her up, and if it gets violent, you might end up slapping her. You can't just go around being bullied. But that's not violence. It's self-defence.'

'Do you see a lot of brutality?'

She shrugged. 'Sometimes. I broke another girl's nose once. I didn't start it. She was bullying me and thought she could turn all her mates against me, so she deserved that.' She wiped the Coke from her lips. 'What about you? Did you get into fights at my age?'

I pictured my teenage years as if they were a lifetime ago, even though I was only twenty-one. 'A few. I won't use it as an excuse, but I drank too much, which led to many stupid things.'

'Is that why you stopped?'

'With the booze? Yeah, that was part of it.'

A car full of young men pulled up opposite us, their eyes melting through the glass. Claudia saw them and shivered.

'I never drink, but Adam does. It helps him sleep.'

'Don't you think it might be harmful to him, to both of you, living this type of life?'

'What choice do we have?'

'When did you last attend school?'

She laughed. 'It's a waste of time. The teachers don't want to know about the bullying or the gangs because it reflects badly on them and the school.'

'But you enjoy reading?'

She nodded. 'I love it. And watching documentaries, mainly history. That's how you learn a lot, especially online. YouTube is great for that as long as you keep away from the racists and conspiracy nuts.'

Two young lads got out of their car, talking to their mates while glancing at Claudia. They must have been in their early twenties, probably only a few years older than me.

I sighed and mentally prepared myself for the

confrontation, exhausted from having to do it again. However, as I clenched my fists, she started the engine and set off, giving them the finger as she did.

'You seem to have everything figured out,' I said as she drove onto the main road.

She grinned at me. 'Girls like you and me, Enola, the rest of the world don't see us as we really are – we're invisible to them.' She tapped her fingers on the steering wheel to match the beat of the music. 'But we're not, are we? We're formidable.'

I returned her smile and hoped she was right.

Chapter 20

Sitting At The Edge Of The World

I told Claudia to drop me off outside Julia's. She smiled as she drove away, with not another word between us. I didn't know what to do about her, but I had other things to occupy me. My clothes were just about dry, and I wanted to talk to Julia about what happened with Becky at school. As I walked in, I took in my surroundings - the small living room with worn-out furniture and a TV playing a daytime show in the background. The air was stuffy and smelled of fried bacon mixed with disinfectant.

Julia was looking at her phone. 'Jesus, Enola, you look like you fell in the ocean.'

I slumped in a chair and tried to get warm. 'It's been a bad day.'

She got up, grabbed towels from the bathroom, and handed them to me. 'Do you want to discuss it?'

I ran a towel through my hair. 'Maybe later. Where's Becky?'

'She's having a nap. She came home from school exhausted, which isn't like her.'

A single damp hair slipped over my eye. 'Did she talk about school?'

Julia shook her head. 'No.'

'And nobody from the school called you?'

She sat forward, her eyelids flickering like butterflies about to take off. 'No. Did something happen?'

I had no choice but to tell her, though I left out my confrontation with Claire King at the boutique. 'The school should have informed you about the fight.'

Julia glanced at Becky's bedroom, and then she put her head in her hands. 'Oh god, Enola, what will I do about this?' She looked up at me. 'Should I take her out of that school?'

It was an option, but I assumed it would cause as many problems as it solved, and there was no guarantee the bullying wouldn't follow Becky to a new school.

'We should speak to her first before you do something drastic.'

Not that I'd done anything like that by destroying one of Claire King's expensive dresses. Maybe I'd have to ask Raven for money to pay for it since he hadn't paid yet for that little trip to Newcastle. Claudia had tried to hint that she and her brother were earning a handsome income from the crime boss, but I doubted it.

'Do you know who the bully is?' Julia said.

Should I lie or tell the truth? And did it matter who the thug was? To me, yes, but not to her. It was more important to talk to Becky about how she felt.

I shook my head. 'No, just some kid, a girl Becky's age.'

'Oh God, Enola. This is all I need right now. There's gossip about them laying off employees at work, and I might be one of the first to go.'

Shit, it was more bad news. I went and put my arm

around her shoulder. 'Let's hope it doesn't come to that, Julia, but we'll think of something if it does.'

She wriggled from my grasp. 'I can barely pay the bills as it is. The dole won't cover everything we need, and if kids are picking on Becky, I don't know what I'll do to help her.'

The kid stepped out of the bedroom, rubbing her face, her cheeks red raw. 'It's Fiona King. She bullies everyone in school, not just me.'

Julia grabbed her kid and squeezed the life from her. When she let go, she brushed Becky's hair from her eyes.

'King? Where do I know that name from?'

'Fiona's Claire King's daughter,' I said.

I saw the anger growing in her. 'She's that stuck-up cow with the boutique on the high street.'

'That's right.'

Julia pulled Becky closer to her. 'Christ, have you been in there? It's all overpriced shite for middle-aged hippy chicks.' She clenched her fingers. 'I should go down there tomorrow and give her a piece of my mind.'

'Can you afford it, Mum?'

We both looked at Becky and burst out laughing.

'You cheeky thing,' Julia said.

They laughed, and I needed the bathroom. 'Can I use your loo, Julia?'

'Of course, Enola. You don't have to ask.'

I left mother and daughter to it and went for a leak, closing the door behind me and turning the hot water tap on in the sink, hoping it would warm all of me up. Instead, the heat kissed my fingertips, sending a tingling sensation through my hand and arm. I glanced at the shower, tempted to throw off my clothes, step inside and turn the temperature up as high as possible without burning me.

That reminded me of what Claudia had said about her

foster parents. It helped me to understand why she believed Raven and his goons were a refuge for her, but I had to get her and her brother away from him. I assumed the journey to Newcastle was him sending me a message about his power in the criminal underworld. Of course, he must have known what had happened with Rook and his county lines gang, but the trip was Raven's way of telling me he was bigger than that. However, I'd learned a lot since my first day in the children's home, including realising that most criminals were never as invulnerable as they thought.

I removed both mobile phones from my jacket and stared at them. All I had to do was call Parker and give him the directions to that factory in Newcastle. Yet, maybe that's what Raven wanted me to do. Perhaps the trip had been a test of my loyalty, and this was my opportunity to prove it or not. If I blew it, it might all blow back on Claudia and Adam, so they'd suffer for my recklessness and stupidity.

But I still didn't know why Raven was interested in me. Was he connected to Rook's gang, and was this some form of elaborate revenge? It wasn't difficult for strangers to discover what happened to my parents, but Raven's knowledge of me seemed to go deeper than that if what Claudia said was true.

I sat on the edge of the bath and considered all my problems, putting my hand near the shower curtain to steady myself. That's when I realised I couldn't have a shower since it was already full of small boxes. I pulled the curtain back and grabbed a box, ripping open the top, shocked to see its contents: perfume. Fake perfume.

There were more than a dozen containers, and they were all packed with designer brand counterfeit fragrances, all famous brands.

'Do you want a hot drink, Enola?' Julia shouted from the other room.

I stood and closed the shower curtain. 'Yeah, I'm coming now.'

I threw water over my face and returned to them, glancing into Julia's bedroom as I made my way and saw what was on her bed. Becky was watching a cartoon on the TV, and Julia was in the kitchen making coffee. I went to her, trudging wet feet through the flat. She must have sensed something was off.

'What's wrong, Enola? Was the hot water dodgy again? I keep telling the landlord, but he does nothing about it.'

I took a deep breath and asked, 'What's with all the fake perfumes in the bathroom?'

She looked at me, surprised. 'Oh, those? They're just a few knock-off fragrances I got for cheap from a mate at work.'

I didn't believe her. 'There are dozens of them. And I saw the fake bags in your bedroom, too.'

She glanced down, ashamed. 'I need the money, Enola. I can't afford to pay for everything, and a friend of a friend offered me the chance to make some quick cash.'

I felt sorry for her, but I couldn't let it go. 'You're putting yourself and others in danger by doing this. You could get caught, and you're supporting an organised crime gang that exploits vulnerable people.' I glanced at the kid and lowered my voice. 'This is dangerous for Becky.'

Julia gazed at me with tears in her eyes. 'I know. I'll stop. I promise.'

I was clueless about what to say. She was struggling, and I didn't want to worsen her situation. But it could hurt both her and Becky. Then I wondered if Raven had set it up on purpose, making them vulnerable to make me vulnerable. If he knew everything about me, he'd know all my friendships.

'I've got to go, Julia.'

'Don't you want your coffee?'

'I should head home, shower, and put some clean clothes on.'

Becky jumped up from the TV. 'You could shower here, Enola, but Mum has all those boxes in the tub.'

Already, the kid had been dragged into a world I was desperate to keep her from.

I ruffled Becky's hair. 'I'll see you tomorrow, and we'll talk about school, right?'

She nodded. 'Okay.'

Julia hugged me and thanked me for checking on her and Becky. I left her flat, conflicted, wondering what the best thing to do was.

However, I knew there was only one decision I could make.

Chapter 21

Europe After the Rain

I returned to the flat to find Bruce and Ginger on the sofa, with Jack Parker by the window. The atmosphere was funereal, and rain was still clinging to my skin. Kronos was staring at Dirty Harry in his tank, so I shooed the dog away and fed my tarantula.

Parker watched me. 'Enola, we need to talk.'

I dropped wriggling insects near my oldest friend in the room, watching as the spider's many eyes lit up. The detective inspector grimaced. 'About what?'

With his shoulders hunched, he turned his back on Dirty Harry. 'We've made some progress in Nora's case.' He glanced at Ginger. 'Somebody hit Nora over the head before she was thrown into the river.'

I watched Harry suck on a cricket. 'Do you have any suspects?'

Jack nodded. 'We're looking into a few leads, including people in the area who might have connections to the organised crime gang running Counterfeit Alley.'

That was the moment to inform him about my day, but I didn't. I sat next to Ginger instead. 'How are you feeling?'

Her shoulder slumped into me. 'It's still so hard to take in, Enola. And then to learn somebody murdered her just makes the whole thing worse.' She squeezed my fingers. 'But you don't need me to tell you how that feels.'

She held a picture of Nora and her from their university days. 'Were you in the same classes?' I asked.

A light shimmered in her eyes. 'No, we met at a psychic evening in the back room of a local pub. The regular drinkers didn't like students much as it was, so you can imagine what they thought about people interested in spiritual matters.'

'Ordinary morality is only for ordinary people,' Bruce said.

I gripped Ginger's hand. 'What?'

'That's what Nora told me the other day, here, in the flat,' he replied.

Parker narrowed his eyes. 'What did she mean by that?'

Bruce shrugged. 'I don't know. She was always very enigmatic with me.'

Ginger laughed. 'That's because you suppress your spiritual side. You need to be more open-minded. There's more to life than what we can see.'

'I saw a ghost once,' I added.

The men peered at me as if I was unhinged, but Ginger's face brightened. 'You never told me this before, Enola.'

I didn't know why I'd brought it up, but I continued. 'It wasn't long after my parents died, and the authorities had dumped me into my first children's home, which was only for girls. It was about as welcoming as a wet weekend in Middlesbrough, and the other kids were quick to tell me about the haunted basement. They dared me to go there, so I did one night.'

'Is that where you saw the spirit?' Ginger said.

I nodded. 'Something moved in the corner amongst the rats and the smell of cat piss. It slipped out of the shadows, a human shape that wailed and drifted into the wall. I just stood there and watched it, thinking that was how my mother and father would be.'

The memory sent shivers through my body. Not because I believed in ghosts, but for that image of my parents still existing somewhere. I'd held onto that belief for a long time, but knew better now.

Bruce grinned. 'Inconveniently, or conveniently, spirits can't be perceived by anything but the naked eye of people who believe in them. Ghosts hate being filmed, as they are notoriously shy and eschew attention. In this, they are much like celebrities.'

Ginger scowled at him. 'Who would want to hurt Nora?'

'You can't think of anybody?' I said.

'No,' she replied. 'Everybody liked her. She didn't have an enemy in the world.'

'What about Nora's former husband?' Bruce asked.

'Frank Miller,' Parker answered. 'He emigrated to Australia two years ago.'

'Couldn't he have come back?' I said.

He shook his head. 'We've checked. He's never left the country since settling there.'

'Has anybody told him about Nora?' Ginger commented.

Parker shrugged. 'I guess so.' Then he turned to me. 'Is there anything else you can remember about that day? Something you may have forgotten when you gave your statement? Any little thing might help.'

I dragged a net through my recent memories. 'I was

there buying clothes for Becky, and I heard two people arguing on my way out. When I got there, I saw it was a bloke shouting at Ginger about the skin cream she'd sold him. He rolled up his sleeve to show it had made things worse, and he was as mad as hell at her.'

'Did her threaten her?' Parker asked.

'Not that I can recall. He went to throw the tub at her, but I pulled him back and tossed him to the ground. Then he was angry at me, but I persuaded him to leave.'

He nodded. 'What did you do then?'

'I chatted with Nora for a while, and she explained why she had a stall there.'

'Which was?' Parker said.

'Because she needed the money,' I replied.

Ginger sighed. 'I wish she'd told me. She knew I had my inheritance, and I'd have helped her.'

Just like Ginger had supported me for months. As Bruce had.

'What happened then?' Parker asked. He'd snuck his notebook out without me noticing, and it all felt official.

'Somebody I vaguely knew approached me, and we got talking. Then we went for a coffee. That's where I was when I heard the sirens blazing towards Counterfeit Alley. So I jumped up and ran back to Nora to warn her.'

'You're such a concerned citizen, Enola,' Parker said, without a hint of sarcasm.

I smiled at him. 'I try my best, Inspector.'

'Who did you go to the café with?' Bruce asked.

I hesitated before speaking. 'Claire King.'

'Claire King?' Bruce replied. 'The woman from the boutique?' I nodded. 'So you knew her before that commotion?'

'What commotion?' the copper inquired.

I repeated the events that started with the fight at the school.

'I'm surprised she hasn't sent you the bill for that dress,' Bruce said.

I looked at Parker. 'She hasn't reported me to the police?'

He shrugged. 'Not that I know, but I don't hear about everything at the station. I have more important things to focus on than two women scrapping in the street.'

'It wasn't in the street,' I replied. 'And it wasn't a scrap. I never touched her, just that crappy dress.'

Bruce sighed. 'This was caught on video in a shop full of witnesses.'

He seemed more concerned about it than I was. I looked at Ginger, who hadn't spoken since I'd mentioned the incident in the boutique.

'Are you okay, Ginger?'

She smiled at me. 'I know that name, Claire King.'

I gripped her fingers. 'Yes, she's had that boutique in the high street for about six months. And she owns a clothes factory on the industrial estate.'

She stared at me. 'No, I recognise it from somewhere else?'

'Where?' Bruce asked.

She got off the sofa, her legs trembling as she walked to the table and grabbed her photo albums. 'She's in here.'

Bruce and I stood and joined her. 'Your old photos?' I said.

Ginger flung open the first one, flicking through the pages at breakneck speed. 'It's in here, I know it is.'

Her eyes were manic, and her face flushed. Parker went to her and touched her hand. 'What's wrong, Ginger?'

She stopped searching and glared at him. 'What's

wrong? I'll tell you what's fucking wrong, Jack. Somebody murdered my friend, and you've done nothing about it. That's what's fucking wrong.'

I moved the first photo album out of the way and pushed the next one towards her. 'You have a picture of Claire King?'

The fire reduced in her eyes as she stared at me. 'Yes, I know I do.'

'From where?'

Ginger opened the album. 'University. I'm sure she was in the same year as Nora and me.'

'Isn't King her married name?' I said.

Parker shook his head. 'She returned to her maiden name after separating from her husband.'

Ginger rushed through the pages until she found it, pointing a shaky finger at a group of students outside a pub. 'There, at the back, in the middle.'

I gazed at the grainy colour photo, recognising younger versions of Ginger and Nora, and there, standing behind them, was Claire King's unmistakable grin.

'Were you all friends at university?' Parker asked.

She laughed. 'God no, she was a right stuck-up cow, she was. We were never good enough for her.' She peered at the picture. 'I don't know why she was with us on that day. But.... fuck.'

'What?' I asked.

Ginger put a hand to her face. 'Nora told me once when she was pissed, so I was supposed to keep it secret, that she'd slept with Claire's boyfriend, and Claire walked in and found them shagging.'

Fuck, indeed.

'Wait,' I said. 'King was in the café with me when the

police arrived. And then I ran to Nora's stall so there was no way she could get to Nora before me.'

Parker nodded. 'Sure, but now we know she had a connection to Nora and was near the crime scene earlier in the day.'

As much as I'd grown to dislike Claire King, I couldn't picture her involvement in Nora's death. Then I looked at the university photos and remembered King's grin from the boutique when she taunted me. She'd seemed capable of anything then.

Perhaps it was possible, after all.

Chapter 22

Running Across Thin Ice With Tigers

I uscd the address Parker gave me to find out who was supposed to be looking after Claudia and Adam. It was easy to locate the names online and delve into their life – the bits they didn't mind people seeing.

'Do nothing stupid,' Parker had warned me.

I didn't commit to anything, spending the rest of the evening with Ginger and Bruce, going through their old university photos and reminiscing about Nora. There had been no more talk of who might have killed her.

'Let's leave it to the police,' Bruce had said, and Ginger seemed content with that. I kept quiet about my new relationship with Claudia and who she worked for.

I trusted Parker and his team to investigate Nora's death. I was more concerned with keeping Julia and Becky safe and helping Claudia and her brother.

That's why I was opposite the foster home early in the morning. I had Kronos with me to blend into the environment, and The Clash played through my headphones. The mutt strained at the lead, trying to chase after the squirrels in the trees, but I concentrated on the house. It was a small two-story building with white siding and black shutters. The lawn was neatly mowed, and a few flowers bloomed alongside the drive.

Pedestrians strolled past me as I sat on a wall, focused on the front door, which hid so much of the trauma Claudia and Adam had endured. I thought it strange how the word pedestrian was sometimes used as an insult, essentially aimed at the lower classes or the so-called common folks. It implied that somebody without a car was a failure in life. "Only Losers Take the Bus," the Fatima Mansions sang in my memory as I peered at the large vehicle in the driveway.

As I waited, the twins' foster mother, Ellen Flynn, stepped out of the house. I recognised her from her Face-book page, where she posted lovely photos of homemade cookies and waxed lyrical about how much charity work she did in the community.

I kept Kronos near me and followed Flynn to the nearby park. She seemed not to have a care in the world as she sat on a bench and fed the birds. The early daylight warmed me as I perched close by, a small bag of breadcrumbs in my lap. After spending the night reading Flynn's many FB posts, I was well prepared for her morning routine.

My mother's voice slipped into my head, a memory of the first time she took me to that park. 'Watch for the dancing birds, Enola.'

Dancing birds? I thought she was playing a joke on me until I saw them, dozens near the trees, planting their feet into the grass and moving as if they were at a disco, their legs going up and down to music only they could hear. I later discovered they were manipulating the earth to bring worms to the surface.

Now, the birds were already gathering around me, chirping and chattering, waiting for me to provide for them.

I tore a tiny piece of bread and threw it forward, watching them swoop to catch it in their beaks. I thought the sight of Kronos might scare them off, but they ignored him for the food.

I watched Flynn, and my mind wandered to my problems. How was I going to escape from the organised crime gang? And what about Becky and Julia? How could I help them get away from the dangers that surrounded them? Who killed Nora? What would I do about Claire King?

And how could I assist Claudia and her brother?

Scrutinising Flynn as she glanced at her phone, I still wasn't sure what I was about to do. I closed my eyes and breathed deeply, inhaling the scent of newly cut grass and the smell of coffee from a nearby café. Then I exhaled slowly, trying to clear my mind. I stopped thinking about dancing birds, remembering all my terrible times in those children's homes.

A cool breeze blew through the park, causing me to shiver. I pulled my jacket tighter, listening to the surrounding noise: the birds, the distant sound of a siren, and the laughter of children playing on the swings. Why weren't they at school?

I opened my eyes and watched gulls drift overhead, their wings flapping in unison, envious of their freedom. They could fly from their problems, whereas mine trapped me.

Flynn mumbled something and pulled her sleeve up, scratching at her skin as if she had fleas. Her eyes twitched while her fingers shook. She'd put her phone away and was talking to herself in an agitated manner. Perhaps she was wearing earphones and was speaking to somebody.

I strode over and sat beside her, seeing the cigarette

burns on her arms. She noticed me looking at them and pulled down her sleeve.

I showed her my hands. 'I was in a fire. So I understand how painful it is.'

Flynn glanced at Kronos and then back at me. 'I don't know what you mean.'

I smiled at her. 'They say that fire is a cleanser, removing unhelpful things so you can move on and start again, but I've never found that.'

Her lips trembled. 'Have we met before?'

'Don't worry, Ellen, I'm not from social services, even though I really should inform them about what you and your husband get up to in that house.' She moved to leave, but I grabbed her arm. 'I'll call them now if you like.'

Her whole body shook. 'Who are you?'

'I'm Enola, a friend of Claudia's. I'm unfamiliar with Adam or his sister, but I bet if I asked, he could tell me some fascinating things about you and Paul, just as Claudia did.'

'I don't know what you're talking about.'

I removed my phone and showed her the story I'd found online, one from twenty years ago, but I was sure she'd remember it.

'They locked your dad up for what he did to you, Ellen. He died in prison, so you don't need to suffer the same from your husband. The world is different now, and people will believe you.'

She glanced at the screen before jerking her head away. 'How do you know about Paul and me?'

'Claudia told me. I understand how terrifying being with somebody like that is, but it's not only you who's suffering, is it?'

Tears streamed down her cheeks. 'No.'

'Claudia and Adam won't return to your house, but others could suffer there, including you, right?'

She nodded. 'I know.'

'So what will you do about it?'

The birds gathered around her feet, nibbling at the bread as Kronos stared at them.

'There's nothing I can do. He'd kill me if he saw me talking to you. I can't tell anybody.'

'Would you like me to hurt him?'

She wiped her cheek. 'You? You're only a girl. What could you do to him? He's an ex-marine and a bodybuilder. He'll eat you alive.'

I lifted my hands to show her my scars again. 'Do you want me to kill him, Ellen?'

Her eyes widened as her lips shook. 'What? No...I...you couldn't do that, could you?'

'Maybe, but there's another option?'

'What?'

I opened the contacts list on my phone and showed her the number of Detective Inspector Jack Parker. 'This is a friend of mine, a copper. He'll help you.'

'No, Paul said the police would never believe me.' She lowered her head. 'They never listened when I told them about my father.'

I put my hand on her arm. 'Things are different now. They'll see the scars on your arms, and they'll listen to what you have to say. I promise you.'

She gazed into my eyes. 'Will you come with me?'

I nodded. 'Of course.'

'Thank you,' she said.

She clung to me as I phoned Parker. Then we sat there and fed the birds before my other phone rang.

I handed her Kronos's lead. 'I need to answer this. I'll be right back.'

She smiled as I moved a few yards away and took the call from Raven.

'Where are you sending me now? Berwick? Scarborough?'

'No, Ms Gray, not too remote, just around the corner from your present location.'

'Where?'

'The police station, Ms Gray. I want you to go to the police station.'

Then he hung up.

Marvellous.

Chapter 23

The Hidden Man

As I led Ellen Flynn into the police station, a wave of commotion greeted us. Phones rang while people typed away at computers and shuffled papers across cluttered desks. The smell of burnt coffee permeated the air. The fluorescent lights flickered, casting an eerie glow over the faces of the officers. Ellen was shaking and scared, and I promised I'd stay with her through the process.

'Where's your friend, Inspector Parker?'

Jack had sent two uniformed coppers to collect us from the park, and neither knew where he was, just that he'd been called out of the station. They showed us to a waiting area, where we sat on hard plastic chairs.

'I'm sure he'll be here soon,' I said to reassure Ellen. She kept scratching at her scars, and I thought she might bolt at any second.

She gripped my arm. 'When Paul finds out, he'll kill me.'

Her fear was genuine, the terror seeping out of her. Part of me wanted to leave her there and head back to that house to deal with Paul Flynn in my own way. Then, a female officer approached us, scrutinising Ellen before turning to me.

'You're Enola, right?' I nodded. 'Jack told me you were coming. You must be Mrs Flynn.' Ellen smiled at her. 'Okay, would you follow me? I'll take Mrs Flynn's statement.'

As we got up, my phone rang - Raven's phone.

'I'm sorry,' I said. 'I have to answer this. Can you start without me?' Ellen looked at me through sad eyes. I touched her hand. 'You'll be fine. I won't be long.'

She left with the officer, and I took the call. 'What do you want?'

'Somebody will give you something soon. Put it in your pocket, say nothing, and leave the station. Do you understand?'

'I'm here with someone. I can't go without them.'

'Do you understand, Ms Gray?'

'You heard what I said.'

'Would you like me to pass that on to Julia Cross and her daughter, Ms Gray?'

I struggled to speak. 'If you hurt them....'

'Do you understand, Ms Gray?'

'Yes, I understand.'

He ended the call, and my heart raced. I took deep breaths, but I couldn't get enough air. My chest grew tight as if someone was squeezing it. I started sweating even though the room was cool. My palms became clammy, and my throat was dry and constricted. The blood pounding in my ears drowned out the surrounding noise. My mind flooded with thoughts that something terrible would happen to Becky and Julia. I felt dizzy and thought I might pass out. My hands trembled. I rubbed them on my legs to warm them up. My stomach churned like a washing machine.

Then, a tall, burly man in a uniform walked over, his eyes scanning the room before landing on me. He came closer, leaning in as he spoke in a low voice.

'I've got something for you.' He pressed a small USB drive into my hand. 'This will help you with your little problem.'

Then he strode away and left me standing alone. I glanced at the drive before slipping it into my pocket. As I did, Jack Parker entered the station.

'Is Mrs Flynn here?' he asked.

My breathing slowed like my heart was trying to burst through my ribs. I nodded towards the door. 'She's in there giving your colleague a statement. I should sit with her.'

'I need to speak to you first,' Parker said. 'In my office.'

'Okay.' Had he seen what had just happened? Did he know the officer who gave me the drive? I looked up, searching for any cameras. CCTV had spotted me in the boutique, so what about in the station?

I followed him into the room. He sat behind the desk, but I stood, putting my hands into my pockets and gripping the USB drive between my fingers.

'How is Mrs Flynn?' he said.

'She should be fine. But will her statement be enough to arrest her husband?'

'I'll need to read it first, but I searched his name on the computer after your call, and he already has a record of violence against previous girlfriends.'

'Fuck!' The fire grew inside my veins, swimming through me like lava. 'So how does he get to be a foster parent?'

'It was over twenty years ago, so I guess nobody checked with us.'

I sat opposite him. 'I thought you were meeting me at the park?'

'I'm sorry, Enola; something came up after I got your call.'

'Was it about Nora?'

He shook his head. 'No. It was two things, but they weren't connected to Nora's murder investigation.'

I noticed the photo of him and Ginger on the desk. 'It seemed tense when we arrived.'

Parker sighed. 'Every station in the country received an urgent message from the Home Office this morning.'

'That sounds important. Terrorist related?'

'In a way. It has to do with security. There have been several breaches within the service recently, not to mention the increase in the discovery of corrupt or criminal officers.' He stared at me. 'I don't need to tell you about that.'

'The government are going to replace you all?'

He laughed. 'Not quite. They will implement new professional standards in the coming months, a tougher vetting procedure for recruits, and tighter security at every station.'

'The police are supposed to deal with criminals, not recruit them.'

Parker nodded. 'Indeed. So that put us all on our toes this morning, and then I had an unexpected visitor.'

I pointed at the photo on his desk. 'Ginger brought you that.'

'I wish it was that, Enola.' He clasped his hands together. 'Claire King came to the station and made a complaint against you.'

I sank into the chair. 'Great. Was it about the boutique?'

'Yes, and she gave us the clip of the incident and the names and addresses of several witnesses. It doesn't look good for you.'

I shoved my hands into my pockets, fingers digging into the USB drive. 'Did she speak to you, Jack?'

'No. I couldn't take her statement because of my connection to you. I've read it, though, and seen the video. I can arrange for an officer to get your side of the story now if it's convenient.'

I gripped the drive. 'It isn't. Did you ask her about knowing Nora and where she was when Nora was murdered?'

'No. That's on my list.'

My gaze dashed between the photo and his face, wondering what my brief outburst at the boutique would cost me, and not just financially.

I got up. 'Is that all?'

'I require your statement, Enola, sooner rather than later.'

'Don't I need a lawyer?'

'It's for you to decide.' He stood. 'With the new security system, I'll need to show you out of the building.'

I followed him out with the drive still between my fingers.

Perhaps I could ask Raven if his organisation had a dodgy lawyer I could use.

Chapter 24

Twilight's Last Gleaming

A thousand problems danced inside. I strode past a couple handing out leaflets from God – I was going to Hell if I didn't mend my ways – and turned the corner, heading back to the flat. Maybe I could take Kronos into the woods to clear my mind.

Then somebody honked a car horn at me.

I looked across the street to the familiar sight of a mud-covered vehicle, and Claudia sat behind the wheel. The Raven phone pinged with a text as I stared at the teenager.

Get in the car.

I did as instructed, slipping into the passenger seat as New Order's "Love Vigilantes" drifted out of the speakers.

'Are we going to Newcastle again?' I said.

She pulled out as I put my seatbelt on. 'No, it's somewhere much nicer this time.'

I watched the city disappear in the rear-view mirror as we drove into the countryside. She lowered the window, bringing a scent of fresh air into the car. The sun was shining, and the sky was a deep shade of blue, a welcome contrast to the grey buildings we'd left behind.

'Where are we going, Claudia?'

Her expression was unmoving. 'You'll see.'

'I spoke to your foster mother.'

The revelation startled her, and she hit the brakes, swerving into a hedge. I thumped forward, glad to have the seatbelt on.

She slammed her hands on the wheel. 'What the fuck?'

My breath came in short bursts. 'I said I'd try to help you.'

Claudia glared at me. 'How the fuck is this helping me?'

'The police will arrest Paul Flynn for what he did to you and Adam. You'll be safe from them.'

She stormed out of the car and screamed at the moon. I followed her outside, feeling the icy wind on my cheeks and recognising the anger in her face.

'All you've done is make things worse, Enola. The coppers won't do anything to them. She was always there helping him, and we'll have nobody to protect us anymore.'

'I promise to do everything to help you, Claudia. You can trust me.'

She laughed and kicked at the grass nearby. Then she returned to the car, and I followed. Claudia reversed away from the hedge and onto the road.

'I didn't think you were this stupid, Enola. Raven said you were clever. That's why he sent you into that cop shop.'

I removed the USB drive from my pocket. 'Do you know what's on this?'

She drove away. 'Nope.'

I didn't entirely believe her as I glanced out the window. We moved down winding country roads, with birds chirping and the rustling of trees filling my ears through the open window. A memory of my parents taking me that way for a picnic rushed back to me. They took me to a petting farm, and I loved being around the animals and getting away from the urban sprawl. After seeing my joy, they promised me a cat, dog, whatever I wanted. They were dead two weeks later.

I pushed the past to the side as we bounced over bumps in the road, and I gripped the door handle to steady myself, watching the countryside slip by. The scenery was breath-taking; fields of vibrant green stretched out for miles, with patches of wildflowers dotting the landscape. Trees of all shapes and sizes cast dappled shadows on the ground. A gentle breeze rustled the leaves, sending them dancing in the wind and a bouquet of nature into the car.

Claudia turned down a small road, and we bumped and swayed along the uneven surface as The Happy Mondays wrote for luck on the radio. I stuck my head out the window; the smell of fresh dirt and grass filled my nose, and the sun warmed my face. We stopped at the edge of a field, and she shut off the engine as I saw the sign for Kane Farm.

'You live here?'

'Used to,' she replied. 'This was my father's until he lost it.'

I never pictured her living on a farm. Hadn't she told me they'd lived in an old, small house? She got out of the car, and I followed. The silence was palpable; the only sound was the soft grass rustling in the wind. The air was cool and fresh, and I took a long breath, filling my lungs with the sweet scent of nature. It was a welcome change from the stifling atmosphere of the town.

I gazed across the field, taking in the rolling hills and the expanse of blue sky. It was calm there, removed from the chaos and danger of the urban jungle. For a moment, I forgot about Raven's gang and what was in my pocket and enjoyed the serenity of the countryside.

'Do you want a tour?' she said.

'Where's your brother?'

'Adam won't come back here, not after what happened.'

Claudia turned away before I could ask what she meant. I followed her from the car, wondering if Raven and his goons were waiting for me somewhere. The land was dry and dusty, with cracks running through the earth. Rusty machines lay scattered throughout the fields, and it was clear nobody had used them in years.

The buildings on the farm were equally chaotic, where the roofs looked like they would cave in at any moment. There were no animals anywhere, and the silence was eerie.

I followed her towards old logs and bits of machinery. She stopped near a rusted axe, resting her fingers on the handle. She took a piece of gum from her pocket and popped it in her mouth, the smell of strawberries puncturing the air as she chewed.

'Why am I here, Claudia?'

She pulled the axe out of the wood, holding it like an expert.

'They own the farm now, the gang.' She glanced over the fields. 'I have a few good memories here from when he was working away and Mum was healthy. Adam loved playing in the countryside and being around the animals.' She gazed at her reflection in the blade. 'Do you think humans can change, Enola? Is it possible for them to still be decent people if they've done something terrible?'

'Didn't you tell me you lived in a small house?'

Claudia nodded. 'That's where we moved to after his gambling and debts meant we had to leave this land. We all loved it here, but it was worse for him, the embarrassment of losing what his family had owned for centuries. It sent him mad, and all the terrible events came from that.' Tears slipped onto her cheeks. 'But I had no control over it.'

'What did you do, Claudia?'

She ran her finger over the axe and drew blood. I watched it slide down the blade. 'It wasn't me, Enola.' Fear and sadness filled her eyes. 'Things might have been different if it hadn't happened that night he dragged us back here. Mum may not have been sent to that hospital, and we'd have stayed with her instead of going to that horrible foster home.'

'Peter Flynn won't hurt anybody else, Claudia. The police have arrested him.'

She slapped the axe in her hand. 'It's people like him who deserve this.' She peered at it as if it was covered in blood. 'Still, so did our father. That's why Adam did it.'

I inhaled deeply. 'Adam killed your father?'

She gazed at me; she was a million miles away, somewhere lost in time.

'He had to, to save me. That's why he did it.' She dropped the axe and fell to her knees. 'But I told him no more.'

I ran to her, took her in my arms, and let her sob onto my shoulder.

Hence, I never heard the footsteps behind me until it was too late.

'My, my, what have we here?' Raven asked. 'Happy families on the murder farm.'

I stood and lifted Claudia with me, turning to observe something that made me go weak in the knees.

'They promised we'd see the animals,' Becky said as she clung to her mother's hand.

Chapter 25

Evidence

I bit my top lip as I spoke, digging my nails into my palms. 'Why are they here?'

Four goons surrounded Julia and Becky, with Raven in the middle.

'Aldous Huxley said that music comes nearest to expressing the inexpressible after silence.'

I looked at my friends. 'What?'

He smiled at me. 'At my secondary school, the headmaster believed that Mozart's music had a calming effect and helped reduce aggression. As we filed out of the main hall every morning after assembly, the orchestra played "Eine Kleine Nachtmusik." After seven years of this, I wanted to smash up all their instruments into little pieces. And then set fire to them.' He put his hand on Becky's shoulder, and I cringed. 'It took me a long time to control my anger, Ms Gray. You don't want me to lose it now.'

'Why do you have them with you?'

'Just insurance in case you double-cross me to the police. I know how pally you are with the coppers, which I find surprising considering their role in your parents' deaths.'

'Let them go.' I said.

He ignored my demand. 'Do you have my package?'

I watched Julia pull Becky closer to her. 'What's on the USB drive, Raven?'

'Names, addresses, contact details, but nothing to bother you. So give it to me.'

I held Claudia as she shivered. 'Whose details?'

He waved a hand at me. 'Just pass it to me, and we can all go on our merry ways.'

Then it hit me. 'Witnesses and informants, their personal details are on the drive, aren't they?'

He laughed. 'Are you worried your name might be on there, Ms Gray?'

'I can't give it to you.'

The thugs loomed over Becky and Julia. 'Are you sure?' he said.

Claudia snatched her hand out of mine. 'Where's Adam?'

'Your brother is safe, as long as you do as you're told.'

Her face flushed red, and she turned her hands into fists. 'Tell me where Adam is.'

Raven sighed. 'He can't escape his punishment, Claudia. You know this, not after what he did.'

Tears streamed down her cheeks. 'It wasn't his fault. She made him do it.'

'It doesn't matter if that's true or not. The boy can't put our organisation at risk and not face the consequences. Are you going to disobey me as well?'

Birds flew overhead, and the wind increased around my head as I saw the tension simmering in Claudia.

Then she raised the axe and leapt at Raven.

He cried, and the closest goon stepped between them, taking the full force of the axe in his shoulder. They staggered back as she screamed, and he howled, trying to drag her off him. The other goons reacted slowly, but Julia didn't, grabbing Becky and running towards me.

'Run for the car,' I shouted at them as Raven's thugs finally acted and advanced on Claudia. The first bloke was on the ground, clutching his wound and crying, as she swung around with the axe held in a defensive position. The next goon charged into her and forced her back, grappling with each other and tumbling into the dirt. The other two went to help their colleague, but I was quicker, kicking one in the knee and burying my elbow in the second one's throat as he turned to me. Then I ran over to the guy pinning Claudia down and kicked him in the head. He crumpled, and I dragged her up.

Raven glared at us. 'Give me that USB drive.'

She held the axe in her trembling hands as the blood dripped from it. 'I'll kill you.'

'Go to the car,' I said to Claudia. 'Becky and Julia should be there.'

'No,' she snarled. 'Not until I know where Adam is.'

Raven's goons steadied themselves, gathering around their boss. The one with the snapped knee couldn't stand, and the thug with blood seeping out of his shoulder sunk to the ground and lay on his back. The other two seemed ready to go again.

'I'll give him up to the police,' Raven said. 'Is that what you want, Claudia? He'll spend the rest of his life in prison, and the only time you'll see him is with bars between you.'

I pulled her towards me. 'Run to the car.'

Raven nodded to his men. 'Take the drive from her and kill them all.'

I ran, dragging Claudia with me. 'Get Becky and Julia safe, and I'll lead them away.'

The goons followed Raven's orders. I pushed Claudia off me and headed in the other direction, hoping the two who could move would come after me and leave her and the others.

And they did.

I heard them on my tail as I scrambled for the barn. They shouted as I burst through the door. The smell of dried hay filled the place as I ducked behind a stack of bales and caught my breath, searching for something to use as a weapon. Adrenaline pumped through my veins as my heart thumped against my ribs, and I waited for them.

However, it was Raven, I heard. 'I don't care about the others, Enola. Just give me the drive.'

I stuck to the shadows and removed it from my pocket. I could have thrown it away or snapped it in half, but I didn't. What if there was more on it than he'd hinted at, something that could implicate any corrupt coppers working with him? I couldn't destroy it if that were a possibility.

'Or we'll take it from you and hurt the others,' he said.

I peered from my hiding spot and saw them searching the barn, their eyes glinting like wolves in a hen house. One of Raven's thugs had a metal pipe, the other a switchblade. They moved cautiously, creeping towards me, and I had nowhere else to go.

So, I stepped out, holding the drive high. 'I'll snap this if you move any closer.'

He shook his head. 'What would that achieve, Enola? My men have Mrs Cross and her daughter. You destroying the USB drive won't help them.'

'You're lying,' I said.

'Do you want to take that risk?'

I waved the USB drive at him. 'Come and get it, then.'

Raven's icy glare sent a chill down my spine as he nodded to his cronies, signalling them to attack. Before I could react, the burlier man lunged at me with a rusted pipe aimed at my head. I darted to the left, narrowly avoiding the crushing blow. The pipe whooshed past my ear, the gust tousling my hair. Seizing the moment, I thrust my palm upward, knocking it from his fist. It clattered to the ground. He stumbled backwards with a grunt, clutching his throbbing hand.

But I had no time to catch my breath as the wiry one pulled a switchblade from his jacket, flicking it open so light reflected off the blade. As he slashed at my torso, I twisted my body and grabbed his outstretched arm. With all my strength, I wrenched his wrist back until he howled in pain, the knife falling to the ground.

Before I could kick it away, a freight train slammed into me. Winded, I careened into the side of the barn as the first thug tried to pin me down. Fuelled by adrenaline, I shoved my fist into his nose. Blood spurted as the cartilage crunched under my knuckles. His hands instinctively flew to his head. Seizing the opportunity, I hit him in the gut, doubling him over.

My hand throbbed as I saw the knife-wielder running at me. I braced for the impact. As he lunged, I sidestepped and stuck out my leg. He tripped over with a squeal, crashing face-first into the dirt. Not missing a beat, I lifted my boot and smashed my heel down on his skull. His body went limp.

My chest was heaving, glancing at my feet before turning to Raven.

And he pointed a gun at me.

Chapter 26

Shadow Memory

Raven's finger was on the trigger, his hand trembling like leaves in the wind. He said something to me, but I didn't hear it because my mind had travelled back ten years, so I crouched in the wardrobe again. The spiders crawled over me, skittering up my arms and legs, aiming for my wide-open mouth as I watched my parents die. I struggled to breathe, my heart crushed against my chest, and the air stuck in my throat. Cold, ghostly fingers wrapped around my lungs, squeezing so hard I expected to pass out. Instead, I peered through the gap in the door, seeing for the thousandth time those thugs draw their knives over my mum and dad's throats. My mother's eyes met mine as her blood slipped onto the floor, and her killers set the room ablaze. The heat was intense as I burst out of the wardrobe and ran to my mother, grabbing her shoulder to drag her from the flames. She was already dead, but my brain wouldn't accept that, even as the fire attacked my hands.

The pain brought me back to the present, and Raven waved the pistol at me.

'Hand me the drive, Enola.'

I stared at my palms, watching the scars shimmer on my skin like wrinkled worms. The drive was between my fingers, and it would have been the easiest thing to give him. But I liked nothing easy.

'What will you do with the names?' I said.

'The names? Some I'll deal with, the others I'll sell to my friends and competitors.'

'Competitors?'

'Yes, you'd be surprised at how many organised criminal gangs there are in this country. The factory you saw in Newcastle costs me a lot of bribes to keep running. Everything is increasing in price, and I must find new financial revenues. So I need that drive from you, and I won't ask again.'

He stood a few feet from me, and the only way out was behind him. I looked nearby, searching for a weapon and finding nothing. Raven raised the gun and pointed it at me.

'Why don't you shoot me and just take it?'

He resembled a demented clown as he smiled. 'There's no need for that, Ms Gray, as long as you behave yourself. Can you do that?'

I considered my options as Claudia barged through the door, screaming as she held the axe above her head. He turned, firing into her chest. The bullet exploded through her clothes. She gasped and crumpled to the ground. I leapt forward, hitting him and taking us both out of the barn. I couldn't get the pistol from him, my hands grasping thin air as he pushed me away and fired. The bullet clipped my ear, and pain fizzed through my face.

The world whirled about me as I bounced off a tractor, blood sticking to my cheek as Raven aimed again. I put my head down and charged like a bull, connecting with his gut and shoving him backwards. His hand jerked up, firing into the air. I continued forward, embracing him and pushing us into a tree. He hit it hard and dropped the gun, his eyes darting everywhere as he reached for my throat.

He thrust his nails into my flesh, pushing on my windpipe while swearing at me. I knocked his hands away and got my fingers around his neck. I dug into his skin, drawing blood and squeezing for all my life. He grabbed my arms to pull me off but didn't have the strength; his eyes bulged like a frog, his cheeks red and puffy. His lips trembled as spit drooled out of his mouth and down his chin. We fell together, and I released his throat. I pushed my knee into his ribs, waiting for the crack as he pleaded for me to stop.

'You'll just repeat this if I let you go,' I said.

Would it be self-defence if I killed him?

No, of course not, but he'd threatened Becky and Julia.

I pressed harder on his chest and dug my nails into his throat again. His blood trickled over my fingers and warmed my skin. Death was no stranger to me, and I was no innocent, but I knew I had no choice if I wanted to keep my friends safe. And all the others Raven had hurt, including Claudia and Adam.

Then somebody grabbed my jacket and hauled me off him. I dangled in the air for a second like a confused puppet before the goon tossed me into a tree. I hit it with my shoulder and crumpled into the grass and broken branches. A swarm of angry bees appeared inside my skull, their buzzing creating a fog over my vision as I saw Raven's man pick him up. Raven coughed before bending over and throwing up. I rubbed at the back of my head, my legs trembling, as I gripped the tree to haul myself up. The bark cut into my hand, and tiny insects crawled over my fingers.

Raven spat blood into the grass and glared at me. 'It will be a slow death, Enola, after I've taken the drive from you.'

I wiped the blood from my mouth. 'I lost it.'

He narrowed his eyes. 'What?'

I inched away from them. 'I must have dropped it in the fight. I guess it's in the grass somewhere.'

'You're lying.'

I kept moving back, but they followed me. I pretended to look for the drive, but it was the gun I wanted. Then I glanced behind me and saw Claudia face down in the barn.

'You need to get help for her,' I said.

Raven shook his head. 'She'll be joining her brother soon.'

'You killed Adam?'

He touched his throat and spat blood again. 'You should worry about yourself, Enola.'

I was getting closer to the barn with no sign of the pistol. I could run, but there was nowhere to go. And I wouldn't leave Claudia.

The buzzing in my skull increased to the point I thought my brain was about to split.

Then I realised the noise was coming from above. The goon ran at me as I looked up and saw the helicopter.

I crashed to the ground when the shouting started.

Chapter 27

A Room As Big As A City

Raven and his goon ran as soon as they heard the police coming. I watched them flee as I grasped the tree to stagger up, my legs trembling as I nearly fell into the dirt. Every part of me ached as I stumbled into the barn, dropping to the ground and peering into Claudia's face. She wasn't moving, and blood leaked out of her chest. I grabbed her wrist and searched for a pulse. There was one, but it was slight.

'Can you hear me, Claudia?'

I squeezed her hand and took rapid, deep breaths. It was loud outside, the police shouting warnings and the thump of the helicopter blades chopping through everything. The shadows increased around us until there was an absence of light. I wiped the hair from Claudia's eyes and gripped her fingers.

Her lips trembled. 'Adam, is that you?'

I moved my head closer to hers. 'It's Enola, Claudia. Help is on the way.'

But was it? The police wouldn't know we were in the barn. I had to leave her and find them.

I stood to go, but she pulled me back. 'Stay with me, Enola.'

'Of course.' I sat with her, holding her hand, screaming in the darkness.

A nurse looked at my bruises when Ginger rushed into the hospital room.

'My god, Enola. Are you okay?'

The nurse scowled, sticking her finger into my hip and making me grimace.

'I'm fine. How did you know I was here?'

'Jack told me,' she replied. 'What the hell happened?'

'I'll get you some painkillers, and your mother can take you home,' the nurse said.

She left, and I laughed, which wasn't clever as it sent more pain speeding through me.

'The cheeky cow,' Ginger moaned. 'I don't look that old.' She peered into the wall mirror, running her fingers over her face. 'Do I?'

Every party of me throbbed as I moved. 'You look better than I feel.'

She dragged herself from her reflection and came to me. 'Oh, Enola, I'm sorry. What happened? I asked Jack, but he wouldn't tell me anything.'

I sat back and hoped those painkillers would arrive soon. Then I told her about the events at the farm. 'They brought Claudia and me to the hospital, but I never saw Parker or spoke to any officers, so I don't know how Claudia is. Do you?'

She shook her head. 'I came straight here when Jack called.'

The nurse returned with the pills, so I asked her. 'The

young girl who was with me – do you know what happened to her?'

'I'm sorry, no.'

She left before I could ask anything else. I turned to Ginger. 'Have you seen Julia or Becky?'

She touched my hand. 'No, I haven't.'

I'd sent them to the car, hoping Claudia would drive them all off that farm, but she'd returned to help me. So, what unfolded with Becky and her mother? Did Raven hurt them while I was in that barn?

I slipped off the trolley, and an uncontrollable spasm of agony erupted through my legs. My body shook, and Ginger steadied me before I collapsed. Those bees reappeared inside my head, and they played electric guitars as if auditioning for a heavy metal band.

'I need to find them and Claudia,' I said.

She eased me back to the trolley. 'You stay here, and I'll ask somebody.'

I didn't argue. The room was dull beige, and the fluorescent lights overhead were harsh and bright. It stank of antiseptic and disinfectant and the heart monitor sound beeped nearby.

The door opened, and Julia strode in. She looked relieved and rushed to my side. 'Enola, thank God you're okay.'

I smiled weakly, still feeling sore. 'What happened to you? Where's Becky?'

'It's okay; she's out there with Jack Parker. She's quizzing him about being a copper.'

'Did you see Claudia on the farm?'

Julia nodded. 'Yes, we were at the car when she gave me the keys and told me to leave with Becky.'

'Was it you who called the police?'

'No. That happened because we were spying on you,' Jack said as he walked into the room with Becky and Ginger.

'Enola!' the kid shouted. She ran over and hugged me. I grimaced but didn't tell her how much pain she was causing my ribs. Julia must have seen the look on my face and pulled her daughter off me.

'Let her rest, Becky,' Julia said.

I ruffled her hair and turned to Parker. 'What do you mean you were spying on me?'

I noticed how Ginger squeezed his hand as he spoke.

'Strictly speaking, we were observing everybody who came into the station. That's how we caught Constable Rice handing something to you at reception.'

I pictured the bloke giving me the drive. 'Why didn't you speak to me in your office?'

'My orders were to see where you took the item.'

'And that's how you ended up at the farm?'

He nodded. 'Imagine our surprise to find what we did.'

'You didn't trust me.'

'No, Enola, that's not it. We had to observe how it transpired.'

I spoke through gritted teeth. 'Becky and Julia might have been hurt. Claudia was.'

'She's fine,' he replied. 'The bullet didn't hit any vital organs, and we arrived before she lost too much blood. She'll spend a few days in the hospital, that's it.'

If I'd had the strength, I'd have jumped off the trolley and gone for his throat.

'We were lucky, Parker, all of us. I won't forget that.'

He didn't take his eyes off mine. 'Noted. What did Rice give you?'

I laughed, and my ribs throbbed. 'It was your phone

number. He claimed you and him have been stepping out together.' I glanced at Ginger. 'You have been a busy boy.'

'Enola!' she shouted. 'Stop messing about.'

I reached into my pocket and removed the drive. 'Raven said it contains the names and addresses of police informants and witnesses.'

'Raven?' Ginger asked.

'He's the guy leading the organised crime gang, the one with my finger marks around his throat.'

Parker took the drive. 'Thanks.' He left without a goodbye to any of us, including Ginger.

Becky ran to me. 'That was so exciting on the farm, Enola. Can we do it again?'

I groaned and lay on the bed, wondering if I could convince the doctors to keep me in the hospital for a few days.

Chapter 28

Your Kisses Burn

I couldn't rest. Bruce cooked for us all when we returned to the flat, including Becky and Julia, and I was half tempted to go straight to bed. My body told me to do that, but my mind had other ideas. I laced up my running shoes and clipped on Kronos's leash.

'You're going for a run?' Ginger asked.

I nodded. 'I need to clear my head.'

'Do you feel up to it?' Bruce asked.

'I'll be fine.'

Ginger scowled. 'You must rest, Enola.'

'Running is how I rest.'

She didn't seem convinced. 'There might be more of those thugs out there. Jack said they probably hadn't got them all.'

'Don't worry. Kronos will protect me.'

She protested some more, but I wasn't listening, pulling on Kronos's collar and leaving the flat. It was dark as I headed out, with the dog keeping up with me and panting. The streets were empty as the moonlight guided me through the town, and I listened to "Babylon's Burning" through the headphones. My bruises ached, but I felt better as soon as I started running, feeling alive again as I entered the woods.

The rustling leaves and twigs snapped under my feet, the trees creating a dappled light effect as we emerged into a clearing. Kronos was puffing and pulling on his leash, eager to keep going. We followed the path towards the river, where I heard the gentle lapping of water against the bank and the air smelt of damp earth and vegetation. Something rustled in the reeds, and the mutt wanted to pull away from me, but I kept a tight grip on the lead.

I slowed as we reached the river, admiring the stillness and beauty of the water. Kronos padded along beside me, sniffing at the water's edge. I took a deep breath, feeling the cool night air filling my lungs. My reflection shimmered back at me, and I pictured Nora in the water. Was it Raven or one of his goons who'd killed her? And if it was, why?

The moonlight sparkled on the surface. I resisted the temptation to crawl into the reeds and relax. Not to lose myself under the water but to float and peer at the stars. A young woman had vanished near that spot before I was born. There were rumours she'd drowned and that her ghost appeared sometimes at midnight. A few months back, a thug had tried to kill me in that dark place, and I'd imagined the dead woman's icy fingers trying to drag me into the abyss. I remembered that moment and pictured Nora's lifeless body floating in the same river. If Raven was responsible for her death, I hoped Parker would discover the truth.

Kronos licked my hand, bringing me back into the present. We continued our run towards the abandoned funfair, and the atmosphere changed. The mouldy scent of decay had replaced the smell of candyfloss and popcorn. The rides were deserted and forsaken, with broken glass scattered everywhere. The dog needed a piss, so I took him to the large clown-face sign in the corner, smiling as he did his business. At least he didn't need a shit.

Then we were off again, with my intended route being the reverse journey, but something in my legs, or my head, took me through the other side of the funfair and into the town's largest industrial estate.

The smell of diesel fuel and metal overwhelmed my nostrils as we sprinted beyond stacks of shipping containers. The flickering lights illuminated the path ahead, casting long shadows across the ground. There should have been security there, but I didn't see anybody as I ran past a micro-brewery, a garage, and a garden centre, stopping outside a clothes factory.

Kronos stared at me. 'Okay, boy, this was just a coincidence.'

I peered beyond him at the sign for King's Clothing

Was it an accident I'd ended up yards from Claire King's business? And what would I do about it?

I dragged Kronos to me. 'Let's go home, boy.'

Then, a car pulled up outside the building, and King got out. She looked around before opening the door and stepping inside. The mutt peered at me through sheepish eyes. I tied his lead to a lamppost and put a finger to my mouth.

'Stay quiet. I'll be back soon.'

I stuck to the shadows and crept across the road, my heart rate increasing with every step. The wind swirled through my hair, and all my bruises screamed at me to leave. As I approached the building, I smelt the pungent odour of chemicals from within. I pressed my head to the door and heard the faint humming of machinery. I pushed the door open, trying to be as quiet as possible.

Rows of empty machines and workstations filled the

factory floor, but I couldn't see King. I crept further inside, drawn towards the voices from the back. The closer I got, the thicker the air became, with the scent of sweat, chemicals, and burning fabric.

I reached a window at the rear and peered through it. King was issuing instructions to a tall, fierce-looking woman. Beyond them were dozens of workers hunched over their machines, their faces strained with exhaustion. And they all looked like children.

Then, out of the shadows, stepped Adam. He grabbed King's hand and stared at her through puppy dog eyes. I didn't hear what he said, but I'd had enough of only observing.

I pushed the door open and went in. 'Are they all on minimum wage, Claire?'

She snatched her hand from Adam's and glared at me. 'You're trespassing.'

I got my phone out. 'Should I call the police?' I nodded at the workers. 'Perhaps minimum wage isn't the concern here, but their age or where you got them from.'

'Get rid of her, Adam,' King said. He hesitated until she touched his cheek.

Then he came for me.

'Claudia's in hospital.'

He stopped. 'What?'

'Claudia took me to your family farm this afternoon, Adam. She told me what happened with your dad.'

'That was an accident.' His hands shook, and I imagined an axe in them. 'Is she okay?'

'Yes,' I replied. 'Raven tried to kill me, but your sister saved my life.'

'Don't mess around, Adam,' King said. 'Get rid of her.'

He gazed at her. 'Like I did with the other one?'

I glanced from him to her. 'Which other one, Adam.'

King pulled him back, so she was between us. 'Why are you here, Gray?'

I ignored the question. 'Who did you get him to hurt, Claire?'

She grabbed a hammer from the bench. 'I don't need him to deal with you.'

I punched her in the face, and she folded like a cheap suit.

Adam dropped to the floor, cradling King's head as I called the police.

Chapter 29

What Kind of Girl

I made the afternoon visiting hours at the hospital. Claudia was in her own room, listening to music on her phone as I entered.

'Anything good?' I asked as she removed the headphones.

'I checked that link you sent me,' she said. 'Joy Division are pretty good, and The Teardrop Explodes are funny, but that Lou Reed album hurt my ears.'

The light was harsh and clinical, and I had to blink a few times to adjust. Claudia was propped up on the bed, her face pale and her hair limp. I pulled a chair beside her and sat, smiling despite the tension.

'How are you feeling?' I said, trying to sound casual.

She managed a weak smile. 'Better than yesterday. The painkillers are working.'

I nodded, relieved. 'Good, good. Has Detective Inspector Parker visited you?'

'Yes.'

'Did he talk about Adam?'

Claudia's face crumpled, and she covered her mouth

with trembling fingers. 'Oh God,' she whispered. 'I knew he was mixed up in something, but I never imagined...'

I took her hand, offering what comfort I could. 'It's not your fault. You couldn't have known what was going on. Claire King manipulated and used him. She groomed him, which will work with a jury in his favour.'

'But why?' she said. 'Why would she make him kill that woman?'

I sighed. 'King held a grudge against Nora for years since their time at university. She believed Nora had stolen her boyfriend. It must have eaten away at her, twisting anything good inside her until all that remained was darkness and bitterness. Unfortunately, your brother and Nora suffered for that.'

Claudia's tears welled up in her eyes. 'If it weren't for me convincing him to leave the foster home, if I hadn't been so desperate, we wouldn't have fallen in with that gang, and Adam wouldn't have met her in Counterfeit Alley.'

I shook my head. 'It's not that simple. He was vulnerable, looking for something to hold on to. Claire King saw that and took advantage of it.'

She wiped her eyes with the back of her hand. 'Even so, I feel like I failed him.'

'You didn't fail him,' I insisted. 'You're here now and trying to do the right thing. That's what matters.'

'What happens to Adam now?'

'I'm unsure, Claudia, but my friends Ginger and Bruce will help him get the best lawyer and legal advice. I promise you that.'

I leaned over and hugged her. She smiled at me when she let go.

'How are you, Enola?'

'Well, the police arrested King on child trafficking

charges, and Jack Parker told me there'll be others to come, including a charge of murder. This means King's accusations against me will probably vanish in a puff of smoke.'

'That's great,' Claudia said. 'What about Raven and his gang?'

'There's good news there. The coppers raided that factory in Newcastle, and several of Raven's goons are already singing to save their own necks, including the bent copper at the police station who gave me the drive. Only two things remain I have to sort out.'

'What are those?'

'First, I have to find a job. I can't keep living off Ginger and Bruce's generosity.' I smiled at Claudia. 'And we need to decide what to do with you when you leave that hospital bed in a few days.'

She narrowed her eyes. 'Won't social services send me back to the foster home?'

'Nope. Peter Flynn is behind bars while the police build their case against him.' I squeezed her fingers. 'And you'll help with that.' I let go of her and reached into my jacket to remove a small parcel. 'And you forgot something while you were slumming it in here.'

Claudia stared at me wide-eyed. 'What?'

I gave her the present. 'Happy sixteenth birthday, Claudia.'

She raised a hand to her face. 'Shit, it was the other day. But, wait, does that mean?'

'Yes, you're an adult now.' I laughed. 'Well, sort of. Anyway, it means no more foster homes for you.'

'That's great, but where will I live?'

'Don't worry. The council should arrange something for you. Parker said he'd make sure of that.' I pushed the parcel at her. 'So open your present.'

She grabbed it from me and eagerly ripped the paper, revealing a small box. She removed the lid and stared at the contents.

'It's a memory chip for a phone.'

I took the chip from the box. 'Yes, but it's not any old memory chip, my young friend.' I held it in front of her face. 'On here, you'll find fifty years of great music, enough to keep you happy for the rest of your life.'

She snatched it from me. 'Is this legal?'

I put my arm around her shoulder. 'I'm proud of you, Claudia. This time last week, you wouldn't have cared and look at you now, an upstanding citizen.'

She got her mobile phone off the desk and removed the back to insert the chip. I watched her do it and felt like a big sister.

Helping others was great.

If only I could help myself.

A. S. FRENCH

THE VANISHING

AN ENOLA GRAY MYSTERY

Chapter 1

Mean to Me

Joe Strummer was shouting in my ears when Becky threw a pinecone at me. It bounced off my cheek as I turned to her, a violent kiss against my skin as I pulled the headphones off me.

'I've been yelling at you for ages, Enola.'

Her cheeks were puffed out like hyperactive tangerines, and she appeared to have a dead rat clutched in her hands. My face throbbed as I looked closer to see it was only a hairy branch. She tossed it to the ground and scowled at me. Becky was a few weeks past her eleventh birthday and seemed to exhibit increased violent tendencies. It was worrying but hardly surprising considering what had happened to her in the last six months, culminating in a criminal gang abducting her and her mother, Julia, to get to me.

'You couldn't come and tell me that instead of throwing things at me?'

'But then it would have flown away.'

'What would?'

She pointed at a bright orange butterfly nestling on a

flower. The smell of damp earth and fresh pine was in the air, and the rustling of leaves surrounded us. The trees were ablaze with golden red and yellow, and the twigs crunched under our feet. It was a splendid day, and I was delighted to have ventured outside to forget about my mounting problems.

Seeing her smile was good, even if she'd assaulted me with the pinecone. I should have been at home preparing for my job interview, but Julia had to work an extra shift, and I was happy to look after Becky while she did. It was an excuse to take the dog for a walk and leave the flat since Ginger was entertaining her boyfriend, Detective Inspector Jack Parker. My relationship with the police had been strained for some time, but Parker and I were friends once, and I couldn't blame her for finding happiness from somewhere.

'Can I take it home, Enola?'

I stared at the butterfly and imagined it pinned to the wall in her house.

'You want to kill it?'

Her eyes bulged. 'No! Why do you say that?'

'How would you keep it in your flat, Becky?'

She screwed up her face and thought about it. 'Some people have birds as pets.'

'Do you think that's fair to the birds?'

She ran her tongue over her lips. 'No, I suppose not.' She peered at me. 'You have Dirty Harry.'

DH was my tarantula. I knelt to get near her, my knees creaking as I did. 'Did you ask your mom for a pet?'

Becky nodded. 'She said the flat was too small for a dog and it wasn't fair to keep a cat in all the time and we couldn't let it out because the road is so close and I don't want a fish, and she won't let me have a spider like you have so I thought something small and pretty like the butterfly would be all right and I can keep it in my bedroom, and it will walk on the ceiling so I can feed it sunlight and whispers.'

She paused for breath after her scattergun speech. I felt old looking at her, and I was only twenty-one.

'Sunlight and whispers?'

Her smile lit up the woods. 'Yeah, I read about it in a book. Humans like us need light to live, so the butterflies and all the insects and other animals must as well.' She scrunched up her face as if trying to remember something difficult. 'It's called an ecosystem.'

I contained my laughter, and it hurt my ribs. 'Okay, that makes sense, but what about the whispers? What are they for?'

She shook her head. 'Don't be so silly, Enola. Every living thing likes chocolate.'

It was impossible to hold it in, and I burst out laughing. 'Right, of course. I forgot. How careless of me.'

Becky scowled and crossed her arms. 'What?'

I waved a hand at her. 'Don't worry about it. It was a bad joke, one before your time.'

I'd forgotten how to be happy, but this excursion into the woods was doing me the world of good. We appeared to be having a great day out, but the laughter was only hiding more serious concerns. The kid was feeling lonely, and I didn't know what to do about it. The bullying at her school had stopped, but I knew she'd made no friends there. And there weren't many kids her age where she lived, which meant I was her only friend.

That probably wasn't a good thing for her.

I thought about that when I noticed something carved

into the oak near my head. I knelt and inched closer to it, peering at the symbol of a five-pointed star inside a circle.

Becky moved in to get a better look at it. 'What is it?'

I put my body between her and the tree. 'It's nothing, kid.' I got my phone and took pictures, my knees digging into the ground. I'd seen the symbol before, but it was usually in movies or books. I couldn't tell her what it was without her asking difficult questions.

'You're not supposed to damage trees like that,' she said.

She must have noticed it before I could stop her. 'Is that right?'

'Yeah, it's bad for the environment. We all have to do our bit to save the world. Don't you know that, Enola?'

I thought about that as Kronos, the crazed whippet, bounded through the trees and jumped on me. I hit the ground as the butterfly fled the scene, the mutt pinning me into the earth as it slobbered over my cheeks. The leaves crunched under my weight as the beast rubbed its wet face into mine. I tasted dirty dog hairs on my lips as I struggled to move. Then another mongrel appeared, a huge Rottweiler that lunged at us. Kronos spun off me and dashed into the bushes as the other dog landed near my head, growling and panting, its sharp teeth close to my throat.

'Caesar, come here,' a bloke shouted as he stepped forward.

I brushed damp leaves off me and stood, watching the hound as it gazed at me like fresh meat. Kronos had disappeared while Becky grinned at the angry mutt in our midst. She moved towards it, but I pulled her back.

'Don't touch the dog,' I said.

The man marched over, as tall as a basketball player, with arms and legs as thick as the trees surrounding us. He looked out of place in the woods, in his expensive clothes and shoes, as if he'd arrived in a personal helicopter.

'Was that ugly thing your mutt?' he demanded.

Kronos returned before I could say anything, and the Rottweiler growled at him.

Steam sizzled inside my brain. 'Can you please control your dog?'

The bloke rolled his eyes. 'He's only playing.'

'He's being aggressive. And he just took a dump. So you need to clean that up.'

He laughed. 'We're in the woods.'

I struggled to contain my temper. 'It's on the path that kids use.'

He shook his head as the Rottweiler lunged at Kronos. Becky screamed, and the two dogs began fighting. I shouted, trying to separate them with my voice, but the Rottweiler locked its jaws onto Kronos' neck.

'No!' Becky howled.

'Get your dog off mine!' I yelled at the unmoving bloke. I ran over and punched him on the shoulder. 'Fucking do it now!'

'Caesar, stop!' he shouted, and the Rottweiler let go.

I sped to Kronos, who was standing but bleeding from the wound. I took a tissue from my pocket and cleaned the blood away to check the damage. He was panting hard, but it didn't look like the other dog had done more than anything superficial. But it would still mean a visit to the vet.

The red mist continued to shimmer before me as I clipped Kronos's lead to the collar and turned to the bloke. The Rottweiler stood near him, its eyes bulging and mouth open to show the blood on its teeth.

'Get your dog on its fucking lead.'

He glanced at Becky. 'You shouldn't talk like that in front of the kid.' Then he strode away. 'Come on, Caesar.'

Becky ran to Kronos. 'Is he okay?'

I rechecked the damage. 'He should be fine. We'll visit the vet on the way home.'

My heart was beating fast enough to power a train, and a tiny version of me was screaming inside my head.

Whoever that fucker was, he'd be paying for the vet's bill.

Chapter 2

Just Like Nothing On Earth

I was lucky to get an emergency appointment with the vet, sitting third in line behind the angry-looking cat and the bored Yorkshire terrier with their owners. My head throbbed, and the tiny dog smelt of strawberries, which irritated my sinuses. I tried to ignore the aroma, still focused on the obnoxious bloke and his Rottweiler. Kronos sat at my feet and seemed okay, but Becky was agitated.

'That man in the woods was horrible.'

I patted her hand. 'Don't worry; we won't see him again.'

I said that even though I was determined to find him and make him pay the vet's bill. The smell of antiseptic and dog fur filled my nostrils, and I heard barking from the back room. The fluorescent lights flickered overhead, casting a sickly glow over everything. None of it did my banging headache any good.

As I sat, my thoughts drifted to when I was a kid and the neighbour's cat, Fangs, took ill. Debbie, the girl next door, had asked me over to play in the garden, and I'd initially been reluctant. Friends had never been easy to come by, and it was no different then, but the thought of playing with the cat had been exciting enough to overcome my shyness.

It had all been going so well until I kicked a football at the cat's head.

I remembered the helplessness that consumed me as Debbie's parents rushed Fangs to the vet. I'd gone with them, sitting in that same room where I waited with Kronos, watching as other animals came and went, their owners just as worried as I was. Or perhaps it was the guilt I felt that day. The moggie recovered, but Debbie never played with me again.

I shook my head, trying to clear the memory, as a man burst into the vets carrying a bulldog. The bloke was bald and squat, wearing a T-shirt saying The Church of the Resurrection. Sweat gushed down his face as he scanned the room before settling on the middle-aged customer holding the irritated cat.

'I should go before you, Julie. This is an emergency.'

The cat hissed at the annoying newcomer. 'My name is Joe,' the cat's owner said.

The bald man grinned. 'See, that's why we kicked you out of the church, Julie. You don't follow the Word of God. Chopping your bits off doesn't make you a bloke.' He moved close to the hissing kitty. Then he grabbed his crotch. 'You need this to be a man.'

He plopped his ample backside in the seat closest to the door and assumed first place in the queue, glancing between the young woman with the terrier and me.

'You've pushed in.' I said.

The sweat dribbled down his cheek as he shrugged. 'It's an emergency.'

I peered at his dog, which appeared perfectly fine. 'Go to the back of the queue.'

He shook his head. 'No chance, love. I'm here now.'

Becky spoke loud enough for all to hear. 'Are you going to hurt him, Enola? I think you should.'

The bald man gave her the finger. 'Fuck you, kid.'

I handed Becky Kronos's lead and stood. Then I took a deep sigh and stepped towards the buffoon. 'Will you go to the back of the queue?'

He laughed and pointed at Joe sitting next to him. 'Are you like this one, unsure if you're a boy or a girl?' He leaned into Joe and sneered at the cat. 'Admit it, Julie; you want to return to the church, don't you? I can help you with that if you confess all your sins.' He smiled at me. 'And we know there've been loads of those, haven't there?'

Joe inched back from the moron, though the moggie looked like it wanted to scratch the idiot's eyes out. I knew how it felt.

I moved closer to the bloke. 'You're a creature of limited imagination.'

He sneered at me. 'What?'

'Your mother should have thrown you away and kept the test tube.'

'Now, look you....'

I raised my hand. 'What?'

The vet nurse stepped into the room. 'Hey, Enola, how are you?'

I turned to her. 'I'm fine, Deb. Kronos got into a bit of a scrap. I think he's okay, but I wanted to bring him in to make sure.'

She looked at Kronos's neck. 'Yeah, it looks like a scratch, but Bob will check him over, anyway.' She glanced through the reception. 'But you'll have to wait your turn.'

'That's no problem.' I grinned at the moron. 'Some folks have manners here.'

The moron clutched the dog to his chest and stood. 'I've changed my mind.'

'Does it work any better?' I said as he left.

'Joe Ripley and Nostromo, the cat?' Deb said.

Ripley stood. 'That's us.' Then they smiled at me. 'Thank you.'

I watched them enter the surgery room as I received a text from Bruce.

When are you coming back so I know when to cook?

I hadn't told him about the incident in the woods and where we were, as it would only have worried him.

It shouldn't be long now, maybe thirty minutes. Make sure there's enough for Becky.

The kid peered at my phone. 'Tell him I want a burger and chips or a pizza, none of that pasta and veggie muck he always makes. And cake. Chocolate cake.'

I used my shoulder to inch her out of the way, looking for something to keep me interested while we waited. I was trying to reduce my internet use, which meant returning to more traditional reading material. Becky grabbed a comic from the magazines on the table, and I sifted through them. There appeared to be two types: ones to make me a better cook and show me how to fit into that dress or instructing me in how to be a superior lover. Since I didn't own any dresses and couldn't remember the last time I was in a relationship, I passed on those mags and picked up the latest copy of the free local newspaper.

Becky hummed some awful pop tune as I peered at the headline - Twenty-Five-Year-Old Mystery: What Happened to Emily Jones?

'Aliens might have snatched her,' the kid said.

'What?' I replied.

She dropped her comic and pointed at the headline. 'That woman who vanished all those years ago, aliens probably took her.'

I turned the paper over and put it on the table. 'Do you believe in aliens?'

Her eyes lit up like the night sky. 'Oh yeah. Mum always watches those programmes about UFOs, aliens, and strange stuff. And there were those videos that NAPA released about those flying Tic Tacs. They were definitely aliens.'

'You mean NASA?'

She shrugged. 'Whatever.'

This was a new side to the kid I hadn't seen before. And for Julia. Still, considering what they'd been through recently, I assumed watching stupid stuff on TV wouldn't harm them.

'Well, I don't think that's what happened here twenty-five years ago. People always go missing, and nobody ever hears from them again.'

Becky nodded. 'See, that's probably the aliens as well. They take folks into their ships to experiment on them. Mum and me watched a show about it. The aliens are breeding babies. Hybrids, they call them, and they have strange powers.'

I hadn't seen her so excited about something in a while, but I wasn't sure if I wanted to go down the rabbit hole with her on the subject. And I needed the toilet.

I handed her Kronos's leash. 'Look after the mutt while I wash my hands.'

She took it, and I went to the bathroom and thought about one bloke who would wish aliens had abducted him the next time I saw him.

Chapter 3

It's A Small World

Becky was peering at my tarantula in his tank as Bruce and Ginger fussed over Kronos and the new bandage around his neck.

'You didn't recognise the bloke in the woods?' Ginger said.

I shook my head. 'No, but I won't forget his face.' I showed her the vet bill. 'And I'll give him this the next time I see him.'

Bruce was seething. 'I keep seeing people online shouting about banning certain dog breeds, but it's the owners who need kicking out of the country.'

Ginger nodded. 'Sure, irresponsible owners and breeders should certainly be banned, but how you go about that isn't simple. Any dog in the wrong hands is capable of harm.'

'We'll get the aliens to take the horrible man with the nasty dog,' Becky said.

Bruce and Ginger looked at me. 'It's a long story,' I replied.

'I saw a UFO once,' Bruce added.

Becky lost interest in the spider and ran to Bruce. 'What? Where was this?'

They sat near each other on the sofa as Ginger checked the food. I slumped in the seat opposite Bruce and the kid with Kronos curled up on the floor between us.

'Well,' Bruce added. 'I was about your age and playing in the woods near the river. It was summer like now and a warm evening, so my mates went swimming, but I didn't.'

'That's because you can't swim,' I said.

He laughed. 'There is that. Anyway, while they were splashing in the water, I went looking for tadpoles and frogs in the reeds, and that's when I saw it.'

Becky clapped her hands. 'Was it an alien with a big grey head and eyes like a bug? Did they take you to their ship for experiments? Did they probe you? Are you a hybrid?'

Ginger brought plates and cutlery for the table. 'Yeah, they gave him a good probing.'

I grinned while Bruce frowned. 'No, I didn't see an alien, but a bright glowing orb flickered yellow and red, hovering above the reeds. It was about the size of a small car, just hanging in the air for about thirty seconds before it shot off into the clouds.'

'It was probably a drone,' I said.

He shook his head. 'There weren't drones then, especially ones so fast.'

'Swamp gas,' Ginger added.

Bruce patted his gut. 'Yeah, maybe.'

My stomach groaned with hunger. 'Why are we only hearing about this now?'

He shrugged. 'It's not something you tell other people unless you want them to laugh at you. When the kids came out of the river, I asked if they'd seen it, but they laughed.

So, my name was a laughing stock for weeks. Fortunately, by the time we returned to school after the holidays, they'd forgotten about it, and there were other things to talk about.'

'When was this?' I asked.

'Twenty-five years ago,' Bruce answered.

The kid yelled. 'That's when that woman vanished! I told you it was aliens.'

I sighed. 'Don't get carried away, Becky.'

'What woman?' Ginger said.

'It was in the local paper,' I replied. 'It's the twenty-fifth anniversary of her disappearance.'

'Don't you remember, Ginger?' Bruce said. 'It was Emily Jones.'

She sat and filled a glass of red wine. 'God, yes, how could I forget that? I was only a kid, but everybody talked about it, even at school.' She poured another drink and handed it to Bruce. 'Wasn't she part of that fundamentalist church? What were they called?'

Bruce nodded. 'The Church of the Resurrection. They were always trying to recruit people on the high street. My dad told me to keep away from them.'

I remembered the moron at the vet. 'There was a bloke in the surgery with that on his T-shirt, the Church of the Resurrection.'

'They were a big thing back then, marching through town protesting against something or other if it didn't meet strict Old Testament conditions,' Bruce said.

Ginger sipped her wine. 'I've nothing against folks and their religious beliefs, but the Old Testament God was not nice. He really enjoyed killing people. And he may have been insane if his willingness to murder devout worshippers like Moses was any indication.'

'The first children's home I lived in had a woman in

charge who used to read us *Bible* text every morning, a few of which I've never forgotten. Eliseus and the Bears was her particular favourite.'

Becky sat next to me. 'I love stories about bears.'

I ruffled her hair. 'Maybe not this one. Eliseus was travelling to Bethel when some kids popped up and made fun of him for being bald. So Eliseus cursed them to God, and with God being a founder member of the baldness club, he sided with Eliseus and sent two bears to maul forty-two of those kids to death for making fun of a bald bloke. Why only forty-two? Nobody knows. Perhaps it had something to do with *The Hitchhiker's Guide to the Galaxy*. Then there's God murdering countless people in horrible ways simply because he's pissed off. God drowning everybody on the planet besides Noah and his family is pretty well known. And he also helped the Israelites murder everyone in Jericho, Heshbon, Bashan, and many more, usually simultaneously killing women, children and animals. Hell, God once helped some Israelites kill 500,000 other Israelites. God's crazy.'

Bruce sighed. 'From what I remember from my parents taking me to church on Sundays, Leviticus bans tattoos, pork, shellfish, round haircuts, polyester and football.'

'And a few other things,' Ginger said.

'Has this Church of the Resurrection always been here?' I asked.

She shrugged. 'I'm unsure. I only heard about it when that young woman disappeared.'

Bruce finished his wine. 'Emily Jones. It's strange, really.'

'What?' I wondered. 'That she vanished?'

'Well, yes, there's that, but I got an email this morning

from an old friend from university, and he's coming here to make a documentary about that case.'

'What old friend?' Ginger asked.

'Tommy Bell. You haven't met him, but you might have heard of his true-crime podcast, *Unsolved Cases*.' Bruce looked at me. 'Do you have a job interview tomorrow?'

I nodded. 'Yeah, with a tech company, though it's only part-time. Why?'

'Because Tommy wants somebody local to help him in the area. He asked me, but I'm too busy, so I thought of you. He pays well.'

My eyes lit up. 'How much?'

He grinned. 'This goes no further than us, but the documentary Tommy's making is for Netflix, so it's a lot of money.'

I glanced at Kronos snoring at my feet. 'At least I'll be able to pay the vet's bill.'

'Don't worry about that, Enola,' he said. 'We'll handle it.'

I waved a finger at him. 'Nope, you won't. I'll settle it. Have you got Tommy Bell's contact details?'

He wrote a mobile phone number and handed it to me. 'Here you go.'

I slipped it into my pocket, ready to eat, and thought about getting a new job. And maybe when wandering around town on a twenty-five-year-old mystery, I might bump into the man in the woods again.

Then I'd make him pay.

Chapter 4

Since You Went Away

When I should have been at my job interview, I drank coffee and scoffed a blueberry muffin in the local café while waiting for Tommy Bell. Only a few people were there: pensioners eating bacon buns and a pink-haired woman reading a book on her digital tablet. I was an hour early because I wanted to research a few things before he arrived; the first was scouring his biography on the *Unsolved Cases* website.

Tommy Bell was born in London, England, on October 15, 1987. Crime stories always fascinated him growing up, and he spent hours reading true crime books and watching documentaries. His parents, both lawyers, encouraged his passion and often discussed legal cases over dinner. He attended the University of Edinburgh, where he studied law. However, he quickly realised that a career in law wasn't for him and pursued his obsession with true crime instead.

After graduating, he returned to London and landed a job as a researcher at a true crime podcast production company. He discovered his talent for storytelling there and started pitching his own ideas for episodes. In 2015, aged twenty-eight, he launched Unsolved Cases. *The show quickly gained a following and became known for its in-depth research and compelling storytelling.*

Over the years, Tommy has investigated many incidents, from high-profile murder trials to lesser-known disappearances. He's interviewed experts, family members, and even suspects in his quest to uncover the truth. In addition, Tommy's accomplishments as a podcaster have led to other opportunities. He's written articles for magazines and has been a guest on several television shows as a true crime expert.

It was good media guff, but it didn't tell me much about the man or what he was like. I'd asked Bruce about him once he'd organised the meeting in the café.

'He was very introverted at uni, keeping to himself most of the time. I only got to know him because we were both big film noir fans. That's where I met him, at a late-night screening of *The Maltese Falcon*. But he was very driven and focused. Once he set his mind on something, he'd never let go until the end.'

I scrutinised his photos on the website, seeing a solid jawline, defined cheekbones, and a slightly rounded face. He didn't smile in any of the pictures.

Unsolved Cases had grown in popularity since its first episode, with its most listened-to episodes focusing on the "Crossbow Cannibal" in West Yorkshire, the serial killer "Bible John" in Glasgow, and the six unsolved deaths known as the "Jack The Stripper" murders.

Yet, he and his work weren't without controversy. His "Student Murder Lessons" podcast received several complaints from people involved. Bell's focus was on a seventeen-year-old girl who had died three months after entering a boarding school that claimed to turn around troubled girls. After a brief investigation, the police decided that the death was accidental, but rumours quickly circulated online about life inside the school and whispers of murder and sexual assault.

Bell focused on these speculations, mentioning student names without explicitly accusing individuals, though it was easy to assume from his reporting – and I use that term loosely – who he blamed for the death. This led to more rumours, comments, and wild theories exploding online. Several people received false accusations, and the young woman's family was hounded online. And many blamed that on Tommy Bell.

I never listened to podcasts, preferring to focus on music to enlighten my life. Crime documentaries were something I rarely watched. Considering what had happened to my parents and how I witnessed it, it felt morally reprehensible to me to use other people's pain as entertainment. Yet I knew millions were hooked on them. The problem was where to draw the line: was it investigative journalism or exploitation of real people?

During my research, I discovered women were likelier to be true crime fans than men and that many popular true crime influencers on YouTube were young women. Was this because we related to the victims? Most of the victims in the documentaries were female.

None of it was sitting easy with me.

Should I get involved in Bell's documentary if it was unethical?

As I considered that, I turned to my next area of research: Emily Jones. Plenty of websites had theories about Jones's disappearance, some of which had appeared in the last few weeks as the twenty-fifth appearance approached. However, I ignored the salacious sites and stuck to the facts about her. Born June 12, 1977, she was the youngest of three siblings and raised in a Christian household. From a young age, she showed a keen interest in music and was an active member of her church's choir, often performing solos during Sunday services. That was the Church of the Resurrection.

She attended the University of Sheffield from 1995 to 98 to study music and was a member of the university's choir. After completing her studies, she returned home and began working at a local music store. She continued to be an active church member and often performed during services. She was well-respected and known for her generosity.

On June 2, 1998, Emily disappeared while jogging by the river. They found her CD Walkman and headphones in the reeds, but no sign of her. Despite extensive searches and investigations by the police, they never solved Emily's disappearance. Instead, her family and friends could only wonder what had happened to her and why she'd vanished without a trace.

Almost immediately, speculations appeared online, from the plausible to the absurd: somebody kidnapped her, she accidentally plunged into the river, and the strong current carried her into the ocean, she escaped, she staged her own demise, and Becky's preferred explanation, extra-terrestrials abducted her. I skimmed most of the websites, and they all had one thing in common – no evidence existed for any of the theories. The family hired a private investigator, and they found nothing. Several psychics and clairvoyants offered their dubious services, but they, unsurprisingly, provided no clues about what happened to Emily.

It moved out of the news cycle within a year, replaced by other crimes, only returning to the media every five years on the anniversary of Emily's vanishing.

Now it was the twenty-fifth anniversary, and Tommy Bell was on his way to make a documentary, and I assumed another episode of his podcast. Would he be keeping it low-key in the community? I didn't see how he could, not with people on social media likely to be all over it once it became known he was in town. And both he and Netflix would crave the attention to promote their product.

Did I really want to be involved in it, regardless of how much it paid?

I did. The money would be useful, but it had more to do with how fascinating the whole thing already seemed. As somebody who had to wait ten years before discovering who murdered my parents, I could understand how Emily's family and friends might feel.

I'd do it for Emily and her family.

That's what I told myself.

I sipped the coffee and ate my muffin while waiting for Tommy Bell.

With murder on my mind.

Chapter 5

Blue Sister

An aroma of coffee filled my senses as I contemplated buying another muffin, chocolate chip this time. Jim Morrison was serenading me through the headphones – yes, people are strange – when two young women entered the café, their faces bundles of joy and happiness. They spoke to the server behind the counter before reaching into their bags and handing out leaflets and pamphlets. When they turned towards me, I noticed the words on their tops: The Church of the Resurrection. Even as an atheist, I took it as a sign of divine intervention since I was just about to research that organisation online.

Their smiles reached me before they did, sparkling white to contrast their green jackets and shirts as if they were a religious wing of Butlins. I popped the headphones out as the one with the glasses spoke to me.

'Hi, is giving you some of our reading material okay?'

'You're from the Church of the Resurrection?' I said.

She nodded. 'Yes, I'm Sister Morgan, and this is Sister Dolby.' They didn't look related, and she must have seen how I glanced between them. 'We are Sisters in Christ for the church.' She pulled out a chair. 'Do you mind if we sit?'

It would be an excellent opportunity to discover something about the church from its members, but I didn't want them to know how keen I was to learn about their organisation.

'Sure, go ahead.' I still had thirty minutes to kill before Bell arrived, and it would be a perfect way to do it.

They sat and placed leaflets on the table. 'Please, take one,' Sister Morgan said.

I did, glancing at the photos of happy, smiling people spreading the word of God.

'Are you new in the community?' I asked.

Sister Morgan shook her head. 'No, we were both born here, but this is our first week of missionary work for the church.'

'Missionary work?'

'Missionary life is one of discipline and commitment and focus,' she said, 'but those are the same attributes we all use throughout our lives, whether in a job or school.'

I slipped the leaflet into my pocket. 'I'm interested in learning more about the history of your church. Could you share some details? I've lived here all my life and hadn't heard of you until recently.'

Sister Morgan beamed at me, her eyes sparkling like shooting stars, and I guessed she wasn't used to such a response. 'Oh yes, of course. Can I ask you your name?'

'Enola,' I said. 'Enola Gray.'

'Well, Enola, I'll try not to bore you too much. Reverend John Williams, a charismatic preacher who believed the community needed a spiritual revival, founded the Church of the Resurrection in 1975. He bought a small chapel on the outskirts of town and began conducting services every

Sunday. Over time, the congregation grew, and in 1982, the church moved to a larger building on the high street. I'm surprised you haven't seen it.'

I shrugged. 'I probably have, but I didn't pay attention to it. I've lacked spirituality in my life, but now I feel I need something more than the same old dependency on material things and stimulants to survive.' It wasn't strictly a lie. 'Do you know what I mean?'

She reached over and touched my arm. 'Oh yes, Sister Dolby and I understand exactly what you mean, Enola.' She looked at her colleague. 'Don't we, Sister Dolby?'

'Of course we do,' Dolby said.

I smiled at them. 'That's great. Have you been church members for a long time?'

They both laughed before Sister Dolby spoke. 'You could say that. Like many church members, Sister Morgan and I were born into it because our parents and siblings are congregation members.'

'I see. And what do you do for the church?'

'Well,' Sister Morgan answered. 'As missionaries, we have a strictly planned daily schedule - of prayer, study, exercise, volunteering in the community and seeking potential converts - starting at six-thirty every morning and ending with a nightly curfew.'

'That sounds like hard work. So what's your hourly rate?'

Sister Dolby shook her head. 'Oh no, we don't get paid for this. Our reward comes when we see the smiles of those we help, in the homeless shelters, at the food bank, and in the outreach work we do with vulnerable people in the community.'

'It does sound very rewarding,' I said. They were both far too young to have known Emily Jones, but their parents must have. I resisted the temptation to ask about Emily, hoping this would be a way into the church to discover more about them. I didn't know if Bell had lined up any interviews with church members, but it wouldn't hurt to show a little initiative before I officially started working for him. Not that I'd had the informal job interview yet.

Sister Morgan left her hand on my arm. 'Does this mean you're interested in attending one of our meetings, Enola?'

'Maybe.' I couldn't be too eager. 'How many people attend your congregation?'

'About eighty to a hundred on a good day,' Sister Morgan said. 'We like to keep things small so folks don't get overwhelmed. Communicating with The Lord is a powerful moment, but you'll find we're all one big happy family.'

'Do you know a little bald bloke who owns a bulldog?'

Sister Dolby's face brightened. 'Yes, that sounds like George Carter. Are you familiar with him?'

'He was at the vet yesterday when I was there. He was rude to a customer.'

The sisters frowned. 'Yes, George can be forthright with his views sometimes.'

'Forthright?' I said.

Sister Morgan lowered her eyelids a little. 'The Church of the Resurrection is traditional with our Christian values, though that doesn't mean our members should condemn others for having different ideals, especially in public. That's not right at all. Deacon Thompson won't be happy to hear about this.'

'I don't want to get him into trouble,' I replied, which was a lie, as I absolutely wanted to get him into trouble.

'No,' Sister Morgan said. 'It has to be mentioned. We can't have church members setting bad examples in the community. Thank you for bringing it to our attention.' The gloom vanished from her eyes, and she smiled again. 'Now, about you attending one of our meetings. When would be good for you?'

'Do you have a mobile phone number?'

She nodded and handed me a business card. 'You can call me at any time, Enola. Any time at all.'

I thanked them, and they got up just as Tommy Bell entered the café. He watched them leave, and I waved him over, wondering if I'd get a bonus for showing such initiative.

<h1 style="text-align:center">Chapter 6</h1>

<h2 style="text-align:center">Who Wants the World?</h2>

'Enola Gray?' Tommy Bell said.

I stood and shook his hand. 'That's me. Would you like a drink? I need another coffee and muffin.'

'I'll get them and add them to the expense account. What do you want?'

I told him and watched him go to the counter. For somebody the same age as Bruce, he looked a good five years younger and much fitter, lean, like an Olympic sprinter. Not that Bruce was out of condition, but he spent most of his life indoors in front of a computer, and the only exercise he got was walking Kronos. And that wasn't a regular thing since I took the dog out most of the time.

He returned with muffins for both of us. 'Thanks,' I said.

'No problem. The woman said she'll bring the drinks over.' He glanced at a leaflet Sister Morgan had left on the table. 'Were you talking to members of the Church of the Resurrection?'

'It was pure coincidence. They were here for their

missionary work, so I thought talking to them might be a good idea. Not that I wanted to step on your toes or anything.'

'No,' he said. 'That's great. I asked for an interview with Deacon Thompson, but they slammed the phone down when I mentioned Emily's name. A few ex-members will speak to me, but if you've got inside the church, that would be fantastic.'

'Deacon Thompson is the leader?'

Bell removed a photo from his pocket and put it on the table. 'He's a leading church member and a successful businessman who owns several local companies, including a construction firm and a real estate agency. He's known for his philanthropic endeavours and has donated large sums to the church over the years. You've never heard of him?'

'No. I never pay attention to religious matters or have any interest in town elders.'

'Didn't you work for the local MP?'

'Bruce told you that, right?' He nodded. 'It was a short-lived employment.'

'Well, if you agree, working with me would last about two weeks.'

'Don't I have to pass the interview first?'

He laughed. 'Is that what Bruce said? The job is yours if you want it, Ms Gray.'

'Call me Enola as long as I can call you Tommy. Mr Bell was a PE teacher at school, and everybody hated him, including me.'

The server brought our drinks over.

'What has Bruce told you about this project?'

'Not much, only that you're looking for somebody local who knows the area and the people to assist you.'

'That's right.'

'Fine, but I wasn't born when Emily Jones vanished. I only heard the full story yesterday.'

He shook his head. 'That doesn't matter. It's important what you'll bring to the investigation.'

'And what's that?'

Bell pointed at the leaflet. 'That - your initiative, quick thinking, and drive. You've already proved how useful you can be. There's a short deadline to finish the filming, and only two of us will work on this.'

'You don't have a crew with you, no camera operators?'

He put a phone on the table. 'That's the Apple iPhone 14 Pro Max, and it's yours.'

I picked it up and ran my fingers over the sleek, slim design. 'These won't be cheap, but surely they can't be as good as a digital video camera?'

'It cost over a grand, but that's not the point. I think people are probably sick of seeing high gloss true crime documentaries and crave something a bit more in your face and street level, and that's what this one will be like.'

It felt great in my hand. 'And you can do a lot of secret filming with this.'

He smiled at me. 'Exactly. See, I knew we'd be on the same wavelength.'

'So what would you need me to do?'

Bell reached into his bag and removed a large folder. 'I have a list of people to interview and locations to shoot at. Some we'll do together and others separately. I'll edit everything when we finish filming. How does that sound?'

I shrugged. 'You're the expert.'

He smiled. 'Well, maybe. I want to review the priorities with you. Okay?'

I'd barely known him for five minutes, but already, I could see how methodical, organised and dedicated he was.

In addition, he had a certain charm that would likely get strangers to talk to him.

'Do you have a focus for the documentary?'

He dropped three sugars into his coffee. 'What do you mean?'

'I listened to some of your podcasts last night, and they always have a theme, usually one of exposing a miscarriage of justice. You don't have that with this. So what concept will you go with?'

'What would you do, Enola?'

'That's simple. You can either try to explain what happened to Emily Jones, which seems unlikely considering how many other people have tried over the years. Or you could concentrate on why she might have disappeared.'

'And?'

I noticed the sparkle in his eyes. 'I don't watch true crime docs or listen to podcasts, but if I did, I'd want to know more about Emily. She was about my age, and with what little I've discovered so far, I'm already fascinated by her. So the focus has to be on her.'

Bell clapped his hands. 'That's also what I think. It's as if we've been working together for years. Bruce was right about you.'

'Do you have any theories about what happened to her?'

'Well, I've looked at them all, but the biggest problem is there isn't one thing that might point in any direction. If everything her family has said over the decades was factual, Emily had a perfect life and no reason to leave. No boyfriends or girlfriends were in the foreground or the background for the police to view as potential suspects. Therefore, the likeliest theory to be true is that a stranger abducted her. The closest road to where she disappeared is the other side of the abandoned funfair, still being built twenty-five years ago. Do you know it?'

I pulled the muffin apart and ate it in bits. 'I do. So where do you want to start?'

He opened the folder and pushed a list towards me. 'These are the people we need to interview, starting at the top with her parents.'

I glanced through the names. 'What about her two sisters? I don't see them here.'

'Samantha, the older one, emigrated to Australia the year before Emily disappeared. The youngest sister, Jane, joined her in 2001. As far as I can tell, they've never returned home since. However, on the phone, I've spoken to Emily's parents, Robert and Elizabeth, and they said they might be able to organise video calls with their daughters.'

'You've arranged a meeting with the parents?'

He nodded. 'It's this afternoon at three o'clock. Are you okay with that?'

'Sure. What will we do until then?'

Bell took a deep breath. 'I need you to do something important for me.'

'What?'

He pointed to the second name on the list. 'Superintendent Roy Crawford ran the investigation into Emily's disappearance. I must talk to him, but he won't speak to me. I was hoping you could arrange it.'

'Me? I don't know the guy, so how could I set it up?'

'Well, because of your connections.'

Then it hit me why he wanted me to work with him. 'You know what happened to my parents?'

'I do.'

I shook my head. 'Why would you think that would give me any leverage with this old copper?'

'It's not just the incident with your parents, Enola. Bruce told me how you found the body in the woods near where Emily vanished. And about your involvement in shutting down two organised crime gangs. You have a wealth of invaluable experience with things like this.'

'That dead man was a relative of a friend of mine, and it was almost twenty-five years after Emily disappeared. Those events are not connected.'

'I understand, but when Bruce told me how you solved that crime, I knew you must be a natural investigator.'

I laughed. 'I'm not sure if I should be flattered or annoyed, but I cannot see how any of that gets you a meeting with Superintendent Crawford.'

'Don't you know who Crawford's nephew is?'

I didn't. Then I did. Detective Inspector Jack Parker.

Bell was using me. I got up to leave.

Maybe there was still time to make that other job interview.

Chapter 7

Always the Sun

I was halfway to the door when Bell shouted at me. 'Wait, Enola. You should look at this first.' I turned to see him with a folded piece of paper in his hand. 'Please. If you still want to leave after, so be it.'

My initial anger had already vanished, so I snatched it from him and stared at its contents: a set of five digits and a pound sign.

'What's this?' I said.

'Your salary, Enola, if you want it. You could start a new career with that.'

'A new career?'

'Sure, whatever you desire. Maybe become the community's only private detective.'

'You've checked.'

'Of course. So what do you say?'

I scrutinised the numbers again. It was a lot of money. A lot. I could finally get off Ginger and Bruce's sofa and find my own place.

'Just because I know Jack Parker doesn't guarantee you an interview with Crawford.'

'No, but it's *our* best chance.'

The way he said *our* wasn't lost on me. 'What do you want me to do?'

'Speak to Parker. Tell him what it's about and how important it is to Emily's family.'

I returned to my seat. 'Is it important to Emily's family or to you?'

'Can't it be both?'

I glanced at the numbers again. 'What do you think Crawford might say that isn't already common knowledge?'

'After doing *Unsolved Cases* for this long, the one constant I've found is that the police always have theories and suspects they never mention to the public. So hopefully, if we speak to him, he'll have something similar for us.'

'Maybe, but you said you wanted to focus on Emily for the documentary – how does speaking to Crawford do that?'

He shrugged. 'We won't know until we talk to him.'

'Do you have a pen?' I asked.

'Sure.' He removed one from his jacket and gave it to me. I turned the paper over and wrote different numbers on the back.

'That's my bank account details. You can transfer the money now. Then we'll start.'

I waited for him to argue, to give me some excuse about waiting until we'd finished the documentary, but he didn't. Instead, he got his mobile and transferred the cash, with my phone receiving a confirmation email immediately.

I offered him my hand. 'Partners, then.'

He shook it. 'Will you call Parker now?'

I did. 'Hello, Enola. How are you?'

'Great, Jack. Are you at the station?'

'I am.'

'Excellent. I need to come over and see you?'

'Is this about Tommy Bell?'

'It is. Did Ginger mention it?'

'Yes, last night. Why do you want to talk to me?'

'It'll be best to tell you to your face.'

He was silent for ten seconds. 'Fine. Is he with you?'

'He is.'

'I'll let the desk know you're on your way.'

Parker ended the call. It had gone well, considering we hadn't been on friendly terms for a few months.

'What did he say?' Bell said.

I stood. 'Finish your coffee, Tommy. We're off to the cop shop.'

It was a twenty-minute walk to the police station, so I showed Tommy Bell the sights. The town was buzzing with life as we strode through the streets. People went to work, went shopping, or just spent time in the town centre. The aroma of fresh bread wafted through the air as we passed a bakery and groups of kids enjoyed the start of their summer holidays. He scrutinised the surroundings, focusing on all the boarded-up shops and failed businesses. The council had done its best to brighten the area, placing posters and artwork over the empty buildings, but the façade didn't fool anybody.

'Bruce said you've lived here all your life.'

'That's right. The first ten years were spent with my parents, and the next six, I drifted between various children's homes until the authorities released me into the wild at sixteen. It's been a barrel of laughs ever since.'

He took out his fancy Apple camera and filmed as he spoke. 'Seeing your colleagues die in that fire at the computer shop where you were the manager must have been hard.'

'Is there anything he didn't tell you about me?'

'I wanted to ensure you were the right person for the job.'

I shook my head and continued past the community centre and the food bank. My phone pinged with a text as I went. I used reading the message as an excuse not to look at Bell, wondering if it hadn't been for the money, would I be putting up with the podcast man?

When are you coming for a visit?

It was from Claudia, a girl I'd helped escape from one of those organised crime gangs Bell had mentioned in my non-interview.

Hopefully, at the weekend. Do you have room for me?

A charity supporting vulnerable teenagers gave Claudia a job and a flat in the next town. She'd been reluctant to go initially, but once I convinced her how much of a fantastic opportunity it was, she took her first step into a new world. Nervousness and excitement had possessed her, but she'd taken to it like a duck to water. We had only a five-year age gap, and I felt like an older sister to her. And that was important since her twin brother Adam was a few months into a ten-year prison sentence for manslaughter.

Yet, I hadn't seen her after she'd left town, and three weeks was a long time when you were a teenager in a strange new place.

You said you'd sleep on the floor, Enola.

It wouldn't differ significantly from a sofa, and I'd slept on worse.

Okay. How are you?

Fine. I'll call later. They need me in the garage.

She was a trainee mechanic, and I couldn't have been

happier for her. I put the phone away as Bell stopped opposite the police station.

'Are you having second thoughts?' I asked.

He filmed the area, shooting up and down the street before returning to aim the camera at the front of the station. 'Why would I do that?'

'I don't know. You had a strange look on your face.'

He grinned. 'Was it wide-mouthed and bug-eyed, like a deranged frog?'

'That's the one. I assumed you might faint.'

'Would you have cared? You'd still have the money.'

'What type of person do you think I am, Tommy?'

He shrugged. 'I thought I'd upset you back at the café.'

I laughed and slapped him on the shoulder. 'You'll know if you upset me. Now let's speak to Parker.'

As we crossed the road, I tried not to picture all that cash in my account.

Chapter 8

It Only Takes Two To Tango

The police station was a large brick structure with tall windows and a grand entrance. The receptionist smiled, handed out our visitor passes, and showed us to Parker's office. It was dimly lit, smelling of old paper and coffee. Detective Inspector Jack Parker sat at his desk, nodding as we entered. He gestured for us to take a seat.

'I understand you're in town for a documentary, Mr Bell.'

Tommy nodded. 'Yes, that's why we're here, Inspector Parker.'

Jack looked at me as I stared at the photo of him and Ginger on his desk. 'How so?'

Tommy didn't speak, so I assumed he wanted me to reply.

'Is Roy Crawford your uncle, Jack?'

'He is. Why?'

I took a deep breath. 'I'm helping Tommy to produce a podcast and documentary about Emily Jones's disappearance since it's coming up to the twenty-fifth anniversary.

We want to talk to Crawford as he was the officer in charge of the investigation, and we're having a problem contacting him. I thought you might help us.'

Parker looked at Tommy before turning to me. 'I didn't realise you were an investigator and filmmaker, Enola.'

I gave him my best fake smile. 'Well, Jack, we all have hidden depths. Who knew you were such an old romantic?'

He shifted in his seat. 'What do you mean?'

'You know it's Ginger's birthday in a few weeks?'

Parker pulled at the top of his shirt. 'Of course, sure.'

'So you must realise how romantic Ginger is and what she really wants for her birthday this year, right?'

'Eh, yeah, maybe. Do you?'

I held out my hands. 'I'm her best friend, Jack – of course I do.'

He turned his attention to Tommy. 'What do you want to ask Roy Crawford?'

The podcast man leaned forward. 'It won't take long, Inspector Parker, I promise. We only need to get his thoughts on the case and his feelings about the investigation.'

'What do you mean by that?'

I could see by how Jack had narrowed his eyes that he was already becoming suspicious about Tommy's motives. And I didn't blame him. Bell had tried his charm on me in the café, and I'd nearly fallen for it before getting up to leave. Then he'd offered me all that money, and my principals vanished like poor Emily Jones. I still wasn't sure how ethical true crime documentaries and podcasts were, but my ethics were currently resting amongst a big wad of cash in my bank account.

'We need to see how he reflects on the case after

twenty-five years,' I said. 'I'm sure you must reflect on some of your investigations and view them differently.'

He scrutinised me. 'When do you want to talk to Roy?'

'As soon as possible,' Tommy replied.

Jack stood. 'I'll be back in a minute,' he said as he stepped outside.

Tommy wiped his fingers across his forehead. 'Well done, Enola. I knew you'd be worth every penny.'

His saying that didn't make me feel any better. 'We haven't got the interview yet.'

I observed Parker through the window, still surprised he and Ginger had got together. Not that there was anything wrong with him – as coppers go, he was okay – but I figured her strong anti-establishment views would scupper any relationship with him.

He returned a few minutes later and sat behind his desk. 'Do you know where the Falcon and Eagle pub is, Enola?'

I didn't, but I'd heard of it. 'Isn't that where all the fox hunters go to cry in their beer because they can't torture and kill animals anymore?'

'Yeah, that's the one. Roy said he'll meet you there in an hour, where you can buy him lunch and drinks, but there's no guarantee he'll talk to you about the Emily Jones case.'

Tommy's hand shot out like a shooting star. 'Thank you so much, Inspector Parker. I'll make sure your name is in the credits of our film.'

Jack didn't shake his hand. 'I don't want my name anywhere near it, Bell. Understand?'

I got up and dragged Tommy to the door. 'Thanks, Jack.'

'Wait, Enola. You promised to tell me what Ginger wants for her birthday.'

I smiled at him. 'Why, it's what every woman wants – a romantic trip to Paris.'

I hauled Tommy out as Parker swore at me, moving through the station quickly enough so his obscenities died in the air behind us before we got outside.

'I left my car near the café,' Tommy said. 'Do you know where this pub is?'

'No, but I'm sure the GPS on my phone does.'

'That was great what you did there, Enola. I was a little unsure about leaving you alone to interview some of our subjects, but you've won me over.'

I grabbed his arm and dragged him towards the entrance to the post office.

'Who should I question? What am I supposed to say? I'm not an investigator.'

He didn't wriggle out of my grasp. 'Look, Enola. We'll do the first few together – Crawford, then Emily's parents, so you can see how it goes and watch my technique. How does that sound?'

All I could hear was the noise of that money being deposited into my account. And how I'd spend it getting a new flat and maybe a foreign holiday. I'd never been abroad and could already picture myself visiting Machu Picchu.

I let go of him. 'Do you have questions for Crawford?'

He wiped the crease from his sleeve. 'One of the lessons I learned early on when creating podcasts was that the better prepared you were, the greater the results would be. Of course, sometimes people say things that throw you, and you must act on instinct, but proper planning is everything in this game.'

'Game?'

'Yes, you have to view it as a game occasionally. Victims, family, and friends are involved in these cases, but you must step back a little while working. If you don't, there's the risk of getting sucked into the darkest parts of humanity you might never escape from. And then your emotional and mental health becomes affected, and you have a hard time getting away from the abyss the investigations have dragged you into.'

There was a hint of darkness behind his eyes I hadn't seen before.

And it bothered me.

Chapter 9

Old Codger

As my stomach grumbled, Tommy parked the car outside the Falcon and Eagle pub.

'Just in time for lunch,' he said.

I stopped him before he got out. 'What are we going to say to Crawford?'

He looked at me. 'I've read the official police reports about Emily's disappearance dozens of times and know them by heart. We need to hear his private thoughts about the case, to learn what he couldn't tell anybody else, especially the media.'

'And if he refuses to disclose those things?'

He grinned. 'At least you get some decent food on me.'

We strode into the pub, greeted by a yeasty beer and pizza aroma. The place was busy, buzzing with chatter and the low drone of the Pet Shop Boys coming from the jukebox. Stuffed animal heads and royal family portraits hung from the walls.

'Do you know what Crawford looks like?'

Tommy nodded. 'There's a video of him online from ten years ago when he retired from the police and gave his last interview about Emily. I don't suppose he'd have changed much since then.'

I was unsure, but my guts told me to eat something soon, or they'd revolt. So I left him to search the pub while I grabbed a menu and went to the bar. I scrutinised the surroundings when I got there, studying the customers and how they drank their wine and spoke about their second homes and holidays in exotic places. It was a world away from where I'd grown up, yet only four miles separated them.

Then I thought of the money recently deposited into my bank and realised I could have this life, if only for a short while, if I wanted.

But I didn't.

Tommy joined me. 'Crawford's in the corner near the fireplace, sitting underneath a huge portrait of Winston Churchill. I have to order food and drink for him, so we might as well get ours. What do you want?'

I told him, scanning the faces in the room while he ordered: mainly middle-aged men and women who looked like they had more cars than children. I watched them smiling and laughing, wondering if reality was an illusion, constantly changing and moulded by our minds rather than something tangible and fixed.

Tommy handed me a Coke. 'Are you ready?'

'Lead on,' I said.

I saw Churchill's giant head first, with a cigar sticking out of his mouth. Roy Crawford, the former superintendent, was just underneath the tip of the cigar, the sunlight beaming through the window and shining off his bonce. He was dressed like Sherlock Homes minus the deerstalker, his face resembling a minor character from a Humphrey Bogart gangster film. He fixed his eyes on me, and I felt his gaze crawl inside my brain.

'You look nothing like Jack Parker,' I said.

He laughed like a drowning horse, nodding so much I thought he might knock the cigar out of Winnie's hand.

'Jack mentioned you had a mouth on you, Ms Gray, and he was right.'

I sat near him. 'Call me Enola.'

Tommy positioned himself opposite the former copper and got his mobile phone out. 'Do you mind if I record this, Ray?'

Crawford inflated his cheeks as if balloons were inside them. 'Yes, I bloody well do. No recordings, I told Jack.'

'Fine, Ray,' Tommy said. 'No problem.' He took two notebooks from his bag. 'Enola and I will take notes. Is that okay?'

He thought about it until a server brought him a large whisky. 'I suppose so.'

Tommy handed me a pen and a pad. 'Great. Let's get started then, shall we?'

Crawford rubbed at his beard, and I could have sworn I saw something crawling through the hairs. 'Might as well while we wait for the food. Fire away, boy.'

I glanced around the room, wondering if anybody was taking a blind bit of notice of us, but it didn't appear they were. Was this the type of place Emily Jones or her family would have frequented? It seemed unlikely since I assumed the Church of the Resurrection likely abstained from alcohol and enjoying themselves.

'The search into Emily Jones's disappearance. You were in charge of it?'

'You know I was,' he said. 'I hope this won't waste my time, Mr Bell.'

Tommy shook his head and appeared nervous. 'No, of course not.' He inched closer to Crawford. 'What can you say about the investigation that I can't find anywhere else?'

He downed his whisky and returned to the pint of beer he was drinking before we arrived. Then he nodded to those stuffed dead heads who judged me from the walls.

'An animal may be ferocious and cunning, but it takes a human to lie.'

'What does that mean?' I said.

'What that means, Enola, is that during the investigation into the disappearance of Emily Jones, several people lied to us, but I could never prove it.'

Tommy scribbled on his pad. 'Who misled the police, Ray?'

Crawford belched so loud he disturbed the country crowd at the bar, and he didn't apologise. 'Not so quick, lad. Let's start with the basic facts, eh? Tell me what you know.'

Tommy placed his pen on the notebook. 'On Tuesday, June 2, 1998, Emily Jones vanished while jogging by the river. Edna Davis, a local woman walking her dog, found Emily's CD Walkman and headphones near the river's edge, but there was no sign of Emily. The last sighting of her was by a group of teenagers as she jogged through the woods on the way to the river at ten to eight. It was a warm evening, and other people were around, but nobody saw her afterwards. Despite extensive searches and investigations by the police, they never solved Emily's disappearance. And now we're a few days away from the twenty-fifth anniversary of her vanishing.'

Crawford raised his glass. 'Indeed, and who knew it was aliens to blame all this time?'

Tommy nearly choked on his Coke, and I pictured Becky pointing at me and laughing.

Chapter 10

Thrown Away

'What?' Tommy said.

Crawford held up his empty whisky glass and nodded to the bloke behind the bar for another. 'I thought you knew all the theories about Emily's disappearance, Mr Bell. Wouldn't that make the best one for your podcast?'

I watched Tommy's cheeks redden. 'Did you bring us here to waste our time, Mr Crawford?'

The old man slapped Tommy on the knee. 'Call me Ray, son. I'm only messing with you.' He winked at me. 'Both your reputations preceded you, and I wanted to see if you had a sense of humour.'

'What reputation do I have?' I asked.

'Why, as someone not to be messed with, Enola. Isn't that right?'

I didn't reply, chewing on an ice cube. It chilled my mouth and irritated my teeth.

'Okay, Ray, that was funny, and now we've broken the ice,' Tommy said. 'So talk to me about the case.'

Ray's smile vanished, replaced with a look you see from a pallbearer at a funeral.

'The uniformed officers and forensic team were the first on the scene, four hours after the dog walker reported what she found.'

I wrote the time in the notebook. 'Why did it take so long?'

'Emily Jones was twenty-one,' Ray said. 'And there was no sign of foul play. She was a grown woman who could have gone anywhere. The police only went when they did because Emily's father, Robert, was in the same Freemason lodge as the chief constable; otherwise, there would have been a forty-eight-hour wait. Nothing in her past indicated she was vulnerable, so that would have been the standard waiting period.'

'Then what happened?' I said.

'I arrived just after midnight,' he replied. 'The search was already underway, but all the early signs were she'd voluntarily left the area or gone into the water.'

I sipped the Coke. 'To swim?'

He nodded. 'Yes, and that's why she abandoned the Walkman and headphones on the edge. It was a warm evening, and she'd run a few miles, so she went into the water to cool off. Then, she was caught in a strong current, and it swept her out to sea, and that's why we never found her body. A riptide took her.'

'What was she wearing?' I asked.

He didn't need to dredge his memory for the answer. 'According to her parents, it was a long-sleeved top and jogging pants.'

I shook my head. 'She wouldn't have gone swimming in those. She'd have taken them off, left them with the Walkman, and swam in her underwear.'

'I'm not convinced,' Tommy said. 'She had a strict conservative upbringing and was a member of a fundamentalist Christian church, so she likely wouldn't remove her clothes before swimming.'

He was right. 'Okay, that's one theory – she went for a dip and got dragged into the sea. But I don't think you believed that, did you, Ray?'

'No,' he said. 'Plenty of my colleagues did, but I had other ideas.'

'Such as?' I asked.

He grinned. 'I told you, aliens.' He raised his hand before Tommy complained again. 'Hear me out. The police received several reports of strange lights in the sky near the river that summer. There was a military base five miles away then - it's closed now - and there were always rumours of secret testing of planes around there. So what if she witnessed something she shouldn't have, and the authorities removed her?'

I remembered Bruce's story of what he'd seen near the river that summer. 'Yeah, that's a stretch. Even if it was true, why would they leave the Walkman and headphones?'

'Why would any perpetrator discard those?' Ray answered.

'Somebody could have carried her off,' Tommy said. 'Maybe more than one person? Where would they have taken her? Behind was the woods, which would have had dog walkers, joggers, etc. Ahead was a two-mile stretch of grass to a six-foot fence between the land and the power station. There were no signs of damage along the fence where anybody might have gotten through, and the route around the river only led back to the trees.'

I pictured the scene in my head. 'Was there any sign of struggle near the Walkman? Any indications in the grass that anyone else was there, no footprints or evidence of a vehicle?'

'Nothing at all,' Ray answered. 'If Emily didn't go into the water, it was as if she'd vanished into thin air.'

'Somebody forced her to leave,' I said. 'Using threats, or intimidation, or maybe a weapon, they marched her out of there.'

'Why abandon the Walkman and headphones?' I assumed it was a question he'd asked himself hundreds of times.

'To confuse the police,' I added. 'It was deliberate.'

'That's what I've always thought,' Ray mentioned.

Tommy nodded. 'If that's the case, there's only one way she could have been taken – through the construction site to the east of the river where they were building the funfair.'

It was the likeliest possibility. 'Unless they had a boat on the river.'

The server gave Ray his whisky, which he accepted with a huge smile. 'The construction for the funfair - people were always there, workers or security guards. There were no sightings of Emily from those we spoke to.'

'So we're back to square one,' I said.

'Not quite,' he replied. He reached down to his side and brought up a small plastic bag. 'I took photos of some of the documents we acquired during the investigation. If anybody had found out, I'd have lost my job, but it doesn't matter now.'

I peered at the bag. 'Why did you do it?'

'Things had a habit of going missing from the station back then, and I didn't want it to happen to these.' He glanced at me as he drank, but there was no need for an explanation about police corruption.

'So what's in there?' Tommy said.

Ray dug into the plastic container and removed a photo he handed me. 'That's from Emily's diary.'

I read it: 'I'll have to change my running route to avoid the construction site. That creepy man was there again, staring at me and grabbing his crotch.'

Tommy snatched it from me. 'This is new.'

Ray pulled out another picture and gave it to me: a list of six female names.

'What is this?'

'Before Emily vanished,' he said. 'Several women and girls came to the police about a bloke harassing and stalking them. However, they made no formal complaints. When my colleagues spoke to the man, he denied everything, and since it was his word against theirs, we didn't take it any further. And he worked at the construction site.'

Tommy puffed out his cheeks. 'Why didn't any of this reach the media during the initial investigation?'

Ray drank more of his beer. 'Because his father was a prominent businessman and local dignitary, a member of the Freemasons, Brian Conway, owner of Conway Construction, who just happened to be the company building the funfair near where Emily vanished. His son Greg was the one we received the complaints about.'

'Greg Conway. Where do I know that name from?' Tommy said.

'When Emily went missing, he was the lead singer in a local band who had some minor national success before it all fell apart for them.'

'Fell apart, how?' I asked.

'Who knows? Drink and drugs, probably. Then Greg Conway inherited the construction site when his father died and sold it, going into property development instead,'

Ray answered. 'Now he owns several major residential developments in the town, streets of houses and flats.'

The server carried our food over, and the smell of my curry was heavenly. I was about to dive into it when Tommy brought a photo up on his phone.

'Is this Greg Conway?'

Ray nodded. 'That's him.'

My hand trembled, and I had to put the fork down before I stuck it into my leg.

'Fuck!'

'What?' Tommy said.

I took several deep breaths before I could speak.

'That's the bastard whose dog attacked mine in the woods yesterday.'

Chapter 11

English Towns

'Y ou're familiar with Greg Conway?' Tommy asked. 'I don't know him. His dog bit the one I was looking after yesterday, and we had to go to the vet, for which he owes me the bill.' Then, a terrible thought struck me. 'You said he owns blocks of flats in the town.' Ray nodded. 'Do you know which ones?'

He ate a chicken breast as he spoke. 'No, but I assume there will be a list on his website. He does like to brag about his property portfolio.'

I grabbed my phone and found Conway's site. It took two minutes to discover what I wanted.

'Fucking fuck fuck!'

'What?' Tommy said.

'Conway owns the flat where I'm sleeping on the sofa.'

He shrugged. 'So? You've got enough money to move out now.'

'That doesn't help Ginger and Bruce if Conway punishes them for our run-in yesterday.'

'He can't just throw people out of their flats, Enola.'

I stared at Conway's ugly mug on the screen. 'The rich

and privileged can do whatever they want and get away with it, Tommy. You know that.' I turned to Ray. 'The police interviewed Conway after the women and girls complained about his behaviour?'

'Yes, my colleagues spoke to him, but his father provided an alibi for every occasion. There was also talk around the station that the alleged victims had targeted him because he was a singer in a band.'

Burning lava swept through me, turning my head into a volcano, and my blood became a firestorm. 'What you mean is you and the other coppers thought they were all lying because he was a bit of a pop star, right?'

The fire in my eyes and voice didn't affect him. 'No, not at all. I dare say some officers believed that, but I didn't.' He pointed at the carrier. 'You'll find photos of the files in that bag and a few other copies of interviews with people I thought were less than forthcoming during the investigation into Emily's disappearance.'

Tommy rubbed at his chin. 'But the police never interviewed him about Emily?'

Ray nodded. 'We didn't, no. I tried, but the higher-ups refused. His old man undoubtedly had a few words and dodgy handshakes with prominent people.'

Greg Conway. I had a name for the fucker, and he was at the top of my list for more than one reason. 'Do you remember his band?'

He grinned. 'Of course not. Mozart and Bach are what I listen to, not that rock rubbish. I'm sure he'll mention it on his website somewhere.'

'Who else did you think lied to you about Emily?'

He stuffed a large potato in his mouth, and gravy dribbled over his chin. 'Emily's parents and her younger sister;

people she knew at the Church of the Resurrection, and some of her work colleagues.'

'That was at the music shop?' Tommy said.

'Yes,' Ray replied. 'That summer, she'd been home from university for a month and was back working where she did every vacation from her studies, at Mack's Musical Instruments on the high street. Of course, it's long gone, but I dare say some of the staff are still around. Most of them were quite young, from what I can remember, apart from Mack, who died tragically two years after Emily vanished.'

'Why tragic?'

'Several heavy boxes fell on him in the back room of the shop – crushed his skull.'

Tommy documented it all. 'An accident?'

'That's what my colleagues believed,' Ray said.

'And you?' I asked.

He narrowed his piggish eyes. 'To be honest, I never gave it much thought. How remiss of me. You think there could be a connection to Emily's disappearance?'

I wrote a question mark next to Mack's name in my notebook. 'You mentioned you believed some of her colleagues might have lied. Which ones and what about?'

Ray reached into the plastic bag and pulled out several photos. He made a big space on the table and placed the pictures side by side.

'Their names are on the back, but the blonde Madonna lookalike is Gwen Casey. She was the total opposite of Emily, a young woman who would break every commandment in the *Bible* if she could. You can imagine how that might cause some friction between them at work. Gwen claimed she and Emily were good friends, but I wasn't sure. They seemed complete opposites to me. The dark-haired older woman in the photo is Denise Rodgers, the shop's assistant manager. She claimed on the morning Emily vanished, Emily argued with Gwen in the shop in front of customers. Apparently, it got quite heated, with a lot of flailing arms and pointed fingers. Gwen said it was about nothing, some silly disagreement over music, but Mrs Rodgers thought it was more than that. And I formed the impression Gwen never told me the truth.'

I peered deep into his eyes. 'Did you think any of them, her work colleagues, might be involved in Emily's disappearance?'

He shrugged, and dandruff drifted off his shoulders. 'It didn't seem likely at the time. Our two main lines of investigation were that she fell into the river or somebody abducted her. And if it were an abduction, it would probably have been one or more men, not a woman. But I know all the women in that shop lied to me for some reason.'

Tommy scribbled away in his book. 'This is all excellent stuff, Ray. We're meeting the parents this afternoon. What can you tell us about them?'

'Robert and Elizabeth? They were long-time members of the church before their daughters were born. Robert worked for the Royal Mail, though I'm unsure if he still does. He's very strict in his attitude, quite Victorian. And he is forthright in expressing his opinions, especially about things he disagrees with. However, when speaking to him about Emily, he comes across as a father who knows little about his children. Outside of making sure they attended church and followed their religious beliefs, I don't think he paid much attention to his daughters as long as they never went against his wishes. Elizabeth was different – she was the person I believed was hiding something about Emily. She was always evasive in her answers, and anytime I believed I might get somewhere with her, Robert would drag her away under some pretence. You should separate them if possible, though it will be hard, as Robert is very possessive, and speak to her alone if you can. Ask her why Emily was out jogging so late?'

'Late?' I said

'Yes. Apart from mentioning the man at the construction site, Emily's diaries contained little of any use. They were mainly about the church, but she mentioned her running routine, usually in the morning before work or between four and five in the early evening. So, for her to be out jogging around eight at night was unusual. When I asked the parents about it, they clamped up, and I knew there was something they weren't telling me.'

Tommy's eyes sparkled. 'What about the people at the Church of the Resurrection?'

Ray laughed. 'Oh, I'm sure they were all keeping things about Emily from the police, but it was impossible to get anything from them. Their dedication to God was unwavering. Most of them would have put their Lord before good old British law.' He pointed to the list of names he'd given me earlier. 'But some have left the church now, either voluntarily or forced, and you might have more luck with them than we did.'

I glanced at my notebook, surprised at how many pages of notes I'd made, and I guessed Tommy's was the same. It meant we had a lot to work with, and even though I had doubts when sitting in the café, I was intrigued about where we would go next. I knew it was likely impossible to discover what happened to a woman who vanished twenty-five years ago, but I was looking forward to learning more about Emily Jones.

And at the back of my mind was an image of me punishing Greg Conway.

Chapter 12

Let Me Introduce You To The Family

It was a short drive to Robert and Elizabeth Jones's house, with the bag of documents in the back seat. Tommy was more excited than a kid in a sweet shop, and I guessed he was pleased with how the encounter with Ray had gone. And that meant he must have been happy with my contribution to his project. Perhaps I should have demanded more money.

'Shouldn't I wait in the car?' I asked. 'Since I'm attending a church meeting later, we don't want the parents telling the other members who I am.'

'It's okay,' Tommy replied. 'When I spoke to them on the phone, Robert mentioned they no longer attend the congregation because of Elizabeth's ill health.'

'What's wrong with her?'

'He didn't say, and I didn't ask. I guess we'll find out once we meet them.'

It was a two-story modern-style building with white siding and black shutters framing the windows. A covered porch extended across the front, with brick steps leading up to a dark door. Large glass panels on either side of the door allowed natural light into the home. Flowerbeds with bright blooms lined the entrance of the house underneath the windows.

Tommy knocked on the door. When it opened, a tired-looking Robert Jones invited us in, and we followed him into the living room. The house's interior was neat and tidy, but the decor hadn't been updated in years. The furniture was old-fashioned, and family photos were displayed on every surface, various scenes of their three daughters. I expected to see a shrine to Emily mounted above an ornamental fireplace, surrounded by candles and verses from the *Bible*, but I was disappointed. The air was heavy with the scent of lavender. Elizabeth Jones was near the window in a wheelchair, her long white hair down to her ankles like Rapunzel.

Robert wheeled his wife close to the sofa, and he sat while Tommy and I settled opposite them in armchairs. I sensed apprehension as I looked at them, knowing we were about to ask about their daughter's disappearance. Neither of them had spoken since we arrived. I gazed at Elizabeth's hair, thinking of all the times somebody had asked me about the murder of my parents and of how I always felt about those questions. I hated them and the intrusion, yet I was there doing the same to those poor people. I added hypocritical to unethical to my list of qualities.

'Is it okay to film this?' Tommy said.

Robert Jones nodded. 'This is for a documentary?'

Tommy opened his backpack and removed a portable tripod for his phone. He set it up as he spoke. 'Yes, Mr Jones. Enola and I hope that bringing Emily's disappearance back into the public eye will generate enough interest for new information to arise and help answer the question about what happened to her.'

I gazed into Elizabeth Jones's unmoving eyes. 'Mainly, we want to get a picture of Emily from those who loved her and knew her best. The world needs to understand what your daughter was like, Mr Jones.'

Tommy focused the camera on them and started recording.

Robert Jones held his wife's hand. 'Growing up, Emily was a shy but talented child with a passion for music. She learned to play the piano at a young age and often spent hours practising. We encouraged her musical talents, but we always reminded her that her ultimate goal should be to serve God. So, most of her time outside of school was with the church, apart from when she got a part-time job at the local music shop. I wasn't happy about it, but she promised it wouldn't interfere with her duties, and to her credit, it didn't.'

'What did Emily do in the church?' I asked.

He started to reply, but his wife stopped him with her pale, withered hand on his arm.

Elizabeth's lips trembled. 'Emily loved her missionary work, getting out in the community and helping people. She even continued with it in Sheffield.'

'Yes,' Robert added. 'In 1995, Emily accepted an offer into the music program at Sheffield University, where she excelled in her studies. She was well-liked by her classmates and dreamed of becoming a teacher after graduation.' His face darkened. 'But during those years at university, she began questioning some of the church's teachings. She explored unusual religious and philosophical ideas, read books we disapproved of, and attended campus lectures that challenged her beliefs. As a result, she was different every time she returned home, and I believe that's where her troubles started.'

'Troubles?' I asked.

Robert sighed. 'Mixing with the wrong crowd, indulging in activities against our beliefs. Those things followed her here and led to her disappearance. I told the police this, but they dismissed it as the ramblings of distraught parents.'

I wrote in my notebook. 'Do you believe somebody Emily might have met in Sheffield was responsible for what happened to her?'

'They must have,' Robert Jones answered. 'It was only when she moved there that everything went wrong in her life.'

'Losing Emily devastated the whole family,' Elizabeth added. 'None of us have gotten over it, especially her sisters, who both looked up to her.'

'How do you feel the police handled the investigation?' Tommy asked.

Robert Jones's expression turned darker. 'They mishandled it from the start, saying she'd gone swimming, with the current dragging her into the sea. Emily was a strong swimmer, but she'd never swim in that filthy river. It was a ridiculous idea.' Thick shadows formed around his eyes. 'That whole place, the woods, and the water were filthy and dirty. None of my girls would remove their clothes to enter such filth. None of them.'

Elizabeth took over, her voice shaking. 'The media hounded us for years after she vanished. They accused us of hiding something or not cooperating with the police. But we were just as lost and confused as anyone else. We wanted nothing more than to find our daughter and bring her home. We still do.' She gazed into my eyes like a magnet drawing me into her. 'Robert didn't want to do this, to speak to you, resurrecting all the bad memories, but those things never leave me, Ms Gray. We're doing this hoping you will finally force this town to reveal its terrible secrets.'

Robert's voice trembled. 'Some people here know more than they're saying.'

As they spoke, a knot formed in my stomach. The pain and grief they felt were palpable, and I couldn't imagine what it must be like to lose a child in such a way. I'd lost my parents and watched it happen, but I wondered if what happened to them was worse.

Tommy questioned if they had any theories about what might have occurred with Emily, and they shook their heads. 'We've spent countless hours going over every detail of that day,' Robert said. 'But we just don't know.'

'What about your other daughters?' I asked. 'Samantha and Jane. Did they have any inkling of what might have happened?'

'They couldn't,' Robert replied. 'Samantha was in Australia, and Jane was only eleven.'

Tommy nodded. 'You mentioned the possibility of arranging a video chat with them.'

Jones shook his head. 'I'm afraid not. I asked, but they wanted to put everything behind them and not dredge up the past anymore. All it brings them is pain. Samantha blames herself for not being here, and Jane still has night-mares about the last time she saw Emily.'

'We understand,' I said. 'Is it possible to look at Emily's room or her things?'

Robert hesitated. 'Well, I don't suppose it could do any harm.'

I poked Tommy in the leg, and he stood. 'That's great, Mr Jones. Thank you.'

He took the tripod and camera with him. They left, and I smiled at Elizabeth. 'How are you, Mrs Jones?'

Her trembling fingers gripped mine. 'I should have stopped him that night.'

'The night Emily vanished?'

'Yes. Robert hated her going to university, so he blamed her time there for what happened, but that was nonsense. We don't know what happened to Emily, do we?'

'Emily didn't usually go running at night, did she, Elizabeth? So why did she venture out that night? Did something happen here?'

Her voice was barely a whisper. 'He ruined her ambitions. I told him not to, but he couldn't help himself.'

'What did he do, Elizabeth? How did he ruin her ambitions?'

Tommy and Mr Jones returned before she could reply.

'It's time I got Elizabeth to bed,' Robert said. 'I'll see you out.'

She squeezed my hand as I stood. We thanked them for their help and promised to do everything we could to solve the mystery of Emily's disappearance. However, as we left, I could only feel the weight of Elizabeth's pain on my shoulders.

And I wondered what it was she hadn't told me.

Chapter 13

Don't Bring Harry

Tommy replaced the tripod in his backpack and put it in the car near the bag of documents we got from Ray Crawford.

'Any luck upstairs?' I said.

He shook his head. 'I took some video, but nothing was in the room to indicate what happened to her. It doesn't look like a typical young woman's bedroom now. They must have changed it since the disappearance.'

I laughed at him. 'How familiar are you with a typical young woman's bedroom, Tommy? And what's a typical young woman, anyway?'

His cheeks turned red, and he pulled at his collar. 'All I meant was I thought they would have left it unchanged, and there would be more of her things in there, like posters on the walls or her CDs and books.'

'Do you know what she liked? Was it ever mentioned in the media what CD the police found at the river?'

'It was a Manic Street Preachers album, *This Is My Truth Tell Me Yours*. She was a big fan and had seen them play live in Manchester the year before she vanished. Music and books were her main interests. Emily loved reading, mainly Terry Pratchett and Alice Hoffman.'

I pictured Emily at a gig, letting her hair down and throwing off years of indoctrination. 'You think she listened to rock music and read fantasy novels in that house with her father?'

He shook his head. 'I assume she fell into that world when she attended university.'

'Where did you learn these things about her?'

'It's all online, Enola.'

'Okay. What did you speak to the old man about upstairs?'

'I asked Robert about Emily's diaries, but he said he didn't know where they went after the police returned them.'

'Did you believe him?'

He shrugged. 'It's hard to tell with the devout. They're so used to believing in things they can't see that I find it difficult to determine if they're lying or not. So, what about Elizabeth?'

'She implied something happened that evening between daughter and father, which sent Emily out of the house for a run, but she didn't give me any details.'

'Okay,' he said. 'We can return to that since I need to convince the sisters to talk to us.' He smiled. 'But it's been a productive first day. Do you want a lift back to the flat?'

'Cheers, yeah. Where are you staying?'

'I have a motorhome near the park. It has my travelling video editing suite waiting for today's clips.'

'Isn't this your car?'

He shook his head. 'No, it's a hire. I go everywhere in the motorhome.'

We got into the car, and he drove off. 'What are tomorrow's plans, Tommy?'

'I'm visiting Sheffield, so why don't you look through the stuff Ray gave us? He said the names of former Church of the Resurrection members were in the bag. Perhaps you can discover if they're still here and will speak to us.'

'Sure, no problem. What's in Sheffield?'

'Hopefully, some of Emily's university colleagues will go on camera. I've contacted two through email. I think they're wavering a bit, so I hope them seeing me will help.'

'Okay. What do we do about Conway?'

Tommy rubbed at the dimple in his chin. 'For now, nothing, but if we could speak to the women who complained about him, it would open up a new investigation avenue.'

I knew what he meant. 'You mean finally having a potential suspect?'

'Yes. It would be a significant breakthrough, don't you think?'

'Sure, but I'm amazed his name hasn't come up before in the last twenty-five years.'

Tommy laughed. 'You're surprised the police or people in power might cover something up?'

'I guess not when you put it like that.'

He went to pat my arm, but then reconsidered. 'You did good today, Enola. Better than good, considering you got in with the church even before we met, and we never would have got that information and those files from Ray without you. Well done.'

'No problem. I'll keep you updated tomorrow.'

He dropped me off and then rushed away to get to his editing suite. I watched him go, still unsure if I trusted him. Then I thought of the money in my bank and pushed all my doubts into the shadows as I climbed the stairs and entered the flat. The place was empty, and I assumed Ginger and Bruce were out walking Kronos.

And that made me think of Greg Conway.

When I'd lived next door, the landlord was a bloke called Simon Kirby. He was the one who kicked me out when I lost my job and I couldn't pay the rent. Or at least he got his solicitor to send me the eviction notice. Had he sold the properties to Conway, or had Conway always owned them?

I took the plastic bag to the table and dumped it there while I fed Dirty Harry. Poor Harry. When I had my own place, I let him out to wander as long as I monitored him, but that was impossible when I was sharing with two people and a dog. I wasn't worried Kronos might eat him – it was the other way around.

I gave Harry food while pondering what I wanted to do with Conway. His behaviour in our brief encounter was that of a fuckwit, but could he have been involved in Emily's disappearance? I didn't know him well enough to decide one way or another. Crawford said six women and girls complained to the police about him but only informally; there would be no record of them. This was twenty-five years ago, and in my experience, blokes who harassed females only stopped when they were in prison or dead. Therefore, if he were doing it then, he'd likely have kept doing it since. Perhaps I could find something connected to his time in that band.

I grabbed the bag and emptied the contents over the table. Crawford was right – it was all photos, pictures he'd taken of documents from the Emily Jones investigation. So, was it legal for me to have them there? Did I care?

No, I didn't.

I left them and headed to the kitchen, my stomach rumbling to remind me I hadn't eaten since the pub. I opened the fridge, finding it lacking any remotely edible food. Still, I was flush with cash and could treat us all to a takeaway.

My guts grumbled again as I went to the living room and got my phone to text Bruce and Ginger to see if they wanted anything.

That's when I heard the scream from Ginger's bedroom.

I ran to the door and burst through, seeing her writhing on the bed.

Completely naked.

Astride a naked man.

Detective Inspector Jack Parker.

'Fuck!'

My legs didn't move, frozen like tree trunks in the Antarctic. Ginger twisted her head enough for me to see Parker gurning, his eyes bulging like a psychotic frog. I'd seen plenty of terrible things in my life, and this was added to those memories that would last forever.

She screamed again, reaching for the bedsheet, but missing. Her fingers found thin air, grasping nothing, falling off Parker, and crashing into the carpet. I made a hasty retreat from the room as she swore at me.

I closed the bedroom door as Bruce entered the flat.

'I wouldn't go in there if I were you,' he said.

My legs shook as I sank onto the sofa. 'Now you tell me.'

Kronos jumped on me, his mouth open and slavering as I tried to remove the picture of Parker's mug from my head.

Bruce threw the dog lead on the table. 'How did it pan out with Tommy?'

I peered at Ginger's door, knowing there was nowhere

to hide. It was just another reminder that I needed my own place. 'Fine. It seems you told him everything about me.'

He went to the kitchen and came back with a beer.

Then Ginger stormed out of her bedroom with a face like thunder, and I wanted a drink for the first time in five years.

Chapter 14

Lies And Deception

'What the fuck, Enola? Don't you knock?'

I dragged Kronos in front of me as a shield. 'I heard a woman screaming.'

Bruce laughed, but Ginger's scowl grew large enough to cover her face.

'Sometimes,' Bruce said, 'you sound as if you're dying, you know, when....'

Jack Parker stepped out of the bedroom, fully dressed. 'Is anybody else hungry?'

I welcomed the opportunity to change the subject. 'I was about to order a takeaway when,' I glanced at Ginger, 'Bruce returned.'

He looked at his phone. 'Indian or Pizza?'

She stomped into the kitchen, opening the fridge with such a thud I thought the door might have fallen off. She came back with two beers and handed one to Parker. He took the seat opposite me.

'How did it go with Ray?'

I tried not to look at his face, remembering what it

looked like in the bedroom. 'He gave us a lot of useful information.'

Ginger glugged half of her beer. 'I remember Emily's disappearance, how my parents freaked out and stopped my mates and me from playing in the woods or near the river.'

Bruce nodded. 'Yeah, my mum and dad were the same, though it didn't stop me.'

Parker laughed. 'That's because you were looking for UFOs.'

Bruce scowled at Ginger. 'You told him that?'

She shot him a fake smile. 'There are no secrets around here. You know that?'

My stomach stopped grumbling, and I lost my appetite. 'Actually, Bruce was right about those peculiar illuminations near the river.'

'What?' he asked.

'Ray Crawford said several people reported seeing unusual lights over the river that summer.'

He shook his head. 'Well, well.'

I laughed. 'Don't get carried away. Apparently, a military base was nearby then, and Crawford reckoned the illuminations were probably some top secret plane or drone.'

'Ha!' Ginger slammed her empty beer bottle on the table. 'Fucking aliens!'

Her anger could only have been because of my part in her coitus interruptus.

'Did my uncle give you anything useful, Enola?'

I glanced at the photos. Should I tell him about them? Maybe. But there was something more important to talk about first.

'Do you know who owns this flat and the building, Bruce?'

He thought about it as Ginger went to the kitchen and returned with more beers.

'Are we ordering food?' she said.

He was still thinking about my question. 'All these flats and the ones opposite changed hands a few months ago. We received a letter about the new ownership, but I paid little attention to it once they confirmed they weren't increasing the rent. Why?'

'Well, the owner's name came up in our conversation with Ray Crawford.'

'How?' Parker asked.

I revealed the harassment claims made to the police, but I didn't mention Conway.

'Fucking hell,' Ginger remarked. 'Shouldn't the coppers have put this bloke at the top of their suspect list for Emily's disappearance?'

'We would if it happened now,' Parker replied.

'Whose name was it?' Bruce asked.

'Greg Conway,' I replied. 'The owner of these flats and the dickhead whose dog attacked Kronos.'

Ginger spat beer over her leg. 'Motherfucker.'

'Tell me what Ray said about him,' Parker asked.

I went to the pile of photos and found the one from Emily's diary where she mentioned the worker at the construction site creeping her out. I gave it to Bruce, who read it and passed it to the others.

'Conway Construction built the funfair, and Greg Conway worked there?' Bruce said. 'And you think he was staring at Emily as she jogged by?'

'I don't know, but Crawford thought it was him, and once you connect that to the complaints made to the police about Conway, it's easy to put two and two together.'

'And they never interviewed him about Emily's disappearance?'

'That's what Ray implied. He also said Greg Conway was the lead singer of a popular local band at the time. Do you know anything about that?'

'What were they called?' Bruce asked.

'Ray didn't know.'

Parker went to the table, studying the images. 'My uncle gave you all these?'

'Yes,' I replied.

'He broke police procedure,' he said.

I shrugged. 'That was twenty-five years ago.'

He grabbed a bunch of photos and sat near Ginger. She continued to scowl.

Parker looked at me. 'What will you do with these, Enola?'

'Sort through them, see if anything jumps out, maybe speak to those who complained to the police about Conway.'

'Why?' Ginger said. 'So you can continue their harassment twenty-five years after Conway did?'

The tension simmering out of her had turned volcanic. There was a fire in her eyes, but I found it difficult to believe it was because I barged into the room when she was shagging the inspector. I'd seen her do worse things than that before. No, there had to be something more to her ire.

Parker answered the question before I could. 'You need to keep quiet about these documents, Enola. You must tell Bell he can't mention them in his documentary.'

'Why?' I said. 'Is it to protect Conway or your uncle?'

He dropped the photos into the pile. 'I'll check the records in the original investigation to see if Conway's name is in there, but I don't want you or Bell going off half-cocked while I do that. If there's a case to be made against him, we have to do it properly.'

'We?' I said.

Parker sighed. 'I've heard things about the Conway family, how their business became successful and what they did to achieve that. I'm also aware of other rumours about Greg Conway and his behaviour towards women, enough for me to believe he might have had something to do with Emily Jones's disappearance. But I stress the word *might*.'

'What?' Ginger said. 'You've known about this fucker's harassment and maybe worse against women and girls, and you've fucking done nothing about it?'

'It's not like that,' Parker replied. 'The police can't act on rumours and hearsay. We need hard evidence or....'

She stormed into her bedroom before he could finish, slamming the door behind her. We sat there in silence as Kronos stared at me through watery eyes. I grabbed my bag from near the sofa and headed to the bathroom to get changed.

'I'm going for a run,' I said, leaving Bruce and Parker to it.

Maybe when I got back, everybody would have calmed down.

Especially Ginger.

Chapter 15

Northwinds

Ginger's unhappy expression was in my head as I left the flat. The sun was setting, casting a warm golden glow over everything. I started running on the pavement, passing people out for a stroll or walking their dogs. There were kids on skateboards, with lycra-clad cyclists, and goth girls laughing outside a pizza shop. A bunch of smokers poisoned my air as I jogged past the Raven Club, with a whiff of stale beer and cold sweat drifting over me.

As I entered the shabbier part of town, the tidy homes and manicured gardens gave way to run-down houses with peeling paint and overgrown yards. Broken pavement and potholes made running tricky as I dodged cracks and debris. The people looked weary, with rigid lines on their faces.

I passed a boarded-up gas station covered in graffiti. An old mechanic shop sat vacant, with a faded sign and oil stains covering the ground. The library had iron bars on its windows, while the grocery had seen better days, with just a few shrivelled fruits in the produce section.

As the sun dipped lower, darkness crept over the town.

Most streetlights were busted or flickering, leaving large swaths of sidewalk in shadow. A couple of stray dogs pawed through overflowing bins. The only open business was a seedy-looking bar with a neon sign buzzing in the window. Music drifted out as a few grizzled patrons sat drinking on the patio.

It wasn't long before I reached the woods. A cool breeze kissed my face, rustling my hair. The trees towered above me, their leaves whispering in the wind. Birds were chirping in the distance, and the occasional squirrel was scurrying through the underbrush. The air became cooler as I entered, and the light faded. The green foliage created a natural canopy overhead, casting dappled shadows on the ground.

I jogged past a couple walking and a kid on a bike, heading towards the river, where Emily Jones vanished. Before I got there, I approached the tree where I discovered a body last year. The memory of the man lingered with me, next to the images of my murdered parents and other memories of violence and death that never left me.

Then something else sprang into my mind, of an image I'd seen in the woods before the confrontation with Conway. I went to the tree, pulling back the bushes to see if it was still there, and it was: the unmistakable symbol of the five-pointed star of a pentagram. I thought it was a satanic sign, but my online research had proved differently. According to the internet, modern occultists employed the pentagram as a protective charm against evil forces. The inverted pentagram was the symbol used for Satanism, sometimes depicted with the goat's head of Baphomet within it, which originated from the Church of Satan.

I touched the carving, feeling the bark nip against my skin. The mark was recent and had nothing to do with Emily's vanishing twenty-five years ago.

Or did it? Perhaps somebody had carved it into the wood with the forthcoming anniversary as a warning. I'd forgotten to ask Parker about it and the possibility that kids were messing about in the woods with Satanism. During my teenage years, which now seemed like a distant memory, kids, including me, were always experimenting with Ouija boards and spiritual shit. In my first children's home, we even had a girl who claimed she was possessed, but I guessed that was only an excuse for everything she broke.

I set off again, relishing the exertion coursing through my legs and how my muscles pulsated. After my parents died, I learned early on that increasing my stamina and running speed would be beneficial in my new life of abandoned children and predatory adults. And I wasn't wrong.

As I ran towards the river, I reached a clearing by the reeds. The river glistened in the last light of the day, rippling gently against the rocks. The sound of the water was soothing, and I stopped to take it in. Then I checked the link on my mobile to the photos of Emily's discarded CD Walkman and headphones to get the correct position. I held the phone up to align myself with where the police had taken the pictures. The vegetation had grown taller, but nothing much else had changed. I rotated to my left, seeing the abandoned funfair in the distance, imagining what Emily would have seen when it was a construction site. And how she would have reacted to the man – presumably Greg Conway – leering and jeering at her.

Then I turned back to the river, peering across the edge alongside the woods. Overgrown trees and bushes presented an impossible path to the water. Yet, it might have been less thick there when Emily disappeared. So, if she'd gone into the river, somebody could have witnessed it from the woodland in that two-mile stretch until it entered the sea. I had to ask Tommy if there were photos from the time for us to check.

I strained my neck and gazed across the river, staring so hard my head hurt. I tried to imagine every perceivable possibility of what might have happened to Emily. I had to admit that her getting into the water, for whatever reason, and then the current dragging her into the sea seemed the likeliest explanation for her disappearance.

Was it that simple? Had the police been right all along?

And if it was, did it invalidate what Tommy and I were doing?

No, it didn't. There was still a story to tell, and it was Emily's, one that was created around her desire to break away from a controlling father and live a modern life without being constrained by her faith. We needed to speak to those who knew her the most, so it was good that Tommy was going to Sheffield to see her university friends. I needed to interview former members of the Church of the Resurrection. It was a shame her sisters had refused to talk to us, but we couldn't do anything about that.

The heat made me think of Australia, and I wiped the sweat from my forehead. Some of it slipped into my eyes, and my vision blurred a little, which must have been why I saw the flickering rainbow lights hovering above the lake.

Bruce and Becky's UFOs?

The sound of a thousand tiny buzzing insects invaded my head as the heat bore down on me. My throat shrivelled up, and I'd brought no water. Such a rookie mistake.

Then, a loud howl assaulted my ears. Only as the fizzing illuminations vanished did I realise the noise was a barking dog approaching.

I turned just in time to see the Rottweiler leaping at me.

Chapter 16

Death And Night And Blood

I lifted my arm as the hound leapt at me, its head smashing into me and sending us both over. We landed in the reeds, the water sinking into my clothes as the headphones tumbled off my ears with Johnny Rotten in mid-rant.

The Rottweiler snapped at me, its teeth dripping with hate and saliva as I stuck my elbow into its mouth. It bit down on my bone, and I screamed. Then, my reflexes erupted, and I threw the dog off me, sending it howling into the river. It hit the water with a massive splash as agony shot through my arm. The mutt scrambled out quicker than I could move, and I expected it to go for my throat.

Instead, it stood on the riverbank, fur matted, sides heaving, watching me warily. In its eyes, I now saw not hatred but fear.

Greg Conway ran towards us, yelling. He grabbed the dog's leash and pulled it back before it could lunge at me again. I stumbled backwards, gasping for air and clutching my bleeding arm. He ignored me and spoke to the mutt.

'Behave, Caesar.'

If I'd had the strength to strangle him, I would have, but all I could think about was the pain and fear consuming me. My head buzzed and my eyes watered. I thought I saw those multi-coloured lights floating over the river again, but I knew it was only shock. As Conway pulled the dog away, I realised he was sweating, and his gaze bore into me.

I grabbed my elbow, with blood smearing onto my fingers. 'You told that fucker to attack me.'

The hound tried to pounce again, chomping at the leash.

'Don't be stupid,' Conway said. 'You did something for him to behave like that.'

I bit my bottom lip. 'You're fucking mad. The mutt ran over two hundred yards to get to me. It must have the best eyesight in the animal kingdom to see where I was.'

'Well, it was an accident. So there's no need to cry about it.'

I shoved my hand towards his face, ensuring I kept my distance from the dog. My elbow dripped blood into the reeds, turning the green into red.

'Your mongrel bit my fucking arm, you cock-sucking moron.'

He shrugged. 'You'll live.' He still hadn't apologised as he walked away.

I swallowed the blood on my lips. 'I know who you are.'

He stopped and twisted his head towards me like the demon child from *The Exorcist*.

'What?'

'I'll go straight to the police, Conway, and tell them how your psycho dog attacked me. Once I show them my wound, what do you think will happen to the mutt?'

It must have known I was talking about it as its eyes blazed like an erupting volcano. Maybe it hated me after all.

'You can't prove that Caesar bit you. It's just your word against mine.'

I smiled through the suffering. 'Of course, that's your signature defence, isn't it, Greg? You always deny it when a girl or a woman complains to the police about you. You've done that for over twenty-five years, haven't you?'

His face darkened. 'What are you rambling about?'

I tried to ignore the pain consuming my arm. 'Weren't you a singer back in the day? Shaking Stupid, is that what they called you? Or maybe it was the Trembling Twat.'

He grinned at me like a psychotic clown. 'The only one trembling here is you, girl.'

The laugh crawled over my lips. 'It must be all the excitement.'

Conway stepped closer, but I didn't move. 'Wait, is that it? Are you some fan groupie for the Biz Boyz?' He shook his head. 'Wasn't it before your time?'

I touched my stomach to stop my sides from splitting. 'The Biz Boyz? Fucking Christ, Greg. Who came up with that shitting name? You might as well have called yourself the Fucking Wankers.'

A chill breeze caressed my cheeks as he waved a finger at me. 'Oh fuck, you aren't, are you?'

My arm hung at my side. 'Aren't what, you moron? Make some fucking sense.'

He lifted his head and laughed, howling like a hyena as the moonlight settled on us. 'You're my kid, is that it? From one of those bints I shagged? Fuck me. Well, there's no chance of you getting any backdated child support, that's for sure.'

The shimmering bright lights returned, and I bent over to throw up. Invisible fingers squeezed my guts to turn them into mincemeat as I took several long, deep breaths. Then I wiped the vomit from my face and stared at him.

'I have the names of those you harassed and hurt. I also know you were here when Emily Jones vanished. Who did your father pay to keep your name from the media?'

Conway loosened his grip on the leash, so the Rottweiler inched nearer to me.

'Who the fuck are you, lady?'

'You're not denying any of it, then? You saw Emily that night.'

His eyes bulged to mirror the dog's. 'What are you talking about?'

The buzzing in my head increased to match the agony in my arm. I strode past him and reached for my head-phones, the movement sending pain through every inch of me. The music continued playing on my phone tucked into my jogging pants.

'That's my dog and me your hound has bitten. You owe me for the vet's bill, and now I'll have to visit the hospital to get a tetanus shot. I can sue you for this if I go to a lawyer.'

The Rottweiler's anger had dissipated, but Conway looked like his face was about to explode. 'Who said I was here the night Emily Jones disappeared?'

'You did with the look of guilt on your ugly mug.'

He laughed at me. 'So, you're just talking shit, then?'

I shook my head. 'Nope. I've got proof.' I was a good liar, even when in pain. 'And several women revealed what you did to them.'

'What women?'

'Have you forgotten them already, Greg? Or have there been so many it's difficult for you to remember them? I bet somebody like you probably kept trophies from your crimes.'

His expression told me he was close to letting the hound go so it could attack again. That's when I got my phone, turned the music off, and set the video recording.

'What are you doing?' he said.

'It's an online live stream.' I aimed it at him, the dog, and then at my elbow. Then I returned it to him and zoomed into his angry face. 'So, Mr Greg Conway, what do you say to reports you were working on the construction site only a few hundred yards from where Emily Jones was the night she vanished? What about the claims several women and girls complained to the police about your behaviour around the time of Emily's disappearance?'

If he could have strangled me and disposed of my body in the river, I'm sure he would have. Instead, he smiled and shook his head.

'You're crazy, lady.'

He pulled on the dog's lead and walked away. I fought the urge to faint but dropped to sit on my aching arse.

Then I waited for the mysterious lights to return.

Fucking UFOs.

Chapter 17

Hanging Around

I sat in the emergency room at the local hospital, my arm throbbing as if plugged into an electricity socket. It had been hours since I arrived, and it was full of people. Some were loud and drunk, while others seemed frail and tired. The fluorescent lights buzzed overhead, casting an unnatural pallor on everyone's faces. A mixed aroma of booze and sweat drifted over everybody, nearly blocking out the lingering smell of antiseptic.

Like everything else in this declining town, the A&E was understaffed and overcrowded. Many doctors had left for better hospitals in the city, while the remaining ones tried their best but were just putting plasters on gaping wounds. A gaunt woman coughed like an asthmatic pigeon into a tissue, then stared blankly at the bloody specks. The drunken man in the corner continued his loud, slurred rant about the failed policies of elected officials. The elderly woman clutched her purse as if expecting somebody to steal it at any moment.

I tried to relax, closing my eyes and taking deep breaths. They gave me painkillers when I arrived and cleaned the wound. Now I was waiting for a doctor to see me. And the longer I waited, the more my mind raced with worst-case scenarios. What if my arm was infected? What if I needed surgery? I tried to distract myself by reading a magazine, but the words blurred together on the page.

The smell of disinfectant hung heavy in the air, making me feel even queasier. I shifted in my seat, trying to find a more comfortable position, but it was useless. My arm was on fire, and my head throbbed.

I watched doctors and nurses rush past me, tending to other patients. They looked harried and exhausted, like they'd been working nonstop for days. I wondered how they kept going, dealing with all the pain and misery.

To ease my suffering, I sent Tommy a copy of the video I'd recorded of Conway and his mutt. He replied immediately.

My God, Enola. Are you okay?

I'm fine. I'm in A&E now. I'm just waiting for a doctor to look at the wound.

Christ, that's terrible. Do you want to take a few days off?

Did I? Fuck no. If anything, I was even more determined to discover if Conway was connected to Emily's disappearance.

No, I'll be fine in the morning. Is there something specific you'd like me to do?

As long as you're sure, then yes. I found a work address for Emily's colleague, Gwen Casey, at the music shop. Maybe you could talk to her about Emily.

He sent me the details for Casey's Dog Groomers, and I recognised the address.

No problem. I'll pop along in the morning. What time are you going to Sheffield?

Early, leaving before eight. I've got three interviews lined up – two former classmates of Emily's and her personal tutor. I might be late getting back, so perhaps we should meet on Wednesday morning to see where we're at. I'm sorry about your arm, but that video footage of Conway will be really useful.

I'm glad I could be of service.

He signed off with a laughing emoji as the painkillers kicked in, with a sense of euphoria sweeping through me. Or maybe that was the first stage of rabies.

After an eternity, a nurse called my name. She led me to a small exam room. Then, she asked me a few questions about what happened and how I felt when the doctor arrived. He examined my arm, poking and prodding as I winced in pain. He prescribed antibiotics to prevent infection and ordered an X-ray to check for bone damage.

'We should see if there's anything embedded in your wound, such as a tooth.'

He left me with that disturbing thought and went to another patient. The nurse took me to the X-ray station and got me to lie on a table, which was cold against my skin. The X-ray device was a tube containing a giant light bulb, and the radiographer aimed it at my elbow. They operated the machine from behind a screen, taking more than one image. It lasted only a few seconds before the nurse returned me to the waiting room.

She left me alone with my thoughts. The pain in my arm had subsided, but my head was still pounding. I wondered how long the X-ray results would take to come back and how much longer I'd have to wait. I thought about calling Ginger but decided not to since she'd been in such a strange mood.

As the minutes passed, I grew increasingly agitated. The noise in the waiting room got louder and more chaotic.

The fluorescent lights became brighter, and the antiseptic smell increased until it was like a blanket smothering my brain. I closed my eyes, trying to focus on my breathing to distract myself from the pain.

I was running by the river in my mind: the clean air, birds chirping, the old factory stacks fading into the distance. There were shimmering lights over the river, seemingly staring at me. They blinked in and out of existence as if sending me a message.

A sudden crash jolted me back to the harsh fluorescent lights of the hospital. Two drunks were now on their feet, yelling and shoving each other. The nurse hurried over, her tone sharp as she tried to separate them. Security arrived, escorting the men out the door. The remaining patients watched with dull expressions, too exhausted to react.

Then I heard a familiar voice.

'What happened to you, Enola?'

My eyes snapped open to see Detective Inspector Parker standing over me.

'I lost a fight with a dog. Why are you here, Jack?'

He nodded towards the uniformed officers behind him and the medics wheeling a young man into a room. 'There was a brawl outside the Raven, punks versus mods.'

My laugh hurt my arm. 'I thought they died out in the 1970s?'

Parker sat near me. 'Everything is resurrected eventually, Enola. Tell me about this dog.'

I did. 'Conway is a real piece of work.'

'Do you want to press charges?'

I shrugged. 'He was right about one thing – it's his word against mine.'

He pointed at the bandage around my wound. 'I could

get a forensic officer here to take photos of that, and then we could compare them to the teeth of Conway's dog.'

'You can do that?'

'Of course.'

I thought about it. 'What would happen to the mutt?'

'It's dangerous, so it would probably be put down.'

He was right; the Rottweiler was dangerous, but I didn't want to be responsible for its death. But what if it attacked somebody else in the future? What if it killed a child?

'I don't know, Jack.'

As much as I hated Conway, could I do that to his dog?

My arm ached again as I considered it.

Bruce

Chapter 18

How To Find True Love And Happiness In The Present Day

'While you think about the dog, I'll tell you what I discovered about Greg Conway in the police files.'

The flutter in my heart overrode the pain in my arm. 'Yeah?'

Parker shook his head. 'Sorry to disappoint you, Enola, but there's nothing on Conway on our system. I haven't had time to check the paperwork from 1998, but if Ray told you there were no official complaints about Conway, then I believe him.'

My excitement vanished, and the throbbing ache returned not only to my arm, but to my head as well. I reached into my pocket and removed the headphones. I plugged them into my mobile, found the video of Conway near the river, and then handed everything to Parker.

'Watch that.'

He did, more than once, before handing them back to me. 'Will you make an official complaint?'

I thought of the women and girls who weren't listened to twenty-five years ago, and who knows how many more since then? I understood I should report Conway and his mutt to the police. However, I was sorry for the dog. And I wasn't sure why I suddenly felt generous to the Rottweiler that had attacked Kronos and me.

My eyes drifted around the room, taking in the other patients. There was an older woman with a bandaged head sitting in a wheelchair, a young child with a cast on his arm crying, and a bloke with a bloodied face slumped in a chair. The constant beeping of machines, moans, and cries filled the air, making it feel like a war zone. An unseen enemy was advancing steadily, leaving casualties in its wake. The child's innocence shattered by a bad fall. The elderly lady, perhaps widowed or alone, concussed and confused. The bloodied man, unconscious but breathing, another victim of drunken street brawls outside shuttered bars. The nurses rushed between those in need, administering what aid they could. But they were outgunned and under supplied for this fight. The best they could offer was temporary relief - stop the bleeding, set the bones, patch the wounds. All the while knowing the cycle would continue.

I glanced down at my dog bite, now neatly wrapped, a minor injury compared to others. Conway's Rottweiler seemed to hate me, but I couldn't be the one to pronounce a death sentence on the animal.

A group of loud, drunk people stumbled into the room, arguing and shouting at each other. They were pushing and shoving, knocking over chairs and equipment. The nurses and security guards tried intervening, but it only worsened things. The noise and chaos escalated until a full-blown fight broke out, fists flying and curses bouncing off the walls.

I looked at Parker. 'Shouldn't you do something?'

He crossed his legs. 'The uniforms will sort it out.'

As he said that, four constables pulled the drunks apart,

wrestling one to the floor with his face all red and puffy as if somebody had inserted a balloon into his head. It would have seemed like watching a reality TV show if it hadn't been so dangerous.

The coppers got the hooligans out, but not before the thugs had caused considerable damage, with overturned chairs and medical equipment scattered on the floor. As the commotion died down, the room fell into an uneasy silence, the sudden burst of violence shaking patients and staff alike. I leaned back in my chair, trying to calm my racing heart. A nurse approached, looking frazzled and tired. She apologised for the disturbance and asked if we were okay. I nodded and thanked her, feeling relieved the fight was over.

'I'm surprised at you, Parker,' I said. 'I thought you were a man of action.'

'When did you stop calling me Jack?'

I shrugged. 'Probably around when you began dating Ginger.'

'I guess you noticed she was a bit upset at the flat.'

I laughed. 'A bit? Look, I'm sorry I stumbled on you two while you were enjoying yourselves, but it wasn't the first time I've barged in on her having sex.'

He raised his eyebrows. 'Is that so?'

I held up my hands. 'It was ages ago, Jack. You have nothing to worry about.'

'You're right, Enola. But that's not why she's upset. It's something else.'

I recognised the concern on his face. 'Oh fuck! Is she pregnant?'

His eyes bulged. 'What? No.'

'So what is it?'

Parker sighed as two of the uniformed officers returned to the emergency room.

'I'm quitting the police. I've got a month left, and that's it.'

'Wow, I'm shocked. I thought they'd have to drag you out in a coffin.'

'Yeah, it surprised me as well,' he ran his fingers through his dark hair, 'but fifteen years is enough. I need something less stressful, and these last few months with Ginger have shown me I can have a normal, happy life.'

'Good for you, Jack, good for you. I thought Ginger would be pleased about that, not sad.' Then I realised what it was. 'You're saying goodbye to this place as well?'

He nodded. 'I am. I've saved enough money to see some of the world before deciding what to do next.'

'Ginger must be gutted you're leaving.' Now I could understand why she was so upset earlier.

'I've asked her to come with me.'

My heart stopped for a second, and the clanging bells returned to bounce around inside my head. 'What?'

'I want her to travel with me, but I think she's conflicted. That's why her emotions are all out of whack.'

'What's there to be conflicted about? She's got the man of her dreams and the chance to get out of this place for some adventure. I'm surprised she hasn't already bitten your hand off.'

'I'm the man of her dreams?'

His grin made me laugh. 'Yeah, and she's the woman of yours. So admit it, Parker.'

He held up his hands. 'Hey, of course she is. And I've told her that repeatedly.'

'Would you leave without her?'

He sighed. 'I would. I need a complete break from this place, Enola.'

I didn't blame him, but I still couldn't see why Ginger

wouldn't jump at the chance to go with him. As I thought about that, the doctor returned with the X-ray results. Thankfully, my arm wasn't broken, and there weren't any foreign objects in the wound, but I'd need to wear a sling for a few days. After that, he prescribed some pain medication and told me to rest.

'Would you like a lift back?' Parker asked.

I nodded, and I left feeling exhausted and relieved. The cool night air was refreshing on my face as I walked out of the hospital and to his car.

'Do you want me to talk to Ginger?' I said.

He opened the door. 'Would you?'

I got into the passenger seat. 'Sure. I'll tell her she needs to go so I can have her room. That sofa is killing my back, and it'll be no good for me now with my arm in this sling.'

Parker grinned and drove away.

But Ginger was my best friend, so did I really want her to leave?

Even if it would make her happy?

Chapter 19

Duchess

I had an awkward night's sleep because of the sling and the painkillers wearing off. I popped more pills as soon as I woke, swinging my legs over the side to see Ginger staring at me.

'What happened to you?'

'Greg Conway's dog attacked me as I jogged near the river last night.'

Her eyes bulged. 'What the fuck? I hope you reported it to the police.'

'It's funny you should mention that as I bumped into Jack at the hospital, and he said the same. He told me a few other things as well.'

Her lips trembled as she spoke. 'Why was he there?'

My arm throbbed as I stood. 'Don't worry, Ginger – he was there as a copper, not a patient. He dropped me here after. I thought he'd come in to see you, but he has a lot of paperwork before he leaves.'

'So he told you?'

'He did. It seemed to have taken a great deal of weight

off his mind. Well, apart from one last thing that's bothering him.'

She sipped her coffee. 'What's that?'

'I think you know.'

She gripped the cup as if it was a comfort blanket. 'He asked me to go with him.'

'And what do you want?'

Ginger tilted her head back and peered at the cobwebs stuck to the ceiling, which reminded me that I had to feed Harry. I went for his food container as she contemplated the question. I dropped several worms into his tank as she replied.

'I should join him, but so many doubts are clinging to my brain. Perhaps I should get one of my friends to do me a tarot reading.'

She'd been into mysticism and psychic readings since the first day I met her but would never do a reading for herself. Apparently, it was a no-no in her profession.

'What are your doubts?'

Ginger put the cup on the table. 'Oh, you know, the usual. Am I too old to change my life? What if it doesn't work out between us? How will I survive without you, Bruce and Kronos?'

'Well, here are your answers to those – no, so what, we'll still be here when you get back. And I'll keep your bed warm for you.'

She smiled at me. 'You only want the room so you can let Harry crawl around in it.'

I held my good arm up. 'You found me out.'

'So you think I should go?'

'I can't tell you what to do. The decision has to be yours, but I'll say just weigh up the pros against the cons and then follow your heart. Now I need to get cleaned up.'

She pointed at my sling. 'Do you want me to wash your hair?'

I wasn't going to bother, but I suppose I needed to look my best for the dog groomer.

And I was glad she offered because I felt better after that and had a full breakfast. She even gave me a lift to the dog groomer. I told her the reason for my visit on the drive over.

'What will you ask her?'

'I'll see if she's willing to speak about Emily, especially regarding what happened between them in the shop the day Emily vanished.'

'What if she won't talk?'

'I'll convince her it's good advertising for her business.'

'Okay. Ring me if you need picking up. I've got a lot of thinking to do.'

I waved her away and peered into the window of the dog grooming salon – it would be just my luck to see Greg Conway and his beast there. I didn't make a formal complaint to the police about the hound, telling myself that once I convinced the world how much of a danger Conway was to women, he'd be separated from his dog soon enough. I didn't have any evidence against him, but my two brief interactions with him told me all I needed to know about what he was like.

Somebody had painted the shop an eye-popping yellow and added photos of famous people and their pooches to the display: Queen Elizabeth II and her corgis, Miley Cyrus and a pit bull, Lorraine Kelly and a Border terrier, and David Beckham with a Cocker Spaniel. None of the mutts resembled their owners, though the Cocker Spaniel looked like it had spent a wild night with one of the Spice Girls.

I pushed the door open, greeted by a cacophony of barking dogs; so many of them howled at me, I assumed they could smell the Rottweiler on my arm. Their owners reined them in as I glanced at the glass showcases highlighting the canine grooming products: hair gels, shampoos, little hats, and even pairs of designer sunglasses. I nearly fainted when I saw the prices, deciding that business must have been booming for Gwen Casey.

The waiting customers, all women who looked like they'd spent the morning being plucked and pampered, glared at me as I strode towards reception. A door was open next to the desk, where a red-faced young woman was scooping up dog shit from a fluffy carpet. The smell invaded my nose as I approached the receptionist.

She was Ginger's age, mid-thirties, with small green eyes that shone like emeralds and dark hair she'd back-combed into an inch of its life.

'Can I help you?'

'I'm looking for Gwen Casey.'

She glanced at my sling. 'Do you have an appointment?' She inched to the side to look behind me and see if I was hiding a dog. 'We're quite busy this morning.'

'No, it's a personal issue I need to speak to Ms Casey about.'

There was a camera just above her head, pointing at me.

'I'm sorry, but you'll still have to schedule an appointment.'

I avoided eye contact with the receptionist and stared straight into the lens. 'Tell her it's about Emily Jones.'

The dogs stopped barking, and the women quit chatting as if an invisible entity had sucked all the air from the room. I wondered if I should take a quick video of the place, thinking it would make a good curiosity shot for Tommy's documentary. However, before I could get my phone out, the door behind the receptionist opened, and a voice shouted: 'Show her in, Liz.'

And I went to meet the queen of the dog groomers.

Chapter 20

European Female

That's what it said on the wall above Gwen Casey's desk: the Queen of the Dog Groomers. She didn't look like a teenage Madonna anymore, with her former blonde hair now so white she could have been an extra from *Game of Thrones*, but for the fact she wore delicate pink glasses and a green pantsuit. A tiny pooch sat near her computer, and the room smelt of flea powder and expensive perfume. There were piles of hairs on the floor and a tub of soapy water in the corner.

'What's this about Emily?' Casey said.

I took the seat opposite her without an invitation and removed my camera.

'I'm part of a crew making a documentary about the twenty-fifth anniversary of the disappearance. Do you mind if I film this?' I saw the doubt in her face. 'It will be good advertising for your business.'

She slipped a vape from her purse and puffed on it, blowing banana smoke at me.

'Who's making this documentary?'

'Tommy Bell. Do you know him?'

Her eyes lit up behind those designer glasses. 'Hell, yeah. I love his podcasts. What's your name?'

I offered her my hand. 'Enola Gray. Is it okay to record an interview with you?'

She shook it. 'Sure, go ahead. Just make certain you spell my name right. The local newspaper wrote an article once and spelt Casey without the Y.' She rolled her eyes. 'What a bunch of morons.'

I set the video running, placed the phone against a coffee cup, and pointed it at her.

'Okay, why don't you tell me who you are and how you knew Emily?'

The mutt eyed the mobile suspiciously. 'What happened to your arm?' Casey said.

I thought it prudent to lie to her. 'I tripped and hurt it. It's fine. Nothing's broken, but doing some things is awkward.'

She took another drag on the vape. 'I bet it is. I'm Gwen Casey, owner and manager of One Pet Beyond Dog Grooming Service. What do you want to know about Emily Jones?'

'You were her friend twenty-five years ago, is that right?'

'Well, I wouldn't say we were friends.' She shifted in her seat. 'We worked together at Mack's Musical Instruments, which used to be a few hundred yards from here, but it's a mobile phone shop now. And not a very good one. I took my phone in to get it fixed, and I'm sure the bloke copied all my pictures. Some are from the beach, and I'm only wearing a tiny bikini.' She patted the dog on the head. 'Don't you think most blokes are right pervs?'

'Did you and Emily have that problem when you worked at the music shop? I've seen the photos of you two together, and I assume you got plenty of male attention.'

Casey grinned at the camera. 'Oh, we sure did – and not only from guys. But it was always an issue for Emily because of her parents and their church.' She took a deep breath. 'I wouldn't normally say this, but it doesn't matter now. Emily going to university changed her life for the better. She learnt more there than just stuff in books, if you know what I mean.'

'Did Emily have boyfriends at university?'

'I never saw them, but she told me she did. According to her, one of them got pretty obsessed with Emily and even followed her here after she finished her degree.'

'A stalker?'

'I don't know about that. I think she encouraged him.' She blew smoke towards the camera. 'Going to university must have been a real eye-opener for her after being stuck in that house all those years. So I don't blame her for getting a little wild.'

'Do you know his name?'

Casey shook her head. 'She kept it a secret from me, but her father knows.'

'Why do you say that?'

'Well, because he stormed into the shop one day, screaming at her for supposedly embarrassing the family with her "goings on" in Sheffield. I asked her about it afterwards, but she wouldn't tell me what it was about.'

'When was this?'

'About two days before she vanished.'

I checked the phone to ensure it was recording, happy to see the red button in action.

'Had you ever seen her dad behave like that before?'

'No, never, but she sometimes mentioned things about him that surprised me.'

'Like what?'

She hesitated for a brief second. 'This is only what she told me. I never saw it myself, but Emily said her dad would occasionally punish his daughters if they disobeyed him.'

'Punish them how?'

'She never said, but I remember seeing the youngest girl once, Jane, when the mother brought them to the shop, and she had a cracking black eye. She claimed her sister had walked into a door, but I knew a punch to the face when I saw it.'

'Was there anything else you thought strange or unusual about Emily's family?'

Casey laughed so hard she nearly spat the vape into the dog's head.

'Strange? The whole thing was strange, what with them believing everything in the Old Testament was the literal word of God and had to be obeyed. I saw her reading the *Bible* here sometimes. She told me God killed kittens.' Her eyes bulged. 'That's why Emily was so happy when she went to university and miserable when she had to return here.'

'Do you think she planned on leaving here before she disappeared?'

She shrugged. 'Probably, if she had any sense. But she never mentioned it to me.'

'Did she ever speak about men harassing her?'

'Apart from her father, you mean?' I nodded. 'Yeah, I overheard her talking to her little sister about staying away from the construction site where they built the funfair because some creepy bloke was working there. Of course, I thought she was just trying to scare the kid, but after what happened, who knows?'

'Did she mention this man's name?'

'Nah, not to me anyway.'

Something in her eyes told me she knew more. 'Did anybody else mention this man?'

She glanced at the phone again. 'I overheard a bunch of women in the toilets at the Raven once, saying there was a rumour going around about this construction worker that woman shouldn't take drinks off him because he, well, you know.'

'Spiked the drinks?'

'That was the gossip.'

'But you don't know his name?'

'Nope.' She managed to lie and keep a straight face. 'Are you done now because I have to clip a Rottweiler's toenails soon, and they're a devil to do? If I make it nervous, the mutt will shit all over the place.'

'Just one more thing, Gwen. Can you tell me what you and Emily were arguing about that afternoon before she vanished?'

She sucked so long and hard on the vape stick I thought she'd eat it.

'What do you mean?'

I gave her my best smile. 'The police have eyewitness reports of the argument between you and Emily in the shop before she disappeared. What was that about?'

Casey's eyes narrowed into pinpricks, and I assumed she'd kick me out, but I guess it was a matter she'd been aching to get off her chest for a long time.

'Devon Pope,' she said.

'Who?'

'He was the delivery guy for Mack's Musical Instruments. And my boyfriend.'

'And?'

'And I caught him in the warehouse delivering something he shouldn't to our dear sweet Emily one day, and I didn't like it one bit. That's what we argued about.'

'Emily was having an affair with this Devon Pope?'

Casey laughed and blew banana vape everywhere. 'It was hardly an affair. He said they'd shagged a few times, and that was it. But I guess he could have been lying.'

'Do you know where he is?'

'Sure. He runs that mobile phone shop I mentioned. Now, are we done?'

I thanked her and got my phone, my head buzzing with several possibilities.

'One last thing. The rumour about the creepy bloke from the construction site – was it Greg Conway?'

'The lead singer from the Biz Boyz?'

'That's him.'

She flashed brilliant white teeth at me. 'You said that, not me.'

Casey returned to her work, and I left her to it, the aroma of wet dog filling my head.

Then I exited the shop, and there was no pain in my arm anymore.

Parker

Chapter 21

Ships That Pass In The Night

I walked down the high street, my arm in a sling and my head throbbing from the painkillers wearing off. The sun blazed, and people bustled about, enjoying the summer day. The scent of freshly baked bread wafted from the bakery, and music from the buskers filled the air. I thought of what Gwen Casey had said, of Emily's hidden life the media hadn't picked up. The internet was in its infancy twenty-five years ago, and I wasn't sure if there was such a thing as social media, but it would be different today. Now, every tiny aspect of her existence would have been scrutinised and dissected, shoved through rumour mills and gossip columns a thousand times over until it was spat out the other side as something unrecognisable.

Alternatively, perhaps a grain of truth would be there somewhere of Emily, the dedicated daughter, sister, and church member, the hard-working student who brought joy to others. Or was it Emily the disappointment to her family, who disgraced her parents, went against her church's teachings and beliefs and had a secret sex life that included sleeping with her friend's boyfriend?

Possibly, she was a combination of all of those things.

Humans have a complex inner world - thoughts, emotions, dreams - that shape who we are. Perhaps Emily had struggled with personal demons the night she disappeared. Maybe she'd acted impulsively in the moment without considering the consequences. I'd told Tommy it was unlikely Emily would remove her clothes to swim in the river, but it was only an assumption based on what little I knew about her.

I entered the mobile phone shop to see a man in his forties talking to a customer. Behind him, a TV showed two men dressed as chickens fighting each other with giant inflatable cucumbers. Amongst the products, there were several framed photos of Devon Pope on the wall participating in various sports: football on a muddy pitch, rugby in front of a baying crowd, riding a mountain bike through the nearby woods, and numerous pictures of him swimming in the sea or rivers, including the local one, where Emily vanished.

Pope's hair was cut short and spiky, resembling a dead hedgehog on his head. His blood-red eyes and three-day-old stubble indicated a late-morning hangover. From the door, I could smell sweat mixed with the aroma of cheap after-shave. While he spoke to the customer, I got my phone and texted Sister Morgan at the Church of the Resurrection.

Hi, it's Enola Gray. When can I come over to meet the rest of your congregation? I'm struggling with a few things right now and could do with somebody to talk to.

It wasn't a complete lie. She replied immediately.

Hi Enola, how lovely to hear from you. There's a meeting tonight at seven – is that okay for you?

That's great. If you text me the address, I'll see you then.

She did, and I recognised the location near the park.

When I completed my task with Sister Morgan, I used my phone to film the premises, catching Pope's attention as he concluded his interaction with the customer, and they left.

'Can I help you?'

'Sure, if you're Devon Pope.'

His defences went up. 'Who's asking and why?'

'I'm Enola, working for the true crime podcaster Tommy Bell. This is for a documentary about Emily Jones on the twenty-fifth anniversary of her disappearance. I understand you were her boyfriend when she vanished.'

Pain shot through my arm, so I took a deep breath, trying to steady myself. The shop was gloomy, and the air was stale with the smell of old electronics. I heard the faint buzz of the few fluorescent lights overhead and the sound of cars passing outside. He looked me up and down like I was an out-of-date tin of beans.

'Who told you I was her boyfriend?'

'Are you denying it?'

He lunged for my phone, but I stepped to the side, my hip hitting a nearby surface and adding to the agony sweeping through me. I'd need to sit down soon before I fainted.

'You're not allowed to film here,' he said.

I leaned against the counter and peered through the open door into the back room, seeing a dog sleeping on the floor. A mutt I knew well.

'Were you in a relationship with Emily, Devon?'

'Why?' he demanded. 'What's it to you?'

'As I mentioned, we're trying to discover what happened to her. Don't you want to help with that?'

'I know nothing,' he said, his voice growing louder. 'And even if I did, why should I tell you? You're just some meddlesome stranger sticking your nose where it doesn't belong. You don't care about Emily or the town.' He pointed his finger at me as if it was about to go off. 'You're just another vulture, like all the others.'

Others? Were more people snooping around the mystery, or did he mean how the media descended upon the town twenty-five years ago?

'If you have any information that could help us, it's your duty to come forward.'

'Who says it's my duty?' he sneered. 'Maybe I need to forget about her and move on with my life.'

'You worked together at Mack's Musical Instruments, so you must have known her well.'

'So, that's where this is coming from? You spoke to that bitch, Gwen, didn't you?'

'She's still unhappy you cheated on her with Emily. Would you like to talk about it?'

'Fuck off before I call the police.'

I couldn't say if it was fear or sadness in his expression. 'This story is getting out with or without you, Devon. It would be better if you got your thoughts out there before people started assuming all sorts of things.'

Pope's eyes softened as he spoke, and the anger vanished from his face. 'We were young and in love, you know? She was always so kind and gentle, but also fiercely independent. I loved that about her. We spent so much time together, just talking and exploring the countryside. It was like we were in our own little world.'

I noticed the change in his attitude. 'Is there anything that might help me discover what happened to her?'

Pope's expression hardened again. 'I already told you, I know nothing. And even if I did, I wouldn't tell you. You're just another person poking around in her disappearance, looking for excitement from it. How much money are you making from this?'

The guilt crawling through my veins increased, but I couldn't leave.

'Look, I get you're protective of her memory, but I'm not trying to exploit her. I genuinely want to discover what happened to Emily. Maybe there's something you remember that could point us in the right direction.'

He shook his head. 'I don't know anything. I wish I did. I've always wondered what happened to her. It's like a part of me is missing, too.'

I felt sympathy for him, seeing the pain and regret etched on his face. 'I'm sorry. I didn't mean to upset you.'

Pope let out a deep breath and rubbed his cheek. 'It's not your fault. It's just hard to talk about her, you know? She was everything to me. Then, one day, she was gone. People don't understand how it feels to lose someone like that.'

I nodded, knowing all too well the feeling of loss and confusion. 'I get it. But if you remember anything, even the smallest detail, it could make a huge difference.'

The door opened, and two blokes entered the shop. Pope left me and went to them. I watched his face change, now enthusiastic as he spoke to the customers, as all his pain vanished as if he was practised at the art of deception.

I stepped outside and considered what he was hiding from me.

And I wondered why he had Greg Conway's Rottweiler in the back room.

Chapter 22

Spectre of Love

Ginger let me nap in her bedroom in the afternoon as the dull throb continued in my arm. I declined any more drugs, reluctant to become too dependent on them. As a teenager, I'd witnessed too many people sinking into the rabbit hole of drug dependency. I'd also dabbled with certain chemicals and stimulants, not entirely falling into an abyss I couldn't escape. However, my tumultuous time between the ages of fourteen and sixteen cemented my determination to live a clean life. Ginger still found it hard to believe I hadn't touched a drop of alcohol in five years, but always raised a glass to me when she was partaking; not to be nasty or sarcastic, but, as she told me, to show her appreciation for my willpower.

I knew she meant well, but her gestures highlighted our different relationships with substance use. Those teenage experiences instilled a conviction to stay sober, a commitment I honoured daily. For her, moderate drinking was still a normal part of life.

Our histories shape us as humans - both the good and the bad. The choices we make, the roads we walk, the trials we endure or evade. Ginger and I emerged from our formative years on diverging paths regarding drugs and alcohol. However, with open minds, we found common ground. I respected her right to imbibe in moderation, and she admired my choice to abstain completely. Our friendship went beyond differences in lifestyle precisely because we invested the time to understand one another's experiences that led us to where we were. Though our stories differed, the shared capacity for growth and redemption united us.

I lost all my family as a kid, and it took me a while to get close to another human. During my two wild years, I had a best mate, Amy, but we eventually drifted apart. Now Ginger was my only female friend. I couldn't really count Becky since she was only a child.

The thought of Ginger going away with Jack Parker worried me more than I was ready to admit, not that I could tell her that. She had to do what was best for her. I pictured her leaving and imagined what it might have been like for Emily's sisters when she disappeared. I'd witnessed death first hand and understood how traumatic it was, but at least I knew what had happened to my parents. The uncertainty must have been devastating for Emily's family.

Ginger and Bruce went to the local pub as I set off for my meeting with Sister Morgan and the rest of the Church of the Resurrection. I entered the park, and a gentle breeze caressed my skin, refreshing me. The sun was setting behind the trees, casting a golden glow over everything. I breathed deeply, the scent of fresh-cut grass and blooming flowers filling my lungs. It was a beautiful evening, but my mind was preoccupied with thoughts of Emily and her relationship with Devon Pope. Had it contributed to her disappearance? What was Pope doing with Greg Conway's dog?

Was this new, or had they known each other twenty-five years ago?

As I strode through the park, I saw couples holding hands, children playing on the swings, and dogs chasing after balls. The laughter and chatter were everywhere, reminding me of happier times. I thought again of Ginger leaving the town and wondered what Amy was doing now. But my mind soon returned to Emily and her struggles.

I was early for the meeting, so I found a bench and took out my notebook, ready to jot down any fresh thoughts or insights. I looked at the sky, the orange and pink hues painting a picture of splendour. I scribbled down my ideas about Emily's secret relationship and how her parents must have reacted. The idea of strict religious parents dealing with their daughter's teenage rebellion was not new to me since I'd encountered something similar during my stay in one of the children's homes. Still, I couldn't help but feel sad for Emily. It seemed like she'd discovered what she wanted at university and was finally breaking away from a life of restrictions when it was all taken from her.

I texted Tommy.

How's it going?

There was no reply, so I got up and headed for the church, fixed on what I'd find there and how they would treat me. I arrived at the Church of the Resurrection, somewhat conflicted since I was about to lie to them regarding why I was there. The imposing stone structure loomed before me as I approached the entrance.

I pushed open the door, hit by the scent of incense and candles. The interior was quiet, contrasting with the bustling park. Rows of wooden pews lined the nave, and at the far end, two tall flickering candles flanked a raised altar. My parents were never religious, but my mother once took me into a magnificent cathedral in Manchester while we sheltered from the rain. I remember being awestruck by the soaring vaulted ceilings and massive stained glass windows that splintered sunlight into fragments of colour. The cold grey stone contrasted with the warm glow inside, a refuge from the storm. My mum just wanted to get out of the downpour, but those moments in the cathedral lingered long after for me.

As a child, I was curious about the towering pipe organ, the intricate carvings, the hushed whispers and the shuffling footsteps that echoed off the stone. Something about the melancholy beauty called to me, contrasting with my ordinary suburban life: in my eyes, it was mysterious, magical - a bridge to histories and beliefs from long ago.

I strode down the aisle, my footsteps echoing in the silence. As I reached the altar, I saw a figure in a black habit seated in a small side chapel.

'Sister Morgan?' I said.

She turned, looking different from when I'd seen her in the café. Her smile added warmth to the chilled surroundings.

'Enola! I'm so happy you could make it. What happened to your arm?'

'I fell over, but it's okay.'

She hugged me, and I didn't resist. 'Come, I'll introduce you to the others.'

Sister Morgan led me through the back into a room large enough for events or gatherings. About a dozen people, including Sister Dolby, turned to me, grinning like Cheshire cats. They were friendly and keen to talk, but never about the church or religion. It was all about politics, social issues, the state of the economy, and even football. I kept quiet and nodded most of the time.

And I wasn't sure how to approach the subject of Emily Jones. Half of the members looked old enough to have known Emily and her parents, and I wanted to speak to them on their own, but it seemed impossible to do with everybody there. I made a mental note of their names, hoping Tommy and I could track them down for interviews later.

Then Sister Morgan pulled me away from the others. She sat me at a table and offered me a pale-looking cake and a glass of water.

'We don't eat sugar or drink tea or coffee,' she said. 'How are you finding us so far? Not too stuffy for you, I hope?'

'No,' I replied. 'It's nice to be around happy people for a change.'

She touched my hand. 'Would you like to talk about it?'

I took a deep breath. 'Well, all this in the news about Emily Jones's disappearance just reminds me of what happened to my parents.' I recounted the tragic events to her. At least none of it was a lie, and it had been on my mind more than usual since I started the investigation. Being inside the church resurrected those memories of my mother in Manchester Cathedral so vividly I could still feel the rain on my face.

Sister Morgan squeezed my fingers. 'Oh, Enola. No wonder you're not feeling well. Do you wish to unburden yourself in the group? Spiritual healing is one of our strengths, and you look like you could use some of that.'

I flexed my sling and winced. 'I should rest, but meeting you all has been lovely.'

Disappointment oozed from her face, but I guessed she didn't want to push too hard on recruiting a new convert.

'Of course, Enola. You go home and take care. You

know where we are should you need anything, and you can call me anytime.'

I said goodbye to the others, and Sister Morgan led me into the night.

Then a miracle happened.

'I'll give you a lift if you need one.'

I turned to see the man from the vet's, George Carter, without his bulldog.

Did he want to get me into his car alone, with only one good arm, for nefarious reasons?

And could I turn down an opportunity to question him about Emily?

Decisions, decisions.

Chapter 23

Four Horsemen

I hesitated, but I didn't have a car and was in no condition to walk home. So, I nodded and climbed into the passenger side. Carter started the engine, and we pulled away from the church. His clothes were worn and dirty, smelling like they'd come straight from the bottom of a rubbish bag; a pungent mix of body odour, cigarette smoke, and motor oil assaulted my nose. I saw frayed hems, stained fabric, and gaping holes exposing skin. Touching the seat, I felt scratchy upholstery and mysterious sticky spots. Dandruff drifted off his shoulder, and his hair desperately needed a comb.

As we drove, the fading sunlight glared through smudged windows, and the rattling engine competed with the radio. Carter's tapping fingers and tuneless humming annoyed me.

He didn't look at me as he spoke. 'So why did you really go to the church?'

Was there any reason to lie to him? I might get something useful from him.

'How long have you been a church member, George?'

'All my life, fifty years. Why?'

'So, you knew Emily Jones?'

He stopped at a red light. 'Is that what this is all about?'

'What do you think happened to her?'

Carter changed the radio station, and it spewed Christian rock.

'Who knows? Maybe she had the operation and turned herself into a man like her mate.' He grinned at me through yellowing teeth. 'Yeah, that's probably it; she's walking around town right now with a fake dick between her legs. Isn't that what they do? Cut their bits off so they can be a proper bloke?'

'Like you?'

He puffed out his chest. 'All those who believe in the word of God are the true representatives of man.'

'You mean humanity?'

Carter laughed. 'Humanity? It's mankind. Man is second only to God, and everything else is below him.'

'What about women and equal rights?'

He rolled down his window and spat out a massive green glob that hit a bird at the side of the road. 'Blasphemous nonsense. God created women from Adam's rib so that they could serve us. They should provide children and keep their men happy. That's all they need to do.' His stare cut through me and dived into my chest, burrowing around with dirty phantom fingers as he tried to rip out my heart. But stronger men than him had tried that before, and they'd all failed. 'That's why that freak left our church, so they could better themselves and become a man, but you can't fool me that way, and you certainly won't fool the Lord.'

'Are you talking about Joe, who you harassed at the vets?'

He laughed as the lights turned green. 'Yeah, *Joe*, right.'

As he drove, I realised I hadn't told him my address, which was a good thing.

'You can drop me off at the woods,' I said. I'd walk through there the rest of the way to the flat.

Carter raised an eyebrow. 'Thousands of people disappear every year. Why do you care so much about a girl who abandoned her responsibilities and her church?'

'It's important to discover what happened to her. Also, Emily's parents are part of your congregation. Don't you want to ease their pain?'

'Robert and Elizabeth? Her mind is too far gone to remember anything, and he was happy enough to claim on Emily's life insurance.'

That information struck me like a bolt of lightning. How come Tommy hadn't known about it? 'Emily's father claimed on her life insurance and got it?'

Carter nodded. 'Aye. He had to wait seven years, but I heard it was a pretty penny. If you find her now, I guess he'd have to pay it all back.'

'You think she's still alive?'

He shrugged. 'It makes more sense than somebody abducting her or that she drowned. Emily was a strong swimmer, and there was talk of her maybe making the Olympics before she broke her parents' hearts and went to university. There was a rumour in the church she was seen swimming naked with some bloke in the river. Poor Robert was livid when he heard about it.'

I struggled with one hand to type the information into my phone.

'Do you know who the male swimmer was?'

He shook his head. 'Nope.'

'Was it Devon Pope?'

'I don't know who it was. You should ask your friend

from the vets as *he* spread that rumour in church.' He turned to me as he drove. 'Julia Case is her real name. I think she had a crush on Emily, so she got all confused about who she was.'

Having only one good arm stopped me from punching him in the teeth.

'Why does it bother you so much?'

'What?'

'You know what? Why do you and the other bigoted simpletons like you get so upset when others live different lives than yours? It doesn't impact your existence. It doesn't affect what you do. So why do you become so bug-eyed and gammon-faced about it? Is it because you can't bear to see other people happy when you're such a miserable fucking bastard?'

Carter slammed on the brakes, just stopping before he hit a woman on a zebra crossing. She gave him the finger, and I wished it was long enough to go up his nose and check for any brain cells, even though I knew there wouldn't be.

His pupils blazed red. 'You'll all burn in the next world for your blasphemies. Only the true converts will feel the joy of the resurrection at the feet of our Lord.'

'Is that in the *Bible*?'

'In Matthew 5:17, Jesus said, "Do not think that I have come to abolish the Law or the Prophets; I have not come to abolish them but to fulfil them." This means we must follow the laws and teachings of the Old and New Testaments. The *Bible* is the only source of truth, and any other interpretation is a perversion of God's word.'

'Do you punish sinners?'

His face rippled with enthusiasm. 'If we must.'

'Was Emily a sinner?'

'Of course.'

'Did you or somebody in the Church of the Resurrec-tion punish her?'

Carter grinned at me as I opened the door. 'Of course.'

I had one foot outside. 'What?'

'The Lord punished Emily Jones, just like he'll punish the rest of you.'

I was out of the car as he sped off, watching him go, and I knew what to do next.

I needed to speak to Joe Ripley.

Chapter 24

In the Shadows

I entered the woods with Carter's bigoted ranting still infecting my head, the pain in my arm throbbing with every step. The trees were dense, and their leaves rustled in the breeze. The only light came from the moon and stars shining through the treetops. I was tired and just wanted to get home and rest.

With each crunching footfall, I tried to shake off his venomous words. But they clung like magnets, welded to my brain and heart. The enveloping darkness around me mirrored the shadows he'd stirred in me - suspicion, fear, a judgment of those unlike me. His vitriol had poured like sewage into my ears, threatening to damage my soul.

I stopped and took a deep breath, inhaling damp soil and pine traces. Somewhere nearby, an owl hooted, beckoning me back to the present. The trees stood silently, witnessing my internal struggle, their weathered bark and steadfast roots centring me once more. Carter's hate may have infected my mind, but it didn't have to take root. I could choose light over darkness.

And I considered what he'd said about the Church of

the Resurrection punishing Emily. He implied it was only a "spiritual" punishment, but there was something deeper in his words, as if he was taunting me. Could Robert Jones and other congregation members have hurt Emily because they believed she'd sinned?

Perhaps that's what Elizabeth Jones was hinting at to me.

As I strode further into the woods, I heard voices. I paused and listened, trying to make out what they were saying. Then, I moved to a group of bushes and stretched on the tips of my toes to peer over the top. Four teenagers, two boys and two girls, about fourteen or fifteen years old, were sitting on the ground in a circle. At first, I thought they were playing spin the bottle just like I'd done at their age until I noticed the Ouija board.

I considered intervening, warning them away from messing with things like that. But I hesitated, not wanting to alarm or lecture them. Those kids probably saw it as a silly game to get adrenaline pumping on a boring night. They looked so young, faces illuminated by their mobile phones that seemed to leach the colour from their skin. Perhaps this was just an act of defiance, a grasping for forbidden mysteries. I knew that urge well.

Were those the kids who carved the pentagram symbol into the tree? In the end, it didn't matter. They were only messing around, and I'd done much worse than that at their age. I turned to walk away, gripping my elbow and regretting not bringing the painkillers.

That's when I heard the girl speak. 'Talk to us, Emily. Tell us what happened to you?'

I froze between the trees, my legs stuck as all the air was sucked out of me.

A boy spoke. 'Yes, Emily. Help us find your killer.'

I pushed through the bushes, scratching my hand and drawing blood. 'Stop messing around with that.'

The kid closest to me jumped up, shrieked, and fell over. The others stumbled back like crabs, pushing their backs into trees.

'What the fuck?' the purple-haired girl asked. 'Who are you?'

'It doesn't matter,' I replied. 'You shouldn't experiment with this stuff. It's dangerous.' During my difficult years, I spent a lot of time poking around with spiritualism, psychics, and mediums. I'd sat in front of my fair share of Ouija boards to recognise it was all nonsense, but I'd also seen that shit mess kids' heads up more than once.

They all stood together and glared at me. 'You can't tell us what to do,' Purple Hair stated.

I shook my head. 'You know it doesn't work, right?'

'Punch her, Bobby,' the girl with a stud in her nose demanded.

He must have been the lad I'd scared into falling over. 'Nah, she's not worth it.' He leaned down and grabbed the Ouija board. 'Let's go somewhere else.'

'Why were you doing it?' I asked.

'What?' Bobby said.

'Trying to contact Emily Jones.'

They looked at each other before Purple Hair spoke. 'We want to see if her killer is still here. We've heard things, you know.'

'What things?'

They glanced at each other.

'Have you any idea how many people have vanished in this town in the last twenty-five years?'

'I don't.' Had there been others reported in the media like Emily had? If there was, I couldn't remember them.

'Dozens,' Bobby said. 'Dozens have disappeared.'

'And most of them were women and girls,' Purple Hair added. 'But nobody hears about them. Do you know why?'

I had a good idea. 'They came from the wrong place or didn't look right enough for the media.'

Purple Hair nodded. 'That's it. And it's all fucked up. We could have a serial killer here, and nobody's doing anything about it.'

Was she right? Was there more to Emily's disappearance than any of us had thought?

'Thousands of people go missing in Britain every year,' I said. 'Not all of them are suspicious. Some just get up and leave their families and friends without saying a word.'

They stared at me as if I was a hundred years old.

'Come on,' Bobby told his mates. 'We're done here.'

I watched them go, adding one more thing for Tommy to include in his documentary. I glanced over my shoulder, peering through the trees at the moonlight shimmering across the river. You'd need to hack through the bushes and branches with an axe or a sword to reach the water now, but what about twenty-five years ago? I had to see if there were any photos of the area from then.

I stumbled through the woods, my arm aching in its sling. Everywhere was in near darkness, but I knew the path by heart.

Then I heard the noise behind me.

I tried to turn but was too late. Somebody grabbed my shoulder, and before I could react, they threw me down. As I rolled towards the trees, I hit broken branches and pebbles that stabbed me in the hip and chest. The musty scent of damp leaves flooded my nose as my body slammed into the earth. Jagged rocks and sticks jabbed my skin through my clothes. I pushed my hand out to break my fall, shredding my palm on the rough ground. Twigs snapped under me like brittle bones.

The darkness shrouded my attacker's face, so all I saw was a looming silhouette lurking above. Their iron grip crushed my shoulder, making me cry out. I lashed out in desperation, my fist glancing off something solid - a jaw, maybe. My ears rang with adrenaline, muting the sounds of the wood.

I scrambled away, every movement triggering waves of throbbing agony where my battered body had hit the earth. Bark scraped my cheek as I tried to push against a tree trunk. The metallic taste of blood filled my mouth. But anxiety drowned out the pain, its icy claws clutching my chest.

Only having one good arm stopped me from leaping up to face my attacker. My hand was in the dirt when he ran over and kicked me in the guts. The pain was unbearable, sweeping through me and blurring my vision. My fingers fumbled through the surrounding debris, grasping a thick branch. My eyesight returned to normal as he crept towards me, masked and stinking of a familiar cheap after-shave. He launched his foot at my gut again, but I rolled aside, twisting around and thrusting the wood into his ankle.

He screamed like a baby, stumbling backwards and falling into the bushes. I coughed and spat blood into the grass, pushing up with one hand and leaning against a tree. He was down and howling, that aftershave overwhelming my senses as I remembered when I'd smelt it before: in Devon Pope's mobile phone shop.

Why had he come after me? And how did he know where I'd be?

He got up with blood dripping from his ankle, and his

masked face turned towards me. I said nothing, not wanting him to realise I knew who he was.

That's when I saw the knife trembling in his hand.

Could I outrun him if I had to?

He only had one good leg, but I couldn't move my arm.

My head throbbed as he inched forward, pointing the blade at me.

'Hey, what's going on?'

That was Purple Hair – the teenagers had returned behind me.

The masked man turned and ran faster than I thought he could with that dodgy ankle.

Then I dropped to the ground and fell onto my back.

The darkness soon followed.

Chapter 25

Midnight Summer Dream

I sat on the ground, surrounded by police and paramedics. The shock of the attack still pulsated through me. Dirt and sweat covered me, my arm throbbing with pain. I focused on the trees and the stars, anything to distract me from what had happened.

The murmur of radios and voices felt far away, drowned out by the ringing in my ears. As gentle hands examined my injuries, I flinched, probing the blossoming bruises and cuts now decorating my body like morbid watercolour paintings. The aroma of antiseptic stung my nose. An emergency blanket scratched my neck, but its warmth barely penetrated the bone-deep chill that had set in.

I inhaled deeply, wincing as my ribs protested. The pain centred me, grounding me in the present. I was alive. Hurting, shaken, but breathing. The rest could come later - the questions, the consequences. For now, I focused on each rise and fall of my chest, taking tiny steps back from the darkness that threatened to swallow me.

A medic removed my sling and looked at my arm. 'How does it feel?' she asked.

'It's fine,' I replied as I raised my top. 'It's this side where I fell.'

She moved around to my hip as a tall man strode towards us.

'Working late again, Jack?' I said. 'Ginger won't be happy.'

He shook his head. 'She'll have palpitations when she learns about this. What happened, Enola?'

I winced as the medic pressed her cold fingers into my rib. Then, I recounted the events. 'His name is Devon Pope, and he runs the mobile phone store on the high street.'

'How do you know it was him? Did you see his face?'

'No, he wore a mask. I recognised his cheap aftershave from his shop this afternoon.'

'Is there a problem with your phone, Enola?'

'No.' I told him why I'd visited Pope. 'He had a relationship with Emily Jones just before she vanished. Is that in the police investigation?'

'I don't know,' he said. 'I'd need to check.'

'And I discovered something else at Pope's place.'

'What?'

'He had Greg Conway's Rottweiler in the back room.'

Parker scribbled everything in his notebook. 'But you didn't see his face. Other people will have that same aftershave. That isn't grounds to arrest him.'

I pointed at the blood in the grass. 'Get a forensic investigator to scoop that up and then speak to Pope. He'll have a fresh wound on his right ankle. The bloodied branch I used should be around here somewhere.'

Parker spoke to a uniformed officer as the medic finished with me. Everything ached as I looked for those teenagers to thank. There was no telling what Pope would have done if they hadn't returned. I couldn't see them anywhere and thought of Devon Pope.

Why would he take the risk of attacking me in the woods?

It had to do with my visit to the shop. It had scared him into such risky action. Or did somebody put him up to it? Was it Conway? They must know each other – what other reason would he have had Pope's dog in the back of his business?

But how did he figure out where I was? George Carter was the only person who knew where I was going since he dropped me off near the woods. Was there a connection between the two men? And if there was, did that mean there was a link between Greg Conway and the Church of the Resurrection?

Or had someone trailed Carter from the church? It would have been easy enough to do. Perhaps they'd been stalking me all day, from my visit to the dog groomers. It was possible, but so was something else – somebody had followed me from the flat. And if they had, they knew where I lived.

This was all leading back to Emily Jones. She was a Church of the Resurrection member, involved with Devon Pope and allegedly harassed by Greg Conway. Now there seemed to be a chain connecting the church, Pope and Conway. Tommy Bell would have a heart attack when he returned and I told him all this. His Netflix documentary might even turn into a series at this rate.

I reached into my jacket and got my phone, meaning to call Ginger, but I didn't. So, I texted Tommy instead.

I have a few bombshells to drop when you return. When and where shall we meet?

There was no immediate reply. I put the mobile in my

pocket, expecting him to be tucked up in bed since it was nearly midnight. The police had cordoned off the area, but I noticed media trucks and bystanders trying to see what was happening in the woods. I turned from them and stared at the spot where Emily had vanished so long ago. Could she have suffered an attack as I did? Was Devon Pope involved in both incidents? What would he have done if those teenagers hadn't returned? Would he have dumped me in the river?

A million things rushed through my head as I watched a forensic officer locate the bloodied branch and pop it into a clear plastic bag. If Parker got his colleagues to Pope's place quickly enough and they swabbed his ankle, they'd probably find bits to match what was in that bag. That would be that. Then Parker could question Pope about his motive for the attack. And Devon Pope seemed like somebody who'd collapse under pressure.

Parker returned to me. 'Officers are at Pope's house now. He'll be in custody soon.'

'Well, they got there quick.'

He nodded. 'Pope is known to us for several minor drug offences.'

Something clicked in my head. 'Using or selling?'

'Both.'

'Do you remember what they were?'

'The usual: cannabis, cocaine, amphetamines and Rohypnol.'

'Rohypnol. Roofies?'

'Yeah. Why?'

'Have you spoken to those teenagers who disturbed the attacker?'

'Not me, but somebody has.'

'You should talk to them, Jack. They think other people

have disappeared over the years, and the police haven't been paying attention.'

'You know I'm retiring in a month, right?'

'So?'

He sighed. 'Okay, I'll speak to them. Anything else?'

I thought about it. 'Has Ginger spoken to you?'

'We talk every day, Enola. Have you told her about tonight?'

'Forget about me. Has she said if she's leaving with you?'

'That's what you're thinking about after somebody tried to kill you?'

'It's not the first time that's happened, Jack.'

He shook his head. 'Do you want a lift home?'

'I thought you'd never ask.'

We headed to his car, and I saw the four kids and their Ouija board. They seemed nervous speaking to a female copper.

'Are those the teenagers?' Jack asked.

I nodded. 'Give me a second.' I went to speak to them as the officer left. 'Why did you come back?'

Purple Hair spoke. 'The board told us to.'

I glanced at it under her arm. 'The Ouija board?'

'Yeah,' she replied. 'We tried it again, and it said you were in trouble.'

'It must have been Emily,' Bobby added. 'She sent us back to save you.'

His words echoed in my head as I got into Parker's car.

Had a dead woman saved my life?

Chapter 26

All Roads Lead To Rome

One positive from the attack in the woods was that Ginger let me use her bedroom to kip as she spent the night at Parker's. I hoped it was a sign she'd made a decision. She was my best friend, and I didn't want her to leave, but I knew she'd regret it if she didn't at least try to make a go with Jack. And I had a good night's sleep for a change, but that might have had something to do with the number of painkillers I'd dosed myself with.

Kronos sniffed around my leg as I sat opposite Bruce and ate breakfast.

The coffee aroma tickled my synapses as I dumped half a blob of butter onto my toast. Then I bit through it as the warm bread washed away the taste of blood lingering at the back of my throat. The rich, nutty flavour coated my tongue, soothing the rawness left behind by the night's trauma. I relished the soft give of the toast between my teeth, grounding me in the safety of the mundane morning ritual. For a moment, the simple pleasure of breakfast eased the tension knotting my shoulders. Sunlight streamed through the window, bathing the kitchen in a tranquil glow at odds with the chaos churning within me.

I sipped the fragrant coffee, and its dark roast bit my tongue with a pleasant sting. The heat seeped through the mug into my hands, thawing fingers still numb from the chill night air. Steam curled upward, carrying an earthy aroma that stirred me to wakefulness.

Closing my eyes, I let the tastes and scents transport me, if only briefly, away from the turmoil of the previous twelve hours. In the sunlit kitchen, savouring the ritual of a new day beginning, I could almost convince myself it had all been a nightmare.

'You had an eventful night,' Bruce said. 'You should avoid the woods for a while.'

'Why?' I said.

He dropped two sugars into his tea. 'Well, let's see – in the last few months while travelling through those woods, you've been pushed into the river, discovered a dead body hanging from a tree, been savaged by a dog, and now attacked by a masked loon. Aren't those enough to give you second thoughts about going there again?'

'It keeps life interesting. Did I tell you about the kids with the Ouija board?'

He nodded. 'Yes, when you got back last night. You owe them big time.'

I did, and it reminded me of a certain teenager I hadn't spoken to for a few days. But before I could ring her, Tommy called.

'How are you feeling, Enola?'

The toast and coffee had warmed my insides, and even though the sling still hampered my movement, I was ready to get going.

'I'm fine. Where are we meeting to collate our information? I want to hear what you discovered in Sheffield.'

He laughed. 'Well, my day wasn't as exciting as yours, but I got some useful bits about Emily that I've pinned on my action board.'

'Action board?'

'Yeah, it's where I put all the points I must include in the documentary. I can drive to you and bring you back here to save you walking.'

'Just tell me where you are. I'll get Bruce to drop me off.'

Bruce raised his eyebrows at me, and Kronos's tail beat against the floor in anticipation of going out.

'Okay,' Tommy said and gave me his location. 'See you soon.'

'What's this?' Bruce asked as I ended the call.

I smiled at him. 'Do you want to visit Tommy's expensive motorhome?'

He did, and we were standing inside it twenty minutes later. Tommy eyed Kronos suspiciously, but Bruce assured him the dog wouldn't piss or shit anywhere. I wasn't so sure.

Tommy gave us a tour of his mobile home. 'The cockpit features a modern dashboard with a ten-inch touchscreen infotainment system that controls the multimedia and navigation functions. The seats are plush, comfortable with armrests, and can be swivelled around to face the living area. A large slide-out with a lavish sofa bed and a booth-style dinette comfortably seats four people. The sofa can be converted into a sleeping space, providing additional room for guests.'

'Impressive,' I said.

He continued. 'The kitchen has a range of high-end

appliances, including a three-burner gas cooktop, a convection microwave oven, and a refrigerator with a freezer. Additionally, it features a spacious sink with high-rise taps, a pantry for storing groceries, and plenty of cabinets and drawers for storing cookware and dishes.

'At the rear, a private main bedroom features a comfortable queen-sized bed with a premium foam mattress. It also includes a large wardrobe with mirrored doors, a chest of drawers, and overhead cabinets.'

'Wow!' Bruce said. 'This is better than our flat.'

I ignored the luxury and went to his action board, which stood on two plush seats near the mobile editing suite. He'd already added notes from his trip to Sheffield. I pointed at them. 'Tell me about those.'

His eyes sparkled like diamonds. 'I spoke to Emily's flatmates, Debbie and Caroline. They said in her first year at university, Emily was shy and reserved, sticking to her strict religious beliefs, so no alcohol, tobacco, tea, coffee, drugs, or premarital sex.'

'What a waste of university life,' Bruce remarked.

Tommy laughed. 'Yeah, indeed. So that meant she rarely went out beyond her classes, shopping, and seeing some of the local attractions.'

'Are there any in Sheffield?' Bruce asked.

I waved a finger at him. 'Pulp, Self Esteem, the Human League, Cabaret Voltaire, and Heaven 17, to name a few.'

He narrowed his eyes. 'Are they pubs?'

'You're such a philistine,' I remarked.

'Anyway,' Tommy said. 'Debbie and Caroline claimed Emily kept to herself that first year but, to their surprise, she was a changed woman when she returned for her second year.'

'How come?'

He pointed to the board. 'First, she had this man, Henry Travis, as her personal tutor and, according to Debbie and Caroline, things became a little too personal between teacher and student.'

Bruce whistled, and Kronos's ears pricked up. 'They had an affair?'

He nodded. 'Yeah. I spoke to Travis, and he confirmed it. It lasted all of Emily's second year at university before she broke it off. Travis, twenty years older than her and married, claimed he still hadn't gotten over it. By then, according to Debbie, Emily was going to pubs and clubs with them and partaking in all those things her religion told her not to. Near the end of her third year, she was getting regular visits from some man she knew from back home. Debbie and Caroline said they never saw this bloke, but they overheard Emily talking to him on the phone, and they were pretty hot and heavy conversations.'

'Devon Pope?' I wondered.

Tommy shrugged. 'Her flatmates never got a name, but after what you told me, it seems likely it was Pope.'

Bruce gazed at the board, which featured other names from the community, including Emily's parents, her sisters, the names of Church of the Resurrection members I'd texted him after my visit there, and Greg Conway.

'How come the police and the media never knew this at the time?' he said.

'Maybe they did,' Tommy replied. 'I'm sure the coppers kept many things from the public during their investigation.'

Tommy had placed Emily's name in the middle of the board, with arrows pointing away from it to other people. I peered at it, happy to see Emily had a life she enjoyed before she vanished.

Nevertheless, we still didn't know what happened to her.

My phone rang, so I answered it. 'Detective Inspector Parker, how lovely to hear your voice again.'

'Where are you, Enola?' he asked.

I told him. 'Tell Ginger her bed is so comfortable.'

'We've charged Devon Pope.'

'I thought you did that last night?'

'This is a new charge.'

'What?' I said.

Parker paused for two seconds. 'Murder.'

Chapter 27

Cruel Garden

I don't know how the word got out, but the media circus had gathered outside the police station when we arrived. Tommy drove us all there, and even Kronos felt stiff with tension when I touched his neck. Camera flashes lit up the morning like paparazzi fireflies as reporters swarmed our car. Microphones jabbed through the windows as voices buzzed with shrill questions. The attention fed on me like vultures on carrion, pecking and prodding for any scrap of reaction.

My eyes flickered as I recoiled from the spotlights aimed at my face, feeling exposed. Their bright glare cast the scene in stark contrast, leaching all colour into black-and-white extremes. The media were ravenous for every salacious detail to feed the twenty-four-hour news cycle.

Pressing closer against the window, their features blurred into a many-headed monster spitting rapid-fire demands. Their breaths left foggy smears on the glass as I shrank away. The stale air in the car felt suddenly stifling, the leather seats clammy beneath me.

Somewhere nearby, a siren wailed, barely audible over

the din outside. I latched on to the sound, letting it drown the questions still hounding me. Its oscillating tones seemed to slice through the turmoil, clearing a path forward. I saw Ginger, so I jumped out of the car and ran through the crowd to her. Her cheeks were red, and she'd been crying.

'Oh, Enola, it's so terrible.'

I squeezed her hand. 'What's happened?'

She wiped a tear from her cheek. 'I'll let Jack tell you. He's waiting for you inside.'

I left her with Tommy and Bruce and rushed into the building. Parker was at the reception, his face dark and haggard as he turned to me.

'Did you give a statement last night, Enola?'

I nodded. 'Yeah, to one of your officers. What's going on, Jack?'

He ushered me through the station and into his office. 'You should sit.'

The concern in his voice worried me. 'Where's Pope?'

'He's downstairs with his lawyer. You were right about the wound. When uniformed officers arrived at his house last night, he was trying to put a bandage on it. And you were also correct about the blood in the woods and what was on that branch – both samples were Popes. When I presented the evidence to him, he cracked like a baby, spilling his guts.'

I took a deep breath. Was the mystery of Emily Jones's disappearance about to be answered? 'What's he said?'

Jack sat on the edge of his desk. 'He admitted to attacking you in the woods, claiming he had no choice because somebody forced him into it.'

'Who?'

'Greg Conway.'

My heart thumped against my ribs. 'How did he make Pope attack me?'

'A lot's happened since I saw you last night, Enola. Pope incriminated two others in criminal activity going back thirty years.'

'Conway and who else?'

'George Carter from the Church of the Resurrection.'

'Fuck! That's how Pope knew I was in the woods. How do they all know each other?'

'They went to school together, where they discovered they all shared the same perverted interest.'

I took a deep breath. 'They enjoyed assaulting women and girls.'

Parker nodded. 'Because of his band, Conway was popular when he was in his early twenties. So, it was easy for him to attract young women and girls, and back then people paid little attention to the behaviour of celebrities. That meant many things went unreported or were just dismissed by those who should have known better.'

'Pope told you all this?'

'Most of it. He alleges Greg recruited him and Carter into Conway's particular hobby. He said he and Carter only watched at first while Conway carried out the attacks, but as time passed, they joined in as well. He says this all began when they left school in 1993. He claims the other two forced him, that he was an unwilling participant, and that he broke away from them in 1997 when he started a relationship.'

'With Emily Jones?'

'Yes. He had photos and videos of them together. She looks happy in them.'

The heat rose in my veins, and ghostly fingers squeezed

my lungs as I struggled to breathe. 'You said you've charged Pope with murder?'

'We have.'

I closed my eyes, seeking calm but not finding it. Then I opened them.

'Is it Emily?'

Parker shook his head. 'No. We went to their houses after Pope gave us Conway and Carter's names. Conway is downstairs with his lawyer, but Carter, well....'

Every muscle in my body stiffened up. 'Well, what, Jack?'

'When the uniformed officers arrived at his home, they found the door unlocked, and he was dead, hanging from the ceiling in his bedroom. They also discovered a note Carter wrote, asking God for forgiveness for his many sins. And he listed all of those, including the location in his garden of a body. Forensics recovered it three hours ago.'

'It's not Emily Jones?'

'No. We're still awaiting identification, but the officers found other evidence at Carter's place – diaries, pictures, and videos. Carter, Pope and Greg Conway are in those photos and videos. I watched some of the clips this morning, and they're horrible, the vilest things I've seen in fifteen years as a copper. We think the body in the garden is of a young homeless woman who vanished three years ago.'

I lowered my head and buried it in my hands. A low humming buzz at the back of my skull slowly increased in volume. A dull throbbing pain possessed my arms and legs, and I yearned for a drink.

'Do you think there will be more bodies?'

'I don't know, Enola. We're still going through the material that Carter left, and Conway has said nothing.'

I thought of what those teenagers had told me in the

woods, of the people who go missing every year, and how nobody seemed to notice. Or care.

'But you asked Pope about Emily?'

'Of course. He says he loved her and would never hurt Emily.'

'How many others?'

'What do you mean?'

'How many others have vanished from this town over the years, Jack? Is it ten, twenty, a hundred? More?'

'We'll do our best, Enola, I promise you. I'll go through the missing persons' reports to see if they had any connection to Pope, Conway, or Carter.'

'What about the Church of the Resurrection?'

'What about them?'

'Carter was an active participant, so I assume you'll speak to everybody in that congregation. Emily was a member, and her parents still are.'

'I'll leave no stone unturned, Enola.'

My legs ached as I stood and went to the door. 'I wonder if the police said that twenty-five years ago, Jack.'

I left the station via the back, finding Ginger with Tommy. Bruce must have taken Kronos for a walk.

'Are you okay?' Ginger asked.

I nodded as a sudden hunger gripped my stomach.

'Come on, Tommy, take us all to lunch, and I'll tell you how your documentary will have the biggest twist of the year.'

Chapter 28

Bear Cage

fter lunch, Tommy took us back to the flat before returning to his mobile editing suite. There were many changes he'd have to make to his documentary. We might have failed to uncover the truth about Emily's mysterious disappearance twenty-five years ago, but we'd found something equally shocking.

'I bet you're glad it's all over,' Ginger said as she poured me coffee.

I warmed my hands on it, with the sling still interfering with my movement.

'It'll never be over without an answer to what happened to Emily.'

She sighed. 'You're right. Did Carter mention anything when you were in the car?'

'He spoke a lot, and most of it wasn't very pleasant.'

'Such as?'

'Oh, you know, the usual bigoted nonsense. I asked why other people's lives bothered him, but he couldn't answer.'

'Didn't you say he was angry with a former church member you saw in the vets?'

'Yeah, how he felt about Joe Ripley was a sore point for him.'

'Wait? Who?'

'Joe Ripley was the name the receptionist used, though they had a different name in the church.'

'Does Joe Ripley have a cat called Nostromo?'

I flicked through my recent memories to find one that didn't include violence.

'Yeah, I think that was it. It's the name of the spaceship in the movie *Alien*.'

Ginger laughed. 'Which was taken from the novel *Nostromo* by Joseph Conrad.'

I shrugged. 'Please excuse my ignorance. I've had a stressful few days.'

'Indeed,' she replied. 'But I might have good news.' She wiped her fingers over the screen on her mobile. 'Yep, here we go. I gave a private tarot reading four months ago to a Joe Ripley, and in the notes, I've mentioned their cat, Nostromo.'

'What, so you have a phone number?'

Ginger nodded. 'Even better, I have an address. Shall we visit them now?'

Ripley's house was an impressive three-storey, two-bedroomed detached property in the leafy suburbs. The warmth of the summer sun enveloped me in a cosy embrace. The scent of recently cut grass and blooming flowers filled my nostrils, distracting me from the itch under my sling. The gentle breeze carried the sweet fragrance of roses and lavender, and the sound of chirping birds and rustling leaves drowned out the buzzing in my skull.

'What does Ripley do?' I asked.

'Something in tech, working mainly from home.'

We approached the front. 'What happened during the tarot reading?'

She raised her eyebrows. 'You know I can't tell you, Enola. It's privileged information.'

'Okay,' I replied. She took her psychic readings seriously, so I didn't press her, knocking on the door instead.

Joe Ripley opened it thirty seconds later, clutching the cat. Ripley's eyes lit up. 'Ginger, how nice to see you.' Then they looked at me. 'Hey, I know you.'

'Yes...'

Ripley stopped me. 'You were at the vets the other day. You spoke to George Carter.'

'Yeah,' I said. 'Have you heard what happened to him?'

Ripley shook their head. 'No. Has he been harassing people again?'

Ginger touched Ripley's arm. 'Can we come in, Joe? We need to speak to you.'

'Sure,' they replied. 'I've just made tea and finished baking.'

Ripley led us inside, and I closed the door. The scent of baked bread and brewed tea wafted through the air and inflamed my senses. We entered the living room, and I glanced at the décor, with modern art on the wall and framed photos on the sideboard and bookshelves. The furniture was plush and inviting, with soft cushions and warm blankets draped over the backs of armchairs.

Ripley let go of the moggie, which jumped onto a chair and peered at me. Its pupils dilated as it watched my every movement, no doubt sensing the turmoil within. I met its unblinking stare, envying the feline's simplicity of instinct. Life held no moral quandaries or existential dilemmas for the cat - just basic drives to guide its actions.

The musty scent of Nostromo clung to my skin. Ginger and I took the sofa opposite as Joe Ripley bundled the cat out of the way before sitting and putting it on their knee. The cat's sandpaper tongue rasped as it nonchalantly groomed its mottled fur. Ripley reached to stroke its back, and it arched reflexively into the touch, craving affection, oblivious to the complexity of human failings.

'We're sorry to turn up unannounced,' I said.

'Please, call me Joe. I know Ginger, but I didn't get your name at the vets.'

'It's Enola. Enola Gray.'

Joe smiled at us. 'Would you like tea? And there's fresh banana bread.'

My stomach grumbled an answer.

Ginger laughed. 'Come on, Joe. I'll help you.'

They stood and headed to the kitchen, leaving me with the cat. I got up and went to the photos, looking at each. Most were of Joe in various places: on a mountain, riding a bike, skiing, and playing football. However, the one at the end caught my attention. I picked it up and stared at a familiar face.

'That was taken the day of Emily's graduation,' Joe said.

I put the photo back. 'You were there?'

Joe nodded. 'I met Emily at primary school, and we continued as friends through secondary and into the church. I saw little of her when she left for university until graduation. But she was a different person then. We both were.'

Ginger placed a tray of food and drinks on the coffee table, and we all sat again.

'Is that where you met George Carter?'

Joe poured the tea. 'Yes. Like Emily, my parents were part of the Church of the Resurrection, so we had no choice but to attend their gatherings. Still, she loved it for many years. It gave her the stability she couldn't find anywhere else.'

'Was it like that for you?' I asked.

Joe laughed. 'No, it was quite the opposite. I guess most teenagers question themselves as they get older, but the answers I needed could never come from something so buried in the past. Emily helped, of course, but the other church members were less than understanding. Carter was the worst, but the others had similar opinions – they just didn't broadcast them as much as he did.' Joe cut three slices from the banana bread. 'So what's he done now?'

I bit the bread and a heavenly taste melted in my mouth. 'George Carter's dead, Joe. He killed himself last night.'

Joe dropped the knife. Studying their face, I couldn't tell if they expressed sorrow or joy.

Chapter 29

Too Many Teardrops

'What happened?' Joe said.

I washed the banana bread down with a gulp of tea and then recounted my encounters with Emily's parents, Devon Pope, the Church of the Resurrection, George Carter, and the events in the woods.

'So, Carter took his own life while the police arrested Conway and Pope. And now Pope is singing like a canary, according to our contact at the station.'

Joe glanced between us both. 'What has any of that got to do with me?'

I peered at the photo of Emily behind Joe's head. 'Well, we thought you might be able to enlighten us about what it was like for Emily twenty-five years ago with her parents and the Church of the Resurrection before she disappeared.'

Joe looked at me. 'You've met all of them, including Robert and Elizabeth. What do you think?'

I pictured my time with Emily's parents. 'Elizabeth Jones is ill, physically and mentally, but she indicated her husband had forced Emily out of the house the night she vanished.'

'Okay,' Joe said. 'And what did you make of the Church of the Resurrection?'

'Apart from Carter, they seemed harmless enough.'

Joe laughed. 'Yes, appearances can be deceptive.'

Ginger reached over and touched Joe's arm. 'Do you want us to leave?'

Joe shook their head. 'No. It's probably time I spoke to somebody about this.' They refilled the cups. 'Fundamentalism thrives on fear. Fear of losing our children, our religious liberty, and being wrong and going to hell. But the problem with fundamentalist fear is that it breeds exclusion and isolation. And Emily and I experienced both.' Joe reached down, opened a drawer in the coffee table, removed a folder, and placed it between us. 'In there, you'll see what Emily's life was like.'

I glanced at the folder. 'And what was it like for you, Joe?'

Joe sighed. 'My relationship with the church declined little by little when they learned I was gay. Two of my favourite lady friends took me into the cry room to pray the gay away and convince me I was not born that way. One evening, I told the *Bible* study group my dad was a narcissistic thug who beat me and only pretended to be a Christian to impress his church friends. You would think everyone there would realise I lived with my dad and knew him longer and better than they did, but because they all loved him, and many of them were his friends, not a single soul believed me. That crushed me, and I was scared. I panicked, thinking it would get to my dad somehow, and he'd be angry and punish me. Which, of course, he did. I eventually left the church, and my dad passed away a few years ago.'

I didn't know what to say. I guess there were even worse things than watching somebody murder your parents.

Joe sipped the tea before continuing. 'I had a tough time existing with my brain in this body. I tried to be what I thought others wanted me to be so as not to risk rejection. Unfortunately, this hiding from myself led to many difficulties in my life. My parents rejected me. The church also, but that was a relief. Emily was the only one who stood by me. It's different now. Most folks are understanding, but there is always a tiny minority who like to criticise.'

'Indeed,' I said.

'So yeah, in my early teens to mid-twenties, I didn't know how to tell people how unhappy I was. Instead, I'd berate myself for it. I struggled with food, intense depression, anxiety, and severe panic attacks. I couldn't function. I couldn't leave the house. I was resigned to living the life I was in until Emily convinced me I didn't have to.' She picked up the folder and handed it to me. 'Emily had her problems, and you can read about them in her own words.'

I opened the folder, removing pieces of paper with writing on them.

'Emily wrote these?' I said.

Joe nodded. 'They're some of the few I got from her room before her parents saw them. I think her father burned all the rest.'

I read the first page aloud. 'OMG, I don't even know what I did, but suddenly my mum's screaming at me, and my heart's pounding so hard it's like my ears can feel it too! And like, I just know that whatever happens next will not be up to me. Will I get hit with a belt? Will she leave me alone to cry and wonder why I'm such a bad kid? Will she go on and on with the verbal abuse for over an hour? Or will I have to wait until my dad gets home to hear how much of a failure I am? Ugh, like any of those things could happen 'cause they're pretty usual in my house, but I feel so helpless right now.'

My heart ached as I stopped reading, catching my breath.

'Christ,' Ginger said. There was no date on the paper. 'How old was she when she wrote this?'

'Sixteen,' Joe replied.

I read from the next scrap. 'You are a female; your body must be covered. Men will look at you and think evil thoughts. You are responsible for that. You disobeyed your father, and you have broken God's heart.'

Then I looked at the accompanying photos of Emily's terrified face as she showed her bruises to the camera: on her arms, legs, back and chest, but always in places that clothes would obscure. There were more pictures and writing, but I'd seen enough.

'Why didn't you give these to the police after Emily vanished?'

'Emily told me she loved Devon Pope but was scared he was getting mixed up with dangerous people,' Joe said.

'Greg Conway and George Carter?' I asked.

'She never mentioned their names, but I knew she was terrified of moving from one abusive relationship to another.'

Ginger squeezed Joe's fingers. 'Do you think they hurt Emily?'

'Lots of people hurt Emily,' Joe said.

I asked again. 'Why didn't you give these to the police after Emily vanished?'

Joe stood and went to the bookshelf, grabbing a laptop.

They opened it, running a hand over the screen so we couldn't see what was happening. Then Joe lowered their voice and spoke into the machine. It was quiet, but I heard one word.

'Samantha.'

Ginger gripped my arm, pushing her head into me. 'Emily's older sister?'

Joe returned to the table, placing the screen facing us. Two women sat staring into the camera; they were in their late 30s or early 40s and were clearly sisters: Emily's sisters. Then they inched apart, and a third woman appeared, smiling as she sat between them.

'Oh fuck!' Ginger said.

Oh, fuck indeed.

Emily Jones smiled at us.

Chapter 30

La Folie

'The police arrested Devon and Greg Conway?' Emily Jones asked.

Ginger, like me, was stuck for words. All I could say was, 'Yes.'

'And Carter is dead,' Ginger added.

Emily hugged her sisters and then spoke into the camera. 'Do you want to tell them everything, Joe?'

Joe shook their head. 'It's your story, Em, but they might need a strong drink first.'

'Rum, if you have it,' Ginger said.

I was sorely tempted as I gazed into the eyes of a dead woman. Supposedly dead. Or just missing for twenty-five years.

'Coffee, please,' I said. 'Strong coffee.'

Emily reached behind her and brought a cup to the table where their laptop was standing. 'One of the first things I did when I arrived in Australia was to find the best coffee shop.'

Joe went for the drinks as I caught my breath.

'Do your parents know where you are?' I asked.

She shook her head. 'No. I had to get away from them. If my father knew where I was, he would have come after me.'

'So you faked your death?' Ginger said.

Emily nodded. 'It was Joe's idea, and Samantha organised my new identity before I arrived in Australia.' She put her arm around her younger sister's shoulders. 'I'm only sorry we had to wait a few years before we could tell Jane.'

Jane Jones smiled. 'You can imagine my shock when I arrived here and saw Emily. I nearly had a heart attack.'

I knew how she must have felt since my chest was pounding like a volcano about to explode. My heart slammed against my ribs as if trying to break free, keeping time with the roaring pulse in my ears. Breathing grew laboured, and each inhale was a battle.

Joe returned with the drinks. Ginger downed half of hers before speaking. 'You did it to get away from your parents?'

'Yes,' Emily said. 'It was mainly my father, but Conway had threatened me as well, and I knew he was friends with George Carter and Devon. I needed to escape, and I was desperate. And then Joe came up with the perfect plan.'

I warmed my hands on the cup. 'Tell us about it.'

Joe sipped at their gin and tonic. 'Emily wanted to return to Sheffield, but we both realised her father would follow her there, and maybe Conway would, too. Then I thought of Samantha in Australia, and we talked it through. It was risky and dangerous, but less so than Em staying here.'

'My father was arranging for me to marry Greg Conway,' Emily announced.

'*What?*' I said.

She sighed. 'Conway's dad and mine were friends,

using me like medieval cattle. I didn't know what was happening until Greg bragged about it one night as I jogged past the construction site.' Her lips trembled. 'He dragged me in there, and I thought he'd rape and kill me. But all he did was laugh and reveal what our fathers were doing. "Then I'll be able to do whatever I want to you every day," he bragged.'

I reeled as the impact of her words sank in. Bile rose in my throat as the depravity she described became horribly vivid.

'Em told me what happened,' Joe said. 'We knew we had to get her away from here.'

'It was more than that,' Samantha added. 'We needed to make sure that neither my father nor Conway would come for Emily ever again. That's why we did what we did.'

I watched the sisters on the other side of the world, seeing their love for each through the screen. The twenty-five-year conspiracy had confused and aggravated many, but I didn't blame the sisters.

'What happened at the river?' I asked.

'I had to leave the headphones and the CD Walkman so people would know I'd been there,' Emily said. 'Then I slipped into the water and swam half a mile downriver. When I got out, Joe was waiting for me in the car with dry clothes. Then we drove to Dover and took the ferry using the fake passport Samantha had sent me the month before. After that, I travelled by train to Berlin and flew to Sydney to start my new life.'

'Did you know what was happening here, how the police searched for you?'

'Joe kept me informed.'

I settled into the sofa, amazed they'd pulled it off. 'Why are you confessing now?'

'Our mother is dying,' Emily said. 'I need to see her.'

Ginger finished her drink. 'Does that mean you're coming back?'

Emily nodded. 'In the next few days. All three of us are returning.'

Joe grabbed the laptop and stood. 'Help yourself to more drinks and cake.'

Then they left the room. Ginger and I sat in silence, my brain in such a fuzz I'd even forgotten about the pain in my arm. Then it returned in a rush, and I groaned.

'I know,' Ginger said. 'I can't believe it either.'

'What do you suppose Inspector Parker will say when you tell him this?'

She sighed. 'He's retiring in a few weeks, but I expect he'll be happy Emily is alive.'

'Don't you reckon the police are going to be pissed off? And the public?'

Ginger shrugged. 'I don't care. Emily's alive; that's all that matters, don't you think?'

'Of course. I just wonder what reception she'll get when she returns.'

She put her empty glass on the table. 'I'm leaving with him, Enola.'

I knew it was coming, and I was pleased for her, but still, it pained my heart.

I took her hand in mine. 'I'm happy for you, Ginger. I'm happy for both of you. But don't tell Parker. He'll think I've gone soft.'

We laughed and hugged. I had to wipe a tear from my eye when we separated.

'So, what do we do now, Enola?'

'That's easy. I'll let Tommy know he has the year's most dramatic true crime documentary.'

An Enola Gray Mystery
Ghosts on Water

A. S. French

Chapter 1

Shell Shock

I stumbled over a dead tortoise in the woods.

My ankle twisted, sending shooting pain through my foot and up my leg. The world spun around me as a swirl of branches and leaves obscured the sun from my vision. Damp earth greeted me as I hit the ground, rolling towards the giant shell.

That's when I saw the rest of them.

My legs trembled as I stood, counting the corpses in the grass. There were seven miniature tombstones, each around two feet long, with rugged shells cracked open to reveal pink flesh. The stench of rotting meat filled my nostrils as I gazed upon their glassy eyes and stiff bodies. My stomach churned at the macabre scene. The air stank of decay and death, the ground wet beneath my shaky hands. Pine needles pricked at my skin, my breath catching at the sight before me. Their limbs hung limply, lifeless. The vibrant hues of their shells had faded, blending with the muted greens and browns of the woods. The distant rustling of leaves, an eerie soundtrack to the mysterious tableau, broke the silence that settled over the scene.

With my knees bent, I touched the shell of the nearest tortoise, the texture rough and cool beneath my fingertips. Nature seemed to hold its breath, waiting for an explanation I couldn't provide. I shivered, struggling to breathe. Invisible fingers clutched at my guts as I stifled a scream of anger. A chorus of insects hummed in the background, contrasting the stillness that enveloped the clearing. The sun filtered through the dense canopy, casting dappled shadows over the deceased creatures. The tang of pine lingered in the air, mixed with an unsettling undertone I couldn't quite place. Death was no stranger to me, but this was unsettling as if someone had displayed the poor animals as some macabre warning.

Then somebody screamed behind me.

Agony swept through my shoulder as I stood, turning to see my neighbour's eleven-year-old daughter running towards me. 'What are you doing here, Becky?'

She pinched her nose and scowled. 'I'm jogging, like you.'

There were grass stains on her baggy trousers, leaves in her hair, and mud on her top.

'You followed me here?'

The kid shrugged. 'You're not as fast as you think, Enola.' She put her hands on her hips, sticking out her chest like a superhero. 'You always say I should stop playing video games and get out of the house. So here I am.'

Yes, there she was.

I dragged her away from the killing ground. 'Does your mother know where you are?'

Becky wriggled in my grasp. 'Who did that to those turtles?'

I held her with one hand while using the other to grab

my phone from my pocket. 'They're tortoises, Becky. Turtles live in the water.'

She pointed over my shoulder. 'The river's over there. They might have come from that. I watched a programme about it on TV once. The mothers come out to lay their babies.' She frowned. 'Some of them get eaten by birds. It's horrible.'

'Well,' I said. 'I'm glad you don't watch those terrible reality shows anymore.' I wanted to distract her from the death behind me. 'It's good to see you're not wasting your summer holidays on that trash.'

She escaped from my grip. 'I saw something last night where a man stuck a pickled onion up his nose.'

The image made me gag. 'Why?'

Becky shrugged. 'Somebody paid him to do it. It's put me right off eating pickled onion crisps it has.'

I ushered her through the bushes and towards the river, but not too close. I could picture her running into the reeds and falling into the water. And there was a dreadful stink coming from it.

Then I rang the local RSPCA.

They arrived twenty minutes later. I'd kept Becky entertained with stories from comic books and Disney movies.

'The talking car and the haunted car were like brother and sister?'

I was about to explain the differences to her when the RSPCA people turned up.

'They're over there,' I told a dark-haired woman. 'Can somebody stay with the kid while I show you where?'

She nodded. 'Sure.' She nodded to a colleague. 'Look after the girl, will you, Sally?'

Sally didn't appear happy about it, but did as instructed. Then, I took the others to the graveyard. We strode through narrow paths bordered by granite hedge banks blanketed in slippery mosses, pennywort and ferns. The lanes twisted downhill. Before this dry spell, rainwater had turned them into streams, funnelling overflow from the swollen, muddy fields down to the river, already high and flooded from the eastern woods. A rough track passed by enormous moss-covered boulders while stunted oaks grew amongst the carved rocks. Swags of bushy lichen hung from the gnarled branches, thriving in the clean, damp air.

'I'm Judy Hartley,' the RSPCA woman said.

'Enola,' I replied. 'I guess this must be new for you, having dead tortoises in the woods?'

Hartley shook her head. 'You'd think so, but no. We discovered a deceased giant tortoise in a National Trust-owned forest near here last year.'

'Shit! How did that happen?'

'We still don't know. After analysing the bodies, we concluded the tortoise had been held in captivity for some time, possibly up to five years, in poor conditions.'

I processed that information as I led her and two others to the corpses. All three sighed at the sight, and I knew how they felt, hoping that the grisly scene hadn't disturbed Becky too much. Hartley and her people did their work as I got my phone, searching for anything online about the other dead tortoise she'd mentioned.

It didn't take long to find. There was a link to an RSPCA report on the unlawful trade in tortoises, titled Shell Shock, saying it was against the law in the UK to import or sell live wild-caught protected species of tortoises or products made from them without a permit for commercial purposes. Breeders could sell only captive animals bred from parental stock in their care. Newborn animals had to be identified with a microdot, and adults with a microchip or other appropriate method. The report said tortoises made "bad pets", explaining the body temperature, humidity and diet required by most species was "virtually impossible" to replicate.

I put my phone away as Hartley returned, shaking her head.

'Their severely deformed shells point to long-term neglect - a condition akin to rickets caused by calcium and vitamin D deficiencies. This often stems from inappropriate housing and poor diet.'

'Damn,' I said.

'It seems whoever got these tortoises struggled to care for them properly. But shockingly, they were abandoned instead of seeking help from an institution or an experienced private owner who could rehabilitate the animals. One would expect even a struggling owner to make efforts to find a suitable home for tortoises they could no longer handle. Yet there was no attempt to reach out before callously leaving these helpless creatures to perish.' Anger simmered in her eyes. 'With the proper care and environment, recovery was possible. This abandonment is tragic and morally reprehensible when alternatives exist that could have saved them. These tortoises deserved far better than the heartless fate they suffered.'

'What will you do now?'

'We'll take them back and report it to the police.'

'Has a crime been committed?' I wasn't sure, even with what I'd read online and what she'd told me.

'These are Aldabras,' Hartley said, 'not native to the UK

and like the one discovered in the National Trust woodland. They're legal to own here, but a permit is required to breed them for sale and exhibition. However, these were unlikely to be bred here.'

'Why not?'

'This particular tortoise species presents immense challenges for breeding in our climate. Only a tiny number of experts and facilities have managed to successfully breed them locally. They grow to be huge adults with specific demands to support mating and egg-laying. Creating suitable conditions for them to breed here is highly complex and demanding. The cool temperatures and lack of space to roam make typical UK enclosures unsuitable for natural courtship and reproduction. Meeting their heating, humidity, lighting, and space requirements stretches the capabilities of even advanced keepers. These tortoises evolved for tropical environments radically different from here. The drastic mismatch poses issues that the few breeders who have conquered them have only accomplished through meticulous effort and purpose-built facilities catering to the species' particular biological needs. For the average keeper, achieving successful captive reproduction of this species in the UK climate remains extremely difficult, if not impossible. Their environmental needs are not easily replicable here.'

I heard the stress in her voice. She continued.

'To answer your question, some criminals trade exotic animals on the side of mainstream criminal activity, such as drug dealing. The cost of keeping just one of the tortoises would have been astronomical. These animals must be kept in subtropical temperatures all year round, so you can imagine the energy costs.' She shook her head. 'The police will determine if a crime has been committed, but it's certainly heartless.'

I gave Hartley my name and contact number as more of her colleagues joined her. I left them to it and returned to Becky. She was throwing stones into the river while holding her nose.

'There's something stinky in there, Enola,' she told me. 'It might be the Loch Ness Monster.'

Sally went to the tortoise graveyard as I dragged the kid away from the water.

'Come on, Becky, let's get you home.'

She held my hand and quizzed me about river monsters.

I kept her entertained on the walk back, more worried about land monsters.

Chapter 2

Ice Ice Baby

After the shock of the dead tortoises, I took Becky for ice cream. We needed a break from the unsettling scene, and nothing lifted the spirits like a sweet treat on a warm summer day.

The gelato shop buzzed with activity as we stepped inside. The air was thick with the scent of sizzling waffles and sugary delights, mingling with the soft hum of conversation and the clinking of spoons against ceramic bowls. Brightly coloured posters adorned the walls, highlighting various flavours, from classic vanilla to exotic tropical fruit.

Becky's eyes lit up seeing the display case, her mouth watering in anticipation. I smiled at her excitement, grateful for this moment of joy amidst the chaos of recent events.

'So, Becky,' I began as we approached the counter, 'how are you feeling about starting secondary school in September?'

Her expression shifted, a mixture of nerves and enthusiasm flickering across her face. 'I'm a bit scared, Enola. I don't know anyone there, and what if they're all mean, like the kids at my old school?'

I squeezed her hand. 'I understand, sweetheart. Starting a new school can be daunting, but you'll make friends quickly. And remember, if somebody bothers you, you can always come to me or your mum.'

Becky nodded. 'Thanks, Enola. I'm just worried about leaving Mum alone while she's always working.'

I sympathised with Becky and her mother. Julia worked tirelessly as a carer, sacrificing much to provide for her daughter. The strain of her demanding job weighed heavily on both of them, leaving Becky to navigate the challenges of adolescence on her own. That's why she spent a lot of time with me.

'When am I getting a pet spider?' she said.

'What?'

'You said when I go to Big School, I could have a tarantula like you do.'

I scrutinised her face, recognising when she was lying. She'd always been a good kid, but her ability for deceit had grown recently.

'Your mum wouldn't like that.' I imagined the look on Julia's face if she got home to find a giant spider in a case waiting for her. 'You'll have to settle for visiting Dirty Harry.'

The sound of the bell above the door interrupted the conversation, and I turned to see the server placing two towering scoops of ice cream in front of us—the sweet aroma wafted from the bowls, tempting us with its sugary allure.

I handed Becky her bowl, watching as her eyes widened in delight. We settled into a corner booth, the chatter of the other customers fading into the background as we indulged in our treats. It took thirty seconds for the kid to get ice cream all over her chin.

'Mum's got that movie in her DVD collection,' Becky said. 'I think somebody from work gave it to her.'

'What movie?'

She scooped ice cream into her mouth, and chocolate sprinkles stuck to her cheek. 'The one you named your tarantula after, *Dirty Harry*.'

'Of course. You can't watch it, though.'

'Why not?'

'You're too young. Wait until you're eighteen.'

Becky narrowed her eyes. 'How old were you when you watched it?'

She was clever, trying to trick me into telling her I was fourteen the first time I saw that Clint Eastwood classic. I changed the conversation.

'You shouldn't go jogging on your own, Becky. You know it can be dangerous, right?'

The kid nodded. 'Because of all the nasty pervs?'

'Yeah, them and others.'

Her gaze sparkled. 'I can go with you then?'

The way she was trying to wrap me around her little finger was impressive.

'I'll think about it.' The ice cream chilled my throat. 'What else have you got planned for your summer holidays?'

'Can I come and work with you in the record shop?'

Chocolate sprinkles tumbled from my lips. 'What?'

'Mum said you have a new job in the record shop. I like music, so I could come and help you.'

'My first day is tomorrow. I'll ask Benjamin, the owner, if you can spend some time there.' It would be good to get her into music early. It was one of the few things that got me through rough times when I was her age. 'Who do you like?'

She scrunched up her face and licked ice cream from

her spoon. 'Little Mix, Taylor Swift, Katy Perry – loads, really. Mum says you like really, really old music, like from a hundred years ago.'

I laughed. 'Yeah, that's right.'

Becky's demeanour shifted as she spooned her sundae, her expression clouded with sadness and longing. I sensed a concern weighing heavily on her mind, something she needed to share. She fidgeted with her napkin, tearing small pieces and rolling them between her fingers.

'Enola,' she began tentatively, her tone barely above a whisper, 'Mum took me to see my dad last weekend.'

My heart clenched at the mention of Becky's father. 'She did?'

Becky nodded, her gaze fixed on her bowl as if seeking solace in the swirling patterns of melted ice cream. 'Yeah,' she murmured. 'It was strange.'

She only discovered recently that her father wasn't dead, as her mother had told her, but was imprisoned. His Majesty's prison service had released William Cross after he'd served a ten-year sentence, but he was soon back inside when he confessed to the police about his part in a local criminal gang. It was a shorter sentence in an open prison, but it still wasn't good for the kid to deal with.

I touched her shoulder. 'Do you want to chat about it?'

Becky hesitated, struggling to find the right words. 'He... he seems distant, like he's not really there, you know? And when he does talk, it's like he's angry.'

My heart broke for her. It was a burden no child should bear, yet there she was, grappling with the harsh realities of life at such a tender age.

'I'm sorry, sweetheart. I know it must be hard.'

'Yeah,' she said without a trace of emotion. 'It is.' She finished her ice cream. 'He likes music and said he used to be a roadie for Oasis.' There was a blob of chocolate on her nose. 'What's a roadie, Enola? He wouldn't tell me what they did.'

'Well,' I replied. 'They do all the heavy lifting for the musicians and sometimes drive them to gigs.'

'It's hard work, then?'

I nodded. 'It can be.'

She smiled, and it was great to see her happy. 'Bruce told me you don't like hard work.'

Bruce was my good friend and flatmate. 'Did he now? I'll have to speak to him about that.'

Becky suddenly changed the subject. 'Did somebody kill those turtles in the woods?'

'Tortoises,' I replied. 'They might have died because it was too cold for them.'

The kid shivered. 'I'm glad it's the summer. Our flat is always freezing in the winter because we can't afford to have the heating on.'

I didn't know how to console her about that. 'Hopefully, it will improve this year.'

Becky grinned. 'Maybe global warming will make things better for us?'

'Where did you hear that?'

She shrugged. 'Mum had the local news on the TV, and some important man on the council said there were benefits to climate change.' She shook her head. 'But he was dumber than a bag of rusty nuts.'

'Becky! Where did you hear that expression?'

The kid wiped ice cream from her face. 'From you, Enola. You said it to that bloke in the park last week, the drunk one who was annoying people. Don't you remember?'

'Yeah, of course.' Perhaps I was a bad influence, after all. My phone pinged with a message, and I checked it. 'Your mum is meeting us at Bruce's flat. He's cooking for us all.' I smiled at her. 'Unless you're full after that ice cream?'

She beamed at me. 'I want a burger and fries!'

My stomach grumbled, and I wondered if I should have had the dessert before my main meal.

Chapter 3

Eat It

The setting sun painted the sky orange and red, bathing the town in a warm, golden light. I guided Becky through the crowded streets, making our way towards the flat I shared with Bruce. The aroma of grilled chicken wafted from a nearby takeaway, mingling with the trace of exhaust fumes. The sounds of traffic and chatter filled the air.

Becky tried to run to the toyshop, but I kept a tight grip on her hand, knowing I'd never get her out if she got inside.

She pointed at the window display. 'I want a Dalek costume for Halloween.'

'That's months away.'

Her eyes bulged. 'I know. So you've got plenty of time to save up for it.'

I laughed. 'There's no need to buy you any cheek, kid.' I dragged her past the shop. 'Aren't you interested in something more traditional, like a ghost or zombie costume?'

She shook her head. 'Daleks are scarier. I fell off the sofa the first time I saw one.'

I pictured her rolling across the carpet as Julia panicked.

Their lives were a struggle, but they loved each other, and that's all that counted. Memories of my parents drifted out of the shadows as we approached the building. Becky wriggled from my grasp and ran up the steps, the sight of the dead tortoises seemingly long gone.

A waft of curry mingled with wet dog hit us as we entered the flat. Bruce was sautéing vegetables in the kitchen while Kronos dozed on his bed.

'Hey, you two!' Bruce shouted. He set down the wooden spoon and came over to hug Becky. At thirty-five, his scruffy beard and kind eyes gave him a fatherly air.

The kid grinned. 'That smells good!' Her love for curry meant she'd forgotten about the burger and fries. 'Is my mum here?'

'She just texted that she's on her way,' I said, sliding my phone back into my pocket. I was relieved Julia could join us for dinner after her long shift.

Becky plopped down to pet Kronos, who awoke with a snort. His tail thumped happily as she rubbed his belly. I settled onto the sofa, gazing out the window at the town bathed in twilight. Sirens echoed up from the streets, the restless sounds of a Sunday evening.

'Did you feed Dirty Harry?' I asked Bruce.

He nodded. 'Sure. Curried insects, right?'

I shook my head while Becky cringed. 'Eh, is that what we're having?'

He laughed. 'It's all good for you, kid – plenty of protein. Didn't your mum tell you that's what you'll get at school in September?'

She buried her face in a cushion and pretended to throw up, emitting large sounds of vomiting. I hoped she was pretending, anyway.

'He's only messing with you, Becky.' I pulled the

cushion off her. 'I wouldn't waste Dirty Harry's food on you lot.'

'Have you had a good day?' Bruce said.

The kid sighed. 'It was okay. We went for a run in the woods and found something strange.'

'Strange?' Bruce raised an eyebrow, setting aside his cookbook. 'What did you find?'

She leaned forward, her eyes wide with excitement. 'We discovered seven dead tortoises, just lying in the grass.'

Bruce's brow furrowed in concern. 'That's not right. Tortoises aren't native to these parts. Someone must have dumped them there.'

'But why would anyone do that?' Becky's voice echoed with genuine confusion, her gaze shifting between Bruce and me.

Maybe I should have tried to explain it to her when we were in the ice cream parlour. 'It could be part of some illegal wildlife trade, criminals trafficking exotic animals for profit.'

Bruce nodded, his expression darkening. 'It's a cruel world, Becky. Climate change is pushing animals out of their natural habitats, making them vulnerable to exploitation.'

A knock came at the door before it swung open to reveal Julia. Though tiredness ringed her eyes, she smiled warmly.

'Sorry I'm late,' she said, embracing me before kissing Becky's head.

'You're right on time,' Bruce assured her. 'Do you want a glass of wine?'

She accepted gratefully and sank into the well-worn armchair. I assumed she was looking forward to a night off from cooking after a double shift.

'Hard day?' I asked her.

'Yeah,' she glanced at Becky. 'I'll tell you about it later. What did you two get up to?'

'It was eventful, to say the least,' I replied, a hint of frustration creeping into my voice. 'We stumbled upon something disturbing in the woods.'

Julia's brow furrowed in concern, her gaze shifting between us. 'What did you find? God, it wasn't drugs, was it?'

She had a never-ending worry that Becky would get caught up in something illegal. There were already rumours going around about school kids being hooked on vapes.

'No, nothing like that.' I recounted our discovery of the dead tortoises, watching Julia's expression shift from confusion to dismay.

'That's awful,' she murmured. 'Poor creatures.' She looked at Becky. 'Are you okay, love?'

Becky squeezed her mother's hand. 'It's fine, Mum. Enola and Bruce are going to figure out what happened.'

Bruce stared at me. 'Are we?'

'We reported it to the RSPCA,' I said. 'We waited for them to arrive, but it was... unsettling.'

Bruce set down his wine, brow furrowed. 'Sounds like the actions of illegal, exotic animal traders. I know the practice is growing.'

I leaned forward, intrigued. 'How does it work?'

He grimaced. 'Ruthless smugglers procure vulnerable species from the wild to sell as pets. But in transit, many die from overcrowding and neglect. The leftovers get dumped wherever's convenient.' He shook his head.

I shuddered at the cruel indifference. Becky looked equally disturbed. I regretted exposing her to such darkness. 'Let's hope the RSPCA and the police find the culprits.' I nodded at her. 'You must be full after the ice cream, so no curry for you?'

She jumped up and ran around the room, her arms stuck out, pretending to be an aeroplane. 'I need more calories.'

That was our cue to eat. Bruce had prepared a fragrant vegetable curry – ginger, coriander, and rich tomato sauce aromas filled the flat. He served it alongside fluffy basmati rice and warm naan bread. I inhaled the comforting blend of spices as he ladled the food into bowls. Diced potatoes, carrots and peas peeked through the vivid orange sauce.

Becky scooped up a spoonful, blowing on it before taking a bite. 'Mmm, this is delicious!' Julia and I echoed her praise after tasting the dish. The vegetables were perfectly tender, with just the right kick from the curry. We ate eagerly, the chatter around the table soon giving way to the simple enjoyment of a good meal.

Bruce rubbed his belly when the last of the food was gone. 'Who's helping me with the washing up?'

Becky tried to run off, but Julia grabbed her. 'This one needs to burn off those calories, or she won't get into her new school clothes.'

The kid frowned. 'That's months away, Mum.'

Julia shook her head. 'It's less than six weeks, kiddo. So scoot into the kitchen, and Bruce will supervise you.'

He raised his eyebrows. 'I will?'

From the look on Julia's face, I guessed she wanted to talk to me about something. 'When Ginger left, you became the oldest resident here, Bruce. That means you have to teach Becky how to clean up.'

He grinned. 'Okay, but that reminds me. Ginger sent me a video message today. Did you get one?'

'Maybe. I haven't checked my phone. Is she still slumming it with the former copper in Australia?'

Bruce nodded. 'Yeah, she and Jack appear to be having a good time. Perhaps you should take a holiday soon, Enola.'

'You tell me this now when I'm starting a new job tomorrow.'

He shrugged. 'You should join the online dating scene like I keep telling you.'

I stood to give him a piece of my mind, but he dragged Becky into the kitchen. 'Can we listen to pop music while doing the dishes?' she said.

'Sure,' he replied, turning the radio on before closing the door.

Julia sipped on her wine, having nursed that one glass throughout the meal. 'I wish I had the time for a bit of romance.' She brushed a stray hair from her eyes. 'God, it's been so long.' She gave me a weary smile. 'I need something to take my mind off the job.'

'Problems?'

'Not for me,' she answered. 'Where I work, we've always been understaffed, and it's getting worse.'

'How come?'

Julia sighed. 'My bosses have had to look abroad for staff, and you know how difficult that is with the restrictions. Still, we've employed four women from Zimbabwe, and they've been a big help. We might have gone under without them.'

'That's good then?'

'Initially, yes, but all four left young kids behind, and now the government is refusing entry into the UK for the children. Despite current rules permitting healthcare workers to bring family members here, single mothers, many of them recruited to work in the NHS and care sector, are routinely having their applications denied.'

'That's terrible. Do they know why?'

'The applications are being refused under a decades-old Home Office rule that a child may only be given a visa if both parents live in the UK unless the parent living here has sole responsibility. My colleagues have supplied extensive evidence showing they're the children's primary caregivers, but the applications have still been refused.' Her face darkened. 'If they don't get it sorted, they'll probably have to leave the country.' The darkness turned to anger. 'They come here to help the most vulnerable in society, working long hours in the most extreme conditions for minimum wage, and then they're treated like this. It stinks, Enola.'

I nodded. 'You're right.' It was a good job Bruce was in the kitchen, or he would have gone on a long political rant about how terrible the government was. 'How old are the kids your colleagues had to leave behind?'

'Small babies to kids like Becky. They stay with grandparents or family friends, but it's not ideal. Children like that should be with their parents, especially if they're single mothers.' She finished her drink. 'I better take Becky home before I reach for the wine bottle again.' Julia stood. 'When I get some time off, maybe you and I should go out for a few drinks.' She grinned. 'You never know – we might meet a couple of nice fellas.' A mischievous smile crossed her face as she winked at me. 'Or a couple of lovely ladies, eh?'

Becky ran out of the kitchen. 'Who's lovely? You and Enola?'

Julia hugged her daughter. 'That's right, love.' She nodded at me. 'I hope your first day in the new job goes well tomorrow.'

I thanked her, and they left. Bruce poured himself

another glass of wine. 'Are you looking forward to getting back to proper work?'

'What does that mean?'

He shrugged. 'Well, your last three jobs were on a true crime documentary, delivering dodgy items for a crime boss, and helping our former local MP. Working in a record shop will be different from all those.'

'You're right,' I said. 'I'm going for a run to burn off this curry, but before I do, I need to ask you something.'

Bruce sipped his wine. 'Sure, fire away.'

'What's this about you telling Becky I'm lazy?'

Chapter 4

Runaway

In the dark, my footsteps reverberated against the wet ground, echoing through the silent town. The streetlights flickered, casting dancing shadows as I navigated the winding streets. Neon signs and distant headlights provided a faint glow, illuminating my path. The air was clammy with the scent of diesel and damp concrete. Faraway sirens added a discordant note to the town's symphony, a constant reminder of the chaos that lurked beyond the edges of perception.

I was glad to be out of the flat, needing to clear my head in preparation for my new job. The interview had gone great – Benjamin had seemed a nice bloke – and, as Bruce said, it would make a nice change from my last few jobs.

Each inhale I took was a desperate gasp, the frigid night air burning my lungs. My muscles throbbed with exhaustion, but I refused to relent, consumed by an insatiable craving for movement, anxious to break free from the suffocating grip of my thoughts. Turning a corner, my breath caught at the sight of the river, its dark waters mirroring the moon's ethereal glow. The water seemed alive, its surface rippling with an unseen energy. After thirty minutes of non-stop running, the exhaustion hit me, prompting me to pause for a drink. Thirsty and still tasting curry, I retrieved the water from my bag and drank it with gusto. I finished and returned the bottle to its original position.

I removed my phone and unlocked it. My excitement grew as I saw a new video message from Ginger. The sounds of the night became distant as I focused on the clip, mesmerised by Ginger's hair tousled by the Australian wind.

'Look, Enola, we're having a picnic at Hanging Rock.' Her smile warmed my heart. 'You'd love it here, but we both miss you.' She pulled Jack Parker into view, and he waved at the screen.

'Hi, Enola. I hope you're staying out of trouble.'

There were several good reasons why I distrusted the police, but I'd started to trust Parker before he and Ginger fell into their relationship. I'd warned him before they left for their round-the-world trip that I'd break his legs if he hurt her.

The video ended, and I put the phone away. Then I ran. My footsteps quickened as I headed away from the river, moving towards the darker parts of the town. The streets were deserted, the town's residents retreating into the safety of their homes as the darkness closed in around them. Yet I pressed on, my senses heightened by the adrenaline pumping through me. I heard the rustle of leaves in the wind, the distant cry of gulls circling overhead, the faint thrum of life pulsating beneath the surface.

As I ran, my thoughts wandered, adrift in a maelstrom of memories and half-formed thoughts. I recalled the faces of those I'd lost, seeing my parents not in all the happy moments we had in my first ten years, but as they were when they were murdered, when I hid in the wardrobe, and the spiders swarmed over me. Their voices echoed in the recesses of my mind like whispers in the wind. I was a solitary figure, adrift in a sea of shadows, yet I found solace in the chaos surrounding me. My chest pounded, each beat a reminder of my mortality. The park loomed ahead, its trees casting eerie shadows in the moonlight. I hesitated, the darkness seeming to swallow me whole, but then I plunged forward, driven by a sense of urgency I couldn't explain.

As I entered the gates, the thick scent of damp earth and decaying leaves assaulted my senses. My footsteps echoed off the trees, a hollow percussion reverberating through the night. I felt the weight of the gloom pressing down on me, a tangible presence that seemed to suffocate my senses.

Then I heard voices up ahead, low and murmuring, punctuated by the occasional laughter. I slowed my pace, seeing the shadowy figures huddled together, passing packages between them with furtive gestures: drug dealers conducting their illicit business under cover of night.

They froze, their eyes widening as they saw me. For a moment, nobody moved, the tension covering me like a blanket. One of them stepped forward, his expression a mask of hostility.

'What do you want, girl?'

I met his gaze. 'I want you to leave. You're not wanted here.'

The biggest one stepped forward. 'And who's gonna make us?'

There were four of them, though the three behind the big bloke looked like they'd been tasting their own product.

'Me,' I said.

They cackled like hyenas. The skinny bloke with the

skull tattoo on his neck approached me. 'Are you one of those modern birds who thinks they're better than men?'

I smiled at him. 'If by modern, you mean do I have a personality not forged by stupidity and bigotry? Then yes. And if the men in question are you four dumb fucks, then it's yes again.'

The skinny one reached for me, but the big goon pulled him back. 'She's not worth it.' He pointed a dirty finger at me. 'If I see you again, it'll be painful for you. Come on,' he told his mates.

They slinked into the shadows. 'Don't return,' I said as they left.

His threat of pain was meaningless to me. Pain was an old friend that never disappeared, always lingering in the shadows of my mind. I pictured strangling him and the others, wondering if I should go after them. Wherever they were headed, it would be to distribute more death and misery. I wasn't one to worry about the pointlessness of removing one criminal because another would soon replace them. Just eradicating them was good enough for me. Sometimes, you could build something meaningful with a hammer if you aimed it at the right people. And by that, I meant the wrong people.

I continued running, thinking of those dead tortoises in the woods. Was that the result of criminal activity, a plan to make money from exotic animals gone bad?

The thought annoyed me, so I pushed it away, worried I was spending too much time with violent images in my head. Bruce had tried to convince me to hit the local dating scene since he'd acquired a girlfriend online. Not that he'd purchased her like a bag of crisps, but they'd met through a dating website.

'You need to interact with other adults more,' he'd told me. 'And stop hanging around with Becky.'

Perhaps he was right, at least about the kid.

I'd kept my heart closed off for a long time, convinced being detached and dissatisfied was safer than letting love in. I thought caring too much would make me lose myself. But maybe I was wrong.

'When you find the right person, love doesn't make you edgy or dangerous—it makes you whole,' Bruce had said after only a few dates with his new paramour. 'With love, your perspective expands, and your vision gets clearer, not more confused. You don't lose your sense of humour; you find someone to laugh with. Falling in love makes you embrace life more fully. It fills you with hope, patience, and understanding. You feel emboldened to face the world's challenges with someone by your side. Far from making you psychotic, love keeps you sane.'

I was thrilled for him, but it wasn't what I needed to bring me joy. Breaking the bones of those drug dealers would have done that.

Maybe tomorrow night, I might get the chance again.

Chapter 5

Uptown Funk

B ruce left for his voluntary work at the community food bank early Monday morning, leaving fresh coffee and bagels for me. I watched the news as I had breakfast, seeing that our local water company, Albion Utilities, was in trouble again because of sewage in the river. Maybe that's what we'd smelt coming off the river yesterday.

Albion Utilities were under investigation by the regulator Ofwat and the Environment Agency for alleged illegal sewage dumping from treatment works, and an independent watchdog was saying that the government and even the regulators themselves might have broken the law by letting firms discharge raw sewage more often than the law allowed.

I increased the volume of the TV. The leader of the council, Mary Martin, was on the news, promising a full investigation into the latest events. There was no mention of the discovery of the dead tortoises, but I wondered if the two things were linked. The footage of raw sewage washing up into the reeds and the woods put me off my food.

A spokesperson for the Rivers Trust said: 'Spilling raw sewage into rivers is terrible news for environmental and human health, sending all sorts of unpleasant substances into waterways that shouldn't be there. As well as bacteria, such as E coli, anything that goes down the drain in our combined sewer system could end up in rivers, so that includes excess nutrients like nitrogen and phosphorus, forever chemicals commonly found in household items, and microplastic particles, which are now ubiquitous in our environment.'

I turned the TV off and cleaned away the plates. We had to swim in filthy rivers and seas, breathe polluted air and eat sub-standard food – and I couldn't see things getting better anytime soon. I fed Dirty Harry and left for my first day at my new job. I took the shortcut through the park, surprised by the noise from the other side. Crowds had flocked to the derelict playground, dozens of mobile phones taking pictures of something I couldn't see.

I sidled up to a woman at the back of the crowd. 'What's happening?'

There was a large plastic box near her feet, and she kicked it to me. 'Stand on that, and you'll see.' She grinned at me. 'We've finally got some culture in town.'

I wondered if it was all some elaborate prank and she'd kick me off the box if I stood on it. People shouted ahead of me, excitement rippling through them.

So I got on the box and peered over the bobbing heads, seeing what everybody was staring at - a colourful sketch of a crowned man eating fifty-pound notes while emaciated children gazed at him. Council workers struggled to erect barriers to protect the art.

'Is that a Banksy?' I said.

The woman nodded. 'So they say. Do you think he'd come this far north?'

I stepped off the box. 'Why not?'

A group of teenagers dragged an ancient boombox into the street, turning the volume up to ear-splitting levels as they danced around the rusted swings as if it were the end of the world. A uniformed police officer, his face a dirty orange from too much time on a sunbed, stormed towards the noisy kids. He shouted at them, and a hundred camera phones pointed at him and away from the town's newest artistic endeavour. The copper looked like he'd rather be eating worms in the jungle.

I studied the community, the crumbling buildings, boarded-up shops, burnt-out cars, and rubbish mountains. There was talk online about forthcoming government investment to regenerate the area and gentrify everything, but nobody was expecting that to go through.

'Thanks,' I told the woman as I left. I wandered through the chaotic scene, scrutinising the excited faces. The crowd's energy was unusual for that early in the day, but many kids were around because the schools were on their summer holidays. I paused at the age of the multitude, studying the urban art, wondering if it would still be there by tonight.

The blaring music hurt my ears, so I moved on. The gyrating teens seemed unbothered, lost in their revelry. Their defiance of the furious copper amused some onlookers, but his reddening face told me it could get ugly fast. The local police weren't known for their community relations. I slipped away before his wrath erupted, heading towards my new dawn.

Past the rubble and litter, I spotted a community garden

bursting with life. Neighbours tended lush plots, children laughing as they helped. It was a small oasis, but vital. Growth still flourished there. I recognised those streets from my childhood, playing with friends who later succumbed to poverty, drugs or crime. Their fate reflected the blight that took root when society dismissed certain lives as disposable. Yet resilience and care persisted if you knew where to look.

I turned into Hope Street, brimming with brand-new shops owned by local people – there were no chains or franchises, no big-name multinational companies. Gone were the crumbling facades and boarded windows - freshly painted storefronts with flowers dotting the sidewalk stood in their place. I peered at the new businesses - a bookshop, a grocer, a café buzzing with patrons. Their wares weren't gentrification-chic or astronomically priced. These were neighbourhood joints run by familiar faces.

Mrs. Howard waved to me from arranging bouquets outside her floral boutique. 'What do you think, dear?' she asked with a gap-toothed smile.

'It's lovely,' I said. She'd been a friend of my parents long ago, and I recalled how she'd dreamed of that shop. Investing in locals was how redevelopment should be done.

At the end of Hope Street, a community mural was underway. Artists stood on ladders painting a vibrant landscape with faces from the neighbourhood gazing up in anticipation.

A young girl grabbed my hand, bouncing on her toes. 'That's our building!' she shouted, pointing excitedly. She reminded me of Becky, and I smiled at her bright eyes. The decaying structures were coming down, but people who called that place home would remain, their spirits unsinkable. They deserved to see themselves in the rebirth.

In the middle of it all was Soundwave Emporium, my

new workplace. The name didn't convince me, but the owner – and my new employer - Benjamin Baptiste, had thirty years of experience in the business, so who was I to argue over a name?

My heartbeat increased, and a thrill of expectation ran through me that I hadn't felt in ages.

It was time to get lost in music.

Chapter 6

Lost In Music

I opened the smudged glass door, and a bell jingled overhead. The rich aroma of aged wood panelling and vinyl records enveloped me. Rows of shelves housed boxes of albums; their gritty texture was worn smooth from decades of handling. It was a treasure trove of CDs, tapes and vinyl. I didn't get to look around the shop during my interview, but now I could drift through all its wonders.

My musical upbringing, crucial for enduring my teenage years, consisted of consuming everything as digital tunes. However, in my last children's home, my friend and mentor, Seraphina, introduced me to decades of music that changed my life. She also showed me how a turntable worked and the treasures you could play on it. I had vivid memories of her bringing stacks of LPs into the home, lumped under her arm as she arrived for work. The other girls would be busy on their phones or computers while I sat in the back room, listening to Donna Summer, The Byrds, Chic, The Stranglers, Kraftwerk, and many others.

My dream came true, and I worked in a record shop. It had been dumb luck to see the job advert online, and I was going to make the best of it. Benjamin looked up from sorting fresh arrivals at the counter. His kind eyes crinkled as he smiled beneath his salt-and-pepper beard.

'Hi, Enola,' he said, his voice a warm rumble. 'Are you ready for your new career?'

Posters covered the walls - Bob Marley, Aretha, Bowie, and others gazing down through the years. The air hummed with the crackling chorus of bluesy rock filtering from speakers overhead. I trailed my fingers along the rows of records.

'Absolutely. This place is great.'

Benjamin chuckled. 'She's got character, that's for sure.'

'She?'

His smile warmed my heart. 'Yeah. She's the ship I sail in, guiding me through turbulent and troubled waters.' He held out his hands. 'She's the goddess of the airwaves, nurturing our minds and protecting our souls with the music that enlightens all who love it. It doesn't matter if it's classical or pop, and everything in between; music lifts us as humans and makes us better people. Isn't that right, Enola?'

I laughed. 'You're quoting me from my interview?'

Benjamin grinned. 'You were very impressive. I knew you were the best person for the job when you told me you spent your spare time searching for records in charity shops.' He shook his head. 'Most young people wouldn't know what a seven-inch single is, never mind how to use a turntable. Digital is everything nowadays.'

I grabbed a copy of The Velvet Underground's first album from a box. 'Peel slowly and see. Isn't this rare, Benjamin?'

He nodded. 'Yeah, I need to get it in a case and on the wall behind the counter. It's my main job of the day once I've shown you around.'

I noticed the origami unicorn perched on the register. 'I can't wait.'

He followed my gaze. 'My granddaughter made that.' His pride was evident.

Benjamin gave me a tour, and we had twenty minutes before the shop opened. I traced my fingers over the records, inhaling the earthy vanilla scent of their cardboard sleeves. An antique turntable played a James Brown track near the counter, and the pops and hisses added texture to the funky tune. Outside, the street bustled by the window. However, in the shop, time slowed to let the music breathe. The place felt alive, its soul embedded in vinyl spirals.

I watched as Benjamin sorted through a box of new arrivals. He showed me the stockroom, an office, plus a small kitchen and toilet out the back.

'This is an impressive collection.' I said, wondering how many hours I'd spend getting lost in the musical treasures.

'It takes some organisation, but you'll get the hang of it,' he assured me. 'And it's not just the two of us.'

This was news to me, though I wasn't surprised. The front door chimed, and a lanky guy around my age stepped inside. His billowy blond hair and worn-in Radiohead tee gave him a laid-back vibe.

'Here's Steve now,' Benjamin said, waving him over. 'Steve, meet our new hire, Enola.'

Steve smiled at me. 'Hey, nice to meet you.' His blue eyes were kind and earnest.

'Enola's a big punk and new wave fan,' Benjamin announced. 'I think she'll be a great fit for our musical menagerie.'

Steve nodded. 'That's awesome. We need more creative types around here.' His gaze drifted to a vintage Pink Floyd poster. 'Music speaks truth, you know? It's a way to shake people out of their apathy.'

I sensed his passion went beyond records. Benjamin must have noticed my curiosity. 'Steve is also one of our local environmental activists.'

Steve shrugged self-consciously. 'I'm just trying to make the world cleaner for future generations. We all have a responsibility to take care of this planet.' He pulled a bunch of leaflets from his backpack. 'We should all be like Greta.'

I peered at the paper, seeing a poorly photocopied picture of Greta Thunberg protesting outside an airport near London.

'Did you see the news this morning?' I said. 'About Albion Utilities in trouble over dumping sewage in the river?'

Steve frowned. 'Yeah, there are dozens like that all over the country. Over 400,000 raw sewage discharges were reported by water companies across England and Wales last year – there's shit everywhere.'

'Mary Martin from the council claimed they'll investigate it,' I said.

He shook his head. 'It'll be a whitewash. You don't get to dump that much crap in the river and sea without involvement from somebody in the government, local or national.'

'Okay,' Benjamin said. 'Enough of putting the world to rights. We've got customers to deal with.'

Two women entered the shop, speaking loudly about adding to their Taylor Swift collections. Steve went straight to them, a beaming smile welcoming them inside.

'I know you've worked in retail before, Enola,' Benjamin said. 'But you can learn a lot from observing Steve. He shouts a lot during his protests, but here, he's perfect with customers.' He touched his nose. 'He has the gift of being able to sell stuff he doesn't like.'

I spent the morning watching, sorting stock, and serving behind the counter. I even helped a woman figure out the name of the song she was looking for as an anniversary present for her husband – Visage's "Fade To Grey" – and discovered some rare reggae tunes courtesy of Benjamin's expert knowledge.

The hours flew by in the Soundwave Emporium. After assisting customers, Benjamin regaled me with tales of his lifelong love of music. Though old enough to be my father, his energy and humour kept pace with mine. It was impossible not to be charmed by him.

'Have a seat. I want to play you something,' he said, eyes crinkling with a smile.

I settled onto the worn leather couch as he selected an album. The crisp pop and hiss filled the air as the needle dropped. Then came the upbeat piano chords and brassy horns of vintage ska.

I nodded along to it. 'It reminds me of The Specials.'

'This takes me back,' Benjamin sighed, leaning against the counter. 'My dad played in a little group in London; it was nothing famous, just local gigs. But I used to fall asleep listening to him practice.'

I pictured a young Benjamin drifting off to those lively rhythms. 'So that's how you got hooked on music?'

'Partly. But it goes back further.' He flipped the album cover over, pointing at the band members' smiling faces. 'See that man on the left? That's my grandfather. He and my grandmother came over on *The Empire Windrush* in 1948.'

I peered closer at the grainy photo. 'He looks like you.'

'They brought their music with them – mento, ska,

reggae, all the songs of home. My parents continued that musical tradition.' The trumpet's vibrato sang out as Benjamin's memories unfurled. I imagined his family's soundwaves echoing through the decades. 'Music's always kept me anchored to my roots,' he mused. 'And it's how I bond with my son and grandkids.'

'It's funny you should say that,' I said. 'My friend's eleven-year-old daughter, Becky, is getting into music, and I thought it might be good for her to spend some time here.' I glanced at all the albums, tapes, and CDs. 'Just to make sure she doesn't listen to too many crappy songs on Radio One.'

He nodded. 'Of course. You've got to get the customers early.'

Steve popped in and out between distributing his leaflets to the other shops in the area. He helped me alphabetise the folk music bin, humming to a Joni Mitchell album spinning on the turntable. His activism was tireless, but his demeanour remained upbeat.

'Every positive action counts,' he said with a shrug when I complimented his dedication.

I wished I had his enthusiasm to improve the world, but my cynicism always got the better of me. Even when he was regaling me with a tale of saving the whales, I could only picture the dead turtles in the woods. Part of me wanted to find the people responsible and make them pay.

We gathered behind the counter during a late afternoon lull, drinking coffee and debating our favourite punk bands. Steve's passion for environmental justice fused with his musical knowledge, and he told me about radical artists using their lyrics for protest.

As the day wound down, I felt a sense of belonging in the store. Surrounded by music and kindred spirits, I found inspiration and purpose. I helped Benjamin close the shop, basking in the golden light angling through the front windows.

'You're a natural at this, Enola. I'm glad you joined our little family.'

'So am I,' I replied.

'We're going to the pub for food. Then there's a gig at the Raven if you fancy it.'

'A gig?'

'Yeah, some people my son went to university with.' He grinned at me. 'You think I'm too old for it, right?'

I shook my head. 'Nope. The woman who introduced me to music was also an old duffer.'

Steve laughed. 'She got you there, Benjamin.'

We stepped outside. He locked the shop door, and we helped him pull down the metal shutters. 'You kids will give me a heart attack.' He slipped the keys into his pocket. 'The first round is on you, Steve.'

Steve grinned. 'Sure, just like always.' He looked at me. 'Are you coming, Enola?'

I considered my options: a night at a gig or going for a jog to see if I could find those drug dealers in the park again.

It was a tough choice.

Chapter 7

Uptown Top Ranking

The heavy bass line vibrated through the crowd as people swayed and danced to the music. Benjamin was at the bar as Steve slipped between the throng, handing out leaflets when he could. I grabbed one from him as I waited for Benjamin and my Coke.

'Say No To Council Cuts!' I read aloud from the leaflet.

He nodded. 'They're planning on cutting essential services and increasing the council tax. Those bastards will break this town while tax cuts make the rich richer.'

Everybody around us seemed to be enjoying themselves except him. 'How do you know the council will cut services?'

He smirked at me. 'Trust me, Enola, it's going to happen.'

I didn't want to think about it, picturing Becky and her mum struggling, so focused on the music as Benjamin returned with the drinks.

'Thanks,' I said. I turned to Steve. 'How'd you get into music?'

His eyes lit up. 'It was borrowing my older sister's Bob

Marley tapes. I must've played them a thousand times. Hearing local bands around town sealed the deal.'

'What about you, Enola?' Benjamin asked.

'A mate of mine introduced me to The Clash, Bowie, Peter Tosh, and others when I was a teenager.' I smiled as memories flooded back. 'When I was fourteen, I snuck into my first punk gig with my friend Amy. I'll never forget pressing up against the stage as the guitars shredded and the singer screamed. The adrenaline of it sparked something in me.'

Benjamin chuckled. 'Ah yes, I remember that feeling well. Once it grabs hold, the music never lets go.'

'Too right,' Steve chimed in. 'As a teenager, when I saw The Manic Street Preachers live, that was it. That night sparked my rebellious spirit.'

I nodded, the camaraderie between us surprising me with its immediacy. I'd only known these men for a few hours, but it already felt like we were lifelong friends.

'Ever since that first gig,' I said. 'I've been chasing that feeling.'

'Some songs grab your soul and shake your world forever,' Benjamin said. 'I feel sorry for people who don't have this.' He beamed. 'I'll educate you properly on reggae history.'

We bantered and laughed, the music and Benjamin's enthusiastic stories transporting us. At that moment, with the joy of the gig swirling around us, I felt a connection growing between us - not just co-workers, but maybe friends. I realised working at the record shop might be more than a job; it was a chance to build a community. The image of the drug dealers in the park faded into the background. Perhaps I'd discovered something to replace that need to deliver justice to those who always seemed to dodge it.

The air was thick with heat and the sweet scent of dope as the mass of bodies pressed close together. On stage, red and green lights illuminated the musicians, casting a colourful glow over them. The drummer pounded out driving beats that vibrated in my chest while the bassist plucked out deep, resonant notes that rattled my bones.

The band started a new song with a syncopated rhythm that got the crowd bouncing. I glanced at Steve, who was moving with eyes closed, lost in the moment. His curly hair was sweaty, and his focus made me smile.

I noticed my reflection in the mirror behind the bar, confused by how I felt. Maybe it was just the music and the euphoria surrounding me, added to the dope slithering its way into my lungs and head. It was unusual for me to be so happy, and it worried me. My happiness usually came when jogging or spending time with Bruce or Becky. Or from hurting people. However, this was different. There appeared to be crazed butterflies beating their wings against my insides.

When the tune ended, Steve opened his eyes, catching me watching him. 'This band is amazing. Their lead singer used to play drums for my favourite group, Ghost Town.'

I nodded, enjoying his enthusiasm. 'I know them – they were named after the song by The Specials.'

'That's right,' he said.

We talked about other bands we loved, realising we shared some favourites from our teen years. The conversation flowed easily. Benjamin winked at me as he went to the bar.

'Another Coke, Enola?'

'Sure.' I hadn't touched alcohol since I was sixteen, but the sugar rush was playing havoc with my emotions.

'You don't drink?' Steve asked.

I grinned. 'My body's a temple.'

That was his chance to reply with a cheesy chat-up line, but he either didn't get it, or his nerves were worse than mine. Was this how Ginger felt when she first saw the former detective inspector, Jack Parker?

A slower tune came on, and people grabbed each other close to sway along.

'You can't beat a bit of lover's rock,' Steve said.

'Absolutely,' I replied.

He pulled at his collar, cheeks flushed. 'Want to dance?'

Laughing, I took his hand and led him between all the other couples. Under the dreamy lights, I noticed the kindness in his eyes. The music surrounded me, pulling us closer. My hand rested on his shoulder as we moved together. With his arm around me, the venue and crowd seemed to melt away. We stayed hand in hand when the song ended, both hesitant to let go. Something had shifted between us. I wasn't sure what it meant and didn't know if I wanted to find out.

Benjamin returned with more drinks. I dropped Steve's hand, feeling self-conscious. Benjamin sidled up next to me, laughter crinkling his eyes.

'I might have to keep you two separated in the shop from now on.'

I felt my cheeks flush hot and mumbled excuses about just dancing as friends. Nevertheless, Benjamin's teasing brought reality back. While Steve was kind, could I let myself get close to someone again?

I'd thrown up walls around me since my parents died, keeping everyone at a distance. It was easier than admitting I still ached from loss and feared more of the same pain. Steve didn't know the wounds I carried. I wasn't sure I knew myself.

He snatched his beer from Benjamin, and I made excuses to visit the ladies, my legs trembling with every step. As I squeezed by gyrating bodies towards the bathroom, my pulse pounded in my ears. Benjamin's joke had cracked open the fortress around my heart. Being with Steve stirred up emotions I thought I'd barricaded away for good. But those feelings left me exposed.

Giggling young women pushed past me as I entered, seeing the red flush consuming my cheeks in the mirror. I gripped the bathroom sink, staring at my reflection. Did I dare lower my defences again? Steve's smile flashed in my mind, warming me. Damn! I'd felt no fear when dealing with those drug dealers, but now it was as if I was about to throw up. Perhaps it was all the ganja floating through the club rattling my nerves.

I splashed water on my flushed face when two women came up beside me.

'You alright, hun?' one asked, her eyes full of concern beneath her pink glasses.

I nodded. 'It's been a long day.'

The other woman smiled, her silver hair glowing under the lights. 'Man troubles?'

I laughed. 'That obvious?'

'Saw you dancing with that dish out there,' the first woman said. 'The cute one with the curls. I'd snatch him up if I were you.'

'It's... complicated,' I sighed.

The older one patted my shoulder. 'Dear, take it from me - don't overthink it too much. The heart wants what it wants.'

'We work together,' I said. 'And I've only known him a few hours.'

Her friend nodded. 'What's life without a little risk in love? You both looked so happy out there.'

Happy? Was that what I was?

Maybe it was time to find out.

I returned to the dance floor. The band's final song ended with a piercing guitar riff that rang in my ears as we funnelled outside. The cool night air was a shock after the sweltering club. Benjamin talked to friends as Steve and I lingered on the sidewalk, neither eager to part ways yet.

'That was an epic show,' he said, smiling at me with bright eyes. His cheeks were still flushed.

I agreed, suddenly bashful. 'One of the best I've seen.'

An awkward silence fell between us. I scuffed my boot against the pavement, unsure what to say. Things had felt so natural inside, but now uncertainty crept in.

'Well, I guess I should head home,' I mumbled. As I turned to leave, somebody knocked Steve, and he bundled into me.

He grabbed my shoulders before moving back, his eyes all apologetic. 'I'm sorry, Enola.'

I grinned. 'Don't worry about it.' I wasn't sure how much he'd had to drink, but his hazy expression might not have been all about the booze.

'You'll have a banging skull tomorrow,' Benjamin said as he approached us.

Steve laughed. 'Nah, I never have hangovers. And anyway, I've got stuff to do when I get home. That will clear my head.'

'Something interesting?' I asked.

He touched his nose. 'It's top secret environmental work. I'll tell you once I know I can trust you.' His hip bumped into mine, and electricity shivered through me. 'Do you want to come on a protest march with me?'

I inched closer to him, smelling the sweat in his hair. 'Are you asking me for a date?'

Steve's cheeks flushed, and he pulled at his collar. 'Eh, no, of course not.' He glanced at Benjamin. 'It would be inappropriate for two work colleagues to do such a thing.'

Benjamin shook his head. 'That's okay, as long as I don't find you snogging in the stock room.'

It was my turn to blush, changing the subject. 'What are you protesting about?'

'The council wants to knock down the old cinema to build flats,' he said. 'But it's a listed building. Charlie Chaplin and The Beatles played there.'

'Who was the headliner?'

He laughed. 'Not together. It's a piece of local history, and we won't let them get away with another example of cultural vandalism.' His eyes sparkled with fire. 'There are dodgy backhanders going on with the council. That's what I'll expose.'

Benjamin patted him on the shoulder. 'That's enough exposing for now. It's time to go home.' He looked at me. 'Are you getting a taxi?'

I shook my head. 'It's only a short walk to my flat. Thanks for the invite – I've had a great day. I'll see you both in the morning.' I glanced at Steve. 'Don't stay up too late.'

Then I headed home, feeling better than I had in a long time.

And I didn't think about those drug dealers at all.

Chapter 8

Police and Thieves

The music was still in my head when I saw the police car outside the building. Panic swept through me as I ran forward, stopping when I noticed Bruce smoking a cigarette while Kronos pulled against his lead.

'What happened?' I said. 'Are you okay?'

He blew smoke above the dog. 'I returned from taking this fella for a walk and found the front door broken. The flat's a mess – somebody broke in while we were out.' He finished the fag. 'How was your day? Good gig?'

I clutched at my chest as my heart steadied. 'Forget about me. What's happening inside?' I couldn't see any coppers.

'The police are checking the flat. Come on, I'll show you the damage.'

I followed Bruce inside, the acrid scent of his smoke lingering over me. The splintered door came into view first, wood shards littering the ground. There were two uniformed coppers in the flat but no forensic officers. My eyes widened at the chaos within - drawers flung open, belongings strewn across the floor, broken glass and ceramics crunching under my boots.

'Mind where you step,' a copper advised in a bored tone. Faint cluttering sounds came from the back rooms as they searched for clues half-heartedly.

I glanced at Bruce, who shook his head. 'They won't find anything. It was probably kids looking for quick cash.' His jaw was tight, eyes troubled. 'My laptop and the money in my bedroom are gone.'

Kronos whined, nosing through shredded papers and overturned furniture. I rested my hand on his back, taking comfort in his familiar warmth. The sanctuary Bruce and I had made was despoiled.

'Fuck!'

'What?' he said.

I ran to the glass enclosure on the sideboard. 'Dirty Harry's gone.'

'Dirty Harry?' a woman said behind me.

My legs trembled as I turned to see a plain-clothes female officer. 'My tarantula. Those fuckers must have taken him.'

'I'm Detective Sergeant Rose Kamara,' she said. 'And you are?'

I examined the container, searching for Harry. 'What?'

'Do you live here?' She glanced at Bruce. 'Are you two a couple?'

I glared at her. 'What the fuck has that got to do with anything?'

She ignored the question. 'Why would anybody steal your spider?'

A volcano burnt through me. 'How the fuck would I know?'

DS Kamara studied the damage in the flat. 'There are

six flats on this block, yet yours was the only place the thieves targeted.'

I dug my nails into my palms. 'What are you implying?'

The copper shrugged. 'I'm not implying anything, Ms...?'

'Enola Gray,' I replied. The three officers glanced at each other as if I was number one on their most wanted list. 'Are you new?'

She raised her eyebrows. 'New at what?'

I lifted my hands to indicate the mess in the flat. 'Investigating crimes. I haven't seen you around town before.'

'Do you have a lot of involvement with the police?' Kamara asked.

My laugh hurt my ribs. 'You could say that.'

She turned from me to Bruce. 'Do you think this may have been a targeted attack?'

'Attack?' he said.

DS Kamara pulled a notebook from her pocket. 'Could somebody have broken into your flat for personal reasons?' She peered at the glass enclosure. 'Stealing a tarantula doesn't seem to be a random event. I'd have thought you'd need a special container to transport it.'

She was right, but I wouldn't admit it to her. 'Fucking fuck!'

'Were you out all evening?' Her gaze was probing.

I bristled. 'Yeah, I was at a gig. Is that unusual on a Monday?'

Kamara flipped open the notebook. 'And when did you leave?'

I rolled my eyes. 'Gee officer, let me think. I departed from Platform 9 3/4 one month ago and just arrived home via the Hogwarts Express.'

Bruce stifled a laugh as Kamara's scowl deepened.

'There's no need for attitude. I'm only establishing a timeline.'

I took a breath. 'Look, I don't know what happened. I was out all day and returned to this mess.' I gestured around. 'Ask the neighbours if they saw anything.'

'We will,' she replied. 'Was anything else taken?'

Bruce scratched at his face. 'I don't think so. As I told your colleagues, a laptop and five hundred pounds in cash are missing.' He glanced at me. 'And Enola's tarantula.'

'Five hundred pounds?' Kamara said. 'That's a lot of money to have lying around.'

I slapped my hand on the sideboard. 'Are you blaming us for this now?'

Kamara's expression was unmoving. 'Of course not, but you seem unhappy with us being here.'

I could have reached over and strangled her. 'Do you get many burglaries like this?'

'What, people stealing exotic spiders? I can't say we do.'

That wasn't what I meant, but I didn't correct her. 'You're never going to find who did this, are you? I'm surprised you even turned up. Don't the coppers ignore most crimes nowadays?'

DS Kamara put her notebook away. 'We'll be in touch when we have any news. You'll get a crime number for insurance purposes.'

She led the others out of the flat. 'Yeah,' I shouted at her back. 'We won't hold our breaths.'

They left, and I sagged against the wall, the adrenaline vanishing. Bruce righted an overturned chair and gestured for me to sit.

'Quite the homecoming, eh?' He tried to sound light-hearted but couldn't mask the violation in his eyes.

I shook my head, anger still simmering. 'Who the hell would do this?'

'Maybe just some random thief. The neighbourhood's gone downhill lately.'

'Oh, come on,' I said sharply. 'They clearly knew we'd be out and were looking for something specific.'

Bruce's expression darkened. 'You think it's connected to your extracurricular activities?'

I bit my lip. 'My what?'

He pulled Kronos to him. 'I know what you get up to when you jog at night, Enola.'

'Yeah, I run a lot.'

'Sure, and you beat up muggers and petty criminals.'

'There's nothing petty about drug dealers, stalkers, and perverts.'

He sighed. 'You're right, but it's not your job to deal with them.'

I laughed. 'What, so I should leave it to the coppers? Like that useless woman who was just here?' I shook my head. 'Anyway, if it were related to that, I'd expect more than smashed-up furniture,' I mused. 'This feels personal.'

Bruce nodded. 'Maybe that's why they took Dirty Harry. Could it be someone from your past, then? An old score to settle?'

My laugh was bitter. 'Take your pick.'

We spent an hour cleaning the mess and checking to ensure nothing else was missing. The rest of the night was me worrying about Harry and wondering how I'd find him.

Chapter 9

Digital Witness

B y the time I finished breakfast, I had a rudimentary plan.

'How do you feel?' Bruce asked as I grabbed my phone and texted an old friend.

'Fine, all things considered. How about you?'

He shrugged. 'I need a new laptop.' When he wasn't helping at the food bank, Bruce spent most of his time trading shares online. 'With all the commotion last night, you never told me how it went at work. And the concert you attended with your new friends.'

'They're hardly friends,' I replied. 'I've known them one day, that's all.' I thought of Steve, wondering if last night's flirting was only a spur-of-the-moment thing. 'And now I have to tell Benjamin I'll be late today.'

'Are you feeling unwell because of the burglary?' We'd cleaned the place up, but there were still signs of what happened.

I shook my head. 'I'm fine. I have to see someone before heading to the record shop.'

'Somebody I know?'

'You've never met her, but you know of her,' I replied.

He laughed. 'That's cryptic. Wait, do you mean Amy?'

I nodded. 'Yep.'

Bruce narrowed his eyes. 'Are you friends again?'

'Hopefully. I need a favour from her.'

Concern gripped his features. 'Is this because she's a criminal?'

I grinned. 'I'm not sure that's how she'd describe herself, but if anyone knows about local thieves, it will be Amy.' My phone pinged as he frowned. I checked it to see her reply.

Meet me at Future Content. It's on Hope Street.

The name rang a bell. Then I remembered seeing it in the row of new shops yesterday.

'Have you heard of a place called Future Content, Bruce?'

He shook his head. 'Nope. What's that?'

I told him. 'All those new shops that opened in town, Soundwave Emporium, and the others. Didn't you tell me it was a government grant that paved the way for creating them?'

He nodded. 'That's right. The money went to the council, and they decided which local opportunities to support. Benjamin Baptiste's record shop was among several lucky applicants, but the council turned down lots more. Lots of people complained online about the process. Why do you ask?'

I used my phone to search for Future Content online, discovering a flashy website offering services where AI tools would create material for organisations and individuals. The site didn't mention Amy, but I sensed her hands behind it. I showed it to Bruce.

'This is where I'm meeting her.'

'Artificial intelligence is taking over the world,' he said.

'Maybe,' I said, wondering what part Amy Sparrow would play in that.

I texted Benjamin as I left, apologising for why I'd be late but explaining about the break-in.

Not to worry, he replied. *I hope you're okay. I can survive on my own.*

Where's Steve?

Not here yet. He might be sleeping off last night's hangover.

Or perhaps he was embarrassed because of what happened between us. But nothing did happen. Yet, I knew it could have.

Maybe it still would.

I pushed that thought from my mind, worrying about Dirty Harry.

Then I headed off to visit my old friend, hoping she'd help me find my stolen spider.

The summer sun caressed my face on the journey. I wanted to feel good, but Dirty Harry's fate bothered me. Did somebody target the flat for him? If so, what did they put him in? Or maybe he slipped out of his container and wandered off somewhere.

Fuck! I didn't know what would be worse. If he were out in the wild, there would be all sorts of dangers. At least if someone had stolen him, he should be in a proper enclosure.

A million worries ran through my head as I strode through the town. The council had erected a barrier around the Banksy, and most locals had moved on to other things. I saw media vans and cameras outside the Town Hall, wondering what was happening. Then I noticed the protestors with their placards, shouting about the shit in our rivers, the crumbling schools and hospitals, and asking why the rich were getting richer while the poorest struggled to pay the bills. I glanced at them, seeing if Steve was there. If he was, I didn't see him.

I thought of Becky and her mother, with Julia working all the hours she could, yet she still couldn't afford to have the heating on during winter. I'd mentioned it to Bruce over breakfast.

'We appear to be existing between two extremes,' he'd said after we cleaned up the flat. 'Empathy versus ego.'

He didn't expand on that, but I knew what he meant. We'd become a country where you are what you have, transforming us into a polarised society of those who have it, flaunt it, and those who don't and must find someone or something to blame for why they don't have it. And social media had only made it worse.

It seemed clear to me that people sat on a spectrum between kindness and selfishness, mixed with a desire for prestige and personal reward. At the extreme end were sociopaths and narcissists who needed no environmental pressure at all. They were the ones who always appeared to rise to leadership positions in society, whether in business or government.

As that thought crossed my mind, Mary Martin stepped out of the Town Hall to speak to the media and the protestors. I kept walking, not interested in what lies she'd spout about the sewage dumped in the river and why the council were slashing public services while the government was cutting taxes for the rich and spending billions on the military.

To take my mind off the terrible things I imagined might have happened to Dirty Harry, I remembered my good time at the gig and how I felt around Steve. I'd known him for only a few hours, but we'd immediately hit it off. And I couldn't blame booze for the flirting.

I texted him, hoping he didn't have too much of a hangover.

Then, I stepped into Future Content to talk with my past.

Chapter 10

Ghost in the Machine

The soft hum of activity and the gentle tap-tap of keyboards greeted me as I entered the shop. Abstract paintings adorned the walls, adding colour to the otherwise modern décor. Approaching the reception desk, I nodded to the young woman behind it.

'I'm here to see Amy Sparrow,' I said. 'I'm Enola Gray.'

The receptionist smiled, her fingers dancing across the keyboard as she checked me in. 'Of course,' she said, her voice professional. 'She's expecting you.'

'Enola,' Amy appeared from a back room, her bold lipstick matching her red blazer. She gripped me in a fierce hug before releasing me.

I leaned in closer to her, out of earshot of the reception-ist. 'Is this your new scam?'

Amy frowned. 'What kind of greeting is that for your oldest and closest friend?'

She was right. There was no need to antagonise her since I needed her help.

'Nice office,' I said, taking in the trendy minimalist decor. 'You've gone up in the world from your last place.'

Amy laughed. 'You mean the back room in the Rusty Nut public house?' I nodded. 'Yes, I required something much more upmarket for this venture.'

I lowered my voice. 'Have you moved into cybercrime?'

She looked offended. 'I'll have you know I'm a legitimate businesswoman.'

I glanced around the humming machines and the young people hunched over them. 'Doing what, exactly?'

Amy grabbed my arm and dragged me to a pink-haired woman staring at a large screen. 'You didn't check our website before coming here?'

With a few clicks of a mouse, the woman generated an image of Humphrey Bogart drinking from a can of Coke.

'Sure, but it made little sense. You're using AI to take over the world, is that it?'

She shook her head. 'I thought you were the computer whizz kid?'

'I am, but I still don't understand why anybody would come to you for their AI-generated content when they can do it themselves.'

Amy wrapped her arm around my shoulder. 'My dear Enola, why do folks hire people for jobs they could do themselves?'

'Pure laziness?' I replied.

'Probably, but whatever the reason, Future Content will be at the forefront of this exciting new enterprise. Our AI excels at creating compelling material tailored to the goal,' she explained. 'It can generate social media posts, articles, ads, you name it. You'd love how much this increases productivity. And the analytics show what resonates with audiences.'

'How long have you planned this?'

'A while,' she said. 'We'd have been up and running

sooner but for difficulties acquiring the appropriate premises.'

'Difficulties?'

She shrugged. 'One reason it took an age to find the right site was that anywhere easy to build on was snapped up by developers, many of them with local authority contacts.'

'Were you part of the funding the council handed out for new businesses?'

'Yes. I gave a fantastic presentation.'

Six staff members were beavering away at computers. 'You have plenty of clients?'

Amy nodded. 'Absolutely. And we just signed a contract with the council this morning, making them our largest client.'

'Doing what?'

She let go of me, and we moved away from her staff. 'Everything and anything – promotional material, videos, photos, web design; it's a long list. But I know this isn't a social visit. What's up?'

I sighed, the levity draining away. 'My place was ransacked last night. They took Dirty Harry.'

Amy's eyes widened. 'No way! Your creepy crawly BFF?'

I nodded, jaw tightening. 'I need your help to get him back. Thought your connections might hear something about who's suddenly peddling exotic spiders.'

Amy held up a manicured finger. 'I'm not in that world anymore, E. I've gone corporate.'

'What?' Was it another of her cons? 'This AI stuff isn't just a side hustle or a front for something dodgy?'

She placed a hand over her heart. 'You wound me, my friend.'

My shoulders slumped. I'd been counting on Amy's ties to the criminal underground.

'I get it,' I said. 'You're legit now. I just hoped.'

Amy cut me off. 'I'll make some calls, anyway. Old habits die hard.' She shot me a sly wink. She must have read the dejection on my face. 'In the meantime, let me show you our secret weapon.' She led me into a glass-walled conference room housing the largest computer I'd ever seen.

'Meet Zeus, our AI content wizard,' she declared. 'Zeus, meet my friend Enola.'

'Hello Enola,' a male voice replied through hidden speakers. 'It's nice to meet you.'

I shot a bewildered look at Amy, who just grinned wider. 'Zeus is our AI system. He can create any content you need in seconds.'

'Pleased to be of assistance,' the machine responded politely. Zeus rattled off his capabilities - research, writing, graph and data analysis. The creative potential was astounding. And a bit terrifying.

'Can you tell Zeus why I'm here?' I asked Amy.

'Zeus is an AI, not a private detective.'

I bit my lip. 'Maybe not. But he's damn good at finding connections in information, right?'

Amy's eyes lit up, catching on. 'Okay, genius, let's see those skills in action.'

Over the next twenty minutes, we fed Zeus all the details of the break-in and Harry's disappearance. His processors whirred, analysing and inferring.

'There is an eighty-three per cent probability the perpetrator possesses advanced knowledge of exotic animals,' Zeus finally reported. 'The targeted nature of the theft and skill in removing a volatile spider point to an experienced handler.'

'I feel like I'm in a science fiction movie,' I said.

Amy laughed. 'You always wanted to be Ripley from the *Alien* movies.'

'Only the first two – the others are shit.'

She nodded. 'You got that right.'

I pointed at the computer. 'How is this information going to help me find Dirty Harry?'

'I always thought that was a stupid name for a tarantula. Godzilla would have been better.'

'He's not a lizard.'

'Luckily for those thieves.'

I asked again. 'How will that info help me?'

She grabbed my arm and dragged me away from Zeus. 'Have you heard of the concept of cognitive miserliness?'

I wriggled from her grasp. 'No.'

'Well,' she said. 'A cognitive miser is anyone who seeks quick, adequate solutions to problems rather than slow, careful ones.'

'Are you insulting me, Amy?'

She shook her head. 'No, I'm referring to professional criminals always looking for quick fixes that don't involve hard work.'

'You're taking the piss, right?'

'No. Populism, nationalism, crime - it's all about not having to think. Having intrinsic values is hard. You worry, have to think about complicated, difficult problems and ideas, and come up against confrontational, challenging people. You have to be able to put forward arguments, and it all takes a lot of energy. Following an extrinsic leader relieves you of all that. And what a relief! Just follow along with your new friends! Don't look at evidence any more, don't listen, facts don't matter. Don't think! You belong now to your clan. You have let your leader do your thinking for you, and it's lovely! So easy! All hail the leader, and Job Done! This also explains why so many thinking, open-minded people turn to extremes and can't be brought back to being thinking humans again. They are in a mental comfort zone, denial if you like, and have to climb up out of that low mental energy state to be a thinker again. It's very much a one-way street. There is no way that reason alone can bring them out because they're not listening, not processing. They'll even protect their bubble.'

'What's your point, Amy?'

She sighed. 'I'm trying to apologise, Enola.'

'Apologise for what?'

'You matured quicker than me, E. I was looking for the easy way out in life, using crime for that. But I've caught up with you now.'

'You won't help me find Dirty Harry.'

'*Au contraire*, my old friend. I'll use my contacts to ask about those trading in exotic animals. You'll get your spider back, don't worry. Just wait for my call.'

I thanked her and left, not wanting to leave Benjamin in the lurch for too long. Amy seemed changed, and I trusted she'd find Harry for me.

But what condition would he be in?

Chapter 11

Sound System

Zeus's near-perfect human voice was ringing in my ears when I strode into the Soundwave Emporium. Benjamin acknowledged me as he dealt with a customer looking through a box of David Bowie imports. I went behind the counter, where the rumbling in my stomach told me it was approaching lunchtime, though it wasn't loud enough to drown out the sound of The Byrds coming from the speakers.

A group of teenagers stumbled inside, which I found surprising. They were probably only a few years younger than me, and I expected them to get their musical fixes through online streaming services and mobile phones.

Seeing them took me back to my first visit to a record shop. It was my fifteenth birthday, and Seraphina thought it was time to introduce me to the magic of retail music therapy. She worked in the latest children's home the local council had dumped me in after the murders of my parents, and it was an excellent excuse to take a trip away from that place.

She led me to Spin Cycle Records, a treasure trove of

music where the scent of old records and the sound of eclectic tunes filled the air. As I stepped inside, the musty aroma filled the air, a blend of dust and ageing cardboard mixing with the fragrance of sandalwood incense burning near the front counter. As I browsed the towering shelves, the scuffed hardwood floors echoed with the squeak of my Converse sneakers. Trailing my fingers along the gritty record sleeves, I scanned the titles and artists, the faint smell of old vinyl filling my lungs. The overhead speakers filled the air with the constant hum of rock music.

Rows of vinyl records lined the walls, their vibrant covers catching the light and drawing me in like a moth to a flame. Each cover was a work of art, a kaleidoscope of colours and images that sparked my imagination. I could feel the music pulsing through the room, a tangible presence that seemed to wrap around me like a warm embrace.

At the rear of the shop, I found the punk section. Flipping through albums, the riot of colour and covers drew me in like a magnet - The Ramones, Sex Pistols, Blondie. I settled on a Siouxsie and the Banshees record, intrigued by the haunting image of Siouxsie with her raccoon-ringed eyes.

'I want to look like that,' I told Seraphina.

'Good taste,' she said. 'You know I met her once.'

'Yeah,' I replied. 'What happened?'

Seraphina leaned against the counter, a wistful smile on her lips as she recounted her encounter with Siouxsie Sioux. 'It was back in 1978, just after the release of "Hong Kong Garden." I lived in London then and stumbled upon a small club where Siouxsie and the Banshees were playing. The energy in that place was electric, like nothing I'd ever experienced. She was a force of nature on stage, commanding the attention of everyone in the room with her raw, unapologetic presence.'

I listened intently, hanging on Seraphina's every word as she transported me back to that moment. The image of Siouxsie, wild and untamed, burned itself into my mind, igniting a spark of inspiration within me. 'What was she like?'

Seraphina laughed, her eyes sparkling with nostalgia. 'She was a force to be reckoned with, that's for sure. But offstage, she was surprisingly down-to-earth. After the show, we chatted for a while, and she struck me as incredibly genuine and sincere. There was a fire in her, a passion for music that burned brighter than anything I'd ever seen.'

The joy of Seraphina revealing something about herself echoed inside me, and I realised how much I missed her.

'Always remember this,' she told me. 'Galleries and bookshops are quiet places, created for contemplation, but record shops are noisy temples to gather, gossip and flirt.'

She was right, but there weren't many of them left. However, at least I was in one. As that thought crossed my mind, Benjamin finished with the customer and approached me.

'Are you okay, Enola? Going home last night to see what happened to the flat must have been terrible.'

I shrugged. 'I've seen worse things.' I assumed he knew the story of my parents' deaths, but he didn't pry. 'Steve didn't turn up?'

He rubbed at his wrinkled chin. 'No, and I've called and texted him several times. It's not like him.'

'He did have a bit to drink last night.'

Benjamin shook his head. 'That was nothing for him. He knows how to hold his booze.' I noticed the worry in his eyes. 'Maybe I should check his flat to see if he's okay.'

'You'd close up the shop?'

He laughed. 'Of course not – I trust you to look after it.'

I glanced at the teenagers at the back, hoping they weren't nicking stuff. 'Sure, I could do that. Or I could go to Steve's after work.'

He considered that. 'Nah, forget about it. I'm probably worrying over nothing. He's a big boy and can handle himself.'

The kids pulled out two Taylor Swift albums and combined their cash to check if they had enough. I nodded in their direction.

'That's good to see, young people buying vinyl.'

Benjamin laughed. 'Young people? What does that make you and me?'

I grinned. 'Lucky. No, I just thought they'd be streaming all their music and not buying physical stuff.'

He scowled. 'Digital streaming has been a catastrophe for most artists - their only real revenue since physical music sales collapsed now comes from concerts. But many still offer physical copies of their music at gigs. You can't say that the rise of digital streaming has benefited artists compared to physical music retailers.'

'You're right,' I said. 'Which is why it's great that Soundwave Emporium is here.' The teenagers took the records to the counter, and I went to serve them. 'And it's great for me as well.'

I spent the rest of the day chatting to Benjamin and dozens of customers, trying to push aside my dark thoughts about DH.

Then, just before the shop shut, Amy texted me.

I had an address for the thieves who might have Dirty Harry.

Chapter 12

When Doves Cry

I texted Amy. *Are you sure that's the correct address?*
Of course. Should I come and hold your hand?
You've got more chance of holding Zeus's hand.
Ha, ha. Let me know how you get on. I already feel sorry for those poor blokes.

I reread her original message with the details of the gang calling themselves The Poachers, led by Ryan Brown. The names meant nothing to me. My focus was on getting Dirty Harry back. And to ask the thieves if they'd targeted me on purpose.

The wind whipped around me as I strode towards the abandoned funfair through the woods. The crisp air stung my cheeks as I trudged through the dense thicket of trees, their gnarled branches reaching out like skeletal fingers grasping at the sky. A symphony of rustling leaves and swaying boughs enveloped me, echoing in my ears like a haunting melody. The scent of damp soil mingled with the sharp aroma of fallen foliage, filling my nostrils with the unmistakable fragrance of the summer.

My footsteps bounced off the ground. The crunch of

twigs and leaves beneath my boots was a comforting rhythm that echoed the pounding of my heart. The path ahead lay shrouded in darkness, illuminated only by the faint glow of the sinking sun filtering through the dense canopy above. The shadows danced around me, twisting and contorting in the shifting light, casting eerie shapes that seemed to beckon me further into the unknown.

A fox ran across my route, darting its head to the side to peer at me, the intruder in its environment. Fox hunting had been banned decades before, but now there were growing calls to bring it back as some supposed return to a great British tradition of natural values. I pictured the fox as large as an elephant – him and others – chasing overdressed buffoons through the woods. That was something I could vote for.

The abandoned funfair loomed ahead; its rusted rides and crumbling facades were a reminder of the joy and excitement that used to ring out there—the air stank of decay, a musty odour that clung to the crumbling structures like a shroud. I heard the distant sound of creaking metal and wailing wood, the remnants of a bygone era echoing in the night's silence.

Bare branches clawed at the overcast sky. A damp, earthy scent filled my nose, overlaying the faint trace of rust from the dilapidated rides. Gravel crunched under my boots, mingling with the squeaking and groaning of the tilting Ferris wheel shifting in the breeze.

Nearby, music thumped, a muffled baseline guiding my path. As I drew closer, laughter and shouting filtered through the trees. My pulse quickened, but I kept my breathing even. I slipped my hand into my jacket pocket, feeling the cool metal of the switchblade.

As I passed the peeling ticket booth, I searched for any

signs of life. A tattered poster clinging to a kiosk depicted a grinning clown, now morphed into something sinister. A cold drop of rain hit my cheek. The wind picked up again with a mournful howl.

According to Amy's intel, the gang operated out of the old haunted house. I steeled myself as the warped entrance emerged, decorated with leering plastic figures. Their bulging eyes appeared to watch me approach.

Then I heard the screaming.

I stuck to the shadows and moved inside, seeing how parts of the building had been ripped out to make way for cages of various sizes. The screams came from the metallic prisons holding dozens of doves, beating their wings against the bars.

'Can't you get them to shut the fuck up?' a bloke said as he wandered into view. He wasn't speaking to me as I hid in the gloom. His hair was as dark as a black hole, and he seemed vaguely familiar. Another man joined him - scars crisscrossed his face, reaching up to his bald head.

'What do you want me to do, Ryan? I'm not Dr Dolittle. They don't listen to me.'

I couldn't see anyone else beyond them, but there were cages full of lizards, raccoon dogs and monkeys. But no Dirty Harry.

Fuck!

In the flickering light of a dim fire, the pens cast elongated shadows that danced across the uneven ground, adding to the eerie ambience of the desolate funfair.

'When's the truck due?' Ryan asked his mate.

Baldy checked his watch. 'Not until midnight.'

Ryan glared at the howling birds. 'You'll have to look after them alone until Tommy and the twins return. I need to speak to a client.'

'Okay,' the goon replied. 'Bring me back a burger, will ya? I haven't eaten all day.'

I clung to the shadows as Ryan strode past me, so close I inhaled his lemony aftershave. Its potency grabbed my lungs in invisible fingers, and I had to put a hand over my nose to quell a violent sneeze.

My breathing returned to normal as he left. I turned to the bald goon, watching him as he inspected the rest of the caged animals. In one cage, a large exotic cat paced back and forth, its muscles rippling beneath its fur as it sought to escape the confines of its prison. Its amber eyes, filled with a mixture of fear and resignation, bore silent witness to the atrocities inflicted upon it by its captors.

Nearby, a group of colourful parrots huddled together, their vibrant plumage a stark contrast to the drab surroundings of their prison. Yet, despite their outward beauty, the dullness in their eyes betrayed the despair that consumed them, a silent plea for freedom echoing through the night.

In another cage, a family of monkeys clung to each other, their expressive faces etched with sorrow and longing. The confines of their prison stunted their agile movements, their once playful antics replaced by a profound sense of resignation.

As I surveyed the scene, despair and sadness rose within me, a mix of emotions fuelled by seeing those suffering creatures. Each cage represented a life stolen from the wild, a soul condemned to a fate of misery and despair at the hands of heartless criminals.

I removed the blade from my pocket and crept behind the bald thug. I pressed the knife against his neck.

'If you move, I'll slit your throat. Nod if you understand.' He did. 'Good. Now tell me where you keep the tarantulas.'

'What?' The word slipped over his trembling lips.

'Don't make me repeat the question unless you want me to cut you a new smile.'

He gulped. 'The spiders are out back, with all the clown heads.'

I kept the knife pressed against him. 'Okay, take me there. And tread carefully. One slip, and I'll slice you.'

He moved slowly towards a doorway at the rear. 'Who are you?'

'You'll find out soon enough,' I replied. 'How long have you been doing this?'

His legs trembled as he walked. 'A few years.' He took a deep breath. 'You don't know who you're messing with.'

I pushed him into the door. 'Neither do you. Now open that.'

He did, and I heard the low hum of electricity as we stepped inside. I saw snakes coiled in tight, twisting masses, their scales shimmering in the dim light like polished gemstones. Their tongues flickered out, tasting the air with an almost palpable anticipation. Their eyes fixated on me with a cold, calculating gaze.

Lizards skittered and scuttled across the barren floor in the neighbouring cages, their rough scales scraping against the metal grating with each frenzied movement. The place was alive with their hissing and chirping, a cacophony of alien sounds that broke my heart.

'Do you have tortoises?' I said.

'Lady, I'm not telling you anything.'

I was ready to cut him when I saw the spiders.

Their hairy legs twitched and wriggled as they scurried about their cages, weaving intricate webs that glistened with dewdrops in the dim light. Their skittering feet echoed in the silence, a haunting melody that lingered in the air.

But I couldn't see Dirty Harry.

Then I did, in a single small pen at the end.

I shoved the goon into the dirt and stepped over him, rushing to Harry. He looked healthy, and I breathed a sigh of relief. I grabbed the cage and turned to leave.

Baldy blocked the exit.

'Who do you work for?' I said. I couldn't imagine a scheme as big as this was run by such low-life local criminals. But where did I know that Ryan bloke from?

He grinned at me. 'It's a good job you came by, love. We've been running low on animal feed.'

'Are you sure you want me to cut you up?'

Baldy laughed. 'You don't have the advantage now, do you? Unless you throw that spider at me?'

I nodded. 'I could, but I wouldn't wish to get shit like you anywhere near him.' I slipped the knife into my pocket and removed my phone. Then I dialled a number and showed him the screen. 'How long do you think it will take before the coppers arrive?'

His answer was to run.

Chapter 13

Send in the Clowns

'Imagine a three-month-old tiger cub drugged in a suitcase, two thousand live animals in the boot of a hatchback car, or eight endangered monkeys placed inside socks and strapped to a male passenger underneath his jumper as he passed through customs. All those things happened.' Judy Hartley spoke as her RSPCA colleagues inspected the captive creatures, and the police officers got in their way.

DS Kamara glanced at me. I smiled as she stumbled into a discarded clown head and swore.

'Do you think these criminals were involved in dumping the dead tortoises in the woods?' I asked.

Hartley shrugged. 'It's possible, but we haven't found any evidence yet.'

I nodded towards Kamara. 'Do you work well with the coppers?'

'It depends on the copper,' she replied. 'And what the crime is. Many police officers aren't interested in crimes like this – solving it doesn't help advance their careers.'

I was stunned by the number of creatures there. 'How would they get all these here?'

She studied the cages. 'It's a big operation, that's for sure.' She watched her colleagues working. 'Most of these animals will have come from abroad, brought in to order.'

'Through the port and up the river to here,' I said.

Hartley nodded. 'That seems the likeliest route. My understanding is that customs checks are quite relaxed at the Freeport.'

A uniformed female officer approached me. 'We need to take your spider as evidence.'

I glanced at the hundreds of imprisoned creatures. 'Are you fucking kidding?'

DS Kamara strode over. 'Is there a problem?'

I shook my head. 'I shouldn't have called you morons and left it with the RSPCA.'

Hartley stepped in to defuse the situation. 'Once the police have catalogued all the animals with photographic evidence, we will transport and store all the specimens.'

Kamara had her notebook out. 'How did you discover this, Ms Gray?'

'As I told one of your colleagues earlier, I was jogging through the woods and saw something suspicious in the funfair, so I came in for a look. That's when I found all these poor animals.'

She looked me up and down. 'You don't appear dressed to go running.'

I laughed. 'You're an expert on fitness and fashion now?'

'Did you see anyone here?' Kamara asked.

I gave her a description of the bald bloke. 'He confronted me when I heard him talking to somebody called Ryan Brown on the phone.' I thought it would be a helpful lie. Then I remembered where I'd seen Brown before. 'I think he works in the town centre vets.'

'Brown?' she said.

I nodded. 'Yeah. I sometimes take my mate's dog there for his appointment, and I'm sure there's a staff member with the same name.'

'There's likely more than one person named Ryan Brown in this town,' Kamara replied.

I shrugged. 'Sure, but it must be worth looking into.' And I knew it was him.

Kamara wrote the name in her book. 'And you scared the other bloke away?'

'He ran when I told him I was calling the police. Coppers are scary people to criminals, DS Kamara.'

She watched the RSPCA staff cataloguing the animals. 'What would you say is the value of this operation, Ms Hartley?'

Hartley glanced around the room. 'From my initial observation, probably tens of thousands of pounds.'

Kamara scribbled in her notebook. 'And how much for a tarantula?'

'That depends,' Hartley replied.

The copper pointed her pen at Dirty Harry in the cage I carried. 'What about that one?'

Hartley peered through the glass. 'Is it a Michoacan?'

I nodded. 'Yep.'

'Between £100 and £150,' Hartley said.

DS Kamara smiled at me. 'That seems small potatoes for an operation like this, wouldn't you say, Ms Hartley?'

Julia Hartley shook her head. 'Your understanding of the workings of the criminal mind is probably greater than mine, DS Kamara.'

Kamara glanced from Harry to me. 'Have you given one of the officers a statement, Ms Gray?'

'Yes,' I lied. 'Can I go now?'

'Do you need a lift home?' the DS asked me.

I pulled the cage closer to my chest. 'Nope. Bruce is picking me up outside.'

Kamara returned to her duties, and I thanked Hartley. I stepped past the clown heads and exited the building. Bruce was in the car waiting for me.

And there was somebody in the passenger seat with him.

I opened the back door and pushed Dirty Harry and the container inside. Then I slipped into the other side, keeping a hand on the cage after I put my seatbelt on.

'Are you okay?' Bruce asked me.

'Fine. Who's your friend?'

The woman turned to me. 'Hi, I'm Mary. Bruce has told me all about you.'

'You're the one he met on Tinder,' I said.

She blushed, and I felt guilty, taking out my frustration with Kamara on her.

'I like your tarantula,' she said. 'Is it a Michoacan?'

'It is,' I replied. 'Do you know spiders?'

She nodded. 'My dad has had exotic pets since he was a kid.' She grinned at me. 'They're much more interesting than cats or dogs.'

'Hey!' Bruce shouted. 'Don't say that around Kronos.'

He drove away, and I settled into the seat. 'Thanks for picking me up.' I smiled at Mary. 'And it's nice to meet you. Forgive my grumpiness – I've had a weird night.'

'What happened?' Bruce asked.

I gave him a short version of the story. 'The leader, Ryan Brown, I'm sure he works at the vets where we take Kronos.'

'Shit!' he said. 'Maybe that's how he knew about Dirty Harry.'

'You mentioned it at the vets?'

He shrugged. 'Probably. I'm always talking to people in there.'

'It seems hardly worth their while breaking into the flat for one tarantula,' I suggested.

'They took my laptop and money as well. Perhaps Harry was a theft of convenience. Did Brown or the other bloke admit to breaking into our flat?'

'I never got the chance to ask. You could be right – the thieves might have just passed Harry on to them.'

'From your description,' Bruce said, 'it sounds like a very lucrative operation.'

I nodded. 'Yeah, something far beyond that baldy goon.'

However, was Ryan, the vet's assistant, clever enough to be the mastermind?

It didn't matter. I had Dirty Harry back; that was all I was concerned about. The police could deal with the rest of it.

Chapter 14

Down by the River

I left early in the morning for a jog to the river, dragging Kronos on his lead. Mary had stayed the night with Bruce, and I wanted to miss that awkward moment where we all stared at each other over the breakfast table. I was happy for him, but was embarrassed because of my response to her in the car.

The streets were empty just before seven as I ran and headed into the woods. I'd fed Dirty Harry before leaving, glad he didn't seem affected by his ordeal. Most of my night was spent researching the illegal wildlife trade online. A criminal organisation bigger than Ryan Brown and his goons had to be behind what I saw at the abandoned funfair.

'Stealing DH must have been a crime of opportunity,' Bruce had said over dinner. 'I don't think they targeted you, Enola.'

I agreed with him but wanted to know more about the illicit market of exotic animals. Wildlife trafficking was the generally accepted term for the illegal trade, with an estimated worth of between ten and twenty billion dollars annually. While I didn't believe Ryan Brown's local operation was anywhere of that magnitude, it was still worth tens, maybe hundreds of thousands of pounds, according to Judy Hartley.

What I discovered online made for grim reading. The wildlife experienced shock at being removed from their habitat, drugging and man-handling, as well as unfathomably cramped conditions without food and water, sometimes for days. This was the life for millions of animals caught in the illegal trade. As many as four out of five of them would die in transit or within a year. All of this was fuelled by money and consumerism: the status of owning an exotic pet or a trinket or animal part for a cure or ointment.

According to the National Network to Fight Wild Animal Trafficking (RENCTAS) via *The Huffington Post*, over thirty-eight million wild animals were captured annually in Brazil, and ninety per cent died in the process of being caught or during transportation. Seventy-five per cent of parrots captured in Mexico to be sold as pets died before reaching a buyer; thirty-one per cent died en route. At least seventy-five per cent of pet snakes, lizards, tortoises and turtles died within one year in the home from stress-related causes of captivity. The world's elephant population was estimated to have dropped from 1.3 million in 1979 to 400,000. A world rhino population of 500,000 at the start of the twentieth century had fallen to 29,000. There were fewer than 3,500 tigers, reduced from 100,000 eighty years ago.

Those statistics clouded my mind as I pictured what I'd do to Ryan Brown when I caught up with him. Dirty Harry was safe at the flat, but that didn't mean I'd forgiven Brown and his masters for what they'd done to me and those caged animals.

Kronos spotted a rabbit and tried to pull away from me. I dragged on the lead and hauled him back, stopping for a drink. 'You'll eat when you get home, boy.'

I kept a tight hold on him, using my free hand to release the bag from my back and get the water bottle. I drank half before emptying the rest on the ground for the thirsty mutt. He lapped it up while I peered into the trees. I glanced at Kronos, his tongue lolling out as he swallowed the water. The woods stretched before me, a tapestry of emerald hues woven together by the dappled sunlight filtering through the canopy above. The scent of damp moss and decaying leaves filled the air, mingling with the crisp aftertaste of pine needles underfoot. As Kronos tugged at his lead, the sound of his claws scrabbling against the ground echoed through the silent stillness of the morning.

As I peered into the dense trees ahead, my thoughts wandered back to the horrors I'd uncovered in my research. The statistics loomed large in my mind, a sobering reminder of the cruelty and greed that fuelled the illegal wildlife trade. My heart ached at the thought of the countless animals suffering at the hands of ruthless poachers and traffickers, their lives sacrificed for nothing more than human vanity and selfishness.

Despite the early hour, the place pulsed with the vibrant energy of life, each tree and blade of grass humming with the promise of a new day. The distant chirping of birds and the occasional scurrying of small animals darting through the undergrowth punctuated the gentle rustle of leaves overhead.

Kronos finished drinking, and I slipped the water bottle

into my bag before checking my phone. I had just over an hour to get back, shower, eat, and then head to the record shop. I assumed Steve would have recovered from his hangover. Last night's activities meant I hadn't given him much thought, but what happened between us at the gig still lingered. What would I do about it?

I hadn't discussed it with Bruce, but I could imagine what he'd say: 'You could go on a double date with Mary and me.'

I shivered at the prospect. It would mean being far too social for my liking. I pushed forward; my footsteps muffled by the thick layer of fallen foliage carpeting the ground. The rhythmic thud of my shoes against the packed earth reverberated through the trees, accompanied by the occasional rustle of wildlife hidden among the underbrush. The place seemed to come alive around me, teeming with unseen creatures.

As Kronos strained against his leash, his eager whines broke the tranquil silence of the woods, a reminder of the world beyond the trees. I paused to control him, the cool morning air filling my lungs with each inhale. The soft caress of the breeze brushed against my skin, carrying with it the faint scent of wildflowers and dew-kissed grass.

That's when I saw the flashing lights ahead.

There were still fancy tales and rumours online of UFO sightings above the river – Bruce had claimed to have seen one there when he was a kid – and I even thought I'd noticed something hovering above the water recently.

But this was far worse. These were police lights.

Against my better judgement, I ran ahead for a closer look, finding uniformed coppers keeping bystanders away from something being pulled from the river.

'Is it more shit from the water company?' I asked the closest woman.

She turned and shook her head. 'No, love. It's body. Someone found a dead bloke floating in the river.'

I pushed past a copper and gasped.

I recognised the dead man.

Amy

Chapter 15

Cry Me A River

I stumbled forward as the copper tried to stop me, dragging Kronos along. His eyes bulged in anticipation, and the police officer stepped back.

'You can't go there,' he said.

'I recognise that man,' I replied. 'The dead body in the river. I know who he is.'

'Let her go, Jenkins,' a familiar voice said.

I turned to see a glum-faced DS Rose Kamara. 'That's Ryan Brown. The bloke who was running the illicit animal trade from that funfair.'

'We know who he is, Ms Gray,' Kamara replied. 'You'll need to come to the station.'

'Me? Why? I told you all I know last night.'

She glanced at Kronos. 'Bring the dog. He can have treats with the police dogs.'

I watched the forensic people move Brown's body away from the prying eyes of the onlookers. 'What do you need me for?'

'It's best to talk about this at the station, Ms Gray.'

'Fuck that. I've got a new job to go to.'

She grabbed me and pulled me close to the reeds with Kronos sticking to my legs.

'I don't want to make this official, but I will if I have to.'

My heart thumped like a hammer as I wriggled from her grasp. 'What the fuck? I'll have you done for assault, you stupid cow.'

She had a phone and showed me the screen. 'Do you recognise that?'

My blood boiled, clouding my vision. I stepped into the water lapping at the reeds and peered at the photo on her mobile. 'There's something in a plastic bag.'

Kamara nodded. 'It's a hairbrush, Ms Gray.' There were three other photos with items in evidence bags. 'And we have a Clash CD, an old ten-pound note and an earring.'

I scowled at her. 'So?'

She put the phone in her pocket. 'You don't recognise any of those things?'

The fire continued to blaze inside my head. 'Should I?'

'All four of them were found in Ryan Brown's clothes after we fished his body from the river. Somebody slashed his throat, probably sometime last night, and then dumped him here. Do you know anything about that?'

I dragged Kronos closer to me. 'Why would I? I told you yesterday I only spoke to his baldy mate. Brown buggered off before I had the chance to question him.'

The photos she'd shown me flashed through my head. 'Wait, those things...'

'Yes, Ms Gray. They're all yours. Are you sure you won't come to the station?'

Twenty minutes later, I sat in a room with her and a uniformed female officer. Kronos was still with me after I refused to let him go. He nibbled at the dog biscuits on the floor.

'Do you want to call somebody?' Kamara asked me.

'Like a lawyer?' I answered.

'Would you like one?'

'Am I under arrest?'

She shook her head. 'No. There are just a few questions I need to ask you.'

I laughed. 'They put you in charge of a murder investigation? Things have really gone down the tubes here since Detective Inspector Jack Parker left, haven't they?'

Kamara ignored my question. 'Who says it's a murder investigation?'

'You claimed somebody slit Brown's throat.'

She shrugged. 'It might be suicide.'

I pushed against the table and stood. 'Right, so I can leave, then?'

Kamara didn't move. 'I said it might be suicide. That's why I have a few questions for you, Ms Gray, but you're not under arrest.' She paused. 'Not yet.'

I sat with a thump. 'Get on with it.'

The uniformed officer approached and placed four large colour photos on the table, the ones Kamara had shown me on her phone.

'The Clash CD, *Sandinista* – inside it says "with love from Seraphina to Enola." The pre-plastic ten-pound note has the words "The property of Enola Gray" on it. Are these items yours, Ms Gray?'

I screwed up my eyes to examine the images. 'They could be. The pictures are too blurry to say for sure.'

'Okay,' Kamara said. 'The other two photos, of the hair-brush and the earring – are those things yours?'

I shrugged. 'Sure, maybe, but they're blurry as well.' I

studied her face. 'How would you know they were mine without DNA tests?'

'We won't,' she answered. 'But I remember seeing an earring like that when we investigated the burglary at your flat the other night. I'm guessing the hairbrush is yours because I can't see Ryan Brown using it on what little hair he had.'

I grinned. 'That's a bit sexist, no?'

She also ignored that question. 'Do you admit the possibility that all four items the police officers discovered on the body of Ryan Brown are yours?'

I stroked Kronos's head and beamed at the coppers. 'Did IQs drop the moment Jack Parker sloped off on a world tour with my best friend?' Kamara glanced at her colleague. 'What, you didn't know that? You'll be telling me next that you're unaware of my eventful experiences with the police officers in this town.'

DS Kamara relaxed in her chair. 'I've read your file, Ms Gray.'

'File?' What did I ever do to the coppers?

'You have several juvenile convictions on record for theft, being drunk and disorderly, and aggravated behaviour.'

I bit into my top lip and tasted blood. 'I'll show you fucking aggravated behaviour if you don't stop messing me around.' I took a deep breath. 'Those happened when I was fourteen or fifteen. They should have been wiped from the records by now.'

'How old are you?'

I assumed she knew and was only asking to wind me up. 'Twenty-one.'

'In England and Wales, juvenile convictions are spent after five and a half years. However, they remain on police computers until a person reaches one hundred years of age; this results in information that is spent being disclosed for a lifetime. There is no pardon system in the UK.'

'Great,' I said. 'But you're missing the most obvious reason for Brown having my things.'

'You mean the burglary at your flat?'

I thumped the table and made Kronos jump. 'And who says coppers are fucking clueless?'

'So,' Kamara said. 'You're claiming Ryan Brown stole the CD, the hairbrush, the ten-pound note, and a single earring at the same time they took your tarantula — is that correct?'

'I'm not claiming anything, numbnuts, but doesn't that make more sense than, well, whatever crazed theories you have slopping around inside your head?'

'Did you report the items missing when the officers attended the break-in at your flat?'

I inhaled deeply to stop myself from punching her in the face. 'No, I had other things on my mind, like finding my tarantula.'

Kamara removed a notebook from her pocket but didn't open it. 'Yes, which you did last night, where you encountered Ryan Brown. Is that correct?'

I bit into my bottom lip. 'I saw him there – it was hardly an encounter.'

She moved her hand over the photos. 'Why do you think the thieves would take these items? Is there any monetary value in them?'

'Who knows why criminals do anything?' I answered. 'They're wired up differently than the rest of us.'

'Indeed,' she said. 'Does that apply to your friend Amy Sparrow?'

'What?'

'Amy Sparrow. Is she your friend?'

I laughed. 'Okay, now I know you're making this all up as you go along, just throwing in random things until something sticks.' I stood. 'There's no need for a lift back – I'll walk.'

Kronos groaned as I dragged him from the room and out of the station.

Fuck!

Brown was dead, probably murdered.

And he had my stuff on him.

Why?

And why did the stupid copper drag Amy's name into it?

But Amy was the one who gave me the details and address for Brown's operation at the funfair.

Could she have killed him?

Fuck!

And I was late for work again.

Chapter 16

Smoke on the Water

Benjamin was smoking a cigarette outside the record shop when I arrived.

I smiled at him. 'I didn't know you smoked.'

His hand shook as he raised it to his mouth. 'I quit for twenty years.' The fag shimmered near his face. 'And now this.'

'I'm sorry for being late again,' I said. 'The police pulled a body from the river when I was jogging through the woods. It threw me off my timing.' That was putting it mildly. It didn't matter how many dead bodies I'd seen; I never got used to it.

Benjamin's eyes widened, and the cigarette tumbled from his fingers. 'Oh, God, it wasn't...'

He couldn't finish the sentence and grabbed my arm. 'What's wrong, Benjamin?'

'The body in the river – was it Steve?'

His shock jumped into me. 'What? No, it was the bloke running the illegal animal factory, Ryan Brown. Why would you think it was Steve?'

He let go and wiped away the sweat dribbling down his forehead.

'After you left work last night, I visited Steve's house to check on him. There was no answer at the door or when I rang him. I spoke to the neighbours, but they said they hadn't seen him all day. I kept texting and ringing with no answer. So I went on his social media accounts – Facebook and Twitter – and there were no posts for two days. I messaged him through them as well, but he didn't reply. I'm worried about him, Enola. He's done this before.'

'Done what?'

'Gone missing for days. I know he gets into trouble.'

Stress consumed his face. 'What kind of trouble?'

He pushed the shop door open. 'Come on, I'll tell you over a cup of tea.'

I followed him, and he placed the CLOSED sign on the entrance. We went through the back, and he put the kettle on.

'I'll make it,' I said. 'You sit and take the weight off your feet.'

He sat at the table, giving me a weary smile. 'Is there any news on your spider?'

I got two mugs and dropped tea bags into them. 'Yeah, he's safely home.' I told him an abridged version of the story. 'How long have you known Steve?' I'd only spent a short time with them in the shop and at the gig, but they seemed more like father and son than employer and employee.

'Three years,' he replied. 'I had a store in Newcastle, and he was at university. He applied for a part-time job in the record shop, and I gave it to him. It was obvious how much he loved music. Steve graduated when I moved here, so he came with me.'

'Neither of you have Geordie accents.'

Benjamin laughed. 'No, Steve's from Yorkshire. He doesn't get along with his family, so he was glad to go to university to escape them. I think I told you about my grandparents coming to England from Jamaica.' I nodded. 'My mother and father met on *The Empire Windrush* as small kids. They lived in London, where they raised me, but as soon as I was old enough, I upped sticks and travelled abroad and in the UK. That's how I ended up in Newcastle when I crossed paths with Steve.'

The kettle boiled, and I made the drinks. 'Tell me about this trouble you said Steve gets into.'

He reached over and opened a drawer in the table, removing a bunch of leaflets and magazines. 'Did Steve tell you he's an activist?'

'Yeah, he mentioned it.'

'Well, it's the one thing he's more passionate about than music – animal rights, the environment, equal rights, everything that oppresses those who can't defend themselves. Sometimes, he vanishes for days, participates in marches, or gets involved in sabotage or protests. He's been arrested before because of them.'

'What do you mean, sabotage?'

His lips trembled. 'He goes with others and breaks into buildings, rescues animals or destroys things that hurt the environment or people. I was worried after his last arrest, so he promised me he wouldn't do it again, but...'

'What?'

He dropped three sugars into his tea. 'I know he was investigating something concerning the council and Albion Utilities.'

'Corruption?'

Benjamin shrugged. 'I don't know. He refused to go into

details and said it was best I didn't know.' He shook his head. 'And now, with that body in the river.'

'Why would Steve have anything to do with that? Ryan Brown was involved with the illegal and stolen animal trade.'

'Yes, and Steve would have fought against that.'

I sipped my drink, the tea warming my lips. 'Maybe, but what's that got to do with the council and sewage dumped in the river?'

He held up his hands. 'I don't know.'

I pondered his remarks and grabbed a leaflet. There was a picture of Mary Martin on it and the words THE COUNCIL ARE LYING TO YOU at the top. I turned it over and read aloud the details on the back.

'Nearly ninety per cent of English rivers have evidence of high pollution from sewage and agriculture. Stinking, toxic sewage is pouring into our rivers, lakes, and seas – and it's all allowed in LAW because of local and national government. Mary Martin wouldn't want raw sewage in her private swimming pool, yet she's happy to let human excrement pollute our waterways. This scandal is the Tories' fault. They cut back enforcement and monitoring of the water companies releasing this filth and are now failing to prosecute them when they are blatantly breaking the law. Let's tell them enough is enough and take our shit to Mary Martin's house!'

I put it down and glanced at the other leaflets: "Climate protest is not a crime" and "Who are the real criminals?"

'You think Steve might be at a demonstration somewhere?'

'He must be. Otherwise, he'd have replied to my texts.' He took a deep breath. 'I think he was feeling guilty as well.'

I narrowed my eyes. 'Guilty? Why?'

Benjamin nodded towards the boxes of albums and singles in the room. 'Vinyl is bad for the environment. Steve knows that, yet he collects it and works here. I know it's been playing on his mind. And I found this in his locker.' He took a piece of paper from his pocket and handed it to me. I read it.

'Climate grief my elbow. People may have a vague ill, ill-formed notion of man-made climate change. But most people show absolutely NO SIGN WHATSOEVER of lifting a finger to do anything about it. Flying, meat-eating, new cars, and even electric are death to the environment. STOP ALL THIS. We are living in a fool's paradise.'

I placed it on the table. 'Steve wrote this?'

'It's his handwriting,' Benjamin replied. He lowered his head. 'I'm worried about him and don't know what to do.'

I finished my tea, put it down, and touched his arm. 'We'll go to his house tonight.'

'What if there's no answer?'

'Don't worry,' I replied. 'I know how to pick a lock.'

Chapter 17

Something Better Change

Benjamin drove in silence, but I saw the sadness in his face.

'Is something else bothering you?' I asked.

He stopped at the traffic lights and turned to me. 'My wife passed away two years ago.'

'I'm sorry,' I said.

'My son and grandkids supported me, but they live three hundred miles away, and they had their own grieving to endure.' The light changed, and he drove on. 'Steve helped me a lot. His best friend died when they were kids, drowned in a frozen river, so he understood what I was going through. I might be a lot older than him, but we have a connection, you know?'

I did. 'My parents died when I was ten.' I didn't mention the murders and how I'd witnessed them as I hid in the wardrobe. 'Then I was shuffled around various terrible children's homes until, at fourteen, I met Seraphina. She was forty years older than me, but we bonded over music, and she became my mentor and a close friend. Her death devastated me.'

We sat with no more words between us until he pulled up outside a large Victorian-looking house. 'This is it.'

'Steve lives here?' The place was massive, three storeys high, with probably four or five bedrooms.

He turned the engine off. 'His maternal grandparents left it for him.' He got his phone and rang Steve again. 'Still no answer.' He glanced at the imposing building. 'You'll break in?'

'Not if you don't want me to.'

He thought about it. 'We have to get inside.'

We exited the car. I stopped him from going to the front door. 'Best to go around the back and hope nobody sees us.'

He followed me as I scrutinised the surroundings. There were four houses similar to Steve's, large buildings that could have housed dozens of flats. As we made our way to the rear of the house, the cool evening air enveloped us in a gentle embrace, carrying the faint scent of fresh flowers and distant laughter echoing through the neighbourhood. The soft glow of streetlights cast long shadows across the pavement, painting everywhere in shades of amber and gold.

The gravel crunched with each step, the sound mingling with the hum of traffic and the occasional chirp of crickets hidden among the bushes. The world appeared to hold its breath as we moved.

As we rounded the corner, the ivy-covered walls seemed to ripple in the faint breeze, casting shifting patterns of light and shadow across the ground. I glanced up at the windows, half-expecting to see a figure watching us from within, but they remained dark and silent, divulging nothing of the secrets hidden behind their panes. It was as if I was staring at the Bates house from *Psycho*.

With a nod to Benjamin, I motioned for him to follow

me as I approached the back door. It was aged and worn, the paint peeling in places, revealing the raw, weathered wood beneath. I reached out and tested the handle, half expecting it to be locked, but to my surprise, it turned beneath my touch, swinging open with a soft creak.

'No need to break in,' he said.

I didn't tell him it wasn't a good sign.

We stepped inside, smelling old wood and dust. The floorboards creaked under our weight, protesting the intrusion as we walked through the dimly lit hallway. The walls were lined with faded wallpaper, peeling in places to reveal the bare plaster beneath.

I paused, listening for any signs of life, but all was silent except for the faint clock ticking in the distance. We moved further into the heart of the house, my senses on high alert for any sign of danger lurking in the shadows. The hallway stretched out before us, bathed in the dim glow of the moonlight filtering through the curtains, casting dark silhouettes across the worn carpet.

As we rounded a corner, a scene of chaos greeted us. Furniture was flipped over, and papers were scattered across the floor like fallen leaves. The place had been ransacked, every drawer pulled open, every surface overturned in a frenzied search for something – or someone. What had Steve been up to?

Benjamin trembled as he surveyed the wreckage, his hands clenched into fists at his sides. 'Who would do this?'

I stepped further into the room, seeing a jumble of broken glass and dishevelled furniture that offered no answers, only more questions. 'Stay here while I go upstairs.'

I nodded to Benjamin before heading up the staircase.

Shadows danced along the walls, casting eerie shapes that seemed to shift and change with every passing moment. The only sound was my heart beating, echoing in my head.

A sudden movement caught my eye as I approached the first door. I froze, my chest pounding as I turned to face the source of the disturbance. A figure clung to the wall, their features obscured by the gloom.

'Steve?' I said.

Everything stood still and quiet.

A masked man stepped from the shadows and lunged at me. I raised my arm, and he grabbed it, shoving us both into the wall. Adrenaline surged through me as we wrestled in the darkness, our struggle echoing through the empty house as we knocked over a table. A lamp crashed to the floor, shattering glass everywhere.

He punched me in the gut twice, but I kept hold of him. I stuck my fingers through the eyehole in the mask and dragged my nails down his cheek. He howled and pushed me away.

I hit the floor, and he fled down the stairs faster than I could get up. I cursed under my breath, my heart racing as I scrambled to my feet and followed him.

Benjamin was down, holding his head and groaning.

My ribs throbbed as I bent to help him. 'Are you okay?'

There was a bruise above his eye, but no blood. 'Yeah, just shaken. He caught me with his elbow before I could do anything. He ran out the front door.'

I helped him up. 'I'm going back upstairs to see if Steve is there. You should come with me in case the intruder returns.'

'Shouldn't we call the police?'

'Later,' I replied.

We went up together. I kept him with me as we checked every room. There was no sign of Steve, but there was plenty of mess.

'What should we do now?' he asked.

I got my phone out. 'Now we call my favourite people.'

Chapter 18

The Culture Bunker

D S Kamara tapped a pen against her notebook.

'Don't you ever go home?' I asked.

'I could say the same for you,' she replied.

Uniformed officers moved around the house. Benjamin sat in the living room with a paramedic dealing with the bruise on his head.

'I've read the statements you gave my colleagues,' she said. 'You came here and found the back door unlocked, entered, and were attacked upstairs?'

'You'll be getting that promotion soon, Kamara.'

'You were worried about Mr Clark?'

'Yes. He hasn't been to work for two days and wasn't answering his phone.'

Kamara wrote in her notebook. 'And the last time you saw him was at the Raven on Monday night?'

'Yep.'

'This was the Culture Vulture gig?' I nodded. 'I had tickets for that but got called into the station. Was it good?'

'Fantastic.'

'Did something out of the ordinary happen at the gig,

something that might have led to Mr Clark's disappearance and what happened here?'

I dug into my addled brain, searching through the memories of that night, remembering how close we seemed to get in that dark, hot, and sweaty atmosphere. Did anything strange happen? Only how my emotions got increasingly screwed up.

'No,' I answered. 'It was a normal night.'

'Do you know why somebody would break into this house?'

I shrugged. 'Nope.'

'Do you have any reason to believe Mr Clark might be in danger?'

Benjamin joined us before I could reply. 'Steve's annoyed a few people,' he said. 'Including the police.'

Kamara narrowed her eyes. 'The police?'

My laughter hurt my ribs. 'Don't you ever do your research?'

'I came straight here when we got the call, Ms Gray. Imagine my surprise when I saw you.' She shook her head. 'I could be at home playing with my cat and watching *Derry Girls*, but I rushed here to help you.'

'Yeah, you must be delighted.'

'Steve's been on a few protest marches,' Benjamin added. 'And the police don't like people protesting in this country.'

'We only enforce the rules,' Kamara said. 'We don't make them.'

'Do you know who killed Ryan Brown?' I asked her.

She studied my face as if I was under a microscope. 'We don't know if it was murder yet; still waiting on the post-mortem report.'

'Justice moves slowly here,' I said.

Kamara was unsmiling. 'Do you think this break-in is connected to the burglary at your flat, Ms Gray?'

I shook my head. 'Am I doing your job now, copper?'

Benjamin stepped in before I blew my top. 'Is there anything else, officer?'

'Did you see the intruder's face?' Kamara said.

'He wore a mask,' I answered. 'But there will be fresh scars on the left side of his face.' I held up my hand. 'I got my fingers inside the mask and dragged my nails down his cheek.'

Kamara moved closer to me and examined my hand. Then she turned to a uniformed copper. 'Johnson, call the station and get a forensic officer here. Ms Gray has evidence of the attacker on her.'

It might have been the only time I'd seen her smile.

My stomach grumbled like a volcano when the forensic officer finished with me.

'Are you hungry?' Benjamin asked me.

I nodded. 'With all the commotion at the river this morning, I missed breakfast.' I rubbed at my gut. 'And this hasn't helped.'

'Do you like curry?' he said.

'Who doesn't?' I replied.

He laughed. 'Philistines. Come on – my flat is behind the shop. I'll cook for us.'

Benjamin's place was a cosy sanctuary, a hidden gem that exuded warmth and comfort, filled with records and books. As we entered, the aroma of spices greeted us like an old friend, wrapping me in a comforting embrace that banished the lingering tension from the day's events.

He grabbed a beer from the fridge. 'Coke for you?'

'Yes,' I replied. 'With plenty of ice, please.' My ribs throbbed like a bastard, but I hadn't told the paramedics about it at Steve's house. It would have been one more intrusion I could do without.

The aromas of turmeric, cumin, and garlic mingled in the air. Benjamin busied himself chopping vegetables while I studied the decor. Vibrant tapestries and artwork adorned the walls, reflecting Benjamin's Jamaican heritage and eclectic taste. The furniture was a mismatched assortment of vintage pieces and handcrafted treasures.

I closed my eyes and let my other senses take over, savouring the tactile sensation of the soft cushions beneath me and the gentle sway of the hanging plants that adorned the windowsills. The air was filled with sizzling pans and bubbling pots, a symphony of culinary delights that promised an unforgettable meal.

'My family moved here from Jamaica when my parents were young kids,' Benjamin said as he worked. 'Things were challenging back then. We weren't welcomed by everyone.'

He described their challenges, overcoming prejudice, and building a life in their new home. Though they struggled, the richness of their culture, especially the food, comforted them. Framed photos showed his smiling family grouped around tables laden with food. My mouth watered as Benjamin finished cooking and brought two heaped plates to the small dining table. The aromas were intoxicating - cinnamon, allspice, nutmeg.

I scooped up a forkful, the textures pleasing my palate - the tenderness of the chicken, the toothsome grains of rice, the crunch of peppers. With each bite, new flavours blossomed - sweet, spicy, savoury. The curry filled my senses, its heat spreading through me.

Through his words, I saw the resilience and strength that had shaped Benjamin into the person he was: a man of integrity and compassion who had overcome adversity with grace and dignity. I listened intently, hanging on his every word, grateful for the opportunity to glimpse into his world and learn from his experience.

I forgot about my recent troubles and thought of my parents, of the times we'd sat as a family, suddenly realising how much I missed sharing life with others. Bruce was my flatmate and good friend, but with his new relationship, I knew we'd likely see less of each other. And as deeply as I loved Becky, she was just a kid.

We finished the meal, and I thanked him. 'That was fantastic, Benjamin. I owe you one.'

He smiled at me. 'Think nothing of it, Enola. It was my pleasure.'

We'd skirted around the question of what had happened to Steve, but there was no escaping it. 'Do you do this for all your staff?'

Some of the sparkle vanished from his eyes. 'Fifteen years ago, just before my forty-fifth birthday, I had what you might call a mid-life crisis or a nervous breakdown.' He gripped the beer bottle close to his chest. 'It wasn't gradual, something that crept up on me over time. It happened overnight. I woke up one morning, and it was like BANG in my face. It was as if there was somebody else inside my head. All I'd been before – confident, assured, happy – was gone, replaced with fear, apprehension, and self-doubt. I examined the story of my life up to that point and found it all wanting, criticising everything I'd done. I was a failure, not a success. Everything had been a lie. My whole life was a deception. I couldn't understand why nobody had seen through me and called me out for the fraud I was, personally and professionally.'

His fingers trembled as he spoke, lifting the bottle to drink as he paused.

'What did you do?'

'I didn't know what to do. I thought it all might go away as quickly and unexpectedly as it had arrived. I should have spoken to someone, but I couldn't burden Felicia, my wife, or my son, Julian. He was at university, and Felicia had the stress of running her florists. The pain was like nothing I'd ever felt before, but I kept it well hidden.' He touched the side of his head. 'Darkness consumed me, my mind overwhelmed by terrible thoughts. It lasted ten months. Then it just went.'

'You never mentioned it to anybody?'

Benjamin shook his head. 'I couldn't. I kept waiting for it to come back. You see, I never understood why I'd felt like that in the first place. I trawled through my mind for explanations, for even one reason for what had happened, but I could never find one. I loved my wife and son, and they loved me. There were no troubles with us as a family.' He finished his beer and got another from the fridge. 'More Coke?' he asked.

'No thanks. I'm on a sugar rush as it is.'

He returned to the table. 'You don't mind me telling you this?'

'No,' I said. 'The longer we hold on to our trauma, the more it hurts us.'

'Thank you, Enola.' He raised the bottle to me. 'I've only ever told one other person about this.'

'Steve?'

'Yes. When Felicia died two years ago, I had another breakdown, but it was different.'

'Grief?'

'Yes, that was the instigator. But it was unlike before. That first time, the pain came from me questioning how successful my life had been. Without Felicia, I asked what kind of person I'd been to her and everybody else. And all I could see were the times when I'd hurt her and others. It wasn't a physical hurt but an emotional one – petty criticisms, meaningless arguments, insults, being unsupportive, judgemental, jealous, and other trivial things that upset me. I remembered all those times, starting with Felicia and then working my way back through my life. I was going mad when Steve recognised my pain and stepped in to help me.' He took a deep breath. 'I wouldn't have survived without him.'

'He encouraged you to talk?'

'He did, and that's what I needed. Would you like to hear what he told me?'

'Please.'

His smile warmed my heart. 'Steve studied philosophy at university and was always pontificating about life. He said there's good and bad in all of us, and we'd only be happy as individuals when we accepted we are capable of both. At the extreme end of the spectrum, the very rare end, there are people who are predominantly bad – psychopaths and sociopaths. But mainly, it's folks like me and you, Enola – we do good and bad, but the bad are usually things we don't really mean, or we feel guilty about them afterwards because we have empathy.'

'Jekyll and Hyde.'

He nodded. 'Yes, Robert Louis Stephenson hit the nail on the head, though Edward Hyde was an extreme example. I've said nasty and horrible things to people, but I'm no Mr Hyde.' He grinned at me. 'How about you, Enola?'

I thought it wise not to tell him I'd killed for revenge or in self-defence. 'As Norman Bates once said, Benjamin, I wouldn't hurt a fly.'

He stood and collected the plates. 'What will we do about Steve?'

'Well, the police have a missing person report for him. Maybe we should leave it to them.'

'Do you trust them to do a good job?'

Of course I didn't, but I couldn't tell him that.

I touched his shoulder. 'Do you want to shut the shop for a few days?'

He shook his head. 'No, I need something to occupy my mind. Do you want some time off?'

'I've only just started working there, Benjamin. I'll be in bright and early tomorrow.'

He gripped my hand. 'Thank you, Enola. Would you like a lift home?'

'No, I'm fine to walk. Thanks for the offer and the food – it was fantastic.'

I left and checked my phone.

It was time to visit the future.

Chapter 19

Are Friends Electric?

It had gone nine o'clock, but the Future Content office was open. I pushed at the door, flinching as the harsh overhead lights and the hum of the computer screens hit me. My eyes were drawn to the colourful abstract paintings on the walls. I moved closer to the largest canvas, a frenzy of jewel tones - emerald, sapphire, amethyst. Running my fingers over the bumpy, thickly layered paint, I felt the ridges and textures left by the artist's bold strokes. Squinting, I traced the faint impressions of shapes - a circle here, a square there - ghostly geometrical forms embedded in the abstraction.

The smaller painting in fiery oranges and reds evoked an aggressive, primal feeling in me, like crackling flames and molten earth. The blurred boundaries hinted at figures just beyond recognition. I imagined its heat pulsing from the canvas.

On the opposite wall, a soothing pale blue canvas offered me tranquillity. Soft bands of colour floated in space, their hazy edges barely touching. It was like gazing at lazy clouds in a summer sky, calming and weightless. I studied the layers of opaque and transparent paint stacked to create this ethereal scene.

'Twice in two days,' a voice said behind me. 'Oh, still my giddy heart.'

I turned to see Amy with one hand on her chest. 'You have a heart?'

'I'm wounded again.' She glanced at the paintings. 'Are you a connoisseur?'

'Only of comic books.'

'Ah, you're still a fellow geek,' she said. She moved closer to inspect the canvases. 'These make me think of comic art. The colours, the exaggerated forms...'

I nodded, seeing her point. The abstract shapes echoed the bold lines and dynamic compositions of comics. 'But comic art often has more concrete narrative and recognisable characters,' I observed. 'These pieces are less representational.'

'True,' Amy mused. She pointed to swirling blues and greens. 'No thought bubbles are giving an inner monologue here. More open to interpretation.'

'The paint textures make them feel alive too,' I added, tracing ridges left by the artist's brush. 'You can't get that tactile quality in print.'

She gestured towards the fiery orange painting. 'Take this one, for example. The bold, aggressive strokes remind me of the action scenes in your favourite comics. It's like the artist is capturing the energy and intensity of a battle.'

I studied the canvas again, seeing it in a new light. 'I see what you mean. It's like the clash of superheroes and villains frozen in time.'

Amy nodded, her eyes lighting up with excitement. 'Exactly! And this one,' she said, gesturing to the tranquil blue painting, 'is like a peaceful moment between the action. It's the calm before the storm, a period of reflection amidst chaos.'

I followed her gaze. 'It's the quiet moments between panels in a comic book, where the characters can catch their breath and contemplate their next move.'

Amy grinned, pleased with my observation. 'Exactly! Art is all about interpretation, whether abstract paintings or comic book illustrations. It's about tapping into emotion and sparking imagination.' Her smile was brighter than the office lights. 'But I don't suppose you're here to talk about art, are you, old friend?'

I glanced around the place. 'Are you alone?'

'Yes, everyone has gone home. It's the perfect time to murder me.'

I frowned. 'Why would you say that, Amy?'

'Whenever I see you, Enola, I don't know if you're going to kiss me or kill me.'

'It's neither. I need to talk to you.'

'Let me guess – it's about Ryan Brown, right?'

'Amongst other things.'

'How exciting.' She went to the door. 'I better lock up. We don't want anybody disturbing us.' She closed the blinds. 'Was it you that dumped him in the river?'

'No. Did you?'

Amy laughed. 'Why would I do that? The poor man never did anything to me.'

'Have you heard anything about who might have killed him?'

She shook her head. 'I told you, Enola. I don't move in that world anymore. I'm a legitimate businesswoman now.'

'Yet, you give me his name and the address where he kept his exotic and illegal animals. You knew the name of the gang.'

'Meaning what?'

'Meaning you may know who'd want to hurt Brown.'

'Apart from you?'

'I only wanted to get Dirty Harry back, and I did that.'

'Yes, you're welcome.' Her eyes sparkled. 'Is it true the coppers discovered some of your personal items on Brown when they hauled him from the river?'

I nodded. 'My *Sandinista* CD from Seraphina, an old ten-pound note, my hairbrush, and one of those earrings you bought me for my sixteenth birthday.'

'What, with the witch on the broomstick?'

'The same.'

She rubbed at her chin. 'Why would anybody steal those things?'

'Perhaps to frame me for Brown's murder.'

'Yeah, but the burglary at your flat was before I gave you the address for the funfair. Framing you with your personal items means somebody thought about it beforehand.'

'Possibly. Or maybe they took that stuff on the off chance and then used it when the opportunity arose. There was no prearranged plan to frame me, but they seized the opportunity when it arrived.'

'Okay, but who are *they*?'

'I came here to ask you that, Amy. Where did you get Ryan Brown's details?'

She scrunched up her lips and studied my face. Then she removed her phone, found something on the screen, and handed it to me. It was an article from the local news website. She summarised the salient points as I read it.

'Michael Morgan, the CEO of Albion Utilities, donated £100,000 to the council earlier this year so they could keep the swimming baths and the central library open. That money came from Morgan's pocket, not the water company's.

But they've dumped tonnes of raw sewage into the river and sea without breaking any laws. Despite several protests, the local council has defended Morgan and Albion Utilities. This may be because our local council is Tory-controlled, and Michael Morgan is a big donor to the Conservative Party.'

I returned the phone to her. 'There are a lot of inferences in that article, but no proof.'

Amy agreed. 'Things get more interesting when you hear how much debt the council has. There's a rumour they're close to bankruptcy and might have to sell certain assets to survive.'

Steve had mentioned that to me. 'What assets?'

'Property, probably to start with.'

'The old cinema?'

'I guess. It's in a desirable location. And there is other land they could sell.'

I pictured my hometown stretching out before me. 'I didn't know they had any land apart from schools and council buildings.'

'You'd be surprised what the council owns.'

'How do you know all this?'

She shrugged. 'I had to do a lot of research before setting up this business. I discovered many interesting things.'

'Such as?'

'Well, the abandoned funfair where you saw Brown and his illegal animal trade — the council owns that land.' That was interesting. 'And they own the neighbouring land, Harrington Woods.'

'Fuck!' I said. 'The town would be up in arms if they sold that.'

Amy agreed. 'Indeed. If the council were forced to sell,

whoever bought it would have direct access to the river and the sea. And the port.'

'And Michael Morgan already has close contacts with the council.'

Amy nodded. 'Closer than you think, Enola.'

'What?'

'There are rumours that the married Michael Morgan and the married Mary Martin are close friends. Very close friends.'

I processed that information. 'Okay, I can see corruption and backhanders rearing their ugly heads there, but what would any of that have to do with Ryan Brown and his criminal activities?'

'What do you know about Brown?' Amy said.

'Not much. He was a vet's assistant.'

'Yes, and while that would give him access to a database of who owned what animals in the town, do you think he's the mastermind behind the operation you encountered in that funfair?'

'Probably not. What I saw wasn't a bunch of stolen pets but a collection of animals shipped into the country from abroad.'

'That sounds right, meaning they'd arrived here through the port.'

'I guess.'

'Who else did you encounter at the funfair?'

'A big bald goon who looked like he eats steroids for breakfast. Do you know him?'

She laughed. 'Do you realise how many bald body-building goons there are in town?'

'Probably too many.'

'Exactly.'

'Who gave you Brown's name and the address you sent me?'

'I can't tell you that, Enola.'

'What, even if it might help me clear my name with the police?'

'Please,' she said. 'The coppers have nothing on you. Those items they found on Brown were obviously stolen from your flat by him or one of his gang. A lawyer would have a field day with that in court.'

'Your confidence in the British legal system doesn't fill me with joy. I need to identify who broke into my place, and you're the only person I know with contacts in the criminal underworld.'

Amy narrowed her eyes. 'We were best friends for two years. Then you abandoned me until last year. Now, you can't keep away, but it's always because you want something from me, Enola. How do you think that makes me feel?'

Was that true? Was I only using her?

'You won't help me, then?'

She shrugged. 'If I hear anything, I'll let you know. How does that sound?'

It sounded like I was still on my own.

'Great,' I replied and left.

All I had to do now was find the bald goon.

Chapter 20

Thursday's Child

I left for work early on Thursday, hoping a meander through town would clear my head. The crisp air bit at my cheeks, inhaling the delicious aromas from the bakery - warm, yeasty bread and sugar-glazed treats. My mouth watered. A busker strummed a guitar at the corner, the chords echoing down the nearly empty street. I dropped a few coins in his case to hear him continue. The melody lifted and anchored me as he sang a version of "This Town Ain't Big Enough For The Both Of Us."

The morning sunlight cast long shadows over the pavement, creating a mosaic of light and shadow that danced with each passing breeze. Soft golden sunlight glinted off darkened windows, scattering reflections everywhere. I turned my face upward, letting the radiant warmth soak into my skin, chasing away the lingering chill. The birds sang around me, and it was as if nothing terrible had happened in my life the last few days.

The morning sun glowed across their faceted surfaces as I strolled past the rows of brick buildings. I reached out to touch the rough surface as I passed, enjoying the sun's warmth against my skin. The cool breeze brushed against my face, carrying the scent of blooming flowers from the nearby park. With each inhale, I filled my lungs with the fresh air, feeling a sense of calm wash over me. The tension coiled tight in my chest unravelled, replaced by peace and clarity.

I wandered past coffee shops, inhaling espresso's rich, bitter fragrance as people readied for the day. My mind felt cluttered, but the walk worked its magic. The kaleidoscope of sensory details - scents, textures, sounds - grounded me in the present. By the time I reached the record shop, the chaotic thoughts that had plagued me earlier had settled.

I pushed open the door, and the aroma of vinyl and paper sleeves welcomed me. Iggy Pop was warbling through the speakers as Benjamin looked up from behind the counter, his brow furrowed with concern.

'Any word from Steve?' I asked.

His face darkened. 'No.' He sighed, his shoulders slumping. 'Have you heard from the police?'

I shook my head. 'Not yet. Are you sure you want to be here?'

'Yes,' he replied. 'I need to keep busy.' He glanced at the spot where Steve had sorted the new CDs the other day. 'He's probably off somewhere on a secret protest with his activist friends. He'll turn up, eventually. Are you okay to work?'

'Of course,' I answered. 'There's nowhere else I want to be.'

My eyes roamed over the boxes of records while we talked, the colourful sleeves contrasting with my worried mood. The sound of a customer entering the shop broke our conversation, and Benjamin turned to greet them with a forced smile. I watched him, admiring his resilience in the face of adversity. Despite his worries, he remained steadfast and composed, a pillar of strength.

I took a deep breath and went to the counter, the worn floorboards creaking beneath my feet. I leaned against the wood, feeling its smooth surface against my palms as I glanced out the window at the bustling street outside.

We spent the morning sorting through fresh arrivals - everything from jazz and blues to 1980s new wave. As the day unfolded, the minutes stretched into hours, and Benjamin and I found ourselves immersed in the store's rhythm. Customers came and went, their voices blending with the eclectic mix of music that filled the air. He worked with purpose and a persistent smile, but I could tell he was suffering.

I left the shop at lunchtime, popping next door for fresh coffee and sandwiches for us both. We worked as we drank and ate, sharing stories of bands we'd seen and obscure music, dancing around the thought of what might have happened to Steve.

Images of Ryan Brown in the river swam through my mind, picturing somebody stuffing his pockets with my stuff. Who had tried to frame me for murder and why?

I found solace in the familiar surroundings, the comforting embrace of the music encircling me like a warm blanket. At the listening station, I cued up a psychedelic rock track on the turntable. As the crackly song flowed from the speakers, I closed my eyes. The shop enveloped me in its sensory cocoon - the fragrance of vinyl and coffee, the tactile sleeves, the melodic tunes.

At four o'clock, a familiar force of nature swept into the Soundwave Emporium.

'Enola!' Becky shouted as she ran to me. Her mother trailed behind her.

'Hi,' I said to Julia. 'Have you had a good day?' She rarely got time off work midweek, so I knew she'd wanted to make it special for Becky.

Her smile warmed my heart. 'Tiring, but it's not over yet.'

'What else have you planned?'

The kid thrust a leaflet at me. 'I'm going to my first gig, Enola. Will you come?'

I scanned the paper and read it aloud: 'Under sixteens gig at the Raven – The Toons supported by Cat People. All children must be supported by an adult. No alcohol allowed.'

'It starts at five,' Becky said. 'What time do you finish here, Enola?'

'Not until five thirty,' I replied.

'It's okay,' Benjamin said. 'You can finish early.' He grinned at Becky. 'We can't have the young lady missing her first live musical extravaganza.'

Becky snatched the leaflet from me and bounced up and down. 'Yeah!' Then she ran through the aisles like a plane about to crash.

'Please come, Enola,' Julia said. 'It will make her day.'

'Sure,' I replied, knowing it would help Julia as well if there were two of us to monitor the kid. 'Have you listened to these bands?'

She shook her head. 'Not really. It's just teen pop, I think. The Toons wear masks of cartoon characters and perform pop versions of kids' TV shows.'

'And Mum said we can go to McDonald's after the show,' Becky said as she danced near us. 'Live music and junk food – what more do you want, Enola?'

Benjamin grinned. 'Out of the mouths of babes.'

Chapter 21

Teenage Kicks

The familiar sights and sounds of the Raven washed over me as I entered with Becky and Julia. The dim lighting, sticky floors, and chattering crowds brought me back to the last time I was there for the gig with Steve and Benjamin.

Inhaling deeply, I caught the mingled scents of overexcited teenagers, stressed adults, and sweat that defined the venue's atmosphere. Roadies were setting up amps and mic stands onstage, clanging and banging echoing through the space. Hundreds of kids and their adults milled around, the sense of anticipation clinging to the children like glue.

Becky vibrated with excitement next to me, her eyes wide as she took it all in. I smiled, remembering the thrilling rush of my first gig. Julia leaned in close so I could hear her over the din. 'Thanks again for coming. This means the world to her.'

My skin prickled with memories and anticipation. Soon, the lights would lower, fog swirl and crunching power chords would hit. I'd be transported, feeling the music's energy coursing through me. It didn't matter what it was, kid's pop or death metal; it still had the power to take me to a better place.

I bought Cokes for us all, and we found a spot to stand as the opening band took the stage. Becky squealed and sang along to every song, her joy infectious. Memories came flooding back about my first show as a teenager, waiting in line with Amy, hoping the bouncers wouldn't realise we were underage. We were giddy with excitement, clutching our tickets, too young to belong in that late-night scene but desperate to be part of it. It was hard to believe it was only six years ago.

The music was raw, aggressive, and liberating. Amy and I were enthralled, swaying and singing along, blending into the passionate crowd. At that moment, I felt truly alive. The outside world, with all its rules and judgments, evaporated. It was just pure emotion distilled into sound. I forgot about my pain that night, of my parents' murders and the miserable life in those children's homes.

We stumbled out hours later, ears ringing, voices hoarse from screaming. A new world had opened to me in those dark moments - a place of uncensored expression, shredded amplifiers, and blazing guitar solos. One transcendent show awakened my love of live music, and I'd never been the same since.

Witnessing Becky's initiation, I hoped for her to seek out moments that would expose her to the enchanting essence of music, allowing herself to be carried away by the pulsating beats and captivating melodies, fearlessly embracing new experiences.

She'd had a difficult upbringing and deserved happiness.

I guess we all did.

Cat People finished their set, and Becky peeled away

from her friends, rushing to see her mum and me. She grabbed our hands.

'You should come down the front with us. There's more sweat there.'

There was a lot of it sticking to her head. 'No thanks, kid. We're okay here. But you go back and enjoy yourself.'

People got the stage ready for the next band. Becky hugged her mother and me before returning to the front, pushing past any kids in her way. She looked more confident than I'd seen her in a while. Perhaps her concerns about going to secondary school had vanished.

'It's good to see her so happy,' Julia said. 'I've been so worried about her attending the new school in September.'

'Because of what happened with the bully at primary school?' I asked.

She nodded. 'Yeah, I thought it might leave a mark on Becky even though that other girl isn't here anymore.'

'She'll be fine, Julia. She's got your strength running through her.' I pointed to where Becky danced with the other kids. 'She's made new friends already.'

Julia gripped my hand. 'And she's got her big sister looking after her.'

I grinned and went to the bar for more drinks. Being in the Raven and not surrounded by drunken punters was unusual. For once, I wasn't the only one not drinking booze. The Toons stepped onto the stage with such screaming I imagined I was at a Beatles concert in the 1960s. I peered at the four of them wearing Disney character masks and wondered how long it would be before somebody sued them.

'It's strange to see Mickey Mouse playing a guitar,' Julia said as I handed her a Coke in a plastic glass.

'And Goofy on the drums,' I added.

We watched the kids enjoying themselves, and I thought that maybe everything was okay with the world. Perhaps Steve was off with his activist mates somewhere, and he'd return to the record shop with a big grin. It was strange to think the last time I'd seen him was outside the Raven.

Yet, if that was the case, who was the bloke who attacked me at Steve's place? And why was he there? Were the police looking for Steve or the intruder? I doubted it, especially if DS Kamara was in charge. She appeared to be lacking competence and ingenuity – those and a personality.

The thug at the house would have fresh scars on his face for a while. I could visit the hospital, nose around at the A&E desk, and check their recent visitors. I could post the details online about the break-in. Somebody might know something. Or maybe Amy would come up with a suggestion.

All I knew was I had to do something, even if it was just trawling the town to find the thug with the scarred face.

That thought crossed my mind as the music and the intensity increased, with the kids screaming so loud it hurt my ears. I peered at the stage, watching Goofy stepping out behind the drums to join Donald Duck at the microphone. The crowd howled, but my heart stopped, focused on the drummer in the mask. The way he strode to the front, swinging his arms and sticking with the sweat glistening on the top of his hairless bonce was something I recognised even though he wore a mask: Goofy was the bald goon from the funfair, Ryan Brown's mate.

'Isn't it great,' Julia said beside me.

I swigged the last of the Coke, letting the warm liquid kiss my lips.

'How did you learn about this gig, Julia?'

She removed the leaflet from her pocket. 'Somebody pushed this through our door yesterday. One of the other mums said whoever organised it wants to make it a regular thing over summer while the kids are off.' She glanced around the club, bursting to the seams with teenage excitement. 'It looks like it's been a success.'

I kept my focus on the drummer. 'What do you know about the bands?'

She shook her head. 'Nothing. I checked online, but they only have Facebook pages. Why? Do you like them? I thought they'd be too teeny-pop for your tastes.'

'I like lots of stuff.' I dropped the empty plastic glass in a bin. 'I'm going to see if I can speak to them when they finish. Tell Becky I'll see her later.'

'You don't fancy a Big Mac?'

'Next time,' I said before moving to the side of the venue to see the back of the stage. I was familiar with the layout of the Raven, including the parts most punters didn't get to see. Once the band finished, they'd exit through the rear to a car or a van. I couldn't move down to the front and let Goofy see me. I had to take him by surprise or follow him.

But I didn't have a car.

I rang Amy.

Chapter 22

Country Life

'You bought a new car,' I said as Amy followed the bald goon in his white van. He'd dropped the others in town and was alone in the vehicle.

She scowled at me. 'You went to a gig without inviting me?'

'I didn't think teeny pop would be your thing.'

'Is Becky your best friend now?'

I ignored the question. 'Can we concentrate on the job at hand?'

She turned the radio on, and The Last Dinner Party guided us out of town and into the countryside.

'Let me get this straight,' she said. 'The goon from the illegal animal horde at the funfair was playing drums at a gig for teens at the Raven this afternoon wearing a Goofy mask, and he's driving that van ahead of me?'

I monitored the vehicle. 'I'm glad you were paying attention. Now, don't lose him.'

As we followed him down winding country roads, the landscape transformed around us; rolling hills stretched out on either side, bathed in the soft glow of the setting sun.

The air was crisp and clean, with an aroma of damp grass. Through the open window, I heard the gentle rustle of leaves and the distant call of birdsong, a symphony of nature, a reminder of the world beyond the concrete jungle we'd left behind.

'Was it any good?' Amy said.

'What?' I replied.

'The gig.' She sighed. 'I haven't been to a concert for ages, too busy with the new business.'

The van was about three hundred yards ahead of us, with no other traffic. 'The kids enjoyed it.'

The road wound through quaint villages and past picturesque farms, each a postcard-perfect image of rural life. Cows grazed in lush green pastures, their gentle breathing blending with the hum of insects and the occasional rumble of a tractor in the distance.

'Are we just going to follow this goon? Then what?'

'I want to see who he works for?'

Amy laughed. 'What, Goofy's manager?'

'Ryan Brown wasn't running that operation in the funfair – he was only a middleman. Hopefully, this bald thug will take us to them.'

'And if he doesn't?'

'I'll let you beat the information out of him.'

She grinned as the music changed to Blondie. 'Finally, something to make the journey worthwhile.'

The van turned off the main road and onto a narrow dirt track. Gravel crunched under the wheels as we stayed back, not wanting to be spotted. The bald goon pulled up to a dilapidated farmhouse, chickens scattering as he parked. I studied the property - a red barn tilting slightly, an empty pigpen with a broken gate flapping in the wind. The air reeked of livestock, with an undertone of manure.

A dense thicket of trees loomed ahead, branches reaching out like gnarled fingers grasping the sky. Silhouettes danced among the leaves, casting dappled patterns of light and shadows on the ground. The land opened into a vast expanse of rolling fields, their golden hues accentuated by the last of the sunlight. I saw a farmhouse, its aged walls and sloping roof standing stark against the horizon. Nearby was a ramshackle barn, its wooden frame warped and weathered with age. The doors hung askew on rusted hinges, revealing a dark interior shrouded in shadow.

Amy stopped, and we watched the bloke get out of the van. The air was heavy with the scent of earth and decay, mingling with the sweet fragrance of wildflowers blooming along the roadside. He didn't look behind him as he entered the house.

'Leave the car here,' I said.

She looked at her watch. 'I can come back in an hour and pick you up.'

I frowned at her. 'You're not coming with me?'

Amy shook her head. 'Do you recall what I mentioned the other day about you only contacting me when you want something?' I assumed it was a rhetorical question, so I didn't reply. 'Well, this is a perfect example.'

I opened the door and stepped out. 'Thanks for the lift.'

She grabbed my arm. 'Do you have a weapon?'

I patted my pocket. 'My lucky blade.'

'The one I got you for your fifteenth birthday?'

'No, that's in the river, remember? I have a switchblade keeping me warm.'

Amy sighed. 'That's no good. There could be others in the farmhouse with him.' She removed something from her jacket. 'You need this.'

I peered at the pistol, fighting the temptation to take it from her.

'Thanks again,' I said as I closed the car door.

The gravel crunched under my feet as I crept towards the building, the trees providing camouflage. The pungent aroma of manure thickened the air, assaulting my nose. Somewhere nearby, a dog barked.

I scrutinised the property - faded red paint peeling from the barn, an ancient rusty tractor near the broken pigpen gate, weeds overtaking the long-neglected garden. Reaching the side of the house, I pressed against the gnarled wall and edged towards the nearest window. Holding my breath, I peered inside. The place was dim and cluttered, faint light filtering through moth-eaten curtains. Dust motes swirled through shafts of sunlight. An antique cabinet overflowed with yellowed papers and books. My eyes roamed over the outdated furnishings of what appeared to be an abandoned living room, frozen in time.

I crept forward, hyperaware of each rustle and footstep. At the back of the house, I discovered a cracked window near the rear entrance. Gripping the frame, I lifted it just enough to squeeze through and gain access. Holding my breath, I lowered myself down.

The floorboards creaked as I shifted position. My heart raced, expecting the bald man to discover me at any moment. However, the house remained still and silent. The only sounds were the ticking of an old clock and the muffled cawing of crows outside.

I crept through the musty interior of the farmhouse, wary of making any noise on the worn floorboards. Cobwebs draped over the doorframes, and dingy oil paintings hung crooked on the walls. Everywhere stank of mildew and mouse droppings.

Rusted pots and pans were stacked haphazardly around the old wood-burning stove in the kitchen. A vintage icebox stood in the corner, riddled with holes and rot. I ran a finger across the Formica table top, leaving a clean streak in the thick layer of dust.

The living room had outdated newspapers and magazines, worn furniture, and an ancient radio. I moved towards the back, past a bathroom with rust-stained fixtures and cracked tiles.

There was no sign of the bald goon or anybody else.

Then I heard muffled sounds upstairs.

I took the knife from my pocket and headed up.

Chapter 23

This Old House

Shadows shrouded the upstairs, the only illumination coming from the faint glow filtering through the grimy windows. I noticed the shapes of furniture covered in dusty sheets; the outlines blurred and indistinct in the low light. Everywhere stank of rot.

Then I heard the mumbling coming from the nearest bedroom.

I took a deep breath and inched inside, ready for any attack.

But the bald goon wasn't there. Laid on the bed was a groaning man, his hands and feet tied and a gag in his mouth. I scanned the room, searching for a hidden menace, but it appeared empty apart from us. I went to the mattress and removed the gag.

He gazed at me through watery eyes. 'Oh, thank God. Hurry, free me before he returns,' he whispered through trembling lips.

I glanced at the open door before returning to the squirming man. His cheeks were flushed a fine shade of red, contrasting the colour of his short, light hair.

'Who are you?' I said.

Panic shot through his eyes. 'I'll tell you later. Just get me out of here.'

'Are you an activist? Do you know Steve Clark?'

'What? Will you please untie me? I'm desperate for a piss.'

I went to the window and peered outside. Where had the bald bloke gone? 'Tell me what's going on first.'

His shoulders slumped. 'My name is William Nelson, an accountant for the council. Yesterday, someone threw a bag over my head and brought me here. That's all I know.'

The floorboards creaked in the corridor. I gripped the knife, waiting for somebody to burst into the room.

But nobody did.

I moved to the door and peered outside. The landing was silent and empty.

I returned to the bloke. 'Okay, William – I'm Enola and a friend of mine, Steve, has gone missing. Considering your present predicament, I thought you might know something about that.' He stared at me blankly. 'Why would anyone do this to you?'

He frowned. 'I've had a lot of time to think about it, and it can be for only one thing.'

A door slammed shut downstairs.

'Go on.'

He took a deep breath. 'Well, I discovered anomalies in the council accounts. It has to be about that.'

'What anomalies?'

William shook his head. 'I can't tell you. It's confidential information.'

I moved to the door. 'Fine. Have a nice day with the bald thug.'

'Wait!' he said. 'I'll tell you.'

I stood near the window. 'I'm all ears.'

'Last year, the council received a large government grant to support new resident businesses. Some council members didn't want to use the money for that since the accounts have a huge financial hole. But Mary said we had to. It was the only reason we got the money.'

'Mary Martin?'

He nodded. 'Nobody argues with her. So the money went to all those new shops on Hope Street. Have you seen them?'

'Yeah.'

'It was great, a big success for the town.' He glanced nervously around the room. 'But I discovered some missing amounts while checking the accounts.'

'Large quantities?'

William shook his head. 'No, not really. It was small things – three or four hundred pounds each time that weren't accounted for, but there were many of them: individual deposits to the shops on Hope Street that added up to a considerable amount – nearly fifty grand. When I checked the details, I discovered the deposits went into different bank accounts we registered for each business. None of it made any sense unless...'

'Unless it was theft?'

'Yes.'

'Did the record shop Soundwave Emporium allegedly receive any of these phantom payments?'

He nodded. 'All the new shops did.'

'Who authorised them?'

'Everything goes through the Finance Department.'

'And who signs off on it?'

'The council leader.'

'Mary Martin?'

'Normally, yes, but it would likely go through the finance officer for small amounts of three to four hundred pounds.'

Several thoughts ran through my head. 'Wouldn't these anomalies be picked up during an audit?'

'Usually, yes, but these are exceptional circumstances.'

'How so?'

He looked at me sheepishly. 'I shouldn't tell you this, but it will be common knowledge soon. The council is about to declare bankruptcy. The shit will hit the fan then.'

'What will happen?'

'Well, councils technically can't go bankrupt. They'll issue a section 114 notice, where they can't commit to any fresh spending and must come back with a new budget within twenty-one days that falls in their spending envelope. They'll have to cut services, increase the council tax and sell council assets. Most of our money is spent on social care, meaning areas such as education, highways, youth services, and the voluntary sector will suffer.'

I used the knife to slice away his bonds. He thanked me and rubbed at his wrists.

'So, it looks like someone has stolen fifty grand from the council accounts by making deposits that appear to be going to local businesses, but aren't?'

'Yes.'

'Can you trace the bank account they went to?'

His lips trembled. 'I hoped to do that when somebody put the bag over my head.'

'Who did you tell in the council?'

'Nobody. I never got the chance.'

'Would anyone have known what you'd discovered?'

He nodded. 'Yeah, if they'd checked the computer logs.'

I ran the information through my head, connecting the

bald goon and Ryan Brown's trade in stolen and illegal pets with what he'd said.

'Could the computer records be altered, so it doesn't look like theft?'

He shrugged. 'Possibly. The software we use is similar to that of the post office scandal, so it might look like phantom payments that were never made.'

I helped him from the bed when I heard a noise outside. I went to the window, seeing a car arrive and four men exit. Baldy stepped out of the farmhouse and welcomed them.

Then they all looked up to the window where I stood.

One of them had fresh scars on his face.

Chapter 24

Rescue Me

I peered out of the window as the men entered the house. I studied the side of the building as the front door closed.

'What's happening?' William said.

I went to the bedroom door. 'Are you afraid of heights?'

He rubbed at the marks on his wrists again. 'What? Why?'

'Four others have just joined the guy who abducted you, and I assume they'll be here soon. So, unless you want to hang around, we must leave now. And we can't go downstairs. That means we'll have to climb out the window onto the sliding part of the roof under the last bedroom. Then we'll drop to the ground and leave the farm while those goons remain inside.'

'Won't they just get into the car and drive after us?'

'Probably, but we should be able to lose them in the trees.'

His hands trembled. 'Should be?'

'Sure. It's better than staying here. Unless you want a rematch with the thug who abducted you.'

Loud voices drifted up from downstairs. William didn't need a second invitation, stumbling out the door before I could warn him to be careful. As I watched him disappear into the corridor, adrenaline coursed through me. I glanced at the window and stepped out of the bedroom. The sounds below increased, mingling with footsteps approaching the staircase. The accountant was a few feet ahead of me, his eyes wide with terror.

Somebody grabbed me and pulled me back. Their fingers dug into my flesh, and an electric shock surged through me before he threw me into the wall. I hit it with my shoulder, adding more pain as I slid to the floor.

The bald goon stood over me and laughed. 'I can't believe you're here. You've saved me from returning to that flat that stank of wet dog. This must be my lucky day.'

'You killed Ryan Brown,' I said.

That stopped him in his tracks. 'Yeah? Where's your proof?'

'And you planted the stuff you stole from my flat on him?'

He shrugged. 'Ryan wasn't up to the job, so I got promoted.' He cracked his knuckles. 'And after I deal with you and that shit accountant, I'll get another promotion.'

I dug my nails into the carpet. 'Who are you working for?'

He grinned at me. 'That doesn't matter, kid. Now you're here, I can frame you for the accountant's murder. And he'll be blamed for the money missing from the council finances.' He shook his bald head. 'Someone is really looking out for me today.'

'What did you do to Steve Clark?'

Confusion crept across his face. 'Who?'

'What are you doing, Tommy?' someone shouted from below.

'Come on up,' he answered. 'I've got some entertainment for you.'

'I know your name now,' I said.

He laughed. 'You're going to know a lot more than that soon.'

Could I get the knife from my pocket before he grabbed me? It seemed unlikely.

He reached for me as William smashed a chair over his head. The wood didn't shatter, bouncing off his skull with a loud crack. He screamed as his legs buckled, falling as the blood sprang from his head. William hit him again for good measure. Tommy collapsed.

William dropped the chair and helped me up. 'Come on. Let's get out of here.'

The floorboards creaked as we ran to the end bedroom. My heart pounded, the men's voices growing louder as they ran upstairs.

We rushed into the room, and I slid the window open. Then I rammed a chair under the handle of the door. It wouldn't stop them for long, but it should be enough.

'Out you go,' I said, bracing myself as William climbed through the narrow frame. When he made it out, I hoisted myself onto the ledge. The roof slanted steeply down, scattered with loose shingles.

William's lips trembled. 'I can't do this.'

I moved slowly, shingles digging into my palms and knees. 'Just slide down carefully,' I coached, keeping my voice low. He took my hand, and I guided him forward. Moving towards the edge, I peered at the ground. William's pale face stared at me, eyes wide.

He peered over the edge. 'How far down is that?'

'About twenty feet,' I said. 'You'll be fine as long as you land okay.'

The wind whipped across us. 'What will happen if I don't?'

'Best case scenario, you break your foot.'

I eased forward, scrabbling for purchase on the slick roof tiles. Heart lurching, I descended just as shouts erupted from inside. I slid faster, shingles splitting under my shoes, and I dropped.

The ground rushed towards me. I prepared myself for the hit, rolling on my side and away from the house. A sharp thud ran through my foot. I sprang up and stared at William, unmoving.

'I can't,' he repeated.

A goon reached the window with a gun in his hand. He fired as William jumped.

He hit the ground harder than I did, twisting his ankle as he landed. He yelped in pain as I dragged him up. The bloke at the window disappeared inside.

'Come on,' I commanded. 'They'll be out soon.'

'My foot,' William said. 'It hurts to move it.'

I put my arm around him. 'We need to get to the trees.' They were three hundred yards away. 'They'll give us a chance to hide. I might be able to deal with them in there.'

He mumbled something as I dragged him forward, the agony etched on his face.

'Leave me,' he said. 'Save yourself.'

I clung to him and moved as fast as I could. He grimaced in pain but kept moving.

The trees were near. With time, we could slip into the shadows to prop William against a tree and get the knife from my pocket. There were four of them with at least one gun.

It didn't seem like good odds.

For them.

Chapter 25

A Forest

We stumbled into the trees. A canvas of leaves above us blocked the light as we staggered into the gloom. The ground was soft and damp, the earth yielding slightly with each step we took. I inhaled the scent of wet grass and decaying foliage, mingling with the faint aroma of pine and moss. Branches snagged at my clothes as we pushed deeper into the trees, their rough bark scraping against my skin.

'Leave me,' William said again. 'Save yourself.'

He sagged in my arms as I dragged him behind dense bushes. 'Stay here.'

I grasped the knife and gazed towards the sounds of our pursuers, their voices growing closer with each passing moment. One of them came into view, a tall man with a thick neck. There was no gun in his hand but a baseball bat.

'Fan out,' he shouted. 'They can't have gone far.'

I couldn't see the others, gripping the blade and steadying my breathing.

He stepped forward over broken twigs and clumps of mud towards me. I crouched near a tree opposite where I'd left William. The forest seemed to close around me, the darkness pressing in from all sides. Every rustle of leaves and snap of twigs sent a jolt through my veins, and my senses heightened to the point of overload. Branches snagged at my clothes as I shifted behind the tree, its rough bark scraping against my skin.

The bloke came closer, with still no sign of his mates. With a few more steps, he'd see William slumped in the grass.

'Can anybody see anything?' he shouted. Nobody answered.

I held my breath, picturing what I needed to do to get us to safety.

Then I sprang forward and stuck the blade into his thigh. His face contorted in agony, ready to scream. I slapped my free hand over his mouth. We fell to the ground together, with me on top of him. He squirmed against me like a frustrated lover. I pushed the blade in further, dragging it up.

Blood seeped from his wound as he bit my fingers.

I left the knife in his leg and cracked his nose with my palm. He sunk his teeth deeper into my fingers before I punched him in the throat. He blinked before releasing my hand and sinking into the undergrowth, unconscious.

My legs ached as I shook my hand and went to William.

'Fuck!' he said. 'That was amazing.'

I ignored my pain, dripping blood into the grass and leaves. 'We can't stay here. The others will come looking for him soon.'

'Okay,' he replied. 'What should we do?'

Light filtered through the branches and caressed my cheeks. 'If they've gone further into the forest, we might be able to double back to the house.'

'Then what?'

'We'll steal a car.'

He frowned. 'Isn't that risky?'

'We can't stay here.'

I put my arm around his waist, taking the weight off his twisted ankle, and guided him through the trees. Silence surrounded us, the only sounds being the pounding of my heart and his laboured breathing.

He gasped for air. 'I can see the path to the farmhouse.'

I could as well.

Then somebody punched me in the head.

Stars exploded behind my eyes as the blow landed, sending me reeling. I let go of William as he shouted my name. Pain radiated through my skull, and I staggered forward, my vision swimming as I hit the ground. Insects skittered over wet leaves, rushing away from me. I saw a figure looming over me through the haze, their features obscured by the darkness. Groaning, I fought to get up, my head pounding with each heartbeat. I tasted blood in my mouth, warm and metallic, as I struggled to focus on the assailant.

William's voice cut through the fog of pain. 'Enola!'

I blinked, trying to shake off the dizziness. The figure lunged towards me, and instinct took over. With a surge of adrenaline, I ducked to the side, narrowly avoiding the blow. But he was relentless, his movements swift and precise. I stumbled backwards, dropping the blade. Everything appeared to swirl around me, the darkness closing in.

He kicked me in the stomach and laughed. 'This is fun.'

Pain surged through me, my lungs clutching for oxygen. I scrambled to retrieve the knife, my fingers fumbling in the gloom as I searched for the weapon. Adrenaline swept through me as I struggled to regain my footing. The figure advanced, their form looming larger with each second. I heard William calling to me, his words a distant echo in the chaos of my mind.

But I couldn't find the blade.

The attacker lunged again, getting one hand around my throat while he punched me in the gut with the other. His eyes glazed over, a manic smile cutting into me. He squeezed harder at my neck and grinned. The pressure sucked the air from my lungs as everything grew darker around me.

I thought of my parents and everything I'd lost and saw images of Becky smiling at me. I pictured Amy and the times we'd shared, the good and the bad.

Then I found the broken branch and stuck it in his face.

He released me and screamed.

My legs trembled as I stood, coughing and spitting blood into the leaves, mixing red with green. William grabbed my arm as the bloke writhed on the ground, flailing at the wood sticking out of his eye. I clung to William as we helped each other out of the trees and into the light. The farmhouse shimmered a hundred yards ahead, my vision blurring, but not enough to stop me from seeing the car nearby.

We stumbled towards it, hanging onto each other.

'What if the car's locked?' William said.

But it wasn't.

The door opened, and bald Tommy stepped out, waving the gun at us. Blood dripped from his head.

'I knew those idiots would flush you out.' He pointed the pistol at William. 'You were always going to die, but now you'll get to suffer longer.' Then he aimed the weapon at me. 'And it will look like a murder-suicide when the coppers find you together.'

'Why did you steal those things from my flat?' I said.

'What?' he answered. 'The spider or the other stuff.'

'All of it. Put me out of my misery before you shoot me.'

He shrugged. 'I've always wanted a tarantula, so it seemed a waste not to take it. For the rest of it, that was just good fortune.' He inched closer. 'I was thirteen the first time I broke into a house, and do you know what I did?'

Keeping him talking seemed like a good idea. 'You stole stuff?'

He grinned. 'Yeah, of course, but it wasn't just about the money and the valuables. I felt close to the people I was ripping off. So I took trophies, something personal for them that became personal to me. Do you understand?'

I didn't. 'Sure – you're a lunatic. Why break into my place and nobody else's? Did you target me?'

'What? No. I didn't even know who you were. Someone came into the building before I could try the next flat, so I scarpered. But I had your spider and knickknacks, so I was happy with that. Ryan didn't like me doing the side gig when I was helping him with the animals, but I didn't care what he thought. And I knew his days were numbered before you turned up at the funfair.'

'Now you'll tell me who you're working for?'

He pointed the gun at my face. 'What, before I kill you?'

William gripped my hand as Tommy squeezed the trigger.

Then he pulled the trigger.

Chapter 26

A Saucerful Of Secrets

I waited for the bullet to hit.

But it never came.

Tommy screamed as his hand shattered. He dropped the weapon, blood and bones spiralling everywhere. He collapsed to his knees, holding his damaged limb as he howled into the wind. My head throbbed, and my vision blurred. Blood dripped from my fingers and onto my leg.

'I'm always late for the party.' I turned to see Amy holding a gun. 'Who's your new friend, Enola?'

I shook the haze from my brain. 'That's William.' He continued to cling to me. 'I thought you'd left, Amy?'

She went to Tommy and kicked his pistol away from him. 'I did, driving back to the main road when a car came past me with four brooding men in it.' She glanced across the path between the farmhouse and the trees. 'What happened to them?'

I nodded at the woods. 'They're in there. Two are injured, but the others are probably armed. We should get out of here. Is your car nearby?'

'It's behind the house,' she replied. 'But you don't have to worry about those blokes. They'll have fled by now.'

'Fled? Why?'

She cupped her ear. 'Don't you hear it, Amy, the siren song of the approaching cavalry?'

I heard it, the howl of police cars. 'Who called the coppers?'

She laughed. 'Did somebody knock you on the head when you were playing in the woods, Enola?' Tommy crawled towards his gun, his blood turning the path red. She stepped on his arm, and he screamed. 'Shush,' she told him. 'The adults are talking.'

'You rang the police?' I could hardly believe it. My lawless Amy was now a respectable civilian.

She shrugged. 'I'm a law-abiding citizen, Enola – an upstanding community member and businesswoman. It was my duty to inform the authorities of what I saw.'

I led William to the car and propped him against it. 'What did you tell them?'

'The truth. I said armed men were on the way to a farm-house to hurt innocent people. Then I gave them directions and returned here to help you out of your pickle.'

I shook my head. 'I thought I'd seen it all, but Amy Sparrow calling the police takes the biscuit.'

She narrowed her eyes at me. 'It wasn't for my benefit, Enola. Besides, only this morning, Future Content signed a lucrative contract with the local coppers to provide media content for them. It's a five-year deal.'

My body ached as I leaned on the car next to William. He appeared to be okay, but I was in shock. 'How the hell did you get that job with your past?'

Amy frowned. 'My past. What do you mean by that?'

My laughter hurt my ribs. 'Come on, Amy. You know exactly what I mean.'

She waved a hand at me. 'Only sad people live in the past, Enola. You should focus on the future. And anyway, my girlfriend works for the police, so she put in a good word for me.'

It was just one surprise after another. 'Your girlfriend's a copper?'

She grinned. 'I think you've met.'

My head throbbed as if there was an angry beehive inside it. 'Wait, what? It can't be. You don't mean?'

'Rose told me you were snappy with her. I explained to her why you don't like coppers.'

'DS Kamara,' I said. 'Your girlfriend is DS Kamara?'

Her smile widened. 'Yes, though the term girlfriend might be a bit juvenile, wouldn't you say? We're in a relationship. Let's put it that way.'

'For how long?'

'A few months. We met in the shop.' Her eyes sparkled. 'It was love at first sight. Are you happy for me, Enola?'

I didn't know how to reply as the police cars appeared, speeding towards the farmhouse as if it were on fire. I pointed at the gun Amy was holding.

'How will you explain that?'

She held it up. 'This? I found it on the path. Then, when I saw what that horrible man was about to do to you and this poor fella, well, I had no choice, did I?'

Three police cars and two vans pulled up. Armed officers jumped out of the vans while uniformed coppers exited the vehicles. DS Kamara was among them. She ran to Amy.

'Are you okay?'

Amy nodded. 'The armed men are in the woods, four of

them. I'm not sure about the house. And there's that bloke on the ground.'

Kamara glanced at me before repeating that information to her colleagues. Then she took the gun from Amy.

'We need an ambulance for William,' I told nobody in particular.

I watched the coppers do their work, wondering how many they'd find in those trees.

Kamara approached me. 'The ambulance is on its way.' She nodded at Tommy as a uniformed officer dragged him from the ground. 'Is that who I think it is?'

'Yeah,' I replied. 'His first name is Tommy. He's the one who broke into my flat, and he planted my stuff on Ryan Brown after he killed him.'

'He told you that?' Kamara asked.

'He did, though he wouldn't say who he's working for. He also abducted William.'

'Why?'

'William is an accountant for the council,' I answered. 'He claims to have evidence of large-scale theft from the council accountants. I assume that's why Tommy took him, probably under orders from someone important in the council.'

She whistled. 'Well, it's been a bad day all round for the council.'

'Why?' I asked.

DS Kamara found something on her phone and showed it to me. 'This is from the *Daily Herald's* website. It was released an hour ago.'

The *Herald* was the local newspaper. I watched the video as somebody from the paper read a statement: 'After months of strenuous investigations, and with the information provided by a whistleblower inside Albion Utilities, we have overwhelming proof that the water company has emptied thousands of tonnes of raw sewage illegally into the river and sea. And all of it was facilitated by Martin, the head of the local council.' He let the information sink in. 'We also have evidence that Mary Martin was preparing to sign off on the council selling land it owns at well under market value to developers owned by Michael Grace, the CEO of Albion Utilities.' Another pause. 'A concerned citizen gathered all this information and then passed it on to the *Daily Herald*. I want to introduce you to him now. Please welcome, Mr Steve Clark.'

My head throbbed, and my lungs ached as I watched Steve appear before the camera. Kamara snatched the phone from me before I could hear him speak.

'Isn't that the bloke you were looking for?' she asked.

I struggled to catch my breath. 'Yeah, we work together.' I had to still my beating heart.

'Okay,' Kamara said. 'I need to do my job. Stay here until the ambulance arrives. We'll get your statements later.'

She left as I fumbled my phone from my pocket.

Amy grinned at me. 'So, he's just a colleague from the record shop?'

I ignored her and phoned Benjamin.

What a strange day it had been.

Chapter 27

Happy Hour

Benjamin placed the Coke on the table near me. The Clash's "Bankrobber" drifted out of the jukebox.

'What time is Steve coming?' I said, trying to keep the butterflies out of my stomach.

'Soon,' he replied. 'He texted to say he had another media interview to finish.'

I slipped an ice cube into my mouth, enjoying the crisp coldness against my lips. 'His head must be a whirl.' Mine was; the same as my guts.

Becky bounded into the pub, holding Kronos's lead as Julia and Bruce followed behind the kid. Becky's smile warmed my heart.

'Enola!' she shouted. 'I've never been to a pub before.'

Benjamin shook his head. 'I'm not a fan of children being around alcohol.'

'Me neither,' I said. There was no need to tell him I started drinking at fourteen. Thankfully, I came to my senses on my sixteenth birthday.

The others joined us, and I introduced everybody.

'I longed to work in a record shop as a teenager,' Bruce said. 'It was my one ambition in life.'

I grinned. 'Was that because you needed early access to all the Take That records?'

He ignored me and plopped a pint of cider on the table.

Julia pulled Becky close to her. 'I wanted to own a bookshop.'

'There's still time,' I replied as Steve entered the pub. It felt as if the moon was sitting on my chest.

Bruce nudged me. 'Here comes the boyfriend?'

'What?' I said. 'You've dumped Mary already?'

He frowned at me. 'Don't be daft. I'm meeting her after work.'

'You never told me what she does.'

'She's a nurse,' he replied.

Steve came straight over. 'Who wants a drink?'

I grabbed his arm and pulled him into the seat next to me. 'Bruce will get you a pint once you tell us where you've been the last few days. Benjamin was worried sick about you.'

His smile warmed my heart. 'I'm sorry, Enola.' He nodded to Benjamin. 'I'm sorry, mate.'

'I saw you on the news,' Becky said. 'Mum thinks you're good-looking.'

Julia blushed. 'Becky!'

Becky shrugged. 'I suppose he's okay, but he's no Harry Styles.'

Everybody laughed as Megan Thee Stallion warbled through the speakers.

'Why didn't you tell us what you were doing?' Benjamin asked.

'I couldn't,' Steve replied. 'The investigation was dangerous, so the fewer people who knew about it, the better. The whistleblower at Albion Utilities contacted me with the information because we were old school friends, and I had to keep everything between us until I was ready to go to the *Herald*.' He gripped my hand. 'Did you miss me?'

'Sure,' I said. 'We needed you to sort out those hundreds of jazz CDs.'

Bruce shook his head. 'Enola doesn't like jazz.'

Steve laughed. 'What? That's blasphemy.'

'No,' I replied. 'That's good taste.'

'What's jazz?' Becky asked.

'Pain in your ears,' I answered.

Steve stood. 'There may be some on the jukebox.'

I dragged him back down. 'Maybe later. Tell Bruce what you want to drink, and he'll go to the bar.'

He wriggled from my grasp. 'No, we're celebrating, so it's my round. What does everybody want?'

'Mucky beer!' Becky shouted.

Steve took the orders and went to the bar, smiling at me as he left. I watched him go and thought of Amy and DS Kamara, still shocked that the former self-claimed Queen of the Underworld was dating a copper.

However, I was happy for her. With that relationship and her new business, maybe she was on the right path to happiness after all.

I stood and went to the jukebox, hoping they'd have what I wanted to hear.

They did.

I selected five tracks, returning to my seat as the first tune burst through the speakers.

Steve glanced at me from the bar as The Buzzcocks sang about falling in love with someone you shouldn't.

Thank You!

Thank you, dear reader for purchasing this book.

Many thanks to my wonderful wife for all her support and patience.

Extra special thanks to Karina Gallagher for being a dedicated reader of my work.

Cover design by James, GoOnWrite.com

Mailing List & Free Books!

If you would like to join my mailing list and receive a free eBook then contact me at mail@andrewsfrench.com

Also by A. S. French

Crime Fiction and Thrillers

The Astrid Snow series

Don't Fear the Reaper

The Killing Moon

Lost in America

Gone to Texas

The Final Girl

Snowstorm: An Astrid Snow Collection

The Ophelia Red series

Ophelia Red

The Detective Jen Flowers series

The Hashtag Killer

Serial Killer

Night Killer

The Killer Inside Them

The Frank Walker series

Where The Bodies Are Buried

Bodies of Evidence

Crime Short Stories

Crime Stories: A Collection

Call Me: An Astrid Snow Short Story

About the Author

Andrew French lives amongst faded seaside glamour on the North East coast of England. He likes gin and cats but not together, new music and old movies, curry and ice cream. Slow bike rides and long walks to the pub are his usual exercise, as well as flicking through the pages of good books and the memoirs of bad people.

Find out more at www.andrewsfrench.com

Facebook:

https://www.facebook.com/A-S-French-Author-15014562500601 8

Twitter:

www.twitter.com/andrewfrench100

Instagram:

www.instagram.com/andrewfrench100

And replies to all his email at mail@andrewsfrench.com

If you have the time, please leave a review at Amazon or Goodreads

Thank you!

www.ingramcontent.com/pod-product-compliance
Lightning Source LLC
Chambersburg PA
CBHW010019200726
48283CB00015B/2967